BELINDA

By the Same Author

Writing as
ANNE RAMPLING
Exit to Eden

Writing as
ANNE RICE

Interview With the Vampire
The Feast of All Saints
Cry To Heaven
The Vampire Lestat

Writing as
A. N. ROQUELAURE
Erotica:

The Claiming of Sleeping Beauty
Beauty's Punishment
Beauty's Release

BELINDA

A NOVEL

ANNE RICE
WRITING AS
ANNE RAMPLING

A Belvedere Book
ARBOR HOUSE   NEW YORK

ISBN: 0-87795-826-2

Manufactured in the United States of America

THIS NOVEL
IS DEDICATED
TO ME.

Bend down, bend down. Excess
is the only ease,
so bend. The sun is in the tree.
Put your mouth on mine. Bend down
beam & slash, for Dread is dreamed-up-scenes
of what comes after death. Is being
fled from what bends down in pain.
The elbow bends in the brain, lifts the cup.
The worst is yet to dream you up,
so bend down the intrigue
you dreamed. Flee the hayneedle in the brain's tree.
Excess allures by leaps. Stars burn clean. Oriole
bitches and gleams. Dread is the fear of being less
forever. So bend. Bend down and kiss
what you *see*.

"Excess Is Ease"
STAN RICE

BELINDA

I

THE WORLD OF
JEREMY WALKER

[1]

"WHO was she?" That was the first thought that came into my mind when I saw her in the bookstore. Jody, the publicist, pointed her out. "Catch your devoted fan over there," she said. "Goldilocks."

Goldilocks, yes, she had hair like that, absolutely right, down to her shoulders. But who was she really?

Photographing her, painting her. Reaching under her short little Catholic school plaid skirt and touching the silk of her naked thighs, yes, I thought of all that, too, I have to admit it. I thought of kissing her, seeing if her face was as soft as it looked—babyflesh.

Yes, it was there from the start, especially once she gave me the age-old inviting smile and her eyes became for a moment a woman's eyes.

Fifteen, maybe sixteen—she was no older than that. Scuffed oxfords, shoulder bag, white socks pulled up over the calves—a private-school kid who had maybe drifted into the line outside the bookstore just to see what was happening.

But there was something strange about her that made me think she was "somebody." I don't mean her poise, the cool manner in which she stood with arms folded just watching all the goings on at the book party. Kids these days inherit that poise. It's their enemy, the way ignorance was the enemy of my generation.

It was a high gloss she had, almost a Hollywood look in spite of the rumpled Peter Pan blouse and the cardigan tied loosely around her shoulders. Her skin was too evenly tanned all over (consider the silky thighs, the skirt was so short), and her hair, though long and loose, was almost platinum. Careful lipstick, could have been done with a brush. All this made the school clothes look like a costume. And a very well chosen one.

She might have been a child actress, of course, or a model—I had photographed a lot of those—young things who will market the teenage look till they're twenty-five, even thirty. She was certainly pretty enough. And the mouth was full, but small, puckered, real babymouth. She had the look all right. My God, she was lovely.

But that didn't seem the right explanation either. And she was too old to be one of the little girls who read my books, the ones crowded around me now with their mothers. Yet she wasn't old enough to be one of the faithful adults who still bought every new work with slightly embarrassed apologies.

No, she didn't quite fit here. And in the soft electric daylight of the crowded store she suggested an imaginary being, an hallucination.

Something prophetic in that, though she was very real, more real perhaps than I ever was.

I forced myself not to stare at her. I had to keep the pen going as the copies of *Looking for Bettina* were put into my hand, see the little upturned faces.

"To Rosalind, of the lovely name," and "For Brenda, of the beautiful braids," or "To pretty Dorothy, with special best wishes."

"Do you really write the words to the stories, too?" Yes, I do.

"Will you do more Bettina books?" I'll try to. But this is number seven. Isn't it enough, perhaps? What do you think?

"Is Bettina a real little girl?" Real to me, what about you?

"Do you do all the cartoons yourself for the Saturday morning Charlotte show?" No, the TV people do all that. But they have to make them look like my drawings.

The line went all the way out the door and down the block, they said, and it was so hot for San Francisco. When San Francisco gets hot, no one is prepared for it. I glanced back to see if she was still there. Yes, she was. And she smiled again in that same calm secretive way, no mistaking it.

But, come on, Jeremy, pay attention to what you're doing, don't disappoint anybody. Smile for each one. Listen.

Two more college kids appeared—oil paint on the sweatshirts and jeans—and they had the big coffee-table book left over from Christmas, *The World of Jeremy Walker.*

Confusion every time I saw that pretentious package, but oh, what it had meant, the grand imprimatur after all these years, the text full of lofty comparisons to Rousseau and Dalí and even Monet, with pages of dizzying analysis.

Walker's work has from its very beginnings transcended illustration. Although his little girl protagonists at first glance suggest the saccharine sweetness of Kate Greenaway, the complex settings in which they find themselves are as original as they are disturbing.

Hate to have someone pay fifty dollars for a book, seems obscene.

"Knew you were an artist when I was four years old . . . cut out your pages and framed them and put them on the walls—"

Thank you.

"—worth every penny. Saw your work in New York at the Rhinegold Gallery."

Yes, Rhinegold's always been good to me, showing me when people said I was just a kid's author. Good old Rhinegold.

"—when the Museum of Modern Art will finally admit—"

You know the old joke. When I'm dead. (Don't mention the work in the Pompidou Center in Paris. That would be too arrogant.)

"—I mean, the trash they call serious! Have you seen—?"

Yes, trash, you said it.

Don't let them go away feeling I wasn't what they expected, that I hadn't listened when they murmured about "veiled sensuality" and "light and shadow." This is an ego-booster all right. Every book signing is. But it's also purgatory.

Another young mother with two battered copies of the old editions. Sometimes I wound up signing more of those old books than the new one from the stacks on the front tables.

Of course, I took all these people home with me in my head, took them with me into the studio when I lifted the brush. They were there like the walls were there. I loved them. But to meet them face to face was always excruciating. Rather read the letters that came from New York in two packets every week, rather tap out the answers carefully in solitude.

Dear Ginny,

Yes, all the toys in the pictures in Bettina's House are in my house, it's true. And the dolls I draw are antiques, but the old Lionel trains can be found in many places still. Perhaps your mother can help you to find, etc. . . .

"—couldn't go to sleep at night unless she was reading Bettina to me—"

Thank you. Yes, thank you. You don't know what it means to hear you say it.

Yes, the heat was getting unbearable in here. Jody, the pretty publicist from New York whispered in my ear:

"Just two more books and they're sold out."

"You mean I can get drunk now?"

Scolding laugh. And a little black-haired girl on my right, staring up at me with the most blank expression—could have been horror or nothing. Squeeze of Jody's hand on my arm.

"That was just a joke, honey. Did I sign your book?"

"Jeremy Walker doesn't drink," said the nearby mother with an ironic but good-natured laugh. Laughter all around.

"Sold out!" The clerk had both arms up, turning right to left. "Sold out!"

"Let's go!" said Jody, squeeze on the arm tightening. Lips to my ear: "That was, for your information, one thousand copies."

One of the other clerks was saying he could send around the corner to Doubleday for more, somebody was already calling.

I turned around. Where was she, my Goldilocks? The store was emptying.

"Tell them not to do that, not to borrow the books. I can't sign any more—"

Goldilocks was gone. And I had not even seen her move out of the corner of my eye. I was scanning everywhere, looking for a patch of plaid in the crowd, the corn silk hair. Nothing.

Jody was tactfully telling the clerks that we were late already for the publishers' party at the Saint Francis. (It was the big American Booksellers Association party for the publishing house.) We couldn't be late for it.

"Party, I forgot about the party," I said. I wanted to loosen my tie but didn't. Before each book came out, I swore to myself I'd do the signings in a sweater and a shirt open at the neck, and everybody would like me just as much, but I never could bring myself to do it. So now I was trapped in my tweed coat and flannel pants in the middle of a heat wave.

"It's the party where you can get drunk!" Jody whispered pushing me towards the door. "What are you complaining about?"

I shut my eyes for a split second, tried to see Goldilocks just as she'd been—arms folded, leaning against the table of books. Had she been chewing gum? Her lips had been so pink, pink as candy.

"Do you *have* to do this party?"

"Look, there'll be lots of other authors there—"

That meant Alex Clementine, this season's movie-star author (and my very good friend), and Ursula Hall, the cookbook lady, and Evan Dandrich, the spy novelist—in sum, the megasellers. The respectable little authors and short story writers would be nowhere in sight.

"You can just coast."

"Like coast home, for instance?"

It was worse outside, the smell of the big city rising from the sidewalks, the way it never does in San Francisco, and just a stale wind gusting between the buildings.

"You could do it in your sleep," Jody said. "Same old reporters, same old columnists—"

"Then why do it at all?" I asked. But I knew the answer.

Jody and I had worked together for ten years on this kind of thing. We'd gone from the early days, when nobody much wanted to interview a children's book author and promotion was just a signing or two in a kiddy's bookstore, to the madness of late, when each book brought demands for guest spots on television and radio, chatter about the animated movies in the works, the long intellectual write-ups in the news mags, and the endlessly repeated question: How does it feel to have children's books on the adult best-seller list?

Jody had always worked hard, first to get me publicity and now to protect me from it. Wasn't fair to back out if she wanted me to do this party.

We were crossing Union Square, weaving through the usual scatter of tourists and derelicts, the pavements filthy, the sky a colorless glare overhead.

"You don't even have to talk," she said. "Just smile and let them eat the food and drink the booze. You go sit on a sofa. You've got ink all over your fingers. Ever hear of ballpoint pens?"

"My dear, you're talking to an artist."

Sad panicky feeling when I thought of Goldilocks again. If I could go home now, I might be able to paint her, get her sketched at least before the details melted in the dazzle. Something about her nose, little upturned nose, and the way the mouth was full but small. Probably be that way all her life, and she'd hate it soon enough because she wanted to look like a full-grown woman.

But who was she? The question again, as if there ought to be a very specific answer. Maybe an allure that strong always creates a feeling of recognition. Someone I ought to know, have known, dreamt up, been in love with forever.

"I'm so tired," I said. "It's this damned heat. I didn't expect to be so tired." And the truth was, I was drained, smiled out, eager to just shut the door on everything.

"Look, let the others have the limelight. You know Alex Clementine. He'll keep them mesmerized."

Yes, good to have Alex aboard. And everybody said his Tinseltown life story was terrific. If only I could get away with Alex, hit some corner bar and breathe easy. But Alex did love this kind of thing.

"Maybe I'd get a second wind."

A flock of pigeons broke for us as we headed toward Powell Street. A man on crutches wanted "spare change." A wraith of a woman in a preposterous silver helmet with Mercury wings attached to it crooned a frightening song through a homemade amplifier. I looked up at the charcoal gray facade of the hotel, the old building stolid and grim, the towers rising cleanly behind it.

Some old Hollywood tale of Alex Clementine's came back, something about the silent film star Fatty Arbuckle accidentally injuring a young girl in this hotel, a bedroom scandal that wrecked his career, all before our time. Alex was probably telling that story now upstairs. Wouldn't miss that opportunity surely.

A jam-packed cable car clanked at the taxis that barred its way. We darted in front of it.

"Jeremy, you know you can lie down for a few minutes, prop up your feet, shut your eyes, then I'll get you some coffee. I mean there's a bedroom up there, it's the presidential suite."

"So I get to sleep in the president's bed." I smiled. "I think I'll take you up on that."

Would like to have gotten the way her "goldilocks" came down to her shoulders in a triangle of ripples. I think she had some of it tied back, but it was so heavy and thick. Bet she thought it was too curly and that's what she would have said if I had said how beautiful. But that was the surface. What about the tempest in my heart when I saw the look in her eye? Empty faces to the right and to the left, but there had been somebody home there in those eyes—how to get that.

"—a good presidential nap and then you'll be fine for dinner."

"Dinner, you didn't tell me about dinner!" My shoulder ached. So did my hand. One thousand books. But I was lying. I had been told about dinner. I had been warned about everything.

The lobby of the Saint Francis swallowed us in a golden gloom, the inevitable noise of the crowd interwoven with the faint strains of an orchestra. Massive granite columns soaring to gilded Corinthian capitals. Sounds of china and silver. Smell of an ice box full of expensive flowers. Everything, even the patterns in the carpet, seemed to be moving.

"Don't do this to me," Jody was saying. "I'll tell everybody you're beat, I'll do the talking—"

"Yes, you say it all, whatever it is—"

And what is there to say anymore? How many weeks has the book been on *The New York Times* best-sellers list? Was it true I had an attic full of paintings nobody had ever seen? Would there be a museum show any time soon? What about the two works in the Pompidou Center? Did the French appreciate me more than the Americans? And talk about the coffee-table book, of course, and the gulf that divided it from the Saturday morning Charlotte show and the animated films that might be made by Disney. And of course the question that irritated me the most: What was new or different about the latest *Looking for Bettina?*

Nothing. That's the trouble. Absolutely nothing.

The dread in me was building. You cannot say the same things five hundred times without becoming a windup toy. Your face goes dead, so does your voice, and they know it. And they take it personally. And lately careless statements had been coming out of my mouth. I had almost snapped at an interviewer last week that I didn't give a goddamn about the Saturday morning Charlotte show, why the hell would I be embarrassed by it?

Well, fourteen million little kids nationwide watch that show, and Charlotte's my creation. What was I talking about?

"Oh, don't look now," Jody said, "but there's your devoted fan—"

"Who?"

"Goldilocks. Waiting for you right by the elevators. I'll get rid of her."

"No, don't!"

There she was again all right, leaning against the wall as casually as she had against the book table. Only this time she had one of my books under her arm and a little cigarette in the other hand, and she took a quick drag off the cigarette in a rather casual way that made her look like a street kid.

"Goddamn, she stole that book, I know she did," Jody said. "She was hanging around all afternoon and she never bought anything."

"Drop it," I said under my breath. "We are not the San Francisco police."

She'd crushed out the cigarette in the sand of the ashtray and she was coming towards us. She had *Bettina's House* in her hand, a new copy but an old book. I'd written it probably around the time she was born. Didn't want to think about that. I pushed the elevator button.

"Hello, Mr. Walker."

"Hello, Goldilocks."

A low voice, that made me think of caramel or melted chocolate, something delicious like that, almost a woman's voice coming out of her little girl mouth. I could scarcely stand it.

She drew a pen out of her leather mail pouch bag.

"I had to get this at another store," she said. Unbelievable blue eyes. "They sold out at the party before I realized it."

You see, she's not a thief! I took it out of her hands, took the pen. I tried to place the voice geographically, but I couldn't. Words almost British crisp but it wasn't a British accent.

"What's your name, Goldilocks? Or may I just write Goldilocks?"

There were freckles on her nose, and a touch of gray mascara on her blond lashes. Skill again. Lipstick bubblegum pink and perfect on her poochy little mouth. And what a smile. Am I still breathing?

"Belinda," she said. "But you don't have to write anything. Just sign your name. That will be plenty." Poise all right. Slow, even-spaced words for all the clear articulation. And the steadiness of the gaze, amazing.

Yet she was so young. Just a baby up close, if there'd been any doubt at a distance. I reached out and stroked her hair. Nothing illegal in that, is there? It was thick, yes, but it gave under my touch as if it were full of air. She actually had dimples. Two little dimples.

"That's very sweet of you, Mr. Walker."

"Pleasure, Belinda."

"I heard them saying you'd be coming over here. I hope you don't mind—"

"Not at all, sweetheart. Want to go to the party?"

Had I said that?

Jody shot me an incredulous glance. She was holding the elevator door.

"Sure, Mr. Walker. If you really want me to—" Her eyes were dark blue, that was the thing. They'd never look anything but blue. She glided past me into the glass car. Small bones, very straight posture.

"Of course, I do," I said. The doors swished out. "It's a press party, lots of people will be there."

Very official, you see, I am not a child molester, and no one is going to grab your beautiful hair in two handfuls. Streaks of yellow in it. It could have been naturally that light. Then you wouldn't call it platinum.

"I thought you were all tuckered out," said Jody.

The elevator shot up soundlessly past the roof of the old building, and the city spread out around us all the way to the bay, frightening in its clarity. Union Square got smaller and smaller.

Belinda was looking up at me, and when I looked down, she smiled again and the dimples came back just for a second.

She held the book close to her side with her left hand. And with her right she fished another cigarette out of her blouse pocket. Gauloises. Crumpled blue pack there.

I reached for my lighter.

"No, watch this," she said, letting the cigarette hang on her lip. Out of the pocket with the same hand she pulled a matchbook.

I knew this trick. But I didn't believe she was going to do it. With the one hand she opened the book, freed a match, bent it back, closed the book, and struck the match with her thumb. "See?" she said as she touched the flame to the cigarette. "I just learned that."

I started laughing. Jody was staring at her, vaguely astonished. I just couldn't stop laughing.

"Yes, that's very good," I said. "You did it perfectly."

"Are you old enough to smoke?" Jody asked. "I don't think she's old enough to smoke."

"Give her a break," I said. "We're going to a party."

Belinda was still looking up at me and she dissolved into giggles without making a sound. I stroked her hair again, touched the barrette that held it in back. Big silver barrette. She had enough hair for at least two people. I wanted to touch her cheek, touch the dimples.

She looked down, cigarette dangling from the lip again, reached into her pouch and pulled out a big pair of sunglasses.

"I don't think she's old enough to smoke," said Jody again. "Besides, she shouldn't smoke in the elevator."

"There's nobody but us in the elevator."

Belinda had the glasses on when the door opened.

"You're safe now," I said. "They'll never recognize you."

She gave me a little startled glance. Her mouth and cheeks looked even more adorable under the big square rims. Skin so brand-new. I couldn't stand it.

"You can't be too careful," she said with a little smile.

Butter, that's what the voice was, warm butter, which I happen to like better actually than caramel.

THE suite was jammed and full of smoke. I could hear Alex Clementine's deep movie-star voice rolling over the seamless chatter. Passed cookbook queen Ursula Hall utterly mobbed. I took Belinda's arm and forced my way through the bar, acknowledging a few hellos here and there. I asked for a Scotch and water, and she whispered that she wanted the same thing. I decided to chance it.

Her cheeks looked so full and soft, I wanted to kiss them, kiss her candy mouth.

Get her off in a corner, I thought, and keep talking as you memorize every detail of her so you can paint her later. Tell her that's what you're doing, she will understand. There is absolutely nothing lecherous about just wanting to paint her.

The fact was I could see her in the pages of a book already, and her name was making strings of words in my head, something to do with an old poem by Ogden Nash: "Belinda lived in a little white house . . ."

Flash of her thin gold bracelet as she pushed at the glasses. The lenses were pink, and pale enough for me to see her eyes. Faint white fleece on her arm, barely visible. She was looking around as if she didn't like it here, and she was starting to get the inevitable glances. How could people not look at her? She bowed her head as if she was really uncomfortable. For the first time I noticed she had breasts under the white blouse, rather large ones. The collar gaped a little and the tan went all the way down—

Breasts on a baby like this, imagine.

I took the two drinks. Best to move out of sight of the bartender before I gave it to her. I wished now I'd ordered gin. No way did this look like a soft drink.

Somebody touching my shoulder. Andy Fisher, columnist from the *Oakland Tribune,* old friend. I was trying hard not to spill the two drinks.

"Just want to know one thing," he said. He gave Belinda the eye, lost a beat. "Do you even like children?"

"Very funny, Andy." Belinda was headed away. I followed her.

"No, seriously, Jeremy, you've never told me that, do you actually like kids, that's what I want to know—"

"Ask Jody, Andy. Jody knows everything."

I caught a sudden glimpse of Alex's profile through the crowd.

"On the twelfth floor of this very hotel," Alex was saying, "and she was a real darling little girl, her name was Virginia Rappe, and, of course, Arbuckle was famous for these drunken—"

Where the hell was Belinda?

Alex turned, caught my eye, waved. I gave him a little salute. But I'd lost Belinda.

"Mr. Walker!"

There she was. She was whispering to me from the entrance to a little hallway. She seemed to be hiding in there. But somebody had my sleeve again, a Hollywood columnist I rather loathed.

"What about the picture deal, Jeremy? This going to happen with Disney?"

"Seems like it, Barb," I said. "Ask Jody. She knows. Probably not Disney though, probably Rainbow Productions."

"Saw that sweet little suck-up piece they did on you in the *Bay Bulletin* this morning."

"I didn't."

Belinda turned her back to me, moved on, head down.

"Well, *I* heard the movie deal was dead in the water. They think you're too difficult, trying to teach their artists how to draw."

"Wrong, Barb." Fuck you, Barb. "Besides, I don't give a damn what they do with it."

"The conscientious artist."

"Of course, I am. The books are forever. They can have the movies."

"For the right price, I hear."

"And why not, I'd like to know. But why do you waste your time with this, Barb? You can write your usual lies without hearing the truth from me first, can't you?"

"Jeremy, I think you're a little too drunk to be at a publicity party."

"Not drunk at all, that's the problem."

Just turn your back and she'll disappear.

Belinda reached out, tugged on my arm. Thank you, darling. We moved down the little hallway. There were two bathrooms there side by side, and the bedroom with its own bath, which I could see through the open doorway. She was looking at the bedroom. Then she looked up, her eyes dark and deceptively grown-up behind the pink lenses. Could have been a woman then. Except that the pink glasses went with the candy-pink mouth.

"Listen, I want you to believe what I'm going to say," I said. "I want you to understand that I am perfectly sincere."

"About what?" Dimples. Her voice made me want to kiss her throat.

"I want to paint your picture," I said. "Just really paint your picture. I'd like you to come to my house. Nothing more to it than that, honestly, I swear to you. Lots of times I use models, all on the up and up. I call reputable agencies. I'd like to paint you—"

"Why shouldn't I believe that?" she asked, almost laughing. I thought she would start giggling again, the way she had in the elevator. "I know all about you, Mr. Walker. I've read your books all my life."

She went into the open bedroom, short pleated skirt swinging tightly with her hips, showing the naked thigh right above her knees.

I slipped in after her, backing away from her a little, just watching her. Her hair was very long down her back.

The noise dropped off somewhat, and the air was cooler here. A wall of mirrors made it seem impossibly enormous.

She turned to me.

"May I have my Scotch now?" she asked.

"Sure you can."

She took a deep swallow and looked around again. Then she took off the glasses and shoved them in her open bag and looked at me again. Her eyes seemed to be swimming with light that came from the low lamps and the reflections of the lamps in the mirrors.

The room seemed overdone to me, padded and draped, as it was, and stretching on through the glass into infinity. Not a sharp edge anywhere. The light was almost caressing. The hotel bed, covered in gold satin, resembled a great altar. The sheets would be smooth and cool.

I scarcely noticed that she had put down her bag and put out the cigarette. She took another swallow of the Scotch without even a wince. And she wasn't faking it. Remarkable poise actually. I don't even think she knew I was studying her.

And a sad realization drifted through my head, something to do with how young she was, how good she looked in any light, how light didn't make the slightest difference with her. And how old I was, and how all young people, even plain young people, had begun to look beautiful to me.

I didn't know whether this was a gift or a curse. It just made me sad. I didn't want to think about it. And I didn't want to stay in here with her. It was too much.

"Will you come to the house then?" I asked.

She didn't answer.

She went to the door and closed it and turned the latch, and the noise of the party simply evaporated. She stood against the door and took another swallow of the drink. No smiles, no giggles. Just that adorable poochy little mouth and the woman eyes above it and her breasts pushing against the cotton blouse.

I felt my heart shut down rather abruptly. Then a painful warmth in my face, and a change of gears from man to animal. I wondered if she had the slightest idea what that shift was like, if any young girl could be expected to. I thought of Arbuckle again. What had he done? Grabbed the doomed starlet Virginia Rappe and shredded her clothes—something like that. Shredded his career in something less than fifteen minutes probably—

Her face was so earnest, yet so innocent. Wetness on her lips from the Scotch.

I said,

"Don't do this, honey."

"Don't you want to?" she asked.

My God. I had thought she'd pretend not to understand me.

"This just isn't very smart," I said.

"Why isn't it?" she asked. Nothing flippant, artificial.

I knew absolutely and positively I wasn't going to lay a hand on her.

Cigarette or no cigarette, Scotch or no Scotch, she was no street kid. The doomed don't look like this, no, never. And I had only helped myself to those sad lost little girls just a few times in my life, just a few times, when desire and opportunity collided with more heat than I'd expected. The shame never went away. The shame of this would be unbearable.

"Come on, honey, open the door," I said.

She didn't do anything. I couldn't imagine what was going through her mind. Mine was sort of letting me down. I was looking at her breasts again, at her socks so tight on her legs. I wanted to peel them off. Strip them off, I think the word is, actually. Forget about Fatty Arbuckle. This isn't murder, it's just sex. And she's what, sixteen? No, just another part of the criminal code, that's all.

She put her drink down on the table. And she came towards me slowly. She lifted her arms and put them around my neck, and the soft babycheek was against my face, her breasts against my chest, her candy mouth opening.

"Oh, Goldilocks," I said.

"Belinda," she whispered.

"Hmmmmm . . . Belinda." I kissed her. I lifted her pleated skirt and slid my hands up her thighs and they were as soft as her face. Her bottom was so tight and smooth under her cotton panties.

"Come on," she said in my ear. "Don't you want to do it before they come and ruin everything?"

"Honey—"

"I like you *so* much."

[2]

I WOKE up when I heard the door click shut. The digital clock on the bedside table told me I'd slept for maybe half an hour. She was gone.

I found my wallet lying neatly on top of my pants, and all my money was still in the silver money clip in the front pants pocket.

Either she hadn't found it or she had not been trying to rob me in the first place. I didn't think too much about it. I was too busy getting dressed, combing my hair, straightening up the bed and getting out into the party to find her. I was also pretty busy feeling guilty.

Of course, she wasn't there.

I was halfway down to the first floor when I realized this was futile. She had too big a head start. Yet I searched the entire maze of dim carpeted hallways, went in and out of the swanky dress shops, the restaurants.

I checked with the doorman out front. Had he seen her, gotten her a cab?

She was just gone again. And I was standing there in the late afternoon thinking, well, I'd done it with her and she was probably sixteen and somebody's daughter. No consolation that it had been simply terrific.

THE dinner was particularly awful. And no amount of Pinot Chardonnay could make it any better. Strictly big bucks, contracts, agents, TV and movie talk. And Alex Clementine had not been there to lend any charm to it. They were holding him back for his own dinner later on this week.

When the subject of the new book came up, I heard myself say: "Look, it was what my audience wanted." And after that I shut up.

A serious writer, artist, whatever the hell I was, has to be smart enough not to say things like that. And the funny thing was the remark surprised me. Maybe I had begun to believe my own hype, or begun to believe that my hype was hype. In any case, by the time the dinner was over, I felt rotten.

I was thinking of her. How tender and fragile she had seemed, and yet so sure of herself. It was not new to her, making love, no matter how new she was. And yet she'd been so delicate, so purely romantic in the way that she'd kissed, touched, let me touch her.

No hint of guilt or old-fashioned shame or the defiance they can produce. No, none of that.

I was going mad over it. I couldn't figure it out.

Too fast it had all been. And then the short sleep afterwards with my arm around her. I had never figured on her slipping away. I hated myself and I was angry with her.

Some rich kid she was, probably, skipping school; and now safe in her mansion in Pacific Heights telling some other brat on the phone about what she'd done. No, that didn't fit. She was too sweet for all that.

I picked up a pack of Gauloises before I left downtown. Very strong, no filter, too short. Just the kind of thing a kid would think was romantic. In my Beat Generation days we had smoked Camels. So with her it was Gauloises.

I smoked the Gauloises in the cab on the way home, my eyes searching every downtown block for her.

IT was still hot after dark, truly unusual for San Francisco. But the big high-ceiling rooms of my Victorian house were cool as always.

I made some coffee and sat for a while, smoking another one of those miserable cigarettes, and I just looked around me at the shadowy living room, thinking about her.

Toys everywhere. Dust and disarray of an antique shop on the worn oriental carpets. I was rather sick of it. Had the urge to sweep it all into the street, just clean the place to the bare walls. But I knew I'd regret it.

It had taken me twenty-five years to collect these things, and I did love them. They were props in those early days. When I did *Bettina's World,* I bought the first of the antique dolls, and the first old standard-gauge railroad train, and the big fancy Victorian doll house because these were Bettina's things, and I needed to have them before me when I painted the pictures.

I'd photograph them in black and white from every angle, in every combination. Then take the photographs up to my studio and work in oil on canvas from the flat patterns that had been created in these photographs.

But I began to like the toys for their own sake. When I found a rare French doll, a porcelain beauty with almond eyes and withered lace clothes, I built the book *Angelica's Dreams* around her. And as the years passed, it continued to work that way, toys generating books, and books swallowing toys, and so on.

The big old carousel horse, fixed on its brass pole between ceiling and floor, had generated *The Celestial Carnival.* The mechanical clown, the old leather rocking horse with the glass eyes—these had sparked the series called *Charlotte in the Attic. Charlotte at the Seaside* had followed, and I'd bought the rusted bucket and pail for that, and the antique wagon. Then a string of books called *Charlotte in a Glass Darkly* had involved almost everything I owned, recycled in new color and juxtaposition.

Charlotte was my biggest success to date, with her own Saturday morning cartoon show. And the toys were always accurately rendered in the background. My grandfather clock was in the background, too, as it was in all the books, along with the antique furniture scattered through this house. I lived inside my pictures. Always had, I suppose, even before I ever painted any.

There were plastic replicas of Charlotte here too in the dust somewhere, drugstore dolls that sold briskly along with packages of tacky little period clothes. But his stiff little creation couldn't compare with the nineteenth-century beauties piled in the wicker baby carriage or lining the top of the square grand in the dining room.

I didn't like to look in on the Saturday morning show. The animation was excellent, the detailing rich—my agents had seen to all that—but I didn't like the voices.

Nobody on that show had a voice like Belinda, a low buttery voice that made its own soothing music. And it was sad. Charlotte ought to have a good voice, because Charlotte was the one who had really made me famous with just a little help from Bettina and Angelica and all my other girls.

Many another children's books artist had redone fairy tales as I had done with *Sleeping Beauty, Cinderella, Rumpelstiltskin.* Many another had created lavish illustrations, suspenseful stories, amusing adventures. But my singular gift was for inventing young heroines and shaping every illustrated page around their personalities and emotions.

In the early days my publishers had urged me to put little boys in the books, to broaden the audience, as they said, but I had never yielded to that temptation. When I was with my girls, I knew where I was, and I could give it the full passion. I kept the focus tight. And to hell with the critics who now and then ridiculed me for it.

When Charlotte stepped into the picture, things began to happen that surprised me completely. Charlotte actually grew older in the books. She went from a tender waif of seven years old to adolescence. That never happened with the others. My best work was Charlotte, even though she too finally stopped at age thirteen or so about the time I signed that television contract.

I could never paint her after she went on the air, no matter how great the demand for books with her. She was gone. She was plastic now. And Angelica might go that way too if this animated movie deal went through. I might never finish the Angelica book I had started a couple of weeks ago.

Tonight I did not care much about it. Bettina, Angelica—I was tired of them. I was tired of it all, and this booksellers convention was only making me face it. The exhaustion went way back. *Looking for Bettina,* what did that mean? I couldn't find her myself anymore?

I SMOKED another one of the Gauloises. I relaxed all over.

The party, the dinner, the noise and bustle were losing their hold at last. And the dingy stillness of the room was comforting, as it was meant to be. I let my eyes drift over the faded wallpaper, the dusty crystal baubles of the chandelier, the fragments of light caught in the darkened mirrors.

No, not ready to throw it all in the street. Not this lifetime anyway. Need it after hotels and bookstores and reporters—

I pictured Belinda on the carousel horse, or sitting cross-legged beside the oval of the toy train track, her hand on the old rusted locomotive. I pictured her slumped on the sofa amid all the dolls. Damn, why did I let her get away like that?

In my head I took her clothes off again. Saw the lattice of marks on her tanned calves left by the ribbed socks. She had shivered with pleasure when I ran my nails lightly over those marks, grabbed the soft mid part of each naked foot. The light hadn't mattered to her. I was the one who had turned it off when I started unbuttoning my shirt.

The hell with it!

You'll be lucky you don't end up in jail someday for this kind of thing, and you're mad at her for skipping out on you. And with the street brats you kid yourself that it's OK because afterwards you give them so much money. "Here, use this for a bus ticket home. Here, this will even make plane fare." What do they buy with it, pot, cocaine, booze? It's their problem, isn't it?

Look, you got away with it again, that's all.

THE grandfather clock chimed ten. The painted plates along the dining room mantel gave a faint musical rattle. Time to try to paint her.

I poured another cup of coffee and went upstairs to the attic studio. Wonderful the familiar smells, the linseed oil, the paints, the turpentine. The smells that meant home, safe in the studio.

Before I turned on the lights, I sipped the coffee and looked out the big uncovered windows in all four directions. No fog tonight, though there would be tomorrow. It had to follow the heat. I'd wake up cold in the back bedroom. But for now, the city was shining with an eerie, spectacular visibility. It was no mere map of lights. There was a muted color to the thick rectangular towers of downtown, to the peaked-roof Queen Anne houses spilling down the Noe Street hill into the Castro.

The canvases stacked all about seemed faded, shabby.

I changed that by turning on the lights. And I rolled up my sleeves and I put a small canvas on the easel and started sketching her.

I don't often sketch. When I do, it means I don't know where I'm going. And I don't do it with a pencil. I do it with a fine brush and just a little oil paint squeezed out on the plate, usually raw umber or burnt sienna. Sometimes I do it when I'm tired and don't really want to get going. Sometimes I do it when I'm afraid.

This was an example of the latter. I couldn't remember the details of her.

I just couldn't see the features of her face. I could not get the *"there there"* that had made me do it with her. It wasn't just her availability. I am not that morally rotten, that stupid, no, not that contemptible. I mean I'm a grown man, I could have fought my way out of there.

Cotton panties, lipstick, and sugar. Hmm.

No good. I had the pyramid of hair all right, thick soft nest of hair. I had the clothes of course. But not Belinda.

I decided to go back to the big canvas I was doing for my next book—a jungle garden in which Angelica roamed searching for a lost cat. Back to the fat glossy green leaves, the bulging branches of the oaks, the moss hanging in streaks to the high grass through which the cat came to reveal its hateful grin—beware Angelica—like Blake's tyger.

It all looked like clichés to me, my clichés. To fill in the background, the ominous sky, the overhanging trees—it was like setting myself on high-speed automatic pilot.

When the doorbell rang around midnight, I almost didn't answer.

After all, it could have been any one of half a dozen drunken friends, and more than likely a failed artist who wanted to borrow fifty dollars. I wished now I had just left fifty dollars in the mailbox. He would have found it. He was used to finding it.

The bell rang again, but not hard and long, the way he always did it. So it could be Sheila, my next door neighbor come to tell me her gay roommate was having a fight with his lover and they needed me to come over at once.

"For what?" I would say. But I'd wind up going if I answered. Or, worse yet, having them in. Getting drunk, listening to them argue. Then Sheila and I would wind up in bed together out of habit, loneliness, compulsion. No, not this time, not after Belinda, out of the question, don't answer.

Third ring, just as short and polite. Why wasn't Sheila cupping her hands around her mouth and screaming my name by now so that I could hear it all the way up here?

Then it occurred to me: Belinda, she'd gotten my address from my wallet. That's why it had been lying on top of my pants.

I ran down the steps, both flights, and opened the front door, and she was just walking away, the same leather pouch hanging from her shoulder.

She had her hair up and her eyes were rimmed in kohl and her lips darkly red. If it hadn't been for the mail pouch bag, I wouldn't have immediately known her.

She looked even younger somehow—it was her long neck and her babycheeks. She looked so vulnerable.

"It's me, Belinda," she said. "Remember?"

I FIXED some canned soup for her and put a steak in the broiler. She was in a mess she said, somebody broke the padlock on the door of her room. She was afraid to sleep there tonight. It was scary somebody busting into her room, and it wasn't the first time it had happened. They'd taken her radio, which was the only damn thing worth taking. They almost stole her videotapes.

She ate the bread and butter with the soup as if she was starving. But she never stopped smoking or drinking the Scotch I'd poured for her. This time it was black cigarettes with gold bands on them. Sobranie Black Russians. And she was looking around all the time. She had loved the toys. Only hunger had got her to the kitchen.

"So where is this padlocked room?" I asked.

"In the Haight," she said. "You know, it's a big old flat, a place that could look like this if somebody wanted to save it. But it's just a place where kids rent rooms. Full of roaches. There's no hot water. I have the worst room because I came in last. We share the bath and the kitchen, but you'd have to be crazy to cook in there. I can get another padlock tomorrow."

"Why are you in a place like that?" I asked. "Where are your parents?"

Under the light I could see the pink streaks in her hair. Her nails were done black. Black! And all that since this afternoon. One costume follows another.

"It's a hell of a lot cleaner than one of those skid row hotels," she said. She laid her spoon down properly, didn't drink the dregs in the bowl. The nails were long enough to look deadly. "I just need to stay here tonight. There's a hardware store up on Castro, where I can get the padlock."

"It's dangerous living in a place like that."

"You're telling me? I put the bars up on the window myself."

"You could get raped."

"Don't say it!" Visible shudder. Then her hand up demanding silence. Was it panic behind the paint? Cloud of smoke from the cigarette.

"Well, why the hell—"

"Look, don't lose any sleep over this, OK? I want to crash here for one night."

That clipped quality was almost gone. Pure California voice. She could have been from anywhere. But it still sounded like butter.

"There's got to be someplace better than that."

"It's cheap. And it's my problem. Right?"

"Is it?"

She broke off another piece of French bread. The makeup job wasn't bad at all, just outrageous. And the soft black gabardine dress was vintage thrift shop. Either that or she got it from her grandmother. It fit snugly over her breasts and under her arms. A few sequins fallen off the tight neck band.

"Where are your parents?" I asked again. I turned the steak over.

She chewed the bread, swallowed it and her face set in a rather stern expression as she looked at me. The heavy mascara made her look even sterner.

"I'll go if you don't want me here," she said. "I'll understand perfectly."

"I do want you here," I said, "but I just want to know—"

"Then don't ask me about my parents."

I didn't respond.

"I'll leave if you mention that again." Very gentle. Very polite. "It's the easiest way you could get rid of me. No hard feelings. I will just go."

I took the steak out of the broiler and put it on the plate. I turned off the broiler.

"Are you going to mention it again?" she asked.

"No." I set the plate down for her with a knife and fork. "Want a glass of milk?"

She said no. Scotch was good enough, especially good Scotch. Unless of course I had bourbon.

"I have bourbon," I said in a small voice. This was criminal. I got down the bourbon and fixed her a weak drink.

"That's enough water," she said.

In between rapid bites of the steak she was looking around the kitchen at the sketches I'd tacked up, the few dusty old dolls that had found their way to a shelf here. One early painting hung above the cabinets. It wasn't so good, but it was of the house where I grew up in New Orleans—my mother's house. She studied that. She looked at the old black wrought iron stove, the black-and-walnut tile.

"You have a dream house here, don't you?" she said. "And this is real good bourbon, too."

"You can sleep in a four-poster bed if you like. It has a canopy. It's very old. I brought it out here from New Orleans. I painted it in my *Night before Christmas.*"

She seemed immediately delighted.

"It's where you sleep?"

"No. I sleep in the back room with the door open to the deck. I like the night air. I use a pallet on the floor."

"I'll sleep where you want me to sleep," she said. She was eating incredibly fast. I leaned against the sink and watched her.

Her ankles were crossed and the straps of the little shoes looked very pretty going over her insteps. The napkin was a perfect white square on her lap. But her neck was the exquisite part. That and the gentle slope of her shoulders under the black gabardine.

She probably thought she looked grown-up. But what the nail polish and the paint and cocktail clothes did, really, was turn her into kiddie porn.

I was thinking it over.

Seeing her got up like this, gulping bourbon and puffing that cigarette, was like watching little child star Tatum O'Neal smoke cigarettes in the movie *Paper Moon.* Children didn't have to be naked to look sexual. You could carnalize them by simply turning them out like adults, having them do adult things.

The problem with this theory was, she had looked just as sexy when I first saw her in the Catholic school uniform.

"Why don't you sleep with me in the four-poster?" she asked. Same simple and earnest voice she had used in the hotel suite.

I didn't say anything. I reached into the refrigerator and took out a beer and opened it. I took a long drink. There goes painting anymore tonight, I thought, rather stupidly since I knew I wasn't going to paint. But I could still photograph her.

"How have you managed to stay alive this long?" I asked. "Do you only pick up famous writers?"

She studied me for a long moment. She blotted her lips very fastidiously with the napkin. She made a little cast-off gesture with her right hand, ripple of slender fingers. "Don't worry about it."

"Somebody ought to worry about it," I said.

I sat down opposite her. She was almost finished with the steak. The paint on her eyes made it very dramatic when she looked down, then up. Head like a tulip.

"I have pretty good judgment," she said, carefully trimming the fat from the meat. "I have to. I mean I'm on the street, room or no room. I'm . . . you know . . . drifting."

"Doesn't sound like you like it."

"I don't," she said. Uneasy. "It's limbo. It's nothing—" She stopped. "It's a big waste of everything, drifting like this."

"So how do you actually make it? Where does the rent come from?"

She didn't answer. She laid her fork and knife carefully across the empty plate and lighted another cigarette. She didn't do the matchbook trick. She used a small gold lighter. She sat back with one arm across her chest, the other raised, curved hand holding the cigarette between two fingers. Little lady with pink streaked hair, blood red mouth. But her face was absolutely opaque.

"If you need money, you can have it," I said. "You could have asked me this afternoon. I would have given it to you."

"And you think *I* live dangerously!" she said.

"Remember what I said about photographing you," I said. I took one of the cigarettes out of her pack. I used her lighter. "Strictly proper stuff. I'm not talking about nude shots. I'm talking about modeling for my books. I can pay you for that—"

She didn't answer. The stillness of her face was a little unnerving.

"I photograph little girls all the time that way for my work. They're always paid. They come from reputable agencies. I take pictures of them in old-fashioned clothes. And I work with these photographs when I make my paintings upstairs. A lot of artists work this way now. It doesn't exactly fit the romantic idea of the artist painting from scratch but the fact is artists have always—"

"I know all that," she said softly. "I've lived around artists all my life. Well, sort of artists. And, of course, you can photograph me and you can pay me what you pay the models. But that's not what I want from you."

"What do you want?"

"You. To make love to you, of course."

I looked at her for a long moment.

"Somebody's going to hurt you," I said.

"Not you," she said. "You're just what I always thought you'd be. Only you're better. You're actually crazier."

"I'm the dullest guy in the world," I said. "All I do is paint and write and collect junk."

She smiled, a very long smile this time. Bordering on an ironic laugh.

"All those pictures," she said, "of all those little girls wandering through dark mansions and overgrown gardens, all those secret doors—"

"You've been reading the critics. They love to go to town on a hairy-chested man who does books full of little girls."

"Do they talk about that, too? How sinister it all is, how erotic—"

"It's not erotic."

"Yes, it is," she said. "You know it is. When I was little, it used to put me in a spell to read your books. I felt like I was leaving the world."

"Good. What's erotic about that?"

"It's got to be erotic. Sometimes I didn't even want to start, you know —didn't want to slip into Charlotte's house. It would give me these funny feelings just looking at Charlotte creeping up the stairs in that nightgown with the candle in her hand."

"It's not erotic."

"Then what's the threat? What's behind all the doors? Why are the girls always looking out of the corner of their eyes?"

"I'm not the one chasing them," I said. "I don't want to lift their long dresses."

"You don't?" she asked. "How come?"

"I hate this," I said gently. "I work six months on a book. I live in it, dream in it. I don't question it. I spend twelve hours a day going over and over the canvases. Then somebody wants to explain it all in five hundred words or five minutes." I reached out and took her hand. "I avoid this kind of discussion with people I don't know. People I do know never do it to me."

"I wish you'd fall in love with me," she said.

"Why?"

"Because you're really someone worth falling in love with. And if we were in love, I wouldn't be drifting. I wouldn't be nobody. At least not while I was with you."

Pause.

"Where do you come from?" I asked.

No answer.

"I keep trying to place your voice."

"You'll never do it."

"One moment it's just California. Then something else creeps in—a trace of an accent."

"You'll never guess it."

She withdrew her hand.

"You want me to sleep in the four-poster with you?" I asked.

"Yes." She nodded.

"Then do something for me."

"What?"

"Wash off all this glamour," I said. "And put on Charlotte's nightgown."

"Charlotte's nightgown? You have that here?"

I nodded. "Several upstairs. White flannel. One of them is bound to fit you."

She laughed softly, delightedly. But there was more to it than delight. I was silent. I wasn't admitting anything.

"Of course," she said finally. "I'd love to wear Charlotte's nightgown." So gracious. Flash of black fingernails as gracefully she ground out the cigarette.

No wonder she had thoughts that the matchbook trick was such a comedy. She was old, polished and suave, and even a little angry. Then she was young and tender. She was shifting back and forth before my very eyes. And it was very disturbing to me. I wondered: Which did she want to be?

"You're beautiful," I said.

"You think so?" she asked. "You wouldn't prefer a darker, more mysterious older woman?"

I smiled. "Been married to two of them. It was interesting. But you're something else."

"In other words, you want me to know it's not always little girls."

"Yes, I want you to know that. I want to remind myself too. But I can't figure you out. You've got to give me a clue on where you came from. A clue on the voice."

"I grew up everywhere and nowhere. Madrid, LA, Paris, London, Dallas, Rome, you name it. That's why you'll never pin down the voice."

"Sounds marvelous," I said.

"You think so?" Little twist to her smile. "Someday I'll have to tell you the whole ugly story. And you think Bettina has it bad in that old house."

"Why not start telling me now?"

" 'Cause it won't make a pretty picture book," she said. She was getting uneasy. She blotted her lips again carefully and put the napkin back in her lap. She drank the last of the bourbon. This girl definitely knew how to put it down.

Ears with the tiniest lobes. Pierced lobes, but no earrings. Just the hurtful little mark. And the skin very tight around her eyes so that there was only a tiny seam running around the lashes. This is the kind of tightness you see in the face of very little children. It usually goes away in the teenage years as the face becomes more modeled. The eyebrows were soft, unshaped, just brushed lightly with gray to darken them. In spite of the paint, her face still looked virginal, the way only a blond face can. And the nose was most decidedly upturned. She would most certainly hate it when she really grew up. But I would love it forever, and the poochy, delicious, puckered little mouth with it. I wanted to touch the loose hair that made fine question-mark curls near her ears.

"Where are your parents? You do have them, don't you?"

She looked startled. She didn't answer; then her face went blank. And it seemed she swallowed. She looked stunned actually, as if I'd slapped her. And when her eyes began to water, I was stunned.

I felt this stab inside as I watched her.

"Thank you for everything," she said. She was gathering up her bag. "You've been very nice." She laid the napkin down beside the plate, and she stood up and went out into the hallway.

"Belinda, wait," I said. I caught up with her at the front door.

"I have to go, Mr. Walker," she said. She had her hand on the knob. About to burst into tears.

"Come on, honey," I said. I took her by the shoulders. No matter what else I felt, what else I wanted, it was unthinkable that she walk out the door at this hour, alone. That simply wasn't going to happen.

"Then don't mention all that again," she said, her voice thickening. "I mean it. Kick me out if you want, and I'll go downtown and drop a hundred bucks for a room or something. I've got money. I never said I didn't. But don't mention parents and all that again to me."

"All right," I said. "All right. Belinda has no parents. Nobody's looking for Belinda." I clasped her neck gently in both hands, tilted her face up.

She was almost crying.

But she let me kiss her, and she was pure warmth and melting sweetness again. The same yielding and the same heat.

"Christ, have mercy," I whispered.

"Where's the nightgown?" she asked.

[3]

In the morning, as soon as I opened my eyes, I knew she was gone.

The phone was ringing, and I managed to mumble something into it as I saw the nightgown, hanging neatly on the hook on the closet door.

It was Jody, telling that they wanted me on a talk show in Los Angeles. It was national coverage. They'd put me up at the Beverly Hills of course.

"I don't have to, do I?"

"Of course not, Jeremy, but look, they want you everywhere. The sales reps say they want you for signings in Chicago and Boston. Why don't you think it over, call me back?"

"Not now, Jody. All wrong for me."

"Limos and suites all the way, Jeremy. First-class air."

"I know, Jody. I know. I want to cooperate, but it's just not the time, Jody—"

Even the collar of the nightgown had been buttoned. Perfume. Clinging to it was one golden hair.

Downstairs I found the ashtray and the dishes washed, everything stacked on the drainboard. Very neat.

And she had found the article on me in the *Bay Bulletin,* and that was spread out on the kitchen table, with me smiling in the big photograph they'd taken on the public library steps.

WITH FIFTEENTH BOOK WALKER CONTINUES TO WEAVE MAGIC SPELL

Forty-four, six-foot-one blond-haired Jeremy Walker is a gentle giant among his small fans crowded into the Children's Reading Room of the San Francisco main library, a gray-eyed teddy bear of a man to the eager little girls who besiege him with questions as to his favorite color, favorite food, or favorite movie. The personification of wholesomeness, he has never given these young readers anything but old-fashioned and traditional images, just as if the garish world of "Battlestar Galactica" and "Dungeons and Dragons" did not exist—

How she must have laughed at that. I threw it in the trash.

There was nothing else of her left in the house. No note, no scribbled address or phone number. I checked and double-checked.

But what about the rolls of black and white pictures we'd taken, still in the camera? *Old-fashioned and traditional images.* I made a phone call to break a dinner date for that night, and went to work in the basement darkroom right away.

I had good prints by the afternoon. And I put the best of them along the walls of the attic and hung my favorites from the wire in front of my easel. They were a satisfying, tantalizing lot.

But she had been right when she had said she was not one of my little girls. She wasn't. Her face did not have the unstamped coin look of my models. Yet her features were so conventionally cute, so babyish.

Like a ghost she looked, actually. Positively eerie. I mean, she suggested somebody who was apart from things around her, somebody who had seen things and done things that others didn't know about.

Precocity, yes, surely that was there, and maybe even a little cynicism. I saw that in the pictures, though I had not seen it when I was taking them.

She'd showered before she put on the nightgown. Her hair had been loose and full of wispy little tendrils, and in the photographs these caught the light. And she had played the light rather naturally. In fact, she had been extraordinarily relaxed before the lense; she would sink almost into a trance as I photographed her, responding just a little now and then as if she were actually feeling my eyes on her, feeling the click when I took the shot.

There was something seductively exhibitionistic about her. And she knew things about how she photographed. Once in a while she'd made some little remark about an angle, about the light. But this was pretty unobtrusive. She had let me do what I wanted to do. And I had never quite had a subject like her. No stiffness, no posing; almost a deep and automatic surrender to the situation. It was distinctly wonderful and odd.

The best picture was one of her sitting sidesaddle on the carousel horse in the living room, her naked ankles crossed beneath the hem of her gown. Key light from above. Then there was a very good shot of her on the four-poster bed with her feet drawn up under her, her knees to the side. These I enlarged and printed right up to poster size.

Another excellent picture was of her on the living room floor kneeling beside the old dollhouse, her face beside the turrets and the chimneys and the lace-curtained windows, and all around her a scatter of other toys.

This one with the toys fairly well ended it for me. We should have gone to bed before we started. I wanted to make love to her right there on the living room carpet, but I didn't want to frighten her, and maybe it wouldn't have if I'd suggested it. But it was frightening me.

The shots of her on the stairway with the candle were supposed to be pure Charlotte. I had gone up ahead of her, shooting as she came towards me. Minimal light. Here she really did look like a child, like a child I had painted a hundred times, except for something in the eyes, something. . . . We almost didn't make it to the bed.

But then taking her in the four-poster was too good to miss. She'd been more relaxed, less anxious to please and more ready to be pleased than at the hotel, which was perfect. The first time I don't think she had enjoyed it really; this time I knew that she had. And it had been a big thing to me that she enjoy it. I had wanted to make her come, and she had, certainly, unless she was world-class at faking it. We'd done it twice actually. And the second time was better for her, though it really left me knocked out and just wanting to sleep after that, the night over too soon.

Sleeping next to her, though, feeling her naked in that usually empty bed, the big cold bed full of faint memories of New Orleans childhood—ah, that was too good.

Her face was smooth in most of these pictures. No smile, but she looked soft, receptive, open.

And when I had them up on the wall, I really began to know the anatomy—the wide cheekbones, the slightly square jaw, and the childlike tightness of the skin around the eyes. I couldn't see the freckles in these photographs, but I knew they were there.

Not a woman's face. Yet I had kissed her breasts, her nipples, her scant smoky pubic hair, felt her bottom in my open hand. Hmmmm. Pure woman.

I thought of a joke I'd heard a few years ago in Hollywood. I'd gone down there to close a deal for a television remake of one of my mother's novels—my mother had died years ago—and I was having a celebratory lunch with my West Coast agent, Clair Clarke, at the new and very fashionable Ma Maison.

The whole town was talking then about Polish film director Roman Polanski, who'd just been arrested for allegedly carrying on with a teenage girl.

"Well, you've heard the joke, haven't you?" my agent said. "She might have been thirteen, but she had the body of a six-year-old!"

I had died laughing.

With Belinda it was the face that was six years old.

I wanted to start painting immediately from these—a whole series was coming into my head—but I was too worried about her.

I knew she'd be back, of course she would, she had to come back here. But what was happening to her now? I don't think a parent could have been more worried about her than I was, even if that parent had known about me.

LATE Saturday afternoon I couldn't stand it any longer. I went down to the Haight to look for her.

The heat wave had not let up, the fog had not rolled in, and I had the top down on my old MG-TD as I crawled through the streets from Divisadero to the park and back again, scanning the shoppers and the drifters, the street vendors and the strollers who made up the crowds.

People say the Haight is coming back, that the new boutiques and restaurants are resurrecting the neighborhood that became a slum after the great hippie invasion of the late sixties—that a new era has begun. I cannot see it. Some of the finest Victorians are in this part of town, true, and when they are restored, they are magnificent, and, yes, trendy clothing stores and toy shops and bookstores are bringing the money in.

But there are still bars across the front windows. The drugged out, the insane, still stand on the corners spouting obscenities. You see the hungry and the dangerous hovering in doorways, sprawled on front steps. The walls are scarred with insipid graffiti. And the young people who drift into the cafés and ice cream parlors are often soiled, disheveled, dressed in thrift shop rags. These places themselves have a desolate look. Tables are greasy. There is no heat. You see the evidence of pain and neglect still everywhere you turn.

The place is interesting. I give it that. But no amount of vitality makes it hospitable.

But then it never was.

Back in the days when I had my first painting studio in the Haight, before the flower children flocked there, it was a hard, cold part of town.

The merchants didn't make conversation. You didn't get to know the people downstairs. The bars were tough. It was a neighborhood of people who rented from out-of-town landlords.

The downtown Castro District, where I eventually settled, was an entirely different place. The Castro has always had the feeling of a small town, the same families owning their homes for as long as a century. And the influx of gay men and women in recent years has only created another community within the community. There is a mellowness in the Castro, a sense of people looking out for one another. And of course there is the warmth, the sun.

The day-to-day San Francisco fog often dies at the top of Twin Peaks just above the Castro. You can drive out of the chill of other neighborhoods and find yourself home under a blue sky.

But it's hard to say what the Haight might become. Writers, artists, students still seek it out for the low rents, the poetry readings, the thrift shops, and the bookstores. It does have a lot of bookstores. And to prowl there on Saturday afternoons can be fun.

If you're not looking for a runaway teenage girl. Then it becomes the proverbial jungle. Every bum is a potential rapist or pimp.

I didn't find her. I parked the car, ate dinner at one of the miserable little cafés—cold food, indifferent service, a girl with sores on her face talking to herself in a corner—and I walked around. I couldn't bring myself to show the pictures to the kids I saw, ask if they'd seen her. I didn't feel I had the right to do that.

WHEN I got home, I found that painting her was the best thing I could do to get my mind off her. I went up to the attic, looked over the photographs, and set to work on a full-scale painting immediately. *Belinda on the Carousel Horse.*

Unlike many artists, I don't grind my own pigments. I buy the best that is commercially available, and I use my paints right out of the tube, since there is usually more than enough oil in them already. I use a little turpentine to dilute, when I need it, but not very much. I like the stuff thick. I like the whole work to be dense and wet, yet moving only when I move it.

As for the canvases, I work almost exclusively in large size with only a few small ones for taking to the park or the yard. And I have them stretched and primed for me. There is always a good supply on hand because I often work on more than one project.

So setting to work on a full-scale painting meant squeezing out a full palette of earth colors—yellow ochre, burnt sienna, raw umber, Indian and Venetian red—and reaching for any one of a hundred prepared brushes. I might sketch a little first, but probably not. I'd go in *alla prima*, painting everything all at once, creating within hours a fully covered surface.

Representing something exactly as it looks—that is automatic with me. Perspective, balance, the illusion of three-dimensional space, all that I learned before I knew what to do with it. I was able to draw what I saw when I was eight years old. By sixteen I could do a good oil portrait of a friend in an afternoon, or in one night cover a big four-by-six foot canvas with realistically rendered horses, cowboys, farm land.

And speed has always been crucial. I mean, I work best when I work fast, on every conceivable level. If I stop to think about how I am rendering a trolly car crowded with people as it rattles downhill under wind-blown trees, I might get blocked, lose my nerve so to speak. So I plunge. I execute. In an hour and a half, voilà, the trolly car.

And then if I don't like it, I throw it out. But time equals output with me. And one of the surest signs that I am doing something bad, that I am on the wrong track creatively, is that something takes too long to finish.

An art teacher I once had—a failed painter himself who worshiped the severe abstract canvases of Mondrian and Hans Hofmann—told me I ought to break my right hand. Or start painting with my left exclusively.

I didn't listen to him. As far as I'm concerned, that was like telling a young singer who has perfect pitch that he has to learn to sing off-key to get some soul into his voice. He doesn't.

Like any representational artist, I believe in the eloquence of the accurately rendered image. I believe in that fundamental competence. The wisdom and magic of a work come through a thousand unarticulated choices regarding composition, lighting, color. Accuracy won't keep life out. To think so is stupid. And in my case weirdness is inevitable.

Despite my craft, no one has ever called me dull or static. On the contrary, I've been labeled grotesque, baroque, romantic, surreal, excessive, inflated, overblown, insane, and, of course, though I didn't want to admit it to Belinda, many people have called me sinister and erotic. But never static. Never overskilled.

All right. I took the plunge. I went at her full sweep with her dense golden hair and her white nightgown and her gorgeous little feet beneath the hem of the gown and the great layers of umber gloom closing in around her, and it was really working and the horse was splendid as always, and her little hand . . .

Something completely unexpected happened.

I wanted to paint her naked.

I thought about it for a little while. I mean, what was this with her sitting there on this glorified toy in this white flannel nightgown? What the hell was she doing there? She's not Charlotte. It was an OK painting so far. In fact, it was better than OK, but it was also all wrong. A detour. I took it off the easel. No. Not her.

And then, without thinking much about it, I turned to the wall the canvases of Angelica for the new book. I laughed when I caught myself doing it. "Don't look, Angelica," I said. "In fact, why the hell don't you pack up and get out, dear? Go to Rainbow Productions in Hollywood." I looked around.

No need to turn around the other canvases. These were the grotesque ones, the ones the reporters often asked about but which no one ever saw in any book or any gallery.

They had nothing to do with my published work or images. Yet I'd done them for years—pictures of my old house in New Orleans and the Garden District around it, mansions rotting, forlorn beings in rooms of peeling wallpaper and broken plaster, landscapes prowled by giant rats and roaches. They all produced in me a kind of giddiness. I mean, I rather enjoyed it when friends came in here and gasped. Childish.

Of course, the lushness of New Orleans is in everything I do. The wrought iron fences are always there, the flowers in threatening profusion, the violet skies of New Orleans seen through webs of leafy limbs.

But in these secret pictures the gardens are true jungles, and the rats and insects are gigantic. They peer through windows. They hover over vine-covered chimneys. They roam the narrow tunnel-like streets beneath the oaks.

These pictures are damp and dark, and the red used in them is always blood red. A stain almost. The secret trick of them is never to use pure black in them because they are already so black.

I paint these pictures when I am in certain moods, and it feels like driving my car at a hundred miles an hour to paint them. My usual breakneck speed is doubled.

My friends tease me a lot about them.

"Jeremy's gone home to paint rats."

"Jeremy's new book is going to be *Angelica's Rats.*"

"No, no, no, it's going to be *Bettina's Rats.*"

"*Saturday Morning Rat.*"

My West Coast agent, Clair Clarke, came up into the studio once, saw the rats, and said, "My God! I don't think we'll sell the movie rights to that, do you?" and went downstairs immediately.

Rhinegold, my dealer, had looked them all over one afternoon and said that he wanted at least five for immediate exhibit. He wanted three for New York and two for Berlin. He'd been excited.

But he didn't argue when I said no.

"I don't think they mean enough," I said.

There was a long silence and then he nodded.

"When you make them start meaning enough, you call me."

They have never started meaning enough. They have remained fragments, which I paint with a vengeful hilarity. Yet I have always known that these pictures have a disconcerting beauty. Yet the lack of meaning in them feels immoral. Rather horribly immoral.

Whatever the limitations of my books, they have meaning and are moral. They have a complete theme.

So much for the roach and rat paintings.

I didn't bother to turn them around when I started painting Belinda naked on the carousel horse. But that wasn't because I thought painting her naked was immoral, either.

No, I had no such idea of that. I could still smell her sweet feminine smell on my fingertips. She was all things naked and good and sweet to me in this moment. She was not immoral and this was not immoral. Far from it.

And it had nothing to do with those rat and roach paintings. But something was happening, something confusing, something dangerous, dangerous to Angelica somehow.

I stopped, thought about it for a moment. The craziest feeling had come over me, and, boy, how I liked it. How I liked feeling this, this sense of danger. If I thought about it long enough—but no matter. Don't analyze.

For now, I wanted to capture a highly specific characteristic of Belinda —the ease with which she'd gone to bed with me, the frankness with which she had enjoyed it. That was the point of the nudity. And it gave her power, that frankness and ease.

But she mustn't worry, ever, about these pictures because nobody would see any of this. I'd be sure to tell her that. What a laugh to think of what it would do to my career if someone did see this, oh, too funny that, but no, it would never happen.

I got her face effortlessly again from the photographic map of lines and proportion. And I was working double fast, as I always did when I did the dark pictures. Everything felt wonderful. I was piling on the paints, creamy and thick and gleaming, and the likeness of her was glaring there, and my brush was racing over the details, all that craft rising up without the slightest conscious hindrance.

Her body of course could only be true to my memory of it, breasts a little large for her small frame, nipples small, light pink, scant pubic hair, truly the color of smoke, no more than a discreet little triangle. There were bound to be inaccuracies. But the face was the crux; the face held the character. The slope of her naked shoulders, the high curve of her calves, all that I reinvisioned, thinking about how it had felt to touch it. And kiss it.

It was working out all right.

AROUND twelve o'clock I had a near-complete canvas of her and the horse, and I was so elated that I couldn't paint for very long without stopping, just to drink coffee, light a cigarette, walk around. I filled in the last details at about two o'clock. The horse was as good as she was now. I'd got his carved mane, the flared nostrils, the bridle with the paste jewels and the gold paint peeling from it.

The thing was done, absolutely done. And it was as photographically real as anything I'd ever painted—her sitting there in a dim bronze Rembrandt light, hallucinatively vital, yet subtly stylized through the even ·attention to every detail.

I wouldn't have changed it then if she had come in and posed naked for me. It was all right. It was Belinda—the little girl who'd made love to me twice, apparently because she wanted to—just sitting there naked, staring at me, and asking what?

"Why do you feel so guilty for touching me?"

Because I am using you, my dear. Because an artist uses everything.

WHEN I got back from my drive through the Haight the next afternoon, there was a note from her in the mailbox.

"Came, went—Belinda."

For the first time in my entire life I almost drove my fist through the wall. Immediately I put the keys to the house in an envelope, marked her name on it and put it in the box. She couldn't miss it. Somebody else might find it, of course, and loot the house. I didn't give a damn. There was a deadbolt on the attic studio, where all the paintings were, and another on the darkroom downstairs. As for the rest of it, dolls and all, they could have it.

WHEN she hadn't come by or called by nine o'clock, I started working again.

This time she was kneeling naked beside the dollhouse. I'd work on her for a while, then on the dollhouse. It took a lot of time, as it always did, to reproduce the shingled mansard roof, the gingerbread windows, lace curtains. But it was as important as she was. And then everything around her had to be done, until the entire background was there with the dusty toys, the edge of the velvet couch, the flowered wallpaper.

By the time the morning light came through the windows it was finished. I scratched the date into the wet oil paint with my palette knife, whispered, "Belinda," and fell asleep right there on the cot under the burning morning sun, too tired to do anything but cover my head with a pillow.

[4]

THE last important party of the booksellers convention was scheduled that evening at a picturesque old mountainside hotel in Sausalito. It was the official sit-down dinner for Alex Clementine to launch the autobiography he'd proudly written—on his own without a ghost—and I simply had to be there.

Alex was my oldest friend. He'd starred in the most successful films ever made from my mother's historical novels, *Evelyn* and *Crimson Mardi Gras.* We'd shared a great deal, both good and bad, over the years. And most recently I'd connected him with both my literary agent and my publisher for his new book. Weeks ago I'd offered to pick him up downtown at the Stanford Court Hotel and drive him across the bay to the Sausalito party.

Fortunately the warm clear weather held out, the New Yorkers were positively moaning over the dazzling view of San Francisco across the water, and Alex, white-haired, sun-bronzed, and impeccably dressed, overwhelmed us with California Gothic tales of murder, suicide, transvestism, and madness in Tinseltown.

Of course, he'd seen Ramon Novarro only two days before he was murdered by gay hustlers, talked to Marilyn Monroe only hours before her suicide, run into Sal Mineo the night before he was murdered, been seduced by an anonymous beauty onboard Errol Flynn's yacht, been in the lobby of the London Dorchester when they'd wheeled out Liz Taylor on the way to the hospital with her near-fatal pneumonia, and "had almost gone" to a party at the house of Roman Polanski's wife, Sharon Tate, on the very night the Charles Manson gang broke into it and massacred all the occupants.

But we forgave him all that for the countless authentic little tales he told about the people he really had known. His career had spanned forty years, that was a fact, from his first starring role opposite Barbara Stanwyck to a regular part on the new nighttime soap "Champagne Flight" opposite the indomitable erotic film star Bonnie.

"Champagne Flight" was the season's camp trash hit. And everybody wanted to hear about Bonnie.

In the sixties she'd been the Texan who conquered Paris, the big beautiful dark-haired Dallas girl who became queen of the French New Wave along with Jean Seberg and Jane Fonda. Seberg was dead. Fonda had long ago come home. But Bonnie had remained in Europe, in seclusion à la Brigitte Bardot, after years of making bad Spanish and Italian films never released in this country.

It had been the hard-core pornographic flicks—*Deep Throat, Behind the Green Door, The Devil and Miss Jones*—that had killed the stylish, often profound erotic films that Bonnie had made in the sixties, driving her and Bardot and others like them from the American market.

Everybody at the table admitted to remembering those old pictures, loving them.

Bonnie, the brunette Marilyn Monroe, peering out from behind big horn-rimmed glasses as she talked existentialism and angst in her soft American-accented French to the cold, callous European lovers who destroyed her. Monica Vitti was never more lost, Liv Ullmann never more sad, Anita Ekberg never more voluptuous.

We compared notes on the rat-hole art theaters where we'd seen the flicks, the cafés in which we'd talked about them after. Bonnie, Bardot, Deneuve—they had had intellectual approval. When they stripped for the cameras, it had been courageous and wholesome. Was there anyone comparable to them now? Somebody still had the *Playboy* in which Bonnie first appeared wearing only her horn-rimmed glasses. Somebody else said *Playboy* was reprinting the pictures. Everybody remembered her famous ad for Midnight Mink with the coat open all the way down the front.

And every single one of us admitted, to our shame, having tuned in the stylish but wretched "Champagne Flight" at least once just to get a look at Bonnie. Bonnie at forty was still first-rate Bonnie.

And though her few Hollywood films had been disasters, she was now in the pages of *People* magazine and the *National Enquirer* along with Joan Collins of "Dynasty" and "Dallas" star Larry Hagman. Paperback biographies of her were in every drugstore. Bonnie dolls were on sale in the madcap gift shops. The show was in the top ten. They were bringing back her old films.

Soulful Bonnie; Texas Bonnie.

Well, Alex had had his arms around her only last Monday afternoon; she was a "darlin' girl," yes, she did need the horn-rimmed glasses, couldn't see two feet in front of her; yes, she did read all the time, but not Sartre or Kierkegaard or Simone de Beauvoir "and all that old foolishness." It was mysteries. She was addicted to mysteries. And no, she didn't drink anymore, they had her off the booze. And she wasn't on drugs either. Who said such a thing?

And would we please stop knocking "Champagne Flight"? It was the best break Alex had had in years, he didn't mind telling us. They'd used him in seven episodes and promised him a couple more. His career had never had such a shot of adrenaline.

The nighttime soaps were bringing back all the worthwhile talent— John Forsythe, Jane Wyman, Mel Ferrer, Lana Turner. Where the hell was our taste?

OK, OK. But we wanted real dish on Bonnie. What about the shooting last fall when she mistook new husband, "Champagne Flight" producer Marty Moreschi, for a prowler and pumped five bullets into him in their Beverly Hills bedroom? Even I had paid attention to that story in the news. Now, come on, Alex, there's something there, there has to be.

Alex shook his head. Bonnie was blind as a bat, that he could swear to. She and Marty were lovebirds on the set of "Champagne Flight." And that Marty, well, he was director, producer, writer of "Champagne Flight." Everybody loved him. That's all Alex could tell us.

The company line, we grumbled.

No, Alex protested. Besides, the best dish on Bonnie was old dish, the story of how she'd picked a father for her kid while she was still big bucks in the international cinema. Hadn't we heard that one?

Soon as Bonnie decided to have a baby, she'd gone shopping for a perfect male specimen. And the handsomest man she'd ever seen was the blond blue-eyed hairdresser George Gallagher, better known as G.G., six foot four and "breathtaking down to the last detail of his anatomy." (Lots of nods from those who'd seen G.G.'s shampoo commercials. And the New Yorkers knew him. You had to book him three months in advance.) Only trouble was, he was gay, absolutely thoroughly and incurably gay, this guy, and had never been to bed with a female in his life. In fact, his most reliable pattern for sexual release, "if you'll pardon my language," was manipulating himself as he knelt worshipfully at the feet of a leather-clad boot-wearing black stud.

Bonnie moved him into her suite in the Paris Ritz, plied him with vintage wines and gourmet foods, had her limo take him to and from work on the Champs-Élysées, and commiserated with him round the clock about his sexual problems, all to no avail, apparently, until she accidentally stumbled on the key.

The key was dirty talk. Real good and steady dirty talk. Talk dirty to G.G. and he didn't care who you were, he could do it! And whispering in his ear the whole time about handcuffs and leather boots and black whips and black members, Bonnie got him into her bed and "doing it" all night, and then she kept him "doing it" all over Spain while she made her last big hit, *Death in the Sun.* He did her hair too, by the way, and her makeup and her clothes. And she talked dirty to him. And they slept in her dressing room together. But when she was sure the baby "had took," she slapped a plane ticket back to Paris in his hand with a kiss good-bye and thank you. Nine months later he got a postcard from Dallas, Texas, and a photocopy of the birth certificate with his name on it as the natural father. The baby was gorgeous.

"And what does this kid look like now?"

Don't ask!

But seriously she was a little doll, that baby, just precious. Alex had seen her in Cannes at the film festival last year during the very lunch on the terrace of the Carlton where Marty Moreschi, on the prowl for "Champagne Flight" had "rediscovered" the woman who soon became his wife, the one and only Bonnie.

And as for G.G., it turned out he loved being a father to the little doll-baby, he'd chased Bonnie and the kid all over Europe just for five minutes here and there with his little girl to give her a teddy bear and take a couple of pix for the wall of his salon, until finally Bonnie got fed up with it and had her lawyers drive G.G. right out of Europe so that he ended up with his fancy salon in New York.

Tell us another one, Alex.

But as the evening wore on, as the stories got racier and funnier and Alex got drunker, an interesting truth emerged: not a single juicy anecdote had been included in Alex's autobiography. Nothing scandalous about Bonnie or about anybody. Alex couldn't hurt his friends like that.

We were hearing a best-seller nobody would ever read. No wonder Jody, my beloved publicist, and Diana, Alex's editor, were sitting there over their untouched drinks looking positively catatonic.

"You mean none of this is in the book!" I whispered to Jody.

"Not a single word of it."

"Well, what is?" I asked.

"Don't ask!"

*   *   *

I SOBERED up over three cups of coffee, then went to the phone booth and
rang my house hoping Belinda had found the keys and let herself in or
that she'd called and left a message on the answering machine.

No score on either account. Just a call from my ex-wife Celia in New
York saying in sixty seconds or less that she needed to borrow five hundred dollars at once.

FINALLY I started the drive back with Alex, and we were arguing almost at
once over the wind in the open car about why he hadn't put the little true
stories in his autobiography.

"But what about the juicy ones that wouldn't hurt anybody?" I kept
insisting. "Forget Bonnie and George Hairdresser What's-his-name, you
know all kinds of things—"

"Too risky," he said, shaking his head. "Besides, people don't want the
truth, you know they don't."

"Alex, you're behind the times," I said. "People are as hooked on the
truth these days as they used to be on lies in the fifties. And you can't kill
a career anymore—anybody's career—with a little scandal."

"The hell you can't," he said. "They may put up with some of the dirt
they didn't want yesterday. But it's got to be the right dirt in the right
measure. It's just a new set of illusions, Jeremy."

"I don't believe that, Alex. I think that's not just cynical, it's a bad
observation. I tell you, things are different now. The sixties and seventies
changed everybody, even people in small towns who never heard of the
sexual revolution. The ideas of those times raised the level of popular
art."

"What the hell are you talking about, Walker? Have you watched any
TV lately? 'Champagne Flight,' you can take it from me is garbage. It's
the step-kid of the fifties 'Peyton Place.' Only the hairstyles have been
changed."

I smiled. Only an hour ago he'd been defending it.

"OK, maybe so," I said. "But any TV show today can handle incest,
prostitution—taboo subjects they wouldn't even touch twenty years ago.
People aren't scared to death of sex these days. They know that lots of
the big stars are gay."

"Yeah, and they forgave Rock Hudson for it because he died of cancer,
same way they forgave Marilyn Monroe for being a sex queen because
she went into the big sleep. Sex, yes, as long as death and suffering comes
with it, gives them the moral overtone they've still got to have. Take a
look at the docudramas and the cop shows. I tell you, it's sex and death,
just like it always was."

"Alex, they know the stars drink. They know they have kids like Bonnie did out of wedlock. It's a long way from the years when they drove Ingrid Bergman out of town for having a baby by an Italian director she wasn't married to."

"No. Maybe for a little while it was really open, when the flower children were big, but now the wheel's turning again, if it ever turned at all. Yeah, we've got a gay guy on 'Champagne Flight' because 'Dynasty' did it first, but guess who plays him, a straight actor, and it's all minor stuff and you can smell the Lysol they sanitized it with a mile off. Just the right dirt in the right measure, I'm telling you. You've got to be as careful with the proportions as you were in the past."

"No, you could have packed your book with the truth and they'd still love you and everybody you wrote about. Besides, it's your life, Alex, it's what you've seen, it's you going on record."

"No, it's not, Jeremy," he said. "It's another part, called movie-star writer."

"That's too cold, Alex."

"No. It's a fact. And I gave them what they wanted, as I always have. Read it. It's a damn good performance."

"Bull shit," I said. I was getting angry. We had glided off the bridge and down the freeway past the ghostly Palace of Fine Arts and into town, and I didn't have to shout so loud now. "And even if you're right, the stories you know are good. They're good entertainment, Alex. The truth is always strong. The best art is always based on the truth. It has to be."

"Look, Jeremy, you make these kid's books. They're sweet, they're wholesome, they're beautiful—"

"You're making me sick. But those books happen to be exactly what I *want* to do, Alex. They are the truth for me. Sometimes I wish they weren't. It's not like there's something else better that I'm hiding or passing up."

"Isn't there? Jeremy, I've known you for years. You could paint anything you want, but what do you do? Little girls in haunted houses. The fact is you do them because they sell—"

"That's not true, Clementine, and you know it."

"You do them because you've an audience and you want them to love you. Don't talk to me about truth, Jeremy. Truth's got nothing to do with it."

"Not so. I'm telling you that people love us more for the truth," I said, really working up a head of steam. "That's my whole point. The stars dish the dirt about their love affairs in books now, and the public devours it because it's authentic."

"No, son, no," he said. "They dish the dirt about certain affairs, and you know what I'm talking about."

Dead silence for a moment. Then he laughed again, his hand lightly squeezing my shoulder. I knew we should lighten up.

"Come on, Walker—"

But I couldn't let it go. It tormented me too much, him blazing away at dinner with all those stories and none of them in the book. And me, what the hell had I said to that reporter two nights ago at the promotion dinner? That I wrote *Looking for Bettina* because the audience wanted it? Did I mean that? That little slip was bound to come back to haunt me, and maybe I deserved it, too.

There was some real important issue here, something that was damned near critical to my life. But I was maybe a little too drunk and a little too tired to really grasp it.

"I don't know what's wrong with me tonight. I don't know," I said. "But I tell you, if you'd put everything you knew in that book, they'd have loved it more, they'd have made a movie out of it."

"They'll make a movie out of it the way it is, Jer," he said with the loudest laugh yet. "We've got two firm offers."

"OK, OK," I said. "Money, the bottom line, all that crap. Don't I know it! I'm going to paint some pictures of money!"

"And you'll sell your little Angelica What's-her-name to the movies, too, won't you? But listen, son, they're calling you a genius for this *Looking for Bettina* book. Saw a window of it downtown. Downtown. Not in some kiddie bookstore. Genius, Jeremy. Got to admit it. Saw it in *Time.*"

"Fuck it. Something's wrong, Alex. It's wrong with me and that's why I'm fighting with you. It's really wrong."

"Ah, come on, Jeremy, you and me, we're both fine," he drawled. "We've always been fine. You've got it made with those kids, and if and when you write your life, you'll lie for them and you know it."

"It's not my fault my books are wholesome and sweet. It's the card I drew, for Chrissakes. You don't pick your obsessions when you're an artist, damn it!"

"OK, OK, OK!" he said. "But wait a minute, smarty pants. Let me give you a damn good example of why I can't tell the true stories. You want me to tell everybody that when your mother was dying, it was you who wrote her last two novels for her?"

I didn't answer. I felt as if he had hit me in the head.

We had stopped at the light at Van Ness and California and the empty intersection was absolutely quiet. I knew I was glowering at the street in front of me, positively glowering, but I could not look at him.

"You didn't know I knew that story, did you?" he asked. "That you actually wrote every word of *Saint Charles Avenue* and *Crimson Mardi Gras?*"

I shoved the car into first and made an illegal left turn onto California. Alex was probably my closest friend in the world, and no, I had not known that he shared that old secret.

"Did the publishers tell you all that?" I asked. They had been my mother's publishers too—twenty-five years ago. But all those editors were now gone.

"I've never heard you talk about that," Alex went on, ignoring my question. "Not ever. But you wrote both those last two books 'cause she was too sick and in too much pain to do it. And the critics said they were her best works. And you've never told anyone."

"They were her outlines, her characters," I said.

"Like hell," he said.

"I read her the chapters every day. She supervised everything."

"Oh yeah, sure, and she was worried about leaving you all those medical bills."

"It took her mind off the pain," I said. "It was what she wanted."

"Did you want it? To write two books under her name?"

"You're making a big issue of something that really doesn't matter now, Alex. She's been dead for twenty-five years. And besides, I loved her. I did it for her."

"And those books are still in every library in this country," he said. "And *Crimson Mardi Gras* plays on late-night television somewhere out there probably once each week."

"Oh, come on, Alex. What's that got to do with—"

"No, it's right to the point, Jeremy, and you know it. You'll never tell for her sake. That biography of her—what was it?—I read that thing years ago, and not a word in there about it."

"Popular junk."

"Sure. And I'll tell you the real tragedy in it, Jeremy. It's about the best story that anybody ever tells about your mother. It may be the only story about her entire life worth telling."

"Well, that's my point now, isn't it?" I said. I turned and glared at him. "That's what I'm trying to say, Alex. The truth is where it's at, goddamn it!"

"You're a scream, you know it? Watch the road."

"Yeah, but that's my goddamn point," I said again. I yelled it: "The truth's commercial."

We were pulling into the driveway of the Stanford Court and I was relieved that this was almost over. I felt scared and depressed. I wanted to be home now. Or go looking for Belinda. Or get dangerously drunk with Alex in the bar.

I stopped the car. Alex just sat there. Then he pushed in the dash lighter and took out a cigarette.

"I love you, you know," he said.

"The hell. Besides, who cares about that story? Tell it."

But I felt a little stab inside when I said that. Mother's secret. Mother's goddamned secret.

"Those kids keep you young, innocent."

"Oh, what crap," I said. I laughed, but it was awful. I thought of Belinda, of reaching under Charlotte's nightgown and feeling this hot, succulent little thigh that was Belinda's. Picture of Belinda naked. Was that the truth? Was that commercial? I felt like a fool. I felt exhausted.

Go home, wait for her to call or come, then take her clothes off. Lay her down on the crumpled flannel nightgown in the four-poster bed and pull off her tight panties and push into her gently, gently . . . like a brand-new little glove—

"It was your mother, you know, who told me about your writing the books," Alex said, his voice rising easily to its dinnertime volume. Lights, action, camera. I could feel him relaxing in the seat. "And she never told me I had to keep it secret either."

"She knew a gentleman when she saw one," I said under my breath as I looked at him.

He smiled as he let out the smoke. He looked immensely attractive even now in his late sixties. His white hair was still full, sculpted in a flawless Cary Grant style. And he carried what little extra weight he'd gained over the years with authority, as if other people were just a little too light. Perfect teeth, perfect tan.

"It was right after the premiere of *Crimson Mardi Gras,*" he said, eyes narrowing, his hand on my shoulder. "You remember we had wanted to fly her out to California and she couldn't come, it was impossible the way she was then, but you came, and then later I flew down to New Orleans to call on her."

"Never forget."

"Jeremy, you don't know how Gothic it all was, that trip south."

"You have my sympathy."

"My car pulls up to this gigantic old rose-colored house on Saint Charles Avenue with all the dark olive green shutters bolted, and the picket fence just holding back the oleanders so they don't fall right down on the front pavements. It took two of us just to push in that front gate."

"No place like home," I said.

"And then I enter this dark cold hallway with the grim bronze pirate's head on the yule post, and a big shadowy oil painting of what was it, Robert E. Lee—?"

"Lafayette," I said.

"—Those ceilings must have been fifteen feet high, Jeremy, and those old cypress floorboards, enormous. I went up and up that Scarlet O'Hara staircase. The old gas light fixtures were still in the walls!"

"They didn't work."

"—And just a tiny little chandelier dangling in the upstairs corridor—"

"It was murder changing the light bulbs."

"—And there she was, *the* Cynthia Walker, in that cavern of a front bedroom. That wallpaper, Jeremy, that old gold-leaf wallpaper! A set designer would have given anything to get his hands on that old paper. Yet even so, it was like being in a tree house when you stood there and looked through the open slats of all those blinds. Nothing but the oak branches and the green leaves. If you peeped out the front, you could barely see the traffic moving down there, just little specks of color and that old wooden streetcar rocking past. It gave off a roar, like the sound in a sea shell."

"Write another book, Alex, a ghost story."

"And there she was in her big old-fashioned bed with the oxygen tanks beside it, the oxygen tanks right in the middle of all this gold wallpaper and mahogany furniture. Big highboy—wasn't it?—with the curly Queen Anne legs, and one of those old French armoires with the mirrored doors?"

"Full of moth balls."

"You can't imagine how it looked to me, that room. And the book jackets and photographs and the mementos everywhere, and those tinkling wind chimes, those dreary brass wind chimes—"

"They were glass, actually—"

"—And this tiny little woman, this mite of a woman, sitting up against all these embroidered pillows."

"Silk."

"Yeah, silk. And she was wearing a lavender silk negligee, Jeremy, beautiful thing, and cameos. She had cameos on her neck and on her fingers, and on her bracelets. I never forgot those cameos. Said they came from Italy."

"Naples."

"And a wig, a gray wig—I thought she had a lot of class to have a wig like that made, natural gray and with a long braid of hair, nothing modern or false for her. And she was so gaunt, I mean, there was nothing left of her."

"Eighty pounds."

"Yet she was so lively, Jeremy, so sharp, and you know she was still pretty!"

"Yes, still pretty."

"She had me sit down and drink a glass of champagne with her. She had the silver ice bucket right there. And she told me how on Mardi Gras day, the king of the Rex parade would stop at every house along Saint Charles Avenue in which a former king lived, and the former king would climb up a ladder to the new king's throne on the float, and they would drink a glass of champagne together while the entire parade waited."

"Yeah, they did that."

"Well, she said that it was like having the king of the Rex parade come to drink champagne with her to have me come to New Orleans to see her. And, of course, I told her what a great writer she was, and what a privilege it had been to play Christopher Prescott in *Crimson Mardi Gras* and how well the premiere had gone and all. She laughed and she said right out that you'd written every word of it. She didn't even know who Christopher Prescott was! Oh, how she laughed. She said she hoped he was a gentleman, this Christopher Prescott, and that he drank champagne with the king of Rex during the *Crimson Mardi Gras.* She said you'd done the last two books under her name and you'd be doing others, lots of others. Cynthia Walker was alive and well in your hands. Cynthia Walker would never die. She was even leaving you her name in her will. You'd be doing Cynthia Walker books forever, saying you'd found the manuscripts in her files and her bank vaults, after her death."

"Well, I didn't do them," I said.

He sighed and crushed out the cigarette. Blessed silence. No sound but the roar of the Saint Charles car in my ears. Two thousand miles away, but I could hear it. Smell of that room.

"I got the call in New York when she died," he said. "That must have been—what?—two months later? We toasted her that night at the Stork Club. Real genuine article she was."

"Undoubtedly. Now get out of my car, you drunken bum," I said. "And next time you write a book, put the story in it."

"I'd like to see you do that," he said.

I thought for a moment.

"And what if I did?" I asked. "Somebody would come along and make a TV movie of just that story. And sales of all her books would go up—"

"But you wouldn't tell it."

"—And so would the sales of my books, and all because people got a little truth. Truth makes art and people know it. Now go on in, you bum, some of us have to work for a living."

He looked at me for a long moment, gave me one of his easy, wide screen smiles. So well kept he looked as if somebody had gone over him with a magnifying glass to remove every blemish, every line, every unwanted hair.

I wondered if he was thinking about the other part of the story, if he even remembered it.

On his way out of the house that afternoon, he'd come by my back porch painting room, and I had invited him in, and he had shut the door and casually slipped the bolt. When he sat down on the cot, he gestured for me to sit beside him. We had made love—I guess you could call it that, he had called it that—for fifteen minutes, more or less, before the big limousine had taken him away.

He had been the leading man then in all his glory, graceful of build with curly jet black hair. I remember he had on a white linen suit with a pink carnation in the buttonhole and a white raincoat over his shoulders which faintly suggested the capes he always wore in his costume roles on the screen. Effortlessly charming. That part had not changed at all.

"You stay with me when you come out west," he'd said. He'd written his private number inside a matchbook for me.

I had called that number three months later when I decided to leave the house.

And there had been the brief affair, a week at most in his splendid, clean Beverly Hills house before he'd said: "You don't have to do this for me, kid. I like you just fine the way you are." I hadn't believed it at first, but he had meant it.

Sex he could get anywhere, and he didn't care if it was the cute little Japanese gardener or the new waiter at Chasen's. What he really wanted around the house was a nice-looking straight kid who could fit in like a son.

When his wife, Faye, had come home from Europe, I'd understood it a little better, staying on with them for weeks after, loving both of them, and pretty much having the time of my life.

Parties, movies, late-night card playing, drinking, talking, afternoon walks, shopping trips, we did all those things easily and comfortably, and the sex was utterly forgotten as if I'd imagined the whole thing. I didn't leave till I had finished a portrait of Faye, which hangs over the living room fireplace down there to this day.

She had been one of those pretty comic starlets that nobody remembers now, her career and her life were swallowed by Alex, but no matter how many "sons" or lovers he had had over the years, she was his one and only true leading lady. He'd gone through absolute hell after her death.

I'd never been to bed with a man after that, though now and then I'd felt a powerful temptation to do it, at least when I was very young. And though many of Alex's "sons" had outgrown his interest, we had become enduring friends.

We'd shared some pretty dramatic moments since those times and would probably share others as the years passed.

"Don't worry, kid," he said now. "I'll never tell that New Orleans tale or any other. The truth is just not my business. It never was."

"Yeah, well," I said bitterly, "maybe you've got a point."

He laughed a little uneasily. "You're cranky tonight. You're crazy. Why don't you get out of the fog for a while, come down south with me?"

"Not right now," I said.

"Go home and paint little girls then."

"You got it."

I LIGHTED one of those horrible little Gauloises because they were all I had left, and I drove down Nob Hill and out to the Haight to look for Belinda.

But I couldn't shake Alex's story. He was right about me not being able to tell that old tale. Neither of my former wives had ever heard it. Nor had my closest friends. And I would have hated Alex had he put it in his book. I wondered what he would think if he knew I'd never set foot in Mother's house since the day I'd left on the plane for California. It was still exactly as he had just described it, as far as I knew.

For a few years I'd rented out the lower floor for wedding receptions and other gatherings through a local agency. You could do that with a Saint Charles Avenue mansion. But when they'd insisted on redecorating, I'd stopped.

The place was kept alive now by an old Irish housekeeper, Miss Annie, whom I knew only by voice on the phone. It wasn't in the guide books anymore, and the tour buses no longer stopped in front. But now and then, I was told, some elderly lady would ring the doorbell asking to see where Cynthia Walker had written her books. Miss Annie always let them in.

FINALLY these dark recollections started to lift as I cruised through the late-night Haight. But other thoughts, just as dark, began to intrude.

Why the hell had I left Alex and Faye so soon to go to San Francisco? Over and over they had asked me to settle down south near them.

But I had to be independent, to grow up, of course. I'd been terrified of the love I felt for Faye and Alex, of the sheer comfort I knew in their home. And how had I become independent? By painting little girls in drafty moldering San Francisco Victorians that reminded me of Mother's old New Orleans house?

It was right here in the Haight, in a Victorian on Clayton Street, that my mother's editor, trying in vain to persuade me to write more Cynthia Walker, had discovered my paintings and signed me up for my first children's book.

The portrait of Faye I'd left on Alex's wall was the last picture of a grown woman that I'd ever done.

Forget it. Drive it all out of mind as you've always been able to do. And think on the exhilaration you feel when you paint Belinda. Just that.

Belinda.

I CRUISED down Haight slowly from Masonic to Stanyon looking for her on both sides of the street, sometimes blocking the little stream of traffic till someone honked at me.

The neighborhood tonight seemed uncommonly forlorn and claustrophobic. Streets too narrow, houses with their round bay windows shabby and faded. Garbage in the gutters. No romance. Only the barefoot, the lost, the crazy.

I made my way back to Masonic again. And then back down to Stanyon and along the park, studying every passing female figure.

I was cold sober now. I must have made the circuit six times before an absolute fright of a kid dashed right up to me at the stoplight on Masonic and leaned into the car to kiss me.

"Belinda!"

There she was under a mess of paint.

"What are you doing down here?" she asked. Blood red lips, black rings around her eyes, gold mascara. Her hair was a shower of magenta-gelled spikes. Perfectly horrible. I loved it.

"Looking for you," I said. "Get in the car."

I watched her run around the front. Horrid leopard skin coat, rhinestone heels. Only the purse was familiar. I could have passed her a thousand times like that and never seen her.

She slipped into the leather seat beside me and flung her arms around my neck again. I shifted gears, but I couldn't really see anything.

"This car's the greatest," she said. "Bet it's as old as you are."

"Not quite," I mumbled.

It was a 1954 MG-TD, the old roadster with the spare on the trunk, a collector's item like the damned toys, and I did get a kick out of her liking it.

In fact, I couldn't believe I had her again.

I turned sharply onto Masonic and headed up the hill towards Seventeenth.

"So where are we going?" she asked. "Your place?"

The perfume must have been Tabu, Ambush, something like that. Real grown-up scent. Like the big rhinestone earrings and the beaded black dress. But she was working hard on a wad of gum that smelled deliciously like Doublemint.

"Yeah, my place," I said. "I have to show you some pictures I did. Why don't we swing by your room and get your stuff so you can stay for a while? That is, if you don't get mad about the pictures."

"Bad news back there," she said. She popped her gum suddenly, then two more times. (I winced.) "The guy and his lady in the back room are having a fight. Somebody's liable to call the cops if they don't stop it. Let's just wing it, OK? I've got my toothbrush. I was by your place a couple of hours ago, you know. Five dollars cab fare. Did you get the note I left you?"

"No. When are you going to give me an address and phone number?"

"Never," she said. "But I'm here now, aren't I?" She popped her gum again three times in succession. "I just learned how to do that. I still can't blow a bubble."

"It's charming," I said. "Who did you learn it from, a car hop? No, don't tell me, the same person who taught you the matchbook trick."

She laughed in the sweetest way. Then she kissed me on the cheek, then on the mouth. In fact, she had me in a clinch, all prickly and soft at the same time with the spikes of hair and the juicy little mouth and her eyelashes like wire and her cheeks like peaches.

"Stop," I said. "We're going to go off the road." We were headed down the Seventeenth Street hill towards Market, and my house about a block past it. "And besides, you just may get mad when you see the pictures I painted of you."

[5]

I KNEW I should take her right upstairs to the attic and get this confession over about painting her nude, along with all the promises that nobody would ever see the pictures.

(Right you are, Alex.)

But when she walked past me into the dusty living room, it was like enchantment. A little light came in from the hall and from the back kitchen. But other than that, it was dark, and the toys looked ghostly. And she was witchy in the black lace stockings and glittering rhinestone heels with her spiked hair and her face painted. She touched the roof of the dollhouse, and then knelt down to move the train on the track. It was better than it had been when she wore the nightgown.

She slipped off the awful fake leopard coat, and she climbed up on the carousel horse. The old black flapper dress she wore was low cut, with only straps over her shoulders. The layers of fringe and beads shivered slightly.

She gathered the fabric up in her lap as she crossed her ankles. And she rested her head against the brass pole with her fingers curled around it above her. She let her eyes move over the objects of the room just the way I often did.

Same pose as the nightgown picture. The naked picture.

"Don't move," I said.

I hit the wall button for the little key light above the horse. Her eyes followed me dreamily. "Don't move," I said again, watching the light on her neck, the curve of her chin, the plump little cleavage of her breasts above the scoop neck. The gold gleamed on her eyelids and eyelashes. Her eyes looked blue as ever, fringed with gold mascara.

I went to get the camera.

I shot her from two different angles. She was very still. Yet she never got stiff. She just drifted into it as I took the pictures, her eyes following me now and then just as I wanted them to do as I circled her.

Then I stood still looking at her.

"Would you take the dress off?" I asked.

"I thought you'd never ask," she said. Little touch of sarcasm.

"Nobody will ever see these pictures, I swear it."

She laughed. "Sure, I've heard that one before."

"No, I mean it," I said.

She looked blankly at me for a moment. Then she said:

"That would be an awful waste, wouldn't it?"

I didn't say anything.

She kicked off the shoes, slipped down to stand on the carpet, and pulled the dress over her head. No slip, no bra, no panties. If I'd reached under the dress, I would have felt moist secret pubic hair. Too much. Don't think about it.

Just a black satin garter belt holding the black lace stockings. She unsnapped it all around, slipped the stockings off. She climbed back up on the horse, assumed the same sidesaddle position, legs closed demurely, wrapping her right hand around the brass pole. She looked softly content—a punk womanchild. She was almost smiling. And then she did smile.

Utterly unselfconscious.

For a moment I couldn't snap it. I was paralyzed looking at her.

A foreboding had come over me, a premonition of disaster that seemed stronger than any dread I had known in years and years. I felt guilty looking at her. I felt guilty being with her and taking these pictures of her. I thought of what I'd said so defensively to Alex, that the talent for children's art was the card I drew, that for me there wasn't anything better. Not true. The pictures of her nude upstairs, they were better. A whole lot better. . . .

And she was so innocently self-assured. So lovely.

Her smile was sweet. No more to it than that. And it was right to the point of everything, her smile, the point of asking her to pose this way. Each element was crucial: her sweetness, the decadent makeup she wore, the carousel horse, her woman's body, even her little cheeks all plumped by the smile.

"Come on, Jeremy," she said. "What's the matter?"

"Nothing," I said. I started snapping the pictures. "Can I paint from these?" I asked.

"Jeremy, really," she said. Then she worked her little mouth for a second and popped the gum. "Sure you can."

I GOT into the shower with her. I soaped her all over, then washed her gently with the sponge as she stood with her head back under the flowing water, letting it come down over her closed eyes and her half-open mouth, her face glossy with it.

Her hair got softer and softer. Then I worked the shampoo into it. I lathered it and I heard her moan, as if it gave her deep pleasure. She pressed her breasts against me. I wanted her so badly. I hadn't taken her upstairs yet, but she had said it was OK to paint her nude. She had said OK. So that could wait until later.

After I'd dried her with the towel, we sat on the side of the four-poster together, and I brushed her hair very carefully. She had on one of my starched cotton shirts. It was open down the front. She looked so small in it.

"Would you braid your hair for me?" I asked. "I don't know how to do it."

She smiled. She said she would. I watched her work at it, amazed that her fingers could do something like that so quickly and easily. She made the braids start up high, pulling the hair back from her temples. Very pretty. Lovely smooth forehead. We bound the plaits with rubber bands. I didn't own any ribbon.

And when she finished, she looked like she was six years old all right. The cotton shirt hid her breasts. I could just see the gentle swell of flesh there, and the smoothness of her belly.

I should have photographed her this way. But that could wait till morning. Right now it was driving me mad, the pigtails and her level gaze.

I kissed her forehead first, then her lips. And then it was all over for the night because we were in bed together. No lights but those of the passing cars, and the room very warm around us.

When she turned over later and sank her face into the pillow, I saw the part in her hair down the back, the way the hair was divided so evenly for the two braids, and that too looked utterly irresistible. Little Becky Thatcher.

But just on the edge of sleep I clapped my hand on her wrist.

"Don't you dare leave here without telling me," I said.

"Tie me to the posts and then I can't go," she whispered in my ear.

"Very funny."

Giggles.

"Promise!"

"I won't go. I want to see the pictures."

In the morning I cut off a pair of my old jeans for her. They were too big in the waist, but she cinched it tight with one of my belts, and she tied the tails of the shirt in front. In this get-up, with the braids, she looked like a Norman Rockwell tomboy. I was still in my robe and slippers when I decided to take her upstairs.

I snapped her several times as we went up, and then I let her just wander into the attic and discover the two nudes.

She didn't say anything for a long time. The sun was coming through the windows, and she had to shade her eyes with her hand. The scant fleece on her tanned arms and legs was golden.

"They're gorgeous, Jeremy," she said. "They're wonderful."

"But what you have to understand is, you're safe," I said. "I meant it when I said no one would ever see them."

She frowned at me for a moment, lip jutting a little.

"You mean, not right away, while I'm on the run."

"No. Never," I said.

"But I'm not going to be sixteen forever!"

There it was. I guess even up till now I'd hoped for eighteen, even though I knew it just wasn't possible.

She was glaring at me. "I mean, I won't be a minor forever, Jeremy. Then you can show them to anyone you want."

"No." I said calmly, a little alarmed by her tone of voice. "Then you'll be a woman and damn sorry you ever posed for anyone in the nude—"

"Oh, stop it, you don't know what you're talking about!" She almost screamed it. Her face went red, and her braids made her look like a fierce little girl who might clench her fists and stomp her feet suddenly. "This isn't *Playboy* for God's sakes," she said. "And I wouldn't care if it was. Don't you realize that?"

"Belinda, all I'm trying to tell you is, even if you change your mind later on, you're protected. I can't show these pictures, even if I want to."

"Why not?"

"Are you kidding? It would ruin my career to show them. It would hurt people. I'm a kid's author, remember? I do books for little girls."

She was trembling she was so upset. I took a step towards her and she backed away.

"Hey, look, I don't understand this," I said.

"Why the hell did you paint these pictures," she screamed, "if nobody can see them? Why did you take the photographs of me downstairs?"

I couldn't figure this out.

"Because I wanted to," I said.

"And never show all this to anybody? Never show them these canvases? I can't stand it. I positively can't stand it!"

"You might not always feel that way!"

"Don't tell me that again, that's a cop-out and you know it!"

She pushed past me suddenly and pounded down the steps, slamming the door to the attic behind her.

She had already stripped off the jeans and shirt when I came into the bedroom. And she was putting on the black sequined dress again. The braids made her look like a kid playing dress up.

"Why are you angry, explain this to me," I said.

"You mean you really don't know!" she said. She wasn't just angry, she was miserable.

She pulled up the zipper easily enough, then snapped the black lace stockings to her garter belt. She snatched up the leopard coat.

"Where are my shoes?"

"In the living room. Will you stop? Will you talk to me? Belinda, I don't understand, honestly."

"What do you think I am?" she flashed. "Something filthy? Something for you to be ashamed of? You come looking for me last night. You tell me you have pictures to show me. They're these two big beautiful canvases of me, and you tell me you'll never show them to anyone. They'd ruin your fucking career if you did. Well, you can get the hell out of my way if that's the way you feel. This trash is getting out of your life, move!"

She shot past me into the hall. I went to take her arm and she drew back furious.

I followed her down to the living room where she found her rhinestone shoes and put them on, her face still flushed, her eyes just blazing with anger.

"Look, don't leave like this!" I said. "You've got to stay here. We've got to talk this over."

"Talk over what?" she demanded. "I'm bad for you, that's what you're saying. I'm jailbait. I'm something illicit and dirty and—"

"No, no, this is all wrong. This is not true. This is just . . . this is too important . . . look, you have to stay."

"No, I don't."

She opened the front door.

"Don't leave like this, Belinda!"

I was amazed at how angry I sounded. Inside I was falling apart. I wanted to beg her.

"I mean it, you walk out on me now like this, I'm through chasing after you, or waiting for you. I'm just through. I mean it."

Really convincing. *I* almost believed it.

She turned and glared at me and then she burst into tears. Her face just crumpled, and the tears spilled down. I couldn't bear it.

"I hate you, Jeremy Walker," she said. "I just hate you."

"Well, I don't hate you. I love you, you little brat!"

She backed away again when I reached out for her. She backed out on the porch.

"But don't try to make me crawl on my hands and knees," I said. "Come back in here."

She stared at me one moment through her tears.

"Fuck you!" she said.

Then she ran down the front steps and up towards Castro Street.

THREE A.M. I was sitting in the attic, looking at the pictures, finishing off her damned clove cigarettes. I couldn't work. I couldn't sleep. I couldn't do anything. Somehow I'd done the darkroom work this afternoon on the punk carousel set. At least until I couldn't stand it anymore.

I sat on the floor with my legs crossed, my back against the wall, just staring at the pictures. Sometimes my mind painted the new carousel nude, the punk nude. But my body didn't move. I was too unhappy.

WHEN I pretended to think, I could see it from her point of view. She had no guilt about it, lovemaking, posing, anything. And I told her the pictures would ruin my career. Ah, how could I have been so stupid? I hadn't fallen into the generation gap, I'd fallen into the guilt gap—assuming she'd want my assurance. But God, she was such a puzzle.

Why did she get so hurt, so angry? Why did she storm off like that? And why hadn't I taken a softer approach with her?

So much for thought.

Behind it was just the pain. A pretty unfamiliar pain after all these years. Like the pain you feel when you're very young, maybe as young as she is.

She might never come back, never, never. No, she had to come back. Just absolutely had to.

THEN the phone rang. Three fifteen. Probably some drunk, some crazy.

I got up, went down to the bedroom, and picked it up.

"Hello."

For a moment all I could hear was some strange little noise, like a gasp. A little cough. Then I knew it was a sob. A woman or a girl crying.

"Daddy—"

"Belinda?"

"Daddy, this is Linda!" Sobbing. But it was she, no doubt about it.

"Linda—"

"Yes, Daddy, Linda. Wake up, Daddy, please, I need you." Crying. "You know I told you about this guy and his lady in the back room here. Well, it happened. It happened. He . . . he—"

"I understand, honey. Slow down. Just tell me—"

"He stabbed her, Daddy, and she's dead and the police are here. They don't believe I'm eighteen." Sobbing. "I gave them my driver's license with my old address, you know, and they still don't believe I'm eighteen. I told them you'd come get me, Daddy, please come. They ran my driver's license through the computer, but I don't have any traffic tickets. Daddy, come!"

"Where are you?"

"If I'm not on the corner of Page and Clayton, I'll be inside. Hurry, Daddy."

Page and Clayton, one block from Haight.

THERE were two prowl cars double-parked on Page when I got there. Every light was on in the big shabby old house, quite impossible to miss, and they were just bringing the dead body out on a gurney. Shattering sight no matter how many times you see it on the evening news, the shiny chrome stretcher on wheels, and the thing under the sheet bound with straps as if it were suddenly going to wake up and start fighting. I watched them put it in the back of the city ambulance.

A couple of reporters were there, too, though they didn't seem too excited by the whole thing. I hoped and prayed it was nobody who had ever interviewed me. Only the old-fashioned flashbulb newspaper cameras, no television equipment.

"Please, I have to get in there," I said to the uniformed cop at the door. "I have to pick up my daughter."

He looked like a waxwork of himself in the dismal light, billy club and gun too shiny, too visible.

"Oh, that's your kid back there?" he said. Faint sneer. But Belinda had come into the hall and she ran towards me, shrinking into my arms.

She was hysterical. Her face was all red and blotched, and her hair was loose and in tangles. She had on the same leopard coat, black dress outfit down to the rhinestone heels, but no stockings.

I held her for a second, vaguely conscious of people shoving past us in the hall, and that this was a dirty place with cracked plaster and urine stink, and that nobody was paying much attention to us. A pay phone hung on the wall. Stack of old newspapers under it and a sack of garbage. The carpet on the floor was like bandages.

"Come on, let's get your stuff," I said. I stroked her hair back out of her eyes. No makeup, ghostly white. "Let's get out of here."

There was a crowd bottlenecked in the back room, a man on tiptoe trying to see over the others. From the street, there came the awful crackling sound of a police radio.

She clutched me so hard her fingers hurt my skin as she pulled me into her room.

It was a perfect hole, loft bed at one end, a tiny window with wooden slats nailed over it. Posters of film stars all over the walls, and a brown suitcase on the bed with a plastic sack next to it. Videotapes sticking out of the sack. The chair and lamp were junk shop. The woodwork was chipped and filthy.

I went to get the sack and the suitcase as she clung to me.

"You Mr. Merit?" somebody said behind me.

"No!" she said shrilly. "Jack Merit's my husband. I'm divorced, I told you. This is my Daddy. His name is different. I'm still Linda Merit on the driver's license."

I turned and saw another policeman in the doorway. Much older than the other one. Heavily wrinkled face, shapeless mouth. He was clearly exhausted but he radiated disapproval.

For once in my life I was glad I was so dull, tweed coat and all. In this setting I couldn't have been anybody but her father.

"Well, I need an address where you're taking your daughter," he said. He had a small notebook in his hand, ballpoint pen.

"Of course," I said. I gave him my address.

"And she sure doesn't look eighteen to me," he said. He wrote my address down in his little notebook. "And she had enough booze in here to run a barroom." He gestured to the trash basket. Bottles of bourbon, Scotch. "The drinking age is twenty-one, you know."

"I told him it was Jack's," she whispered, her voice hoarse, struggling. "Jack still comes around, you know that, Daddy." She pulled a Kleenex from the pocket of her coat and blew her nose. She looked like she was twelve. She was terrified.

"Look, this has really been a nightmare for her, and I would like to just get her home," I said, trying not to sound scared. I picked up the suitcase and the sack.

"I know you from somewhere," the cop said. "I've seen you on TV. Did you say Seventeenth Street or Seventeenth Avenue? Where have I seen you?"

"Seventeenth Street," I said, trying to steady my voice.

Someone bumped into him from behind. They were carrying something out of the back room. It looked like a couch. Flashbulbs were going off back there.

"And this is the address where she'll be if we need her?"

"I didn't know them," Belinda said, struggling not to cry. "I didn't hear anything."

"Can I see some identification, please," the cop asked me, "with this address on it?"

I took out my wallet and showed him my driver's license. My hand was shaking badly. I could feel the sweat breaking out all over my face. I looked at her. She was in a silent panic.

If he asks me her birth date, I am up shit creek, I thought. I haven't the slightest idea what it really is, let alone what she told them. And this guy is recording my identity in his little book. And I am standing here lying and saying she's my daughter. My hand was sweating on the handle of the suitcase.

"I know who you are," the cop said suddenly, looking up. "You wrote 'Saturday Morning Charlotte.' My kids are crazy about your books. My wife loves them."

"Thanks, I really appreciate it. You'll let me take her home now, won't you?"

He closed his notebook, and stared at me rather coldly for a moment.

"Yeah, I think that would be a damned good idea," he said contemptuously. He was looking at me as if I were dirt. "Do you know what kind of a place your daughter's been living in?"

"Terrible mistake, terrible—"

"That guy in the back, he knifed his girl, watched her die before he called us. Says God told him to do it. Stoned out of his head when we got here. Track marks on his legs and his arms. Doesn't even remember calling us, let alone killing her. And you know what's across the hall—?"

"I just want to take her out of here—"

"Two hard-bitten little hustlers who work the queers on Polk Street. Want to guess who lives upstairs? Dealers, man, the penny-ante juvenile brand we find dead with a bullet in the back of the head after a rip-off."

Nothing to do but let him finish. I stood there, rigid, feeling the heat in my face.

"Mister, you may write terrific books, but when it comes to being a father to this little girl, you need to read a few."

"You're right, absolutely right," I murmured.

"Get her out of here."

"Yes, sir."

* * *

SHE broke down completely when we got into the car. Through her sobs I didn't catch all of what she said, but this much came clear. The killer was the same guy who'd ripped off her radio, a real mean son of a bitch who had hit on her all the time, beating and kicking the door of her room when she wouldn't open it.

As for her Linda Merit driver's license, it was fake, but the police couldn't prove anything. She'd scored it with the real birth certificate of a dead Los Angeles girl whose name she'd gotten from old newspapers in the library.

But the police kept saying they didn't believe her. They made her stand there while they checked the name through their computers. She kept praying the dead girl never left an unpaid traffic ticket in San Francisco. Only when she told them she had a father who'd come get her did they leave her alone.

I kept assuring her that was the right thing to do. And she was safe now. I tried not to think about that cop writing down my name and address or recognizing me.

WHEN we got home, I practically carried her inside. She was still crying. I sat her down in the kitchen, wiped her face, and asked her if she was hungry.

"Just hold on to me," she said.

She wouldn't even let me get her a glass of water.

In a little while she was quiet. It was almost five now. And the morning light was just coming through the kitchen curtains. She looked stunned and broken. She talked for a little while then about a drug bust, when the narcotics agents had kicked in both the back and front doors of the flat above her. Every piece of furniture in the place had been ripped to shreds. She should have moved immediately.

"Let me fix you something to eat," I said.

She shook her head. She asked if she could have a drink.

I kissed her. "You don't really want that, do you?" I asked. She got up and went past me and got the Chivas Regal and poured herself half a glassful. I watched her drink it smoothly, just the way she always drank, as if it was nothing to her. It hurt me to see it, the Scotch just going down her throat.

She wiped her mouth, set the bottle and the glass on the table, and sat down again. She looked dreadful and vulnerable and lovely all at once. When her blue eyes finally fixed on me, I found her irresistible.

"I want you to move in here," I said.

She didn't answer. She looked dazed. I watched her pour herself another glass of Scotch.

"Don't get drunk," I said softly.

"I'm not getting drunk," she said coldly. "Why do you want me to move in? Why do you want jailbait living with you?"

I studied her, trying to figure the angle of the rage. She took a pack of Garams out of her pocket, stuck one on her lip. The book of matches she'd left at breakfast was still there. I opened it, struck a match, and lighted the cigarette for her.

She sat back, glass in one hand, cigarette in the other, hair all free and messy, and the leopard coat still on, just a little womanshape and black sequins showing between the lapels.

"Well, why do you want me here?" Her voice was raw. "You feel sorry for me?"

"No," I said.

"I can find someplace else to live," she said. Hard, woman's voice coming out of the babymouth. Puff of smoke. Incense smell of the clove cigarette.

"I know that," I said. "I wanted you here after the first night we were together. I wanted you here this morning when you took off. Sooner or later I would have asked you. And whatever I feel about it all—guilt, you know, that kind of thing—I'm sure of this. You're better off with me than living in a place like that one."

"Oh, so you feel this whole mess lets you off the hook, is that it?"

I took a deep breath.

"Belinda," I said, "I'm a pretty square guy when you get right down to it. Call it dull, call it unsophisticated, call it what you will, I think a kid your age should be at home. I think somebody somewhere is crying over you, looking for you—"

"Oh, if you only knew," she said, her tone low and bitter.

"But I can't know until you tell me."

"My family doesn't own me," she said harshly. "I own me. And I'm with you because I want to be. And the old rule still holds. I'll walk out the door if you ask me about my family."

"That's what I figured. You're saying you won't go home, not even after what happened tonight."

"That's not even a possibility," she said.

She looked away for a moment, biting a little at her fingernail, a thing I'd never seen her do before, the pupils of her eyes dancing as she looked around the room. Then she said:

"Look, I bombed as an American kid."

"How do you mean?"

"It didn't work for me because I am not a kid. So I have to make it on my own, either with you or without you. And I'm going to do it. I have to!

If I move in with you, it's not because I'm scared. It's because, it's because I want to—"

"I know, honey, I know."

I reached across the table. I took her hand off the glass as she set it down, and I held her hand tightly. I loved the smallness of it, the tenderness, the way the fingers curled around mine. But it was pain to see her eyes squeeze shut, to see the tears spill down her cheeks just the way they had before, at the front door, when she was storming out.

"I love you too, you know," she said, still crying. "I mean, I wanted to be an American kid, I really did. I wanted it. But you're like a dream, you know, you're like some fantasy I made up that's better than that and, and—"

"So are you, little girl," I said.

AFTER she'd gone to sleep in the four-poster, I put her suitcase and things in the guest room. That could be her private place.

And I went upstairs to work on the punkchild carousel nude, the one of her with the witchy hair, and I painted into the afternoon without stopping, thinking the whole time about the strange things she had said.

What a trio this would be, these carousel pictures.

Now and then I thought of the policeman who had recognized me. I thought of him writing down my name and address in his little notebook. I should have been afraid. I should have been a nervous wreck over all that, in fact. I was a man who had never gotten so much as a speeding ticket.

But it thrilled me. In some dark and secret way it thrilled me. She was here with me now, and I knew it was OK for her, had to be, and I was painting with a speed and power I hadn't known in years. Everything felt good to me.

[6]

ABOUT eleven that morning she woke up screaming. I came down as fast as I could. For a moment she didn't know where she was, who I was. Then she closed her eyes and put her arms around me.

I sat there beside the bed until she was asleep again. She looked tiny, curled up under the quilts. I smoked a cigarette, thought a lot about her and me, about falling for her, and then I went back to painting.

ABOUT two o'clock she came up into the attic.

She looked relaxed and absolutely cheerful.

I was still in the middle of some detail work on the punk nude figure of her on the carousel horse and she stood watching me quietly. The main part of the painting was done and I thought it was spectacular. She didn't say anything.

I put my arm around her and kissed her.

"Look, there's a gallery opening this afternoon for a friend of mine," I said. "A good sculptor name of Andy Blatky. It's his first one-man show, Union Street, fancy, sort of a big break. You want to go with me?"

"Sure, I'd love to," she said. She tasted like vanilla wafers.

I started to wipe the brushes.

She moved away and spent a long time checking out the roach and rat pictures. Barefoot in her flannel gown, she looked like an angel. Seems the little girls of long ago in my church parish had dressed like that for a procession at Christmas midnight mass. Only thing she needed was paper wings.

No comment on the roach and rat paintings either. Just her warm sweet presence and the knowledge, the splendid knowledge that she was here to stay.

I told her I'd put her things in the guest room. That could be her private place. Yes, she said, she found all that. Beautiful brass bed in there. Like a big crib with the side rails. Everything in the house was beautiful, like the sets for an old-fashioned play.

I smiled, but her comment made me feel uncomfortable. Settings for a play, Alex talking about Mother's room in New Orleans—I wanted to put all that out of my mind.

AFTER a quick shower she came down looking splendid. She had on a beautiful old tweed suit, a little worn in spots but exquisitely tailored. She looked very jaunty in the little tapered jacket. Snow white turtleneck sweater underneath. Pair of vintage alligator pumps probably made before she was born.

I had never seen her like this before, without a costume. And she was the shining expensive girl I'd only glimpsed that first afternoon, her hair brushed free, her makeup only a little blush on her cheeks and the perfectly applied candy lipstick.

She gobbled a bowl of cereal, smoking all the time, belted down a Scotch with precious little water, in spite of my protests, and then we took off in the late afternoon sunshine for Union Street.

I was pretty high from the lack of sleep. I felt wonderful, maybe even as wonderful as she looked.

"I want you to know something," I said, as we were coasting along Divisadero Street. "No matter what I said about never showing those paintings, it's pretty damned exciting for me doing them."

Silence.

I glanced over to see her smiling at me in a rather knowing way, her hair blowing softly around her face in the breeze, her eyes glistening. She took a drag off her cigarette and the smoke disappeared.

"Look, you're the artist," she said finally. "I can't tell you what to do with your pictures. I shouldn't have tried."

But it had a defeated sound to it. She had moved in with me, she wasn't going to fight with me anymore, she felt she couldn't.

"Say what you really feel," I said.

"OK. What's the big excuse for never showing all those others? The stuff with the bugs and the rats?"

Here we go again, I thought. Everybody asks. They have to. And so would she, of course.

"I know all your work," she said. "I've seen it in Berlin and Paris and I had the big coffee-table book before I—"

"Ran away from home."

"—Right. And I used to have every book you ever did, even the early stuff, *The Night before Christmas* and *The Nutcracker*. I never saw anything like those grotesque things back there, the ones with the houses falling apart. And you've dated them all. They go all the way back to the sixties. So why are they locked up like that?"

"Not fit to show," I said.

"Ruin the old career because the little girls would scream 'Eeek, a mouse!' "

"You know much about painting?" I asked her.

"Probably more than you think," she said with a little teenage bravado. Just a tiny crack in the adult poise. Subtle lift to her baby-soft chin as she exhaled the smoke.

"Oh, yeah?"

"Grew up in the Prado for starters," she said. "Used to go there every day with my nurse, practically memorized Hieronymus Bosch. Spent a couple of summers in Florence with a Nanny who didn't want to do anything but go to the Uffizi."

"And you liked it?"

"Loved it. Loved the Vatican, too. When I was ten, I used to hang out at the Jeu de Paume in Paris. I'd rather go there or the Pompidou than go to the movies. I was sick of the movies. Damned sick of the movies. When I was in London, it was the Tate and the British Museum. I've put in my time on capital A art."

"Pretty impressive," I said.

We were making all the green lights, and the sad, faded Victorians were giving out now to the restored mansions of the Marina. Ahead was the sight that never fails to stun me, the distant mountains of Marin under a perfect sky, cradling the brilliantly blue water of San Francisco Bay.

"All I'm trying to say is, I'm no Valley girl who can't tell a Mondrian from a place mat."

I broke up. "That puts you ahead of me," I said, "by a long way. I don't know what the hell to think about abstract art. I never did."

"You're a primitive, you know it?" she said. "A primitive who knows how to draw. But back to the roach and rat paintings—"

"You sound like *Newsweek* magazine," I said. "And you're hurting my feelings. Little girls shouldn't do that to old men."

"Did *Newsweek* really say that?"

"*Newsweek* and *Time* and *Artforum* and *Artweek* and *Art in America* and *Vogue* and *Vanity Fair*. And God knows who else, and now even the love of my life."

She gave me a little polite laugh.

"And let me tell you something else," I said. "I don't understand Andy Blatky's sculptures anymore than I do Mondrian. So don't get me into any over-hearable discussions in the gallery. I'll make a fool of myself. Abstract art is just plain over my head."

She laughed in a sweet genuine way, but she was definitely surprised by what I was saying. Then she said:

"Soon as I've had a look around the gallery, I'll answer any questions you might have."

"Thanks, I knew I was a good judge of character. I can spot a girl who's made the grand tour when I see one. And I bet you thought it was your charm."

Union Street was bustling with the usual sunny day expensive shopping crowd. Florists, gift shops, ice cream parlors swam with well-heeled tourists and locals. This was the place to buy a silk-screened hand towel, every brand of semisoft cheese known to the Western world, a painted egg. Even the corner grocery had turned its fruits and vegetables into artifacts, heaping them into pyramids in baskets. The fern bars and the outside cafés were packed.

The gallery doors were open. People blocked the busy sidewalk—usual mixture of the bohemian and the well to do complete with the inevitable plastic glasses of white wine. I slowed, looking for a parking space.

"OK," she said, tapping my arm. "I've done the grand tour and I know the territory. Now back to the rat and roach paintings. Why are they locked up?"

"All right. The stuff looks good, but it lacks something," I said. "It's an easy kind of ugliness. The pictures don't mean like my books mean."

She didn't say anything right away.

"It's seductive, Jeremy, it's more interesting," she said.

I had spotted a parking spot right on Union. Now the trick was to get into it. She was silent while I pulled up, then back, then angled, slamming the bumper in front of me only twice.

I turned off the ignition. I was aware that I felt very uncomfortable.

"That is not true," I said.

"Jeremy," she said, "everybody knows what you've done, transcending the children's books, making art and all that."

"*Newsweek* magazine," I said.

"But the little girls in your books aren't even in original clothes.

They're in drag in a way, all got up like Victorian kids, the whole frame-work is Victorian—it's Lang and Rackham and Greenaway and you know it."

"Watch your mouth, Belinda," I said. I was kidding. But underneath I didn't like her challenging me. "The girls aren't in drag," I said. "They're in dream clothes. It's all dream images. When you understand that, you'll understand why the books work the way they do."

"Well, all I know is, the rat and roach paintings are original. They're crazy and completely new."

Again I didn't respond. We were sitting with the sun coming down warmly on the black leather cockpit of the little car, the sky above blue and open. I wanted to argue, but then again I didn't.

"You know," I said, "sometimes I think it's a hell of a mess. I mean the whole thing. Books, publishing, the critics. I think it's a series of traps. And what makes me mad about my friends always praising those rat and roach pictures to the stars is this: I know they don't work. And nobody wishes more than I do that they did. If I thought they'd blow the lid off for me, I would have shown them a long time ago."

It felt like taking a deep breath to admit all that.

"What do you mean, 'blow the lid off'?" she asked.

I thought for a second. I watched her light another one of the clove cigarettes, and I gestured for her to give me one. She gave me a light from her own.

"I don't know exactly," I said, looking into her eyes and trying not to be distracted by how pretty she was. "Sometimes I feel reckless about it all. I feel like just—throwing it all up."

"But how?"

"I told you. I don't know. But I wish something violent would happen, something unplanned and crazy. I wish I could just walk away from it all —you know, like one of those painters who fakes his suicide or some-thing so he can slide off and go all the way back to square one as some-body else. If I were a writer, I'd invent a pen name. I'd get out."

She studied me, not saying anything. But I don't think she understood. How could she? I didn't understand myself.

"Sometimes," I went on, sort of taking advantage of her silence, "sometimes I think my greatest achievement has been to make success out of a failure, to make an evasion into art."

She hesitated for a moment, then she nodded.

"And what makes me mad," I said, "is when people point out the failure involved as if I don't know it. And when they don't recognize the power of the art I've made."

She took that in. Then she said:

"So you're telling me to get off your case."

"Maybe. Maybe what I'm saying is that if we're going to really know each other for a long time, get used to me. Get used to the evasion. It's me."

Again she smiled, nodded. She said, "OK."

I got out of the car, and she was out before I could come around to open the door for her. I kissed her. She slipped her arm in mine, and we moved into the crowd in front of the gallery. I was getting addicted to these damned cigarettes.

Through the open doors I could see the Spartan white rooms and Andy Blatky's mammoth enameled sculptures exquisitely lighted on their severe white rectangular pedestals. How hard this must be for Andy, I thought, watching the crowd flow and shift, backs often turned to the works themselves, glances almost covert as if it wasn't proper to admire the exhibit. I had the urge to turn around and split. But I wasn't going to do that.

We went through the first room and into an open courtyard, and here was a giant work, its baked pearlescent surface seemingly alive in the sun, its bulbous arms almost tenderly embracing each other. Modern art, I thought bitterly. I love it because Andy did it, and it is beautiful, it really is, this huge, muscular, powerful-looking thing, but what the hell does it mean?

"I wish I did understand it all," I muttered, still holding tight to Belinda. "I wish I was connected. I wish I wasn't just a primitive to these people, just a primitive who knew how to draw. Roaches, rats, dolls, kids—"

"Jeremy, I didn't mean that," she said suddenly, tenderly.

"No, honey, I know you didn't. I was thinking about the other two thousand people who've said it. I was thinking about the way I always feel at moments like this, kind of on the outside."

I wanted to touch Andy's sculpture, to run my hands all over it, but I didn't know if that was allowed. And then I spotted Andy himself in the room behind the courtyard, sort of slumped against the wall. Anybody would have known he was the artist. He was the only one wearing sneakers and a fatigue jacket. He was stroking his small black rabbinical-style beard, eyes vague behind tiny wire-rimmed coin-sized glasses. He looked really upset.

I headed for him, vaguely aware that Belinda had veered off in another direction, and by the time I was shaking his hand, she was lost in the crowd.

"Andy, it's great," I told him. "Terrific mounting, everything. The turnout looks awfully good, too."

He knew I didn't really understand his stuff, never had. But he was glad to see me, and he started mumbling right off about the damned gallery and how they were bawling out people for putting out cigarettes in their damned plastic cups. They were washing out and reusing the damned cups. How could they carry on about a thing like that, the plastic cups? He had half a mind to give them twenty dollars to cover it and tell them to shut up, but he didn't have twenty dollars.

I said I did and would gladly do it for him, but then he was afraid to make them mad.

"I know I should let it ride over me," he was saying, shaking his head, "but goddamn it, it's my first one-man show."

"Well, the stuff couldn't look better," I said again, "and I'd buy that big mother in the garden if it wouldn't mean hiding it where nobody would ever see it in my backyard."

"Are you putting me on, Jeremy?"

I'd never bought anything of his because we both knew it didn't go with the Victorian gingerbread and the damask and the dolls and all the other trash in my house. (Stage set for a play!) But I felt so sick of that suddenly. I'd always wanted one of his pieces. And why the hell not put my money where my head was for once?

"Yeah," I said, "I want that one. I like that one. I could put it down in the grass out there behind the deck. I'd like to see the sun come up on it. It's beautiful, that much I do know."

He studied me trying to figure if this was just talk. He said if I bought it and would lend it back to him with my name on it—courtesy of Jeremy Walker—for future exhibits, he didn't care if I put it in the bathroom. It would be a terrific thing.

"Then it's sold. Shall I tell them, or do you want to tell them?"

"You tell them, Jeremy," he said. He was smiling and stroking his beard even faster now, "but maybe you ought to think it over for a couple of days, you know, like maybe you're not in your right mind right now."

"I've been doing some new work, Andy," I said. "Some really wild new things."

"Oh, yeah? Well I caught *Looking for Bettina,* and you did it again there, Jeremy, you gave me a couple of real moments there—"

"Forget that stuff, Andy. I'm not talking about that at all. Someday soon I want you to come over and see—" I stopped.

Someday soon?

I just drifted for a second. Yeah, that piece would look great out there in the garden.

I caught a glimpse of Belinda far away from me, the pink sunglasses hiding her eyes now, and in her hand was an illegal glass of white wine. My Belinda. I spotted other friends, Sheila, a couple of writers I knew, my lawyer, Dan Franklin, in fast conversation in the corner with a pretty woman two inches taller than him.

People were looking at Belinda. Babymouth, white wine, pink glasses.

"Yeah?" Andy was waiting for me to finish. "What kind of new stuff, Jeremy?"

"Later, Andy, later. Where's the honcho? I want to buy that piece now."

[[7]]

THERE was time to hit the Union Street boutiques afterwards. She didn't want me to spend money, she kept protesting, but it was too much fun taking her into one fancy store after another, buying her all the things I wanted to see on her. Little pleated wool skirts, blazers, delicate cotton blouses. "Catholic school forever," she teased me. But pretty soon she was having fun, too, forgetting to protest the high price tags.

We drove on downtown and made Neiman Marcus and Saks. I bought her frilly dresses, pearls, the lovely froufrou stuff that the new female rock stars had made popular. But it was clear that she had a good eye, was used to good things, and thought nothing of the attentive sales-woman clucking over her.

Slacks, bikinis, blouses, suede coats—all the interseason things you can wear year-round in San Francisco—went into the fancy boxes and garment bags.

I even got her perfumes—Giorgio, Calandre, Chanel—sweet, innocent scents that I liked. And silver barrettes for her hair, and little extra things she might never have bothered with, like kid gloves and cashmere scarves and wool berets—finishing touches, you might say, that would make her look like one of those beautifully turned-out little girls in an English storybook.

I even found a lovely princess-line coat with a little velvet collar. She could have been seven or seventeen in that. I made her buy a mink muff to go with it, although she told me I was crazy, she hadn't carried a muff since she was five years old and that had been in the dead of winter in Stockholm.

Finally we ended up at the Garden Court of the Palace Hotel for dinner. Service slow, food not great, but the decor absolutely lovely. I wanted to see her in that setting, against the mirrored French doors, the gilded columns, the old-world elegance. Besides, the Garden Court always makes me happy. Maybe it reminds me of New Orleans.

It reminded her of Europe. She loved it. She looked tired now, last night finally catching up with her. But she was excited, too. She stole sips of my wine, but otherwise her table manners were exquisite. She held her fork in the left hand, Continental style. She asked for a fish knife—and used it, which I had never actually seen anyone do before. And she hardly noticed my noticing it.

We talked easily about our lives. I told about my marriages, how Andrea, the teacher, had felt small on account of my career, and Celia, the free-lancer, was always traveling. Now and then they got together in New York, had a few drinks, and called me to tell me what a bastard I was. It was what Californians call family.

She laughed at that. She was listening in that marvelously seductive way that young women can listen to men, and my realizing it didn't make me feel any less important.

"But did you really love either one of them?" she asked.

"Sure, I loved them both. Still do in a way. And either marriage could have lasted forever if we hadn't been modern Californians."

"How do you mean?"

"Divorce is de rigueur out here once the marriage is the least bit inconvenient. Psychiatrists and friends convince you that you're crazy if you don't split up for the smallest reasons."

"You're serious, aren't you?"

"Definitely. I've been watching the action out here for twenty-five years now. We're all proudly enjoying our *acquired* lifestyles, and pay attention, the key word is acquire. We're greedy and selfish, all of us."

"You sound like you regret the breakups."

"I don't. That's the tragedy. I'm just as selfish as the rest of them. I never gave my wives an emotional fifty percent. So how can I blame them for walking out? Besides, I'm a painter."

She smiled.

"Such a mean guy," she said.

"But look," I said, "I don't want to talk about me. I want to talk about you. I don't mean about your family, all that. I've got the rules down, relax on that."

She waited.

"But what about you right now?" I asked. "What do you want besides wearing punk clothes and not getting busted?"

She looked at me for a moment, almost as if the question excited her. And then a shadow passed over her face.

"You talk in big crayon-style print, you know it?"

I laughed. "I didn't mean to sound so harsh," I said. "I mean, what do you want, Belinda?"

"No, it wasn't harsh. I like it. But it doesn't make much difference what I want, does it?" she asked.

"Of course, it does."

"Isn't making you happy enough?" She was teasing. A little.

"No, I don't think so."

"Look, what I mean is, I can't do what I want till I'm eighteen. I can't be anybody. You know, I'd get caught if I really did anything."

I thought about that for a moment.

"What about school?" I asked.

"What about it?"

"You know there are ways we could fix it. I mean, get you into some private school. There have to be ways, names, lies, something—"

"You're crazy," she laughed. "You just want to see me in one of those pleated skirts again."

"Yeah, I'll cop to that. But seriously—"

"Jeremy, an education I have, can't you tell that? Nannies, tutors, the works, I had it. I can read and write French, Italian, and English. I could get into Berkeley now, or Stanford, just by passing an examination."

She shrugged, stole another drink of my wine.

"Well, what about Berkeley or Stanford?" I asked.

"What about them? Who would I be? Linda Merit, my fake person, she'd rack up the credits?"

Her voice trailed off. She looked very worn out. I wanted to wrap her in my arms and take her home to bed. The long day was obviously telling on her.

"Besides," she said, "even if I wasn't on the run, I wouldn't go to college."

"Well, that's my question. What would you do? What do you want? What do you really need right now?"

She looked at me in a slightly distrustful way. And I sensed a defeat in her again, as I had in the car on the way to Union Street. It was a sadness bigger than being just tired, bigger than not knowing me very well.

"Belinda, what can I give you besides pretty clothes and a roof over your head?" I asked her. "Tell me, honey. Just tell me."

"You crazy guy," she said. "That's like the moon and the sky right now."

"Come on, honey, this whole thing is a little too convenient for me. I'm getting what I want and what I need but you—"

"You still feel guilty about me, don't you?" She looked as if she was going to cry, but then she smiled in the sweetest, gentlest way. "Just . . . love me," she said. She shrugged and smiled again, her freckles showing for a moment in the light, very pale, very cute. I wanted to kiss her.

"I do love you," I said. Catch in the throat. Catch in the voice. Did she think it was like some sixteen-year-old telling her?

We looked at each other for a long private moment, oblivious to the crowded, brightly lighted room, the waiters moving among the white-draped tables. Candles, chandeliers, reflected light—it was all melded around us.

She formed her lips into a silent little kiss. Then she grinned and cocked her head.

"Can I listen to rock music real loud and put posters on the walls of my room?"

"Sure, you can have all the bubble gum you want, too, if you'll lay off the Scotch and cigarettes."

"Oh, boy, here it comes."

"Well, wasn't it bound to sooner or later? You want a lecture on nutrition and the needs of the teenage female body?"

"I know what this teenage body needs," she purred, leaning over to kiss me on the cheek. "Why don't we get out of here?"

HALFWAY home I remembered I had to send Celia five hundred dollars right away—that phone message I'd never answered. We drove back downtown to Western Union.

As soon as we got in, she hit the Scotch. Just one drink, she said. Half a glass, going down her gorgeous young throat as I watched. Well, bring it up to bed, I said.

AFTERWARDS I made a fire in the grate and went downstairs for a bottle of sherry and two crystal glasses. I mean, if she had to drink, at least it wouldn't be the Scotch. I poured her a glass of sherry and we sat snuggled up against the pillows in the four-poster, watching the fire in the darkness.

I told her again she could do anything she wanted with the room down the hall. We should have taken her movie posters out of the Page Street dump.

She laughed. She said she'd get some more. She was all soft and warm and drowsy beside me.

"You want a stereo, go get one," I said. I'd set up a bank account for her, for Linda Merit. She said quietly that Linda Merit had one. Good, I'd put money in it for her.

"You got a VCR?" she asked. She had some videotapes, hadn't been able to watch them in a long time. Yes, two, I said, one in the back den up here, one down in my office. What were the tapes? Just old things, odd things. I told her about the big rental places on Market.

We sat there quiet for a while. I was running a mental tab of all the things she said about herself. Quite a puzzle it was.

"You have to tell me something," I asked. I was reminding myself to be gentle.

"What?"

"What you meant last night when you said you'd bombed as an American teenager."

She didn't answer for a while. She drank another half glass of sherry.

"You know," she said finally, "when I first came—to America, I mean —I thought that just being an American teenager for a while would be wonderful. Just being with kids here, going to rock concerts, smoking a little grass, just being in America—"

"And it wasn't like that?"

"Even before I ran away, I knew it was a crock. It was a nightmare. Even the shiny-faced kids, you know, the rich brats who were going on to college, they're all criminals and liars."

Her voice was slow, no teenage bravado.

"Explain."

"Look, I had my first period at nine. I was wearing a C-cut bra by the time I was thirteen. The first boy I ever slept with was shaving every day at fifteen, we could have made babies together. And I found out the kids here are just as developed. I wasn't any freak, you know? But what is a kid here? What can you do? Even if you're going to school, even if you're a goody-two-shoes who hits the books every night, what about the rest of your life?"

I nodded, waited.

"You can't legally smoke, drink, start a career, get married. You can't even legally drive a car till you're sixteen, and all this for years and years after you're a physical adult. All you can do is play till you're twenty-one, if you want to know. That's what life is to kids here—it's play. Play at love, play at sex, play at everything. And play at breaking the law every time you touch a cigarette or drink or somebody three or four years older than you."

She took another sip of the sherry. Her eyes were full of the red light of the fire. "We're all criminals," she went on. "And that's the way it's set up, that's the way people want it. And I'll tell you this much, you play by the rules and you're a shallow person, a real, real shallow person."

"So you broke them?"

"All the time. I came here breaking them. And all I saw when I tried to join in and be one of the crowd is that everybody else was breaking the rules. I mean, to be an American kid you had to be a bad person."

"So you ran away."

"No, I mean, yes, but it's not why." She hesitated. "It just . . . came to that," she said tentatively. "It all blew up. There was just no place for me."

I could feel her stiffening, drawing away. I took another drink. Ought to hold off, I thought, take it very easy. But she started to talk again.

"I'll tell you this," she said. "When I first hit the streets, I did think, well, it would be an adventure. I mean, I thought I'd be with the really tough kids, the real kids, not those rich slick little liars. That was stupid, let me tell you. I mean the rich kids were adults pretending to be kids for their parents' sakes. And the kids on the streets are kids pretending to be adults for their own sakes. Everybody's an outcast. Everybody's a faker."

Her eyes shifted anxiously over the room, and she bit a little at her fingernail again, the way I had seen her do last night.

"I didn't belong on the street any more than I did with the others," she said. "I mean, guys who stole car radios every day to score food and dope, girls selling themselves in the Tenderloin, and the hustlers, my God, convincing themselves it was a big deal if some gay guy took them to a fancy hotel for an hour and bought them dinner. It was the world, sixty minutes in the Cliff Hotel, imagine! Same as the rich kids, everything unreal. Unreal. And the cops, they don't really want to bust you. They don't have any place to put you. They hope you'll up and disappear."

"Or Daddy will come—"

"Yeah, Daddy. Well, all I want is to grow up. I want my name back. I want my life to begin. I want this shit to be over."

"It is over for you," I said.

She looked at me.

"Because you're with me," I said. "And you're OK now."

"No," she said. "It's not over. It just means you and I are criminals together."

"Well, why don't you let me worry about that part of it?" I bent forward to kiss her.

"You crazy guy," she said. She lifted her glass. "Here's to your pictures in the attic."

FIVE A.M. I saw the glowing numbers on the face of the bedside clock before I was even awake. Now the grandfather clock was chiming the hour, and in the vibrating silence that followed I heard her voice very far away. Downstairs. Talking to someone on the phone?

I got up slowly and went to the top of the stairs. The hall light was on down there. And I could hear her laughing, an easy cheerful little laugh. "Prince Charming," she was saying, and then the words were lost. Car passing in the street, even the ticking of the grandfather clock came between us. "Just don't let them hurt you!" she said. Anger? Then the voice went down to a murmur again. And I heard her say: "I love you, too." And she hung up the phone.

What was I doing? Spying on her? Should I sneak back to bed as if I hadn't come this far?

I saw her come into the lower hallway, and then she saw me.

"Is everything all right, baby darling?" I asked.

"Oh, sure!" She came up towards me with her arms out, slipped them around my waist. Her face was open, full of simple affection. "I was just talking to an old friend of mine, had to tell him I was OK."

"It's so early," I said sleepily.

"Not where he is," she said, offhandedly. "But don't worry, I made the call collect."

She led me back to bed, and we climbed under the covers together. She was nestled in my arms.

"It's raining in New York City right now," she said, her voice low, already drowsy.

"Should I be jealous of this friend?" I asked her in a whisper.

"No, never," she said. Slight scoffing tone. "Just my oldest buddy in the whole world, I guess. . . ." Voice trailing off.

Silence.

The warmth of her; and then finally her deep, even breathing.

"I love you," I said softly.

"Prince Charming," she whispered, as if from the deepest sleep.

BY noon the next day she had posters all over the guest room walls: Belmondo, Delon, Brando, Garbo, as well as the new faces, Aidan Quinn, Richard Gere, Mel Gibson. The radio blared Madonna by the hour. She played with all the new clothes, neatly stacking sweaters on the closet shelves, ironing blouses, polishing old shoes, experimented with new bottles and jars of expensive makeup.

I only looked in now and then on my way down from the attic to the coffee maker in the kitchen. The three carousel pictures were almost complete, and I was lettering in the titles at the bottom of the canvases, as I'd done years ago with my first paintings: *Belinda on the Carousel Horse One, Two,* and *Three.* The effect of the trio, set up to dry, was making me giddy.

I COOKED dinner for us around six—steaks, salad, red wine—the only meal I know how to cook. She came down with her hair braided and the braids tied across the top of her head. I kissed her a lot before we started eating.

"Why don't you watch those videotapes tonight?" I asked. I told her she could have the den to herself. I almost never went in there. Maybe, she said. She'd watch some TV, if I was going to work, or read some of my books on painting.

She went down to the basement library after we cleaned up, and I could hear the click of the pool balls down there as I sat at the kitchen table with my coffee letting the wine wear off, gearing up to go to work again. Last bit of background, then done on those three up there.

The whole house smelled like her perfume.

SHE was sound asleep in my four-poster when I came down. She had taken off the flannel gown and pushed the covers away, and she lay on her face, her mouth only a little open, her long slender hand limp beside her face on the pillow.

Her naked bottom was small, almost boyish, a glint of gold pubic hair showing there. I touched the silky backs of her knees, the little crease that was so sensitive to touch when she was awake. I touched the silky soles of her feet. She didn't move. She slept with the perfect trust of childhood.

"Who are you?" I whispered. I thought of all the things she'd said.

At dinner she'd mentioned something about a trip to Kashmir, traveling by train across India with two English students, her companions for that summer. "But all we talked about was the States. Imagine there we were in one of the most beautiful sports on earth, Kashmir, and all we talked about was LA and New York City."

I bent down and kissed the back of her neck, the little bare patch of skin that showed through her thick hair.

Sixteen.

But how can you give me permission, my love, how can I give myself permission? If only there was no one else, no one who cared. But then you wouldn't be running, would you?

Dark in the hallway.

The guest room, her room. All these new faces staring at each other across the dark, the brass bed glimmering, her purse open, things spilled out. A hairbrush.

Closet door open.

Videotapes. Why tote them through the world when she had so little else? A sack, a suitcase. Something to do with a past life? What was in the suitcase?

I was standing in her doorway. Of course, I wouldn't pry a lock, wouldn't even lift a suitcase lid. I mean, these were her things. And what if she woke up, came down the hall, discovered me here?

Just look in the closet. Crammed now with new clothes.

But there was the suitcase on the floor, and it was locked. And the videotapes now stood in a neat stack on the shelf behind an empty purse, folded underwear, a hair dryer.

I examined them in the light from the hall.

Strange labels on these cassettes. Only the name of the dealer in New

York: Video Classics. And on one a check mark had been scratched in the black plastics as if with a ballpoint pen or a bobbie pin. Nothing else to say what they were or why she would want them.

Her magazines: quite a stack. And many of them foreign. *Cahiers du Cinema* on top, *L'Express,* copies of German *Stern,* more French, some Italian. And film the theme always. What she had in English was Andy Warhol's *Interview, Film Arts, American Cinematographer.*

Fairly sophisticated for a girl her age it seemed. But then with her background, maybe it wasn't so unusual.

Many of these journals were old. In fact, they had secondhand store price labels on them. Only the *Film Arts* was new, with a picture on the front of "Up-and-Coming Texas Film Director Susan Jeremiah."

Inside was tucked an article torn out of *Newsweek,* also on Ms. Jeremiah—"Thunder in the Southwest"—a tall, lean, dark-haired Houston woman with deep-set black eyes, who actually wore a cowboy hat and boots. I didn't think Texans really did that.

As for the older mags, there was no immediate clue to why she had bought them. Film and film and film. Some went back ten years. No marks anywhere that I could see.

I put all of this back carefully. And only then did I notice an old *TV Guide* under the tapes. And when I pulled it out, I saw Susan Jeremiah again, smiling under the shadow of her white cowboy hat. Handsome woman. The issue was two months old. I scanned quickly for the article.

Ms. Jeremiah's first television movie, something called *Bitter Chase,* had premiered in April. The article was short, said she was one of the new generation of talented women in film. Her first theatrical feature, *Final Score,* had gotten a standing ovation at last year's Cannes festival. She'd grown up on a Texas ranch. Ms. Jeremiah believed American film was wide open for women.

There was more, but I was getting nervous. Suppose Belinda woke up. I thought I heard a noise, and that was it. I put the magazine back and closed the closet.

The key to the suitcase might be in her purse. Her purse was on the brass bed. But I had done enough. And I could not bring myself to snoop in her purse, no, there had to be a limit to this.

But these little discoveries were tantalizing. Just like her chatter about Europe. Just like her, whoever she was.

No surprise that a girl her age was interested in film, no surprise that her tastes would be good. But why this focus on a female film director?

Of course, it was just the sort of thing to interest a modern girl—the strong independent Texas woman not out to be an actress but a filmmaker. Rather irresistibly American. The press certainly liked the hat and the boots, that was obvious.

The fact was, none of this explained anything much about Belinda. It only added to my question.

I LOCKED up the house for the night, put out the lights, went into the bathroom, and felt my face. Real scratchy beard, as always this time of night. I decided to shave.

When she woke up in the morning in my arms, I didn't want my face scratching her babycheeks.

As I lay there in the dark, I kept thinking: Who is looking for her? Who is crying over her? Dear God, if she were my little girl, I'd move heaven and earth to find her.

But then, she is my little girl. And do I want them, whoever they are, to find her?

No, you can't have her back. Not now.

AT nine A.M., I was sitting in my office and she was still asleep. I picked up the phone on the desk and called my lawyer, Dan Franklin. He wouldn't be back from court till eleven, his secretary said, but, yes, he could probably see me then. Come on over.

Now, my lawyer and I went to school together. He's probably as good a friend as I have, and the one person in the world I trust more than any other.

Agents, no matter how much they love you and how hard they work for you, are really go-betweens. And they often know the movie people and the publishers better than they know their authors. Often they like the movie people and the publishers better. They have more in common with them.

But my lawyer worked only for me. When he went over a contract or an offer for rights, he was on my side completely. And he was one of the few really good entertainment lawyers who did not make his office in New York or Los Angeles.

Not only did I trust my lawyer, I also liked him, personally. I trusted his judgment, I considered him a nice guy.

And I knew now that I'd avoided him at Andy Blatky's exhibit the other day because I hadn't wanted to explain Belinda.

I made the appointment to see him at eleven. Then I showered, shaved again, put two good head shots of Belinda in a manila envelope, and put that in my briefcase.

I had hoped to have more for a start. But the more could come later.

* * *

BELINDA was eating potato chips and drinking a Coke when I came down. She'd gone across the street to the corner store for them while I was in the shower.

"That's breakfast?" I asked.

"Yeah, cuts through the smoke," she said. She gestured to the lighted cigarette.

"That's trash," I said.

"Cereal's got just as much salt, do you know that?"

"What about eggs and toast and milk?" I said. I went to work fixing enough for both of us.

Yeah, gee, thanks for the eggs, but she was full of potato chips. She opened another can of Coke and sat down to tell me how wonderful it was being here.

"I slept last night, I mean, slept without thinking somebody was going to climb in the window or start playing the drums in the hallway."

I got an idea.

"Have to see my lawyer downtown," I said. "Some stuff about one of my mother's books, a movie deal."

"Sounds exciting. I loved your mother's books, you know."

"You're kidding, you never read them."

"Not so! Read every one, absolutely loved *Crimson Mardi Gras.*"

We stared at each other for a moment.

"What's wrong?" she asked.

"Nothing," I said. "Just business on my mind. I'm taking the van downtown. Do you really know how to drive a car?"

"Of course, how do you think I got the fake license? I mean, the name's fake, but I was driving on . . . driving in Europe when I was eleven."

"You want the keys to the MG, then?"

"Jeremy, you don't mean it."

I tossed them to her.

Bait taken.

She was down not ten minutes later, dressed in a new pair of snow white wash pants and a white pullover. It was the first time I'd seen her in pants since she wore the cutoff shorts around the house, and I was unprepared for my reaction. I didn't want her to venture out the front door like that.

"You know what that makes me want to do?" I said giving her the eye.

"What?" She missed the point. "How do I look?" She was brushing her hair in front of the hall mirror.

"Rapable."

"Thanks."

"You going to wear a coat?"

"It's eighty degrees out there, you must be kidding. First time this city has warmed up to a civilized temperature since I got here."

"It won't last. Take a coat."

She threw her arms around my neck, kissed me. Soft hot crush of arms and cheeks. Babymouth succulent, sweet.

"Don't need a coat."

"Where are you going?"

"Tanning studio for fifteen minutes under the hot lights," she said tapping her cheek with one finger. "It's the only way to stay brown in this town. Then riding, Golden Gate Park stables. I called from upstairs. I've wanted to do it since I got here."

"Why didn't you?"

"I don't know. Didn't seem appropriate, you know, the way I was living." She was digging in her purse for a cigarette. "You know, I was on the street. All that. Didn't seem to mix with horses."

"But it mixed with the tanning studio."

"Sure." She laughed. Her hair was beautifully full from the brushing. No paint, just the cigarette on her lip.

"And now you can go riding again."

"Yes!" She laughed in the most open, delighted fashion.

"You are truly beautiful," I said. "But the pants are too tight."

"Oh, no, they feel fine," she said. Snap of her lighter.

I took out several ten-dollar bills and gave her that with the keys to the car and the house.

"You don't have to, really—" she said. "I have money—"

"Look, don't bother saying that ever again," I said. "It's like when I ask you questions about your parents. Don't mention money. I hate it."

Another sweet soft tight hug and she was off, just dashed out the front door, in fact, like an American teenager.

And probably with the key to the suitcase in her purse. But—

I WAITED till I heard the car roaring up the street before I went upstairs and opened her closet.

The key was in the damn suitcase and the suitcase was open.

I took a deep breath, then knelt down, laid back the lid, and started going through it.

Fake Linda Merit passport! My God, she was thorough. Two New York Public Library books, one a Vonnegut novel, the other a Stephen King. Typical enough, I figured. Then there was my signed copy of *Bettina's House* and a picture of me over a notice of the booksellers autograph party cut out of the *San Francisco Chronicle*.

Lingerie—even that looked second-hand—old-fashioned midnight blue taffeta slips, lace brassieres with wire, which I don't think girls wear much anymore. Cotton panties, beautifully plain. A brown paper sack and in it programs from several recent Broadway musicals. *Cats, A Chorus Line,* Ollie Boon's *Dolly Rose,* other things. The Ollie Boon program had been autographed, but no personal note above the signature.

Absolutely nothing here that was personal.

I mean, not a clue to who she was. And for some reason this made me feel all the more guilty for what I was doing.

Had she deliberately obliterated her past? Or had she bolted on the spur of the moment?

I went over the clothes in the closet—the old things she brought with her.

Except for the school uniforms, of which there were three, it was class in every case, as I had figured. Tweeds were Harris or Donegal. Skirts and blazers were Brooks Brothers, Burberry, Cable Car. Nothing frivolous as we'd bought yesterday on our little downtown spin. Even the shoes were respectable.

But all of it was used, definitely, some of it probably made before she was born. Not likely any of it had been hers before she had hit the street. This was too puzzling.

In the pockets I found New York theater ticket stubs, something from a recent concert in San Francisco. Matchbooks from the big hotels. The Fairmont, the Stanford Court, the Hyatt Regency.

It troubled me, this. I didn't want to think about what she'd been doing in all those hotels. But maybe she was simply roaming the lobbies, homing to places like those in which she'd once lived. Looking for some way back into the adult world.

But her recent past wasn't the point. We were going to destroy all that together. It was the real past that mattered. And there was nothing here to tell me the slightest thing about her. It was downright scary.

Even the tapes had only those commercial labels.

The best clue so far was Susan Jeremiah.

I got out the magazines, sat down on the side of the brass bed, and read through them.

Well, this was an interesting woman all right. Born on a Texas ranch, went to school in Dallas, later in LA. Was making movies with a home camera when she was ten. Worked in her teens for a Dallas TV station. *Final Score,* which had won accolades at Cannes, was described as atmospheric, fast-paced, philosophical. Done on location in the Greek islands, it concerned a gang of nihilistic young Texan dope smugglers. Film buff talk about handheld cameras, artistic debts to Orson Welles, the Nouvelle Vague, philosophical approach, that sort of thing. All too short. On to another woman director, New Yorker, featured in the same article.

The *Newsweek* piece wasn't much better. Focus on the April television film *Bitter Chase,* praised for "a high quotient of visual beauty, something often altogether absent from films made for television." Jeremiah would make two more for United Theatricals, but didn't want to be stigmatized as a television director. Heavy praise for the star of the film, Dallas girl Sandy Miller, who had also starred in Jeremiah's "arty and often self-indulgent erotic film," *Final Score,* never released in this country. But oddly enough, the only picture in the magazine was of Jeremiah. I think that Texas getup and that lean frontier face really got them. Too bad for Sandy Miller.

I sat there more confused than ever and feeling pretty damned guilty.

I wanted to take those videotapes down, run them through the machine in my office. Or better yet, the machine in the den. The den door had a lock on it. And that way if she came in—

Oh, but how would she ever forgive me if she found out what I was doing? And what if I just brought up the tapes in conversation? She might explain everything. No need to betray her at all this way, because maybe this stuff had nothing to do with who she was.

It was ten forty-five. I had to get going.

DAN didn't show until noon. I apologized for keeping him from lunch.

"Look," I said. "This is client–lawyer privilege."

"What's that supposed to mean? You kill somebody?" He sat down opposite me behind the desk. "You want some lunch? I'm sending out for a sandwich."

"No. I'll make this as quick as I can. I want you to do some detective work."

"You're kidding."

"You have to do it yourself. You can't hire anybody from an agency. You have to do what you can by phone, and then if you have to travel, I'll pay for it."

"Do you know what that will cost you?"

"Doesn't matter. You have to find out something for me."

"Which is what?"

"The identity of this girl," I said. I handed him my photos of her.

He studied them for a moment.

"This is absolutely confidential," I said. "You cannot let anyone know who wants to know all this."

"Come on," he said impatiently, shaking his head. "Fill me in. What am I looking for?"

"She's sixteen," I said.

"Uh huh." He was studying the picture.

"Till two days ago she was on the street. She says her name's Belinda. That may or may not be true. She's been all over Europe, grew up in Madrid, she said, spent time in Rome, Paris. She was in New York this winter, I'm pretty certain of that. I don't know when she got here."

I described the theater programs, the top-price tickets.

"She's maybe five foot four. No taller than that. One hundred pounds, maybe a little more. Hair, face, you can see. Her body is very grown-up. Full breasts. Her voice is grown-up, too, very grown-up, but no accent except for a touch of something I can't place. I don't know if that would help anyway."

"What's your connection with her?"

"I'm living with her."

"You're what!"

"I don't want to hear about it. I want to know who she is, where she came from—"

"—You don't want to hear about it! She's sixteen? And you don't want to hear about it?"

"—But I want to know more than that. I want to know why she ran away, what happened. I'm pretty sure there's money mixed up in it. She's too well educated, her taste is too good. There has to be a family somewhere with money. Yet it doesn't add up. It's strange. I want to know everything you can possibly—"

"Jeremy, this is crazy."

"Don't talk, Dan. I'm not finished."

"Do you know what this could mean if you're caught with this kid?"

"I want to know how she got to be where she is. Who she's hiding from? I'll tell you the strangest thing. I went through her belongings and there's not a single clue to her real identity."

"You crazy son of a bitch. Do you realize what this could do to you? Jeremy, do you remember what happened to Roman Polanski?"

"I remember."

And what was all that rot I had told Alex Clementine about scandal not hurting anyone anymore? And he had said the right dirt in the right measure. Well, I knew in my case this was the wrong dirt, never mind the measure.

"Polanski got nailed for one lousy afternoon with a minor. You're telling me you're living with this one?"

I told him quietly and calmly about the Page Street address, the police, them writing down my address and the fake name Linda Merit in their notebooks.

"I wish the cop hadn't recognized me."

"Put her on a plane for Katmandu. Immediately! Get her out of your house, you idiot."

"Dan, find out who she is. I don't care what it costs. There must be people you can ask, on the qt, without revealing anything, maybe some way to ask around at the street down there. I am almost one hundred percent sure someone is looking for her."

"So am I. Europe, money, education—" He picked up the picture. "Christ!" he muttered.

"But remember, I have to know everything, who are her parents, what did they do, why did she take off?"

"Suppose they didn't do anything and she's a rich bitch who decided she wanted some excitement."

"Out of the question. You wouldn't say that if you talked to her. In fact, the funny thing is, she's too poised to be rich, yet she's gotta be."

"I don't get it."

"Rich kids are sheltered. They're soft. There's always a little naiveté shining through, no matter how precocious they are. The girl's poise is deep and almost hard. She makes me think of the poor girls I knew when I was a kid, I mean, the ones who had big diamond engagement rings on their fingers by sixteen and two kids by a piano mover husband by the time they were twenty. You know the kind of girl. She can hardly read or write, but she can run the cash register in the all-night drugstore for five hours without ever breaking one of her long manicured fingernails. Well, there is something sad and tough about this little girl which is like that, something old. But she's too educated, too refine for the rest of the image."

He was giving me angry glances in between studying the picture.

"I've seen this girl somewhere," he said.

"At Andy's exhibit the other day," I said. "She was with me."

"No, I didn't even know you were there. Missed you completely—"

"But she was wandering around, in a pair of pink sunglasses—"

"No, no, I mean I know this girl. I know this face, I know her from somewhere."

"Well, then, get on it, Dan. Because I have to know who she is and what happened to her."

"And she won't tell you."

"Nothing, not a word, made me promise never to ask or she'd walk out. I know it's something terrible."

"You mean, you hope it's something terrible to get you off the hook with your conscience!"

"Maybe. Maybe so."

"You think it will get you off the hook with anyone else, you're crazy."

"Dan, I just want to know—"

"Look, I'll get on it. But in exchange you listen. This could demolish your career. Demolish, as in obliterate, annihilate, disintegrate, do you understand me? You're not a European film director. You're a children's book author."

"Don't remind me."

"You are putting it on the line, every nickel of it, if this gets to the press. And if her parents are rich, it could be kidnapping on top of everything. There could be charges I haven't even thought of. I gotta look this up. I gotta—"

You should see the paintings, I thought. But I said:

"Dan, that can wait. Find out all about her."

Yes, definitely the wrong dirt in the wrong measure.

So why did I feel exhilaration, this warmth all over, this sense of being alive suddenly? It was like that day when I walked onto that jet plane at the New Orleans airport and knew I was headed for California.

"Look at me, Jer! You'll get the Lewis Carroll Kinky Old Man Award of the Year, you hip to that? They'll pull your books off the library shelves and burn them. The bookstores in the South and Midwest won't even stock them. And any Disney movie deals you can kiss good-bye forever. You're not listening to me. You're not listening!"

"Dan, I have an imagination. Imagining things is what I get paid for. I love this little girl. And I have to know if somebody is out there looking for her. I have to know what they did to her."

"This is not the sixties, Jeremy. The flower children are gone. The feminists and the Moral Majority are joining ranks these days to get the child molesters and the pornographers. This is no time for—"

I had to laugh. It was Alex Clementine all over again.

"Dan, we are *not* in court, I *am* impressed. My rights have been read to me. Call me when you have something—anything!"

I locked the briefcase and started towards the door.

"They'll cancel the Saturday morning show!"

"Lawyer–client privilege, Dan."

"Disney is bidding right now against Rainbow for the rights to Angelica!"

"Oh, you reminded me. Belinda's interested in movies, very interested. *Cahiers du Cinema,* magazines like that. Film buff stuff."

"She's sixteen, she wants to be a star, so did Lolita. Get rid of her, the little bitch."

"Come on, Dan. Don't talk like that about her. I mean, she reads serious film things. And she has a special interest in a woman director, someone named Susan Jeremiah."

"Never heard of her."

"Up-and-coming Texas woman. Did a TV film in April for United Theatricals. There just might be a connection."

"I'll get on this all right, you better believe I'll get on this, just to show you how dangerous this is!"

"Be careful, whatever you do, when you call me. She's there all the time."

"No shit."

"If you leave a message on the machine, make it sound like book business."

I STOPPED in the lobby long enough to take a deep breath. I felt like an absolute traitor. Please, let it be something rotten. Let them be corrupt. Let her belong to me.

I WENT to a phone booth on Market Street and looked up the address of a riding apparel shop. It was on Divisadero.

I knew her sizes from the day before, and the woman assured me I could bring back anything she didn't like. So I bought her everything. A red wool hacking coat, and a black hunting jacket, and two beautiful black velvet hard hats with chin straps. Breeches, gloves, a couple of quirts. Some very pretty little shirts and things. I knew it was the sort of thing people didn't use everyday for riding. It was for shows. But I wanted to see her in it, and I hoped she would like it.

Then I went home, put all of this out on the bed, and went upstairs. The palette was still loaded with wet paint from last night, and the brushes were still wet, too, so I went right to work instantly. Last bit of gold on the lettering of the last picture: the punk-waif picture.

I scarcely looked at the work I'd done. I got paint all over my wool pants, but it didn't matter.

Only when I looked at the shadowy little V between her legs did I have to stop, have to detach. She was too alive for me. I stood back, and when I saw the amount that was done—the size of the three canvases, the detail all finished—I was a little overawed. Even for me this pace was wondrous.

ABOUT four I went out for some beer, milk, the dumb little things I needed from the corner market. I got her five different brands of foreign cigarettes. Jasmine, Dunhill, Rothmans, anything unusual that she might like. I also got plenty of apples, oranges, pears, good things she might eat on the run instead of garbage. I mean, here I was buying a kid cigarettes. I doubled up on the milk, grabbed a few boxes of dry cereal.

The car was in the drive when I came back.

When I shut the front door, I saw her standing at the top of the staircase.

There was only a weak light from the stained-glass window there, and my eyes had to get used to the shadows before I could really see her.

She had on the black velvet riding hat and the high leather boots. And she was posed like an old-fashioned portrait, with one hand on her hip and the other holding the black leather riding quirt. She was otherwise naked. She smacked the side of the boot with the quirt.

I went down on my knees at the bottom of the stairs. I shoved the groceries aside.

She held the pose for as long as she could, but then she was shaking with half-repressed giggles. I doubled over with laughter before I got to her.

I climbed on top of her at the top of the stairs and started kissing her.

"No, in the bed," she said. "In the bed. It's too good in the bed."

I picked her up and carried her. She was still laughing when I set her down. I kissed her, cradling her chin with the little leather strap, and feeling her boots against my legs—the hard leather and the soft thighs.

"Tell me you love me, you little witch," I said. "Come on, tell me."

"Yes," she said, kissing me back. "It's going to be perfect, isn't it?"

Just before I stopped thinking altogether of anything rational, I thought: I have my next picture.

[[9]]

It was all right with her in the attic, too.

For three nights, as I worked on the riding portrait, she was quiet, reading *French Vogue* or *Paris Match,* dozing off then watching me. She wore tight jeans, cotton T-shirts, liked keeping her hair in braids, made it much easier to care for. She had laughed when I bought the little plastic barrettes in the dime store for the ends of her braids. But she wore them.

(Don't look at the taut wrinkles of cloth between her legs, or her nipples showing through the sheer bra under the shirt. When she rolls over on her stomach on the polished wooden floor and her breasts hang down, don't go crazy. She kicks her feet a little, crosses her ankles. Crushes out a cigarette, drains the Coke, which, thanks to my nagging, has no slug of Scotch in it. Don't look. The brand of lipstick is Bronze Bombshell.)

With and without this inspiration, I was actually finishing before midnight of the third night.

And it was just the way she'd suggested when she posed at the top of the stairs. Boots, hat hand on hip, nude, of course, with riding crop. Splendid.

I'd taken half a roll of film for it. In spite of her narrow hips there was something about it that could only be described as voluptuous. But the face, always the face, that was the issue. Bud mouth, upturned nose, yet so much maturity in the eyes.

Midnight. The grandfather clock sent its chimes up through the old floors.

My right arm ached. The light glaring off the canvas was getting to me. I was getting tired of painting the details with a tiny stiff camel's hair brush. But I wouldn't quit. Wanted to deepen the color of the drapery behind: essential to get the rough texture of antique velvet there. Little prestidigitation there, and the gleam of the light on her right boot. Some fool would stand in the gallery later—the gallery? later?—and say, why it looks just like she's going to reach out and touch you!

Kiss you. Take you in her arms, crush your face to her breasts like she does mine. Right. Exactly.

She lay on her back looking at the ceiling. Yawned. Said she had to go to bed. Why didn't I come too?

"Soon."

"Kiss me." She stood up, pounded on my chest with her fist. "Come on, stop just long enough to kiss me."

"Do this for me," I said. "Sleep in the brass bed in the middle room. I want to take pictures there . . . later." It had those side rails that could be raised, like a baby bed, only lower.

OK, she said. As long as I came to bed there with her afterwards.

I went downstairs with her.

There was an old brass lamp there, an oil lamp wired now with a little bulb—very gentle light to photograph her by.

I put the nightgown on her myself and buttoned the tiny pearl buttons to her throat.

I watched her undo the braids and brush out her rippling hair. Something about the white fabric and the pearls, it was déjà vu—a swoon almost—having to do with churches, candles.

For a moment I couldn't attach it to anything—then a lot of forgotten things came back, those long lush church ceremonies I'd witnessed a thousand times when I was a little boy in New Orleans. Banks of white gladiolas on the altars, the satin vestments so carefully embroidered, sometimes even painted it seemed. Watered silk. Purple, deep green, gold. Every color had its liturgical meaning.

I didn't know whether they even did elaborate things like that anymore in the Catholic church, whether they'd ever done them in California. I'd passed a Catholic church here one evening and they had been singing "God Bless America."

What I heard now was *Veni Creator Spiritus*. And these were children's voices. And it was intimately of the past, of the big moldering old houses of the Garden District streets, of the giant Gothic and Romanesque churches built lovingly by immigrants to the old European scale, full of imported stained glass, marble, finely carved statues.

Miles from there to here, yet some elusive point of convergence in the light as it fell on the tight, virginal skin of her face, her babylips.

Her hair spilled down on the white flannel. The brush lifted it, seemed to stretch it and straighten it, then let it go, the tight rippling waves eating up the strands immediately.

I could almost feel those moments in church—all the little girls in white lace and linen up in the cloister outside waiting to go in. We had on white suits. But it was the girls I remembered, the girls with their little cheeks and lips rouged. Rustle of taffeta. Finger curls. Satin ribbon.

Processions, little girls strewing rose petals out of little white papier mâché baskets, all down the marble aisle of the church before the priest passed under the swaying canopy. Or the ranks in the dusk as the May Procession moved through the narrow back streets of the old parish, class after class marching together, all dressed in white, our Hail Marys rising in a chant, the people out on their front porches to watch, and the little altars to the Virgin with flickering candles set in the little front windows of the narrow railroad-flat duplexes. Women in pale shapeless flowered dresses walking beside us on the sidewalks as they said their rosaries.

No, I think it was something else, something very distinct in the church itself and there was this light: Holy Communion.

An idea was coming to me, another tableau. And it seemed more bizarre than anything yet—the carousel horse, the dollhouse, the riding boots. But I knew, if I could do it, it would be extraordinary, raptuous.

And it probably wouldn't frighten her. Not her. She lay down on the pillow, and I raised the brass sides of the bed. Thin bars on all sides. Like an old hospital bed or a gilded cage.

Like a crib truly.

She was giving me that soft dreamy pacific smile. This extraordinary awareness of happiness came over me. This certainty of happiness and completeness.

Her hair was all out on the pillow, pale yellow. She said she didn't mind falling asleep with the lamp on. I wouldn't wake her when I came in to photograph her.

"Good night, my darling dear," she said. My little girl. Her mouth, the lipstick wiped away, was irresistibly puckered, succulent. Never would be a woman's mouth. Promised a lifetime of felonious kisses.

* * *

SHE was asleep by one o'clock.

I spent an hour photographing her through the brass bars of the bed. The awareness of happiness was still there—an acute awareness.

I don't think that happens often in life, at least it has not happened to me very often. The awareness of happiness comes after, in memory, with the belated appreciation of the moment.

This was close to joy, this feeling. Loving her, painting her—it made a cycle and shut out the world beyond completely.

The world seemed even less than the poster faces all over these walls —her actors and actresses. Just for one moment I studied them through the gloom. Susan Jeremiah up there now in her white cowboy hat—one of those quickie blowups from the *Newsweek* picture. Susan Jeremiah squinting into a Texas sun?

She disappeared as I looked down into the light from the lamp, adjusted the camera.

No, I wasn't a traitor for what I'd done, trying to find out who she was. Rather I felt a certainty that nothing I found out would separate us. I'd discover things about her that would make me want to keep her close to me forever.

I tiptoed around the bed, kneeling down to catch her through the bars, get the feeling of a big brass crib. All I had to do was touch her, lean over and kiss her lips or her eyes, and she would stir in her sleep, move, shift into another languid and yielding position. I brushed her hair down over her face once so that only her eyes were uncovered. I lifted it back and turned her head and got her profile perfectly.

When the pearl buttons would catch the light, that strong positively haunting sense of the church would return. Flowers, incense, white dresses. It was First Communion or Confirmation, and what had they called Confirmation then? Big Communion. We wore white suits again, probably for the last time. And the girls looked like little brides, breathtaking. The bishop put oil on our foreheads, spoke Latin. We were all now, boys and girls alike, soldiers of Christ. What a mad mixture of imagery, metaphors.

I pulled up her nightgown very gently, very gently, until the soft flannel was gathered in my hands and her breasts were uncovered. Then I kissed them, watching the nipples get small, stiff, erect. They seemed to darken slightly.

"Jeremy," she said in her sleep. She pulled on my arm, reached up groggily without opening her eyes and pulled my head down towards her.

I kissed her mouth very lightly, then felt her gliding back into sleep again.

I wasn't ready to sleep yet.

I went back down to the basement and opened one of my trunks from New Orleans. It was the one in which I kept old personal things. I hadn't opened it in years.

The smell of camphor was rather unpleasant. But I found what I wanted. My mother's prayer book. It was the Latin missal she'd used when she was a little girl—the cover was simulated pearl, and there was a golden crucifix on it. Pages edged in gold. Her rosary was in a little white jewelry shop box with it. I took it out and held it up to the light. The blue paper had kept the silver links from tarnishing. The Hail Mary beads were pearls, the Our Fathers rhinestones, each capped in silver.

My mother hadn't much loved these things. She'd told me once that she wished she could throw them all out, but it seemed wicked to throw away rosaries and prayer books. So I saved them.

My father's picture was in the trunk, too, the last one he had taken before going overseas. Dr. Walker in uniform. He had volunteered the day Pearl Harbor was bombed, died in the South Pacific. That was two months after I was born, and I don't think my mother ever forgave him. We lived in Dr. Walker's big Saint Charles Avenue house. But I never knew him.

I put him back, closed the trunk, and took the rosary and prayer book upstairs with me.

The exhilaration was there again, the sense of being alive. Connected.

SHE was ready to go riding when I woke up, looking absolutely adorable in the red coat and breeches. Said she'd found a stable in Marin that would rent her a jumper.

Sure, take the car. Be back for dinner.

I watched her drive away. Positively dashing as she nestled down in the old black leather seat of the dark-green MG-TD. The gears were screaming for mercy by the time she shifted into third. Kids, I thought.

The kitchen was totally fogged in with cigarette smoke.

And the clutch would fall out in a week.

And I had five paintings upstairs. I felt absolutely marvelous.

I drove downtown in the van, taking one of her shoes with me.

I had this plan in mind, which had to do with the white cloth and pearl buttons. But I wasn't sure I could carry it off. Didn't know where to find everything.

But as soon as I wandered into the bridal department of one of the downtown stores, I saw some of what I needed. Not only sheer white bridal veils on sale, but delicate white floral wreaths. Too perfect. I stood looking at these things in one of those dimly lit utterly private corners that exist all over big stores—all the noise was swallowed up by the carpets. The atmosphere of the church came back with bittersweet power. Things utterly lost, gone forever.

I bought a veil and wreath immediately, but the dresses were all wrong for my purposes. And the ones in the little girls' department would never fit her.

In the lingerie department, quite by surprise, I spotted exactly what I wanted: lovely European nightgowns of white linen, all done up with white lace and ribbons. There were many different lengths, styles. And all achieved the same general effect. Very fancy, pure, old-fashioned.

I chose a short full gown with no waistband or gathering. It had an exquisitely stitched yoke and, yes, the pearl buttons, the very thing I wanted, pearl buttons. And the sleeves, the sleeves were too good to be true. They were short puffed sleeves, trimmed with tiny ruffles of satin ribbon. Ribbon on the hem. It was the thing all right. A little dress.

I bought the two smaller sizes to be safe. And I bought a number of other gowns, too. Gowns would never go to waste in my house.

For the shoes I did have to go to the little girls' department. And apparently there are little girls with very long feet. Size 7 triple A. I got what I wanted. A plain white leather shoe with an instep strap. Rather wide I thought, but she really didn't have to walk in it.

The white stockings were no problem. I bought some lace ones, but that was not right. Plain white was what I remembered.

Then I called up the florist on Eighteenth Street around the corner from my house and ordered the flowers. I'd be there in my van to pick them up myself. Just have them ready. I wanted lilies, gladiolas, roses, and everything white. Carnations OK too, but principally the church flowers.

I had a light lunch in the upstairs restaurant at Saks, bought the wax candles I needed, and was about to catch a taxi when I thought perhaps I should call Dan.

I didn't really want to do it, but I thought that I should.

Luckily, Dan was in court. Wouldn't be back till tomorrow. But his secretary said that he'd been eager to reach me. My message machine hadn't been on. Did I realize that?

Yeah, I guess I did. I was sorry. Did she know what Dan had to say?

"Just something about remember his warning."

Which meant what? I had half a mind to tell her to tell him to drop everything. But I didn't.

I hung up. And on a hunch I tried to reach Alex Clementine.

He had checked out of the Stanford Court and gone on with his book tour to San Diego.

I called Jody, the publicist, in New York. She said Alex had a packed schedule. She'll tell him I wanted to get in touch with him.

"It's not important, don't bother him."

"You know his book's number eight this week on the list," she said. "We can't keep it in the stores—"

"Marvelous."

"They want him on every talk show in the country. I tell you, it's all that awful 'Champagne Flight.' I mean, these nighttime soaps have hooked everybody. They're selling dolls of that actress Bonnie here, can you believe it? Twenty-five dollars in plastic, one hundred twenty-five in porcelain."

"So sign up Bonnie for a book," I said. "Make sure it has plenty of pictures from her old movies."

"Sure, sure. Why don't you and Alex have a drink with her and you guys talk her into writing her life story."

"That's over my head. Alex will have to deliver that one."

"Looking for Bettina's still rolling at a solid five thousand copies a week," she said.

"I know, I know."

"So how about loosening up and doing some more bookstores? Remember you promised me you'd think about it?"

"Yeah . . . Look, give Alex my love in case I don't catch up with him."

"They're begging for you in Berkeley and Marin. Just an hour away, Jeremy."

"Not right now, Jody."

"We'll send you a big stretch limousine and two of our sweetest little elves to take care of everything."

"Maybe soon."

"That woman at the *Chronicle*'s furious that you canceled her interview."

"What woman? Oh, that. Yeah. Can't talk to people right now."

"OK, you're the boss."

SHE was still out when I got home. The house was quiet and very warm from the afternoon sun, about the warmest it would ever get regardless of the weather.

There was a different smell to it, and I don't mean the cigarettes only. Her perfume, soap. Something. Something rather lingering and sweet and different.

All the toys in the living room were lying under a veil of dust and sun, and there were changes there, too. Sometime or other she had arranged the dolls neatly in the wicker carriage, spread them out on the sofa. She had opened the glass doors to the big three-story dollhouse and straightened all the little furniture inside. Polished the glass. Dusted all the little bits and pieces in there—the tiny hardwood tables and chairs, the little patches of handwoven oriental carpet. She'd even put the little china dollhouse people in different positions. Now the little man stood by the little grandfather clock. And his corseted wife sat primly at the dining table. In the attic the dollhouse child played with the tiny train that really ran on its thread of electric track if you touched the little wall switch.

Before, it had looked like World War II in there.

I wish I had caught her in the act with the camera. Gotten her when she was deep into it, with all her hair tangled with the afternoon sun the way it was now, maybe in sock feet in that plaid skirt.

Well, there was time now for everything.

I hung up my coat, then brought in everything from the porch—the flowers, the packages—and took them upstairs and started to arrange things.

I put an old white chenille bedspread on the four-poster. I stood the white floral wreaths around it. And I brought the silver candelabra up from the dining room and put the candles in them and set them on the night tables. The wreaths pretty much concealed the night tables. With the shades drawn and the candles lighted, the effect was as I had imagined it: the church at mass. There was even the delicious floral scent, though it could never be as sweet or as strong as it had been in New Orleans. That could never be duplicated.

I set the camera on the tripod at the foot of the bed, laid out the new things and the white prayer book and the pearl rosary. I stood inspecting everything. In afterthought I went downstairs, got a bottle of good Burgundy out of the cupboard, opened it, and brought it up with two glasses. Set it aside on one of the hidden night tables.

Yes, it was lush, gorgeous. But I was impressed very suddenly with the utter madness of it.

The other pictures I'd done of her had formed themselves rather spontaneously. The props had been here. And the riding portrait had been her idea.

This was contrived in an almost insane fashion.

And as I stood there looking at the flowers and the flicker of the candles on the white satin canopy above—the tester, as we called it—I wondered if it wouldn't frighten her. If I wasn't wrong about that. It was sick, wasn't it, to go this far? It had to be. And these wreaths of flowers on their spidery black wire stands, they were funeral wreaths. No one else ever used such flowers, did they? But that wasn't what they meant here.

Yet a person who could go to these lengths to see her this way, maybe such a person could hurt her.

Imagine her telling me that she had done this with a man. "And then he bought a white veil and white shoes and . . ."

I would have said, he's crazy, stay away from him. You cannot trust someone who does something like this.

But it wasn't merely the degree of contrivance. There was the obvious blasphemy. The prayer book, the rosary.

My heart was beating too fast. I sank back against the wall for a moment, folded my arms. *I loved it!*

I went downstairs, poured a cup of coffee, and took it out on the back deck with me. One thing is for certain, I thought. I would never hurt her. It's madness to think I would. I'm not hurting her, asking her to put on these clothes, am I? It's merely a tableau. And it fits perfectly, doesn't it?

The pictures could be a book so far—the carousel horse trio, the riding portrait, now the Holy Communion.

WHEN I heard the front door shut, I didn't move. In a few moments she'd see these things. She'd come down and tell me what she thought. I just waited.

The water went on upstairs. The pipes along the side of the narrow house were singing with it. She was taking a shower. Think of her in the hot steam, deliciously pink—

Finally the water went off. I could hear even the faint vibration of her moving in the house.

I walked inside very slowly, put down the cup.

No sound.

"Belinda?"

She didn't answer.

I went upstairs. There was no light from anywhere but the bedroom, and that was the candlelight, throwing its flicker on the old wallpaper and the white ceiling.

I went into the room.

She was standing at the foot of the bed, dressed in the full costume, with the white wreath around her head and the veil down over her face. She was holding the prayer book and the rosary. Her feet were right together, heels of the white shoes touching. And the short gown just reached her knees like a little girl's First Communion dress a long time ago. She was smiling through the veil. Her naked arms coming out of the puffed sleeves were very round, yet her fingers threaded through the pearl rosary beads were thin and fine and tapered.

It knocked the breath out of me utterly. Her grave blue eyes shining through the veil, her bud of a mouth set just on the edge of a smile. Only the hands were a woman's hands. That is, until I noticed the thrust of her breasts under the yoke, the pink nipple showing through the sheer linen.

I felt the passion come up between my legs. I felt it go to my brain instantly.

I came towards her. I lifted up the veil and threw it back over her hair, over the white wreath. That was the right way. The little girls had never worn veils down. Always back. Her blue eyes were flowing with the candlelight.

I took her in my arms, clasping her bottom through the thin linen. I lifted her up and back on the bed. I pushed her back, until she was seated against the pillows. Her legs were out straight and she held the prayer book and the rosary in her lap. I kissed her knees, ran my hands down her calves.

"Come here," she said gently. She beckoned with both hands for me to come up on the bed. I climbed up and she went back into the pillows. "Come on," she said again. She opened her mouth and started kissing me very fast, very impatiently. I could see the movement of her eyes under her closed eyelids. I ran my thumbs across her eyebrows—silk. And her body pumping slightly beneath me.

I was going to come before I was into her. I got off my pants and shirt, and then I pulled off her white stockings in one rough quick gesture.

There was her sex under the heap of crumpled linen, all but hidden, the shy little lips under the ashen shadow of hair. A seam of frightening dark peach pink flesh. A core I wanted to touch—

Her face was flushed. She pulled me close to her, and then she lay back, drawing the dress up so that I could see her breasts. I pressed my face to her stomach, then I went up on my arms and I gathered up her breasts and started kissing them, sucking them. Her nipples were tiny, stone-hard. She was moaning softly. Her legs lay open.

I reached for the crystal glass of wine I had set beside the bed. I poured just a few droplets onto her sex, saw it flow down into the moist secret little creases. I smoothed it with my fingers, feeling her open more, feeling her invite, feeling her hips rise slightly. I poured the wine in her. Saw it stain the white coverlet, saw her quivering under it.

And lying there with my hands curled around her thighs, I drank wine out of her. I pushed my tongue deep into her and drank the wine, and felt the taut muscles there contracting. Her thighs closed against the side of my face, hot, clamping onto me. She seemed to be throbbing, shivering.

"Come on," she said.

Her face was very red, her head turning back and forth against her tangled hair. The veil was all over under her.

"Come on, Jeremy," she said again in a whisper. I went into her, and felt her legs really lock around me this time. But I had to be free to thrust into her hard and she let me go and lay back, sprawled out, her head crushing the nest of white veil, white silk flowers.

When I knew she was coming, absolutely could feel it as her body clamped down on me, I let go inside her.

One two three four five six seven. All good children go to heaven.

[11]

WE slept a long time. I noticed later the candles had burnt down quite far. It was dark outside. When I opened my eyes, she was sitting beside me, looking down at me. She'd taken off the dress and the stockings, but she had the wreath and veil properly in place and the veil fell down to the bed forming a triangle of white light covering her. Her breast in profile and her bent leg were divinely lovely. I ran my hand down her leg. The pink of her nipples was exactly the pink of her mouth.

To look at her eyes frightened me a little. She was peering out from this body and I don't think she knew what a miracle it was. How could she? How could any child know?

"Let's take the pictures," she said gently.

"Doesn't anything scare you?" I asked softly.

"Of course not, why should it?"

Priceless, the expression on her face, better than I'd ever be able to paint it.

And there was the camera staring from the foot of the bed.

I was so sleepy, positively drugged. The fragrance of the flowers was all around us. On the ceiling above I saw the shadows dancing, delicate shadows, like those of the frilled petals of the carnations, everything shivering as the candle flames were shivering.

"Get the wine, would you?" I said. "Over here." That will wake me up, won't it?

I watched her fill the glass with Burgundy. When she looked down, she looked younger than at any other time, because you saw her blond eyebrows brushed and soft and her lower lip jutting just a little. As soon as she looked straight ahead again and her face relaxed, she was ageless: the nymph who'd had this same body for a hundred years.

She sat beside me with one knee up, her hair tumbled down over her shoulders, over her breasts. She seemed to glow in the light of the candles.

"Holy Communion," I said.

She smiled. She bent down with the red wine on her lips and kissed me and she whispered:

"This is my body. This is my blood."

DAN called while we were still shooting. When I heard that voice coming through the bedside phone right next to her, I felt the blood rushing to my head.

"Look, I can't talk now," I said.

"Well, you listen to me, stupid. Somebody's looking for your little girl. And the whole thing looks weird to me."

She was looking through the prayer book. Her shoulder was touching my arm.

"Not now. Call you later," I said.

"You go out and call me back now."

"Impossible."

I glanced at her, and she looked up at me. Something stirred in her face. I couldn't hear what he was saying. I felt as if I didn't know what to do with my mouth to look natural.

"—photograph of her I want you to see!"

"What? Look. I have to go now. Right now."

"—my office, eight o'clock, before I go to court. You listening to me?"

"Twelve," I said. "I work late."

"Jeremy, this is weird, I'm telling you—"

"In the morning, OK?"

I hung up. My face was burning all right. I knew that she was looking at me.

It was the hardest thing just to turn and look back at her. And I knew she was sensing something, and that I wasn't pulling this off.

And then I saw the suspicion plainly there, her little mouth set, her skin slightly flushed too.

"What's the matter?" she asked. Right to it, of course.

"Nothing. My lawyer, that's all. Book business." Yeah, hit close to the truth and you might be able to make it convincing.

I was fumbling with the camera. What had I been doing? Changing the ASA for the new roll of film, what?

She studied me for a long moment.

"Let's break," I said. "Can't work after an interruption like that." I went right downstairs and threw on the answering machine with the sound down. *That* wasn't going to happen again.

SHE'D been drinking for a while before we left for dinner. Maybe the first time I'd seen her just a little drunk. Her hair was pinned up and she had on a velvet suit, white blouse. Very grown-up. The ashtray was full of butts. She didn't say anything when I suggested a little place around the corner. She tossed down the last of her Scotch and got up languidly.

White wicker tables, overhead fans, good food. I kept trying to make conversation. She was stony.

And Dan, what the fuck had he been saying about a photograph of her? Another photograph of her?

"Who was that who called?" she asked suddenly. She had just lighted another cigarette. She hadn't touched the scampi.

"My lawyer, I told you. Taxes or something." I could feel the heat again in my face. I knew I sounded like a liar. I put down the fork suddenly. This was just too ugly.

She was eyeing me downright coldly.

"I have to go down, see him at noon, I hate it."

She didn't respond.

"All these things in the works, Disney thinking about buying the Angelica books. Rainbow Productions wanting them. It's a tough decision to make." OK, good, latch onto that little misplaced speck of truth. "Don't much want to bother with it right now. My mind's on you, it's a million miles from those things."

"Big bucks," she said with a slight lift of her eyebrows. "Rainbow's a new company. They do exquisite animation."

Now how would she know that? And the tone, all the California girl had dropped away. There was that crisp articulation I'd noticed the first time I met her.

Her eyes were strange. The wall had come down again.

And what did I look like to her?

"Yeah, Rainbow . . . they did a a—" I couldn't think.

"Knights of the Round Table. I saw it."

"Yeah, exactly. So they want to do two films of Angelica."

But this wasn't working. She knew something was out of wack.

"But then Disney is Disney," I said. "And whoever does it has to make sure the animation is true to the drawings. You know, if they want to add characters, they have to fit."

"Don't you have agents and lawyers that handle all that?"

"Sure. That's who called me. The lawyer. I have to sign on the dotted line finally. Nobody can do that but me."

Her eyes were frightening me. She was drunk. She really was.

"Are you really happy with me?" she asked. Small voice. No drama. She crushed out her cigarette in the uneaten food on her plate. She never did things like that.

"Are you happy?" she asked again.

"Yes, happy," I said. I looked up at her slowly. "I'm happy, probably happier than I've ever been in my life. I think I could write a new definition of happy. I want to go home and develop the pictures. I want to stay up all night and paint. I feel like I'm twenty-one again, if you want to know. Do you think I'm a fool for that?"

Long pause. Then the smile, tentative, then growing brighter, like a light coming down a dark passage.

"I'm happy, too," she said. "It's all happened just like I dreamed it could."

To hell with Dan. To hell with all of it, I thought.

I DID the whole roll of Communion shots before I went to bed. For a little while she came into the basement darkroom with me, a cup of coffee in her hand.

I explained everything I was doing and she watched carefully. Asked if she could help next time. She seemed tired from all that Scotch earlier, but otherwise OK. Almost OK.

She was fascinated by the process, the pictures coming clear magically in the developing tray. I told her how a real photographer might do it, take more time with every step. For me it was like squeezing out oil onto the plate, cleaning brushes, it was mere preparation.

I made three enlargements, and we took these up to the attic.

I knew this was going to be the best picture of all. *Holy Communion* or *Belinda with Communion Things*. Just the veil and the wreath, no other clothing, of course. And the prayer book and rosary in her hands. Formal as the riding picture, as the little black-and-white photographs that the mothers would take of the little girls on that day outside the church before the procession. The trick was the background.

At first glance you had to think you saw cloisters or Gothic arches. Maybe the flowers of an altar with candles. Then you would realize you were seeing a bedroom, a four-poster bed, wallpaper. Had to make this illusion seamless: it was a matter of texture as well as lighting. And I was going beyond the practiced applications of my craft here into a new depth of illusion.

I wanted to start then; keep the pace going. But she said she wanted me to come to bed with her, really snuggle with her.

Desperate, her eyes. Her voice.

"OK, darling baby," I said.

She was stiff when I put my arm around her.

"You know there's a place we could go," I said suddenly. "I mean, we could get away from San Francisco for a little while. House in Carmel I have, rarely use it. We'd have to clean it up, but it's small, wouldn't be hard. Just a block from the ocean."

ABOUT four in the morning I woke up and realized that she was crying. She had been shaking me, trying to wake me up. She was standing by the bed and she was sobbing, wiping at her eyes with a Kleenex. "Wake up," she was saying.

"What's the matter?" I said.

I switched on the small light by the bed. She was wearing only a cotton slip. She was really drunk now. I could see it, smell the Scotch on her. She had a glass in her hand, full of ice and Scotch, and her hand holding it was a woman's hand.

"I want you to pay attention to me," she said. She was gritting her teeth, and her eyes were all red. She was really frantic. The thin little triangles of white cotton barely covered her breasts, and they were heaving.

"What is it?" I said. I took her in my arms. She was actually choking, she was so upset.

"I want you to understand this," she said.

"What?"

"If you call the police on me, if you try to find out who I am, if you find my family and you tell them where I am, I want you to know, I want you to know, I'll tell them what we've been doing. I don't want to do it, I could die first, to do something like that. But I mean it, if you ever betray me, goddamn it, if you ever do that to me, if you ever betray me like that, if you ever ever do that to me, I will, I swear I will I will tell them—"

"But I wouldn't, I wouldn't ever—"

"Don't you ever betray me, don't you ever do it, Jeremy."

She was sobbing in spasms. I was holding her tight and she was just writhing against my chest.

"Belinda, how could you think I'd do that?" That wasn't it at all, not at all.

"I don't want to say horrible things, it kills me to say I'd hurt you. It kills me to say I'd use these things to hurt you, twist it all around for them and their filthy morality, their stupid idiotic morality. But I would, I would, I would, if you betrayed me—"

"You don't have to say it, I understand." I stroked her hair, held her tighter. I was kissing the top of her head.

"But, so help me God, if you betrayed me—"

Never, never, never.

WHEN she was finally calmed down, we lay there curled in each other's arms. It was still dark outside. I couldn't sleep anymore. It was going round and round in my head that what I was actually doing was not betraying her. Lying, yes, betraying, no.

She whispered, "I don't ever want to talk about it. I don't ever ever want to think about it. I was born the day you saw me. I was born then, and you and me were born then."

Yes, yes, yes.

But I only wanted to know what happened, so that we could both put it behind us, both know it was OK, OK, OK . . .

"Jeremy, hold on me. Hold on to me."

"Come on," I said finally. "Let's get up, get dressed, get out of here."

She seemed numb. I pulled the little wool skirt and blazer out, dressed her. Buttoned the white blouse myself up to her neck, kissed her. Got the cashmere scarf and put it around her neck. Put the little leather gloves on her.

She was a doll all dressed up, a little English girl. I brushed her hair even, put it back in the barrette so I could see the flawless plane of her forehead. I loved to kiss her bare forehead.

She watched silently as I gathered up the photographs of *Holy Communion,* carried the canvases down to the basement, opened up the back of the van, slid the canvases into the rack. I helped her up into the high front seat.

I DROVE south out of San Francisco in the early morning darkness, down the clean silent stretch of highway towards the Monterey Peninsula, the morning coming slowly through the gray clouds.

She was sitting beside me looking very stately with her hair blown back from her face and her arms folded. The lapel of her jacket flapped silently in the wind, just touching the hollow beneath her cheekbone.

An hour, an hour and a half, and the sky was brightening behind the clouds. The sun coming suddenly through the high windshield. Blessed warmth on my hands.

I made that turn into the wind, towards the ocean, into Monterey, then south through the piny woods to Carmel.

She didn't know where we were, I don't think. She'd never seen this strange still little beach town, like a stage set before the day's tourists, never seen the little thatched cottages behind their white picket fences beneath the towering gray Monterey cypresses with their gnarled limbs.

I led her along the gravel path to the rounded door of the cottage. The earth was sandy, the brilliant yellow and red primroses scattered in the clumps of green grass.

In the little house of raw redwood beams and stone floors the sun spilled through the little windows. Green leaves high against the leaded glass.

I climbed the ladder to the loft bed with her, and we sank down together in the musty down covers.

The sun was breaking in shafts through the webbing of branches above the skylight.

"Dear God," she said. She was shuddering suddenly and the tears came back and she looked past me into the light overhead. "If I can't trust you, there is no one."

"I love you," I said. "I don't care about any of it, I swear. I love you."

"Holy Communion," she said squeezing her eyes so the tears came out.

"Yes, Holy Communion, my darling," I said.

[12]

"WHAT this requires is a decision," she said. "I mean, a commitment. That you want this, you want me here and I want to be here. That we are going to do this now, live together, be together. And then it's settled."

"It's settled, then, it's decided."

"You have to see me as someone who is free, who is in control of what is happening to her—"

"But let's be absolutely frank. You know what's bothering me. That someone is grieving, that someone is going crazy, worrying about you. That they think you're dead—"

"No. This will not work. This will not work. You have to understand that I have walked away from them. I made the decision to go. I said to them and to myself this will not continue. And I decided that I would leave. It was my decision."

"But can a kid your age make that decision?"

"I made it," she said. "This is *my* body! This is *me*. I took this body and I walked with it."

Silence.

"You got it? Because if you don't, I walk again."

"I got it," I said. "You've got it."

"What?"

"The commitment. The decision."

[13]

On the third day in Carmel we started arguing about the cigarettes:

What the hell did I mean, die of cancer, all that rot, would I listen to myself the way I sounded, like somebody's father for God's sakes, I mean, did I think she was born yesterday? And it was not two packs a day and she did not chain smoke or smoke on the street that much. Didn't I know she was experiencing things, this was a time of life for going overboard, making mistakes, didn't I understand she wasn't going to puff like a stove pipe all her life, she didn't even inhale most of the time?

"All right, then, if you won't listen, if you want the prerogative of making the same stupid mistakes everybody else makes, then there have to be ground rules. I won't watch you poison yourself on a routine basis in either the kitchen or the bedroom. No more smoking in the rooms where we take our meals or take each other. Now that is fair, isn't it?"

Red-faced glare, almost slammed the kitchen door, obviously thought better of it. Stomp of feet going up the ladder to the loft. Tape of rock queen Madonna suddenly thumping through the cottage at deafening level. (Did I have to buy her a Carmel machine as well as a San Francisco machine?)

Tick of cuckoo clock. This is awful, awful.

Creaking sound of her coming back down the ladder.

"OK, you really don't want me to smoke in the bedroom or the kitchen."

"Really don't. Really—"

Lower lip jutting deliciously, back to the door frame, cutoff jeans very tight on her brown thighs, nipples two points in the black T-shirt with ghastly logo of the rock group Grateful Dead on it.

Quiet voice:

"OK, if it makes you happy."

Silk of inner arms around my neck, hair coming down me before the kiss like a net.

"It makes me very happy."

THE Holy Communion canvas was exploding. The whole living room of the cottage was the studio, the easel sprawled on the rumpled drop cloth. New air, new sky, even new coffee cup exhilarating. Nothing stood between me and this picture. I painted until I literally could no longer hold the brush.

The argument about the booze erupted on the seventh day:

OK, now I was really getting out of hand, who did I think I was, first the smoking and now this, did I think I was the voice of authority that I could just tell her what to do, did I talk this way to Cecilia or Andrea or whatever their names were?

"They weren't sixteen and they didn't drink half a bottle of Scotch for breakfast on Saturday morning! They didn't drink three cans of beer while driving the van to Big Sur."

That was outrageous, that was unjust, that was not what happened.

"I found the cans in the van! The cans were still cold! Last night you poured half a pint of rum into your Cokes while you were reading, you think I don't see this, you're putting down quarts of booze a day in this house—"

I was uptight, puritanical, crazy. And if I wanted to know, it was none of my business what she drank, did I think I owned her?

"Look, I can't change being forty-four, and at my age you don't watch a young girl—"

Just hold it right there. Was she supposed to join Alcoholics Anonymous just because I didn't know the difference between two drinks and dipsomania? Well, she knew the difference. She'd lived all her life around booze and people who poured it down, boy, what she could tell me about booze, she could write the book on booze, on cleaning up vomit and dragging drunks up to bed and lying to bellhops and room service and hotel doctors about drunks, don't tell her about drunks—

She stopped, staring at me.

"So you're going to go through it all, too? What is that, loyalty or something to this drunk whoever it was? Is this person dead that he or she deserves that kind of loyalty?"

Crying. Saying nothing. Foxed.

"Stop it!" I said. "Stop all of it, the Scotch, the wine with dinner, the goddamned beers you think I don't see you putting down."

ALL RIGHT GODDAMN IT! THIS WAS THE BARRICADES. IS THAT WHAT I WANTED? Was I telling her to get out of my house, was I?

"No, and you won't leave either, because you love me and you know I love you and you will stop, I know you will. You will stop the drinking now!"

"You think you can just order me to stop!"

Out the front door. Off towards the ocean. Or to the highway to hitch-hike to GONE FOREVER?

I threw on the overhead light and looked at *Holy Communion.* If this isn't the breakthrough of my career, then I don't have one. Everything I know about reality and illusion is there.

But what the hell damn difference does this make? Never felt so much like getting drunk myself.

Eight o'clock, nine o'clock, she's gone forever. I'm leaving notes for nobody when I walk on the beach. Not a single figure approaching in the sugar white sand is Belinda.

Ten thirty. The loft without her, lying there on the giant floppy mattresses and comforters.

Front door opens down there.

Then she is at the top of the ladder, holding onto the sides, face too dark to see.

"I'm glad you're home. I was worried."

Smell of Calandre, cold fresh air. Her cheek would smell like the ocean wind if she came over and kissed me.

She sat near the top of the ladder, profile against the little window.

Light from the skylight milky and chilling. I can see the red of the cashmere scarf. One of her black leather kid gloves as she pulls on the end of the scarf.

"I finished the Holy Communion canvas today."

Silence.

"You have to understand that nobody ever paid that much attention to what I did," she said.

Silence.

"I'm not used to taking orders."

Silence.

"To tell you the honest fucking truth, nobody ever cared, I mean, they just figured I could handle whatever I was doing, you know, they just didn't give a fucking damn."

Silence.

"I mean, I had teachers and all the clothes I could want and nobody bugged me. When I had my first affair, well, they took me to Paris to get me on the pill, you know, just nothing to it, like don't get pregnant and all. Nobody—"

Silence. Hair white wisps in the moonlight.

"And it's not like you're saying I can't handle it, because I can! I can handle it perfectly. I always handle it. You're just saying it would make you feel better if I didn't drink so much and then *you* wouldn't feel so guilty."

Silence.

"That is what you're saying, isn't it?"

"I'll settle for that."

Soft crush of her against me suddenly, smell of cold salt wind, her luscious mouth, just like I knew it would be.

Eight A.M. the next morning.

Slices of apple, orange, cantaloupe on a china plate. Scrambled eggs, a bit of cheese.

"This must be an hallucination. Are you actually eating real food for breakfast? Where's the Coke and potato chips?"

"Honest to God, Jeremy. Get off my case. I mean, nobody can live on Coke and potato chips."

Don't say anything.

"And there's something else I want to talk to you about, Jeremy."

"Yes?"

"How about letting me buy you a couple of tweed jackets that actually fit?"

AN innocent little remark like that in a place like Carmel can turn into a shopping marathon. Which it did.

[14]

As soon as we came back into the San Francisco house, I had another picture. Next step from *Holy Communion.* I knew it when I went into the living room and looked at the dolls. *Belinda with Dolls.*

The mailbox was full of crap from Dan, New York, Hollywood. I dumped it on the desk unopened, unplugged the answering machine, turned down the bell on all the phones, and went back to work.

"Take off your clothes, will you?" I said to Belinda. We'd do it right here in the living room on the Queen Anne sofa, the one that had been in all the Angelica books.

She laughed.

"Another one of these magnificent pictures never to be seen by anybody!" she said, as she stripped off her jeans and sweater.

"Bra, panties, all off, please," I said snapping my fingers.

That brought another little riff of laughter. She pitched all the clothes into the hallway, then pulled the barrette out of her hair.

"Yes, perfect," I said, adjusting the lights and the tripod. "Just sit in the middle of the couch and I'll pile the dolls around you."

She stretched out her arms to receive them.

"Do they have names?" she asked.

"Mary Jane and Mary Jane and Mary Jane," I said. I told her which were French, German. This was the priceless Bru, and this smiling child, what they had called the character baby. That made her smile, too.

She was playing with their matted wigs, their faded little dresses. She loved the big ones, the girls with their long locks. Such serious expressions they had, dark painted eyebrows. Stockings and shoes were missing here and there. She'd have to fix them up. Get them new hair ribbons.

Actually they were just fine without their shoes and stockings, most of them, rather bashed and ancient-looking in wilted tulle, but I didn't tell her.

I watched her delicate fingers struggle with the tiny buttons.

Yes, this was what I wanted.

I started snapping. She looked up startled. Got it. Now the big blue-eyed long-hair Bru doll pressed to her naked breasts, both of them staring at me, yes. She gathered them all onto her lap, got it. Then rolled over slowly, stretching out on the couch, the dolls tumbling around her, little bonnets and feathered hats fluttering, her chin resting on her elbow sunk into the puce velvet, her naked bottom baby-smooth, got it.

She rolled over on her back, knee raised, picking up the biggest doll, the German Bebe with the red curls and the high-button shoes. And all the dolls around her glared with their brilliant glass eyes.

I saw her fall into the usual trance as the shutter kept clicking.

And then, as she eased down off the couch onto her knees and turned to the side with the Bru in her arms, the others all heaped behind her, I knew we had the picture. It was in the dreamy expression of her face.

This and the brass bed picture were the future. Go away, world.

SHE popped up early the next afternoon, on her way out to see a new Japanese film. "Nothing is going to get you away from these pictures that nobody will ever see, right?"

"I can't read all those subtitles. Go on."

"You're incredible, you know it? You fall asleep during the symphony, you think Kuwait is a person, you can't follow foreign movies, and you worry about me getting an education. Good grief!"

"It's terrible, isn't it?"

She zeroed in on the doll photos.

"The one where you're kneeling," I told her. "And the brass bed series, I'm going to do six panels, like the page of a comic book, all different angles of you through the bars."

"Terrific." She popped her gum, hands on hips, black sweater tight over her breasts. "And all this goes in a vault somewhere, or do you burn it finally?"

"Don't be a smart aleck. Go to the movies."

"You're crazy, you know it? I mean it this time, I do, I do."

"And what if I did show them?" I asked. "What if the whole world saw them? What if they were plastered all over *Time* and *Newsweek* and the papers, and *Artforum* and *Art in America,* and the *National Enquirer* and you name it, and they called me a genius and a child molester and the reincarnation of Rembrandt and a kidnapper? Then what would happen to you? Miss Belinda with no last name, no family, no history? With your picture in every newspaper in the country? And make no mistake. It would be like that. It's that kind of story."

That steady look, that serious look. I'm not sixteen. I'm old enough to be your mother. Except when I pop my gum.

"Would you have the guts to do it?" she asked. Not a mean voice. Just on the line.

"What if I said I knew it was just a matter of time? What if I said that no artist works like I'm working on paintings he never intends to show to anybody? What if I said it was like walking closer and closer to a cliff, knowing at some point, when you weren't looking, you'd go over? I'm not talking tomorrow. I'm not talking next week or next month, maybe not even next year. I mean, there is a whole lifetime of work to be undermined here, a whole lifetime to be destroyed, and that takes guts, yes, guts, but sooner or later—"

"If you said all that, then I'd say you have more guts than you let on sometimes."

"But let's keep the focus on you. What happens if these parents or whoever they are open *Time* magazine and see your picture there, painted by Jeremy Walker?"

Sober, reflecting.

"What could it prove?" she asked. "That we'd met? That I'd posed for some pictures? Is that a crime, to pose for pictures? They wouldn't have anything on you unless I supplied it, and I will never never supply it."

"You're still not understanding me. What happens to *you?* Do they come to collect their little girl posthaste from the dirty old man who's been painting her pictures?"

Eyes narrowing. Mouth getting hard. Looking at me, then away, then back at me again.

"A year and a half!" A voice so low it sounds like somebody else inside her body. "Less than that, actually, until I'm eighteen and then there is nothing, absolutely nothing, they can do to me! And you can show those pictures! You can hang them on the walls of the Museum of Modern Art, and there is nothing, absolutely nothing they can do to either one of us!"

But who are they? Who are they and what did they do to you?

Quiet.

"Show them!" she said. "You have to show them."

Silence.

"No. I take that back. If it's falling off a cliff, then you have to make that decision. But when the time comes, don't use me as an excuse!"

"No, I'll just go on using you, period," I said.

"Using me? *You?* Using *me?*"

"That's how anybody in his or her right mind would see it," I said. I glanced at the canvases surrounding us. And then I looked at her.

"You think it's all cut and dried?" she asked. "You think you're grown-up and everything, and so I've got to be the one who's being taken advantage of? Well, you're nuts."

"It scares me, that's all. The way I accept your word for it that it's OK you're with me—"

"And whose word could you accept!"

Silence.

"Don't get mad," I said. "We have years to argue about it."

"Do we?"

I didn't answer.

"Stop talking about being a kidnapper or a child molester. I'm not a child! For God's sakes, I'm not."

"I know—"

"No, you don't. The only time you don't feel guilty is when we're in bed or you've got the paintbrush in your hand, you know it? For God's sakes, start believing in us."

"I do believe in us," I said. "And I'll tell you something else. If I don't fall off that cliff, books or no books, I'll never be anything."

Steady from her.

"Never be anything? Jeremy Walker, the household word?"

"That's right. That's what I said."

"Then let me tell you something," she said. But she hesitated; then: "I can't explain it, but just remember. The people who are looking for me? They wouldn't *dare* try to do anything to you."

What the hell did that mean?

THE day they came to install Andy Blatky's sculpture she did a disappearing act. I didn't know she was leaving until I heard the MG pull out.

Andy's big-shouldered work looked good on the back patio. It seemed to be reaching up towards the decks and the house, the fluid lines of the piece accentuated against the dark bricks beneath it, the plain whitewashed fence on three sides.

Andy and I took an hour or more to rig up the small nighttime spotlights. Then we sat at the kitchen table, talking, drinking beer.

"How about showing me that new work?" he said.

I was so tempted. I just sat there, thinking soon, very soon.

THREE days later Dan came banging on the door.

"Where have you been? Why the hell aren't you answering my messages?"

"Look, I'm working," I said. I had the brush in my hand. Halfway through the brass bed canvas. "I don't want you coming in right now."

"You what!"

"Dan, look—"

"Is she here?"

"No, she's out riding, but she'll be back any minute."

"That's terrific!"

He came storming into the front hall.

"I don't even want to come in this house with her here."

"So don't."

"Look at this picture, idiot!" he said. He took it out of a manila envelope. I shut the front door behind him, then turned on the hall light.

It was Belinda most definitely. A Kodachrome five by seven of her in a white dress, leaning against the stone railing of a terrace. Blue sky, sea behind her. Shocking to see her in another world. I hated the sight of it.

"Turn it over," he said.

I read the small clear felt-tip writing on the back: her height, weight—age, sixteen. No name. "Have you seen this girl? She's wanted for an important part in a theatrical feature. Reward for any information leading to her whereabouts. No questions asked. Contact Eric Sampson Agency." A Beverly Hills address.

"Where did you get this?"

He took the picture and returned it to the envelope.

"Halfway house in the Haight," he said. "This guy Sampson flies up here, passes these out at the youth shelters, on the street. Anybody finding Miss Up-and-coming gets a reward for it. Just call his number. I called his number. He says a big studio wants her, she tried out for a part, then vanished. He doesn't have a name."

"I don't believe it."

"Neither do I. But he's tough, this guy. And he knows a lot about her, that much I can tell you. I tried a couple of phony possibilities on him immediately. No, his kid is quite educated, trilingual, as he puts it. And her hair is definitely not bleached. And I'll tell you something else. Couple of calls to New York turned up just what I thought they would. Sampson's been on the East Coast passing these out too."

"What do you make of it?"

"Money, Jer, lots of it. Maybe a big name. These people want her back bad, and they're spending a bundle on it, but they won't go public. I checked and rechecked with missing persons, missing juveniles, absolutely zilch."

"Crazy."

"They aren't about to hang a sign on her that says 'Kidnap me.' But that doesn't mean they won't pour their money into hauling you into court on every conceivable morals charge from—"

"We've been through that."

"And I checked out this Sampson by the way, and he's not an agent, he's a lawyer, in the business affairs end of the agency. People like that don't scout."

"The funny thing is—"

"What?"

"It's not impossible. She could be some kind of movie star. I mean, it wouldn't be out of the question at all."

"Then why doesn't he have a name for her? No, it's bullshit all the way."

"What about the director I mentioned, that Susan Jeremiah?"

"Dead end. Oh, she's hot, real hot, did some arty thing that got raves at Cannes, turned in a good TV flick, so she's the genius of the week down there. But she's got no missing sisters, cousins, nieces, or daughters. Big Houston family. Just plain folks with loads of real estate money. She's Daddy's girl, drives a big shiny Cadillac, if you can believe it. She's really on her way."

"But nothing—"

"Not a thing."

"OK. You did your best. Now we should drop the whole thing."

"What? Are you out of your head? Get out of this mess, Jeremy. Give her some bucks, send her on her way. Burn everything she leaves behind her. Then get on a plane for Katmandu yourself. Take a nice long vacation where nobody can find you. If the shit hits the fan and she tells all, it's your word against hers, you never heard of her."

"You're getting carried away, Dan. She's not Mata Hari. She's a little girl."

"Jer, this Sampson hands out hundred-dollar bills to anyone on the streets that gives him even a clue to this little girl's whereabouts."

"Does he have clues?"

"If he did, you'd be dead in the water. But he's been here twice this month! All he has to do is connect with the kids in that Page Street address or the cop who put your name in his little book—"

"Yeah, but that's not as easy as it sounds, Dan."

"Jer, the cops down there saw her with you! They wrote down this address. Pick another runaway, Jer, some waif from the sticks that nobody ever wants to see again. The police don't even bother picking them up unless they can nail them for shoplifting. There's lots of free kids out there for the taking. Just go down to the Haight-Ashbury and stick out your hand."

"Look Dan. For now I want you to call it quits."

"No."

"You like working for nothing? I'm telling you it's closed."

"Jeremy, you aren't just a goddamned fucking client to me, man, you're my friend."

"Yeah, Dan, and she's my lover. And I can't sneak behind her back again on this. I can't. I don't even want to know this much and not tell her, but how can I tell her that I snooped?"

"Jer, this guy may very well trace her to your door!"

"Yeah he might. And if he does, well, she's not going anywhere with him or anyone else unless she wants to."

"You're flipping out! You've fucking lost your mind. I ought to have you committed for your own sake. You think this is one of your story-books, you've—"

"Look, Dan, you're my lawyer. I'm saying you're off the case. Tear up the picture and forget everything I told you. When she gets ready, she'll tell me herself all about who she is. I know she will. Until then . . . well, we've got what we've got just like anybody else, I guess."

"You're not hearing me, old buddy. Your agents have been trying to get you all week about this Rainbow Productions deal for Angelica and you're blowing it. Blowing everything. They don't make animated cartoon movies of books by kidnappers and child molesters."

"I am hearing you. I love her. That's what matters to me right now." *And what is happening to me matters, the painting that is up in the attic right now matters, goddamn it, and I want to get back to it.*

"Don't give me this song and dance, Jer! My God, is this kid a witch? What are you going to do next, the plastic surgery routine, dye on the gray hair, start wearing shirts open to the waist and gold chains and hip-hugger jeans and doing cocaine 'cause it makes you feel as young as she is?"

"Dan, look, I trust you, and I respect you. But you can't change what's happening here. You've done your duty. You're off the hook now."

"Like hell."

He was really steaming. He glanced around at the hallway, the living room crowded with toys. His eyes were moving critically over stuff he'd seen a thousand times before. "Jer, I'm going after this guy Sampson, I'm going to crack this little story of his, if I have to go down south to do it in person."

He opened the front door. Blast of traffic noise from Seventeenth Street. She might be coming around the corner any minute.

"Look, Dan. I realized something a long time ago. I don't really want the truth about Belinda. I just want to hear something that will make me feel OK about having her with me."

"I'm hip, Jer, I caught that the first time around."

"Well, Dan, when you can handle only one kind of answer to a question, it is really better not to ask."

"When I find out something else, I'm calling you," he said. "And you answer your damn phone. And you call your agent, for God's sakes. She's been trying to reach you for three days!"

THE house was still vibrating from his voice it seemed. I stood there holding the brush. OK. One call. It had been almost three weeks.

I went in and called Clair Clarke. Break out the champagne. The deal was all set with Rainbow Productions for the eight Angelica books to be made into two feature animated films. They had agreed to all our terms. Movies to be substantially based on the plot of the books, all character rights retained by us. Contracts in a week.

"How's it coming by the way?" she asked.

"What's that?"

"The new book."

"Oh, I don't know about that, Clair. Let's celebrate this little turn of events for a while, not rush things."

"Nothing's wrong."

"No! Everything's fine actually, better than ever." Over and out.

I went back to the attic and the six panels of number seven: *Belinda in Brass Bed.*

Belinda, always seen through the bars, slept in a nightgown in the first. In the second she had shifted position, nightgown pushed up. Third, nightgown draped over her, breasts bare. Fourth, full nude. Fifth, close in on her profile waist up. Six, very close full face turned to us, only framed by the bars, asleep on the pillow.

My brush was moving as if my right hand had a mind of its own. I'd say, Do it. My hand would do it.

Don't think about anything else.

FOUR o'clock in the morning. She was down in the kitchen again. I could hear her faraway voice.

I went to the railing, the way I'd done that first time. I kept thinking of the things Dan had said.

I could hear her laughing a little. Cheerful, intimate like before.

I made my way down slowly until I stood at the yule post at the bottom of the stairs and I could see her through the kitchen door. She said something quickly in the phone and then hung up.

"I woke you up again, didn't I?" she asked, as she came towards me.

"Don't tell him where you are," I said.

"Who?" A shadow falling over her face, her lip quivering slightly, look in her eyes I've never seen before.

"The guy you were talking to, the oldest buddy in the world, the one in New York. It was him, wasn't it?"

"Oh, yeah. I forgot I told you." Eyes dulling, distracted. If she is a liar, she gets the Sarah Bernhardt award.

"Somebody could be looking, a private detective. He could question people. They could tell."

"You're half asleep," she said. "You sound like a bear. Come on back upstairs." She looked tired, as if her head hurt her, that kind of dullness in her eyes.

"You didn't tell him the address, did you?"

"You're getting excited over nothing," she whispered. "He's my buddy, he'd never tell what I told him."

"Just stay away from the street kids, will you? Don't see them anymore or call them, OK?"

She didn't look at me. She was tugging, trying to get me to go back up the steps.

"I don't want to lose you," I said. I took her face in my hands and kissed her very slowly.

She closed her eyes, letting me kiss her, opening her mouth, her body becoming limp in my arms.

"Don't be afraid," she said in the softest whisper, her eyebrows knitted. "Don't be guilty and don't be afraid."

[16]

On August 15 I was out of stretched canvas. I took out the bucket of flat white paint and went over the two I had started for the Angelica book.

Odd to see those images covered up by the thick white coat, to see Angelica disappearing. I had to stop, stare at the whole process for a moment.

Angelica through a veil of white. Good-bye, my darling.

Inventory of what has been done.

One, two, and three, *The Carousel Horse Trio:* Belinda in nightgown on the horse; Belinda nude on the horse; Belinda with punk hair and makeup nude on the horse.

Four, *Belinda with Dollhouse.*

Five, *Belinda in Riding Clothes.*

Six, *Holy Communion.*

Seven, *Belinda in Brass Bed.*

Eight, *Belinda with Dolls.*

Nine, *Artist and Model*—small canvas, not good, work in progress. Artist can not paint himself nude. Doesn't turn him on even minimally. Love scene is a fake, besides, because artist could not do it with camera clicking away. Belinda could.

("I don't understand your hang-ups about sex, just sex, you know. I wish I could make it go away, that I could kiss you the way the Prince kisses Sleeping Beauty and you would open your eyes and feel no more pain.")

Ten, *Belinda Dancing*—another small canvas, of her naked, hair in braids, beads around her neck, whirling on the kitchen floor to rock music. Bratlet. Very very good!

I'd continued painting in the titles themselves so that they were part of the work. And now I was going back and putting in the numbers. The continuity would be inseparable from the parts.

The miracle here wasn't merely the speed. I'd had bursts like this before, right after I was first published, when I created so many books that I became my own industry.

No, it was a deepening of the style. The pictures were cleaner, harsher, and utterly free of the Jeremy Walker clichés that had encrusted everything before this. The automatic cobwebs, the inevitable dirt, the expected decay was not there.

Yet never had I painted anything as dark and frightening as these pictures of her. She burned like an apparition amid solid objects. Pure fire exploding suddenly in the claustrophobic gloom. She reproached the onlooker with her frankness, her cleanness, that was it. In the First Communion veil, she announced: This is the sacrament, this is clean; you don't like it, it's your problem. All of these pictures, really, said this.

But what is the next step? I kept staring at *Belinda Dancing.* Braids and beads. Bratlet, almost woman, except the braids pushed it in the other direction—

I had half a mind to call up Andy Blatky, say: Look, come over here and look at these damned pictures. Didn't.

But about an hour later I made another decision. Quit for the day and maybe plan to go ahead and do a book party somewhere out there, accept an offer for a signing. yes, it was time to do that.

Called Jody in New York.

"If they still want me at Splendor in the Grass in Berkeley, I'll do it." She was delighted, would set up a date. We were still number seven on *The New York Times* list.

"You know, if you went on tour right now, Jeremy, we could broaden that base—"

"Start with *Splendor in the Grass,* I'm pretty busy. And I'll take the limo, it's just so much easier—"

"Star treatment all the way."

I wasn't off the phone five minutes when Dan called from LA. I almost didn't pick up. But Belinda was out, had been since morning. And he was uttering his usual threats into the answering machine. I picked up the receiver.

"Look," I said, "knock it off. I told you I don't want to play it this way. I want to wait until she tells me herself—"

"Do you want to know what I found out or not?"

"OK, what?" I said.

"This whole deal is getting weirder still. This guy Sampson honestly doesn't know who she is. He thinks the studio execs who sent him on this goose chase are wacko, but the order has come from the very top at United Theatricals. Find her and on the qt, no expense should be spared."

United Theatricals, a monster establishment. Old as Tinseltown. They'd done three of the movies made from my mother's books. They did TV shows, released foreign films, they did everything.

I'd been on the lots years ago with Alex, seen the famous Big City Street, as set where they had shot a thousand New York scenes that I had thought were done on location. And there was the tank where they did the boat scenes against an endless blue sky.

"I'm trying to get the name of the top brass involved," Dan was saying. "But even drunk this guy doesn't budge. The studio sends the check. He might not even know who he's working for. It's crazy as hell."

"Jeremiah, does she work for United Theatricals!" I said. "Somewhere, something I read—"

"Yeah, but so do thousands of other people, and she isn't top brass, she's the Monday-night movie right now, she's nothing. And besides, Sampson doesn't know who she is, I ran that by him, on the sly, sort of. He never heard of her. And I can't get to her because she's off shooting the Monday-night movie in Europe. As for Sampson, he doesn't seem to have a clue as to where Belinda is."

"How do you know that?"

"He's headed for New York with more pix next Friday, then down to Miami, if you can believe it, Miami, and then up to Frisco again. He's canvassing LA too, that much I can tell you, but he is real sly about LA. I mean he says it's real hush hush down here. And he does not know why. I mean you don't hear of him going up to kids on Sunset. He says LA is a special aspect of the case."

"Meaning what, for God's sakes?"

"You want my guess? Her family's here. What else could it be?"

"But do they want to find her or don't they! I mean what is this?"

"Good question. Because I can assure you the LAPD knows nothing about a runaway fitting that description."

"Makes no sense."

"Well, you don't either if you want my opinion."

"Look, Dan, I'm sorry about acting this way. I just . . . I'm fucking confused if you want to know."

"Look, I'll be here at the Beverly Wilshire for the next few weeks. I'll call again when I have something. But take my advice, will you, and get out of this, *before* we figure it out?"

SHE came home later that afternoon. Lots of packages. I was sitting at the kitchen table, kind of comatose. I'd been thinking about those video-tapes in her room. She'd never played them as far as I could figure. Never. The VCRs went night and day with rental tapes. Those unmarked tapes were hidden behind her sweaters. I knew because I had just checked.

"I spent scads," she shouted on her way up the stairs.

"I hope so," I said. And did I put the sweaters back properly?

A few minutes later she was back:

"Like this?"

Oh, yes. Huge swallowing black wool sweater and little skirt, very dramatic. High black boots disappearing under the hem. Barrette clasping her hair on top of her head so it flowed down behind her ears to her shoulders. Corn silk on the black wool. *A starlet. United Theatricals.*

"You don't have a wet paintbrush in your hand, you realize that?" she asked.

I nodded. *Belinda Dancing.* It was different from all the others, like the punk carousel nude. Just not part—

"Let's go have coffee," she said. "Come on."

I shrugged. Sure. Would like that. My hand was cramped a little from painting in those numbers up there, whiting out those canvases. I was feeling light, crazy. Too many nights of no more than five hours sleep.

She stood in front of the hall mirror. She was putting on pearl earrings. Now she reached into her purse, drew out a long silver wand, uncapped it, rolled it under her eyelashes.

Ladylike, beautiful. Was she a starlet? Did they want her for the part of her life?

I slipped on my jacket and went into my office and got the camera. I snapped her there by the mirror.

"I want to take this with us, OK?"

She glanced at me. "Oh, yeah, sure," she said. "Something without the kiddie things, you mean? Yeah, right on."

Yeah, right on. So immediate, thoughtless. Yet my heart was pounding.

WE went down to the Café Flore on Market and Noe, and I photo-graphed her at one of the marble top tables with a cup of coffee. She had one of her Black Russians between her uplifted fingers. Nothing affected. Quite natural. Quite charming.

People were watching us of course. A couple of writer friends were in there, good buddies, but a real nuisance. I didn't introduce her. They kept making wisecracks to get her attention, making real fools of themselves. She was civil enough, too civil. They finally gave up and split. I finished the roll.

"Do I take my clothes off now?" she whispered.

"Shut up," I said.

OF course, number eleven—*Belinda in Café Flore*—did not have any clothes on. Except for the high black boots. They matched the black cigarette.

I got that same fantastical, undeniable rush of energy when I started the canvas. By midnight that night I knew it was the next step.

"Want to hear something funny?" I asked when she came up to the attic.

"Sure, tell me."

I gestured to the picture:

"This is the first time in twenty-five years that I have painted anything that even faintly resembled a grown woman."

SPLENDOR in the Grass was one of those dream bookstores for kids, full of posters of white unicorns, and giant stuffed animals on which the toddlers can play, and little tables and chairs for reading, and every book that could conceivably be of interest to boys and girls from babyhood to twenty.

The limousine pulled up at three in the afternoon on the last Friday in August.

The crowd would have been, under normal circumstances, absolutely terrific for the ego. At least a hundred and fifty parents and children crammed into the four connecting rooms of the store, which had once been the lower floor of a private house and still retained fireplaces, wainscoting, window seats.

I sat down in the easy chair by the log fire in the first room and for an hour straight just signed, and answered the quick, simple questions.

Berkeley children are in general brilliant children. Their parents teach at the university, or they go there to study. Or they are merely the kind of people who live in a world-famous radical community—people who prefer big old gracious houses to new tract homes, and well-trafficked tree-lined streets to the more remote and protected mountain roads of the suburbs of California's Contra Costa County.

The kids asked wonderful things about the pictures in the books as well as the stories. They had intelligent complaints about the Saturday morning Charlotte show; they were suspicious of the up-and-coming animated movie.

Their bohemian parents, well scrubbed, in wash pants and sandals with babies in back carriers, talked easily of Jung, and my little girls being my feminine soul, and the "allegory" they found so delightful.

But it has gone on too long, my soul wandering through these dark rooms. It has become a pattern that is a dark room in itself.

"Sometimes, you know, I feel it has to come to an end," I heard myself say aloud. "The old houses in the books have to fall down, and I have to stop repeating this quest for freedom. I have to be outside at last."

Nods, patter, an attentive circle of the parents forming if I showed the slightest tendency to hold forth.

"And what is outside?" Question from an art student, red hair, granny glasses, jeans.

I thought for a moment.

"Contemporary life itself," I said. "Life, just life!" My voice was low, I could hardly hear it.

"But you can be an artist all your life celebrating a particular step in human development."

"True, very true, and that is what's here, of course. But it's not enough anymore."

Questions pulling it this way and that.

But I knew now why I had wanted to do this party. I was saying farewell to these kids. I was saying farewell to their proverbial shiny faces and their unbounded trust and their innocent uncensored enthusiasm, farewell to their parents who had read my works to them.

"—love the way you paint the hands, such detail to the hands."

"—and the way Angelica's shadow changes its size with each step up the stairs to her father's attic."

"—Balthus, no, much more florid than Balthus, don't you think? But you must have some response to his work—"

"Of course, of course."

More coffee, thank you.

I have used you all these years as I hid behind my mask. And yes, this is farewell. But what if now I am simply not good enough to make it as a painter?

Fear. But, above all, that thumping exhilaration. Go home, work.

And then looking at these kids I felt sadness. What if they were hurt by the Belinda pictures? What if they felt betrayed? What if it made a darkness inside them that someone they trusted had turned out to be bad and dirty? Did I have the right to do that?

"Well, your work has always been erotic." Erotic, erotic, erotic.

Just the right dirt in the right measure.

Oh, it was so important that the world, whatever the world was, understand what I did when I did it. But this was farewell to all the little girls to whom I had said the right thing for so long, the little girls that I had never never indecently touched or kissed or frightened.

Yeah, I'd come here to say good-bye, and *I* was frightened. Yet I felt better than I ever had in my life.

SHE didn't get home till later that evening—she'd had so much fun out there at the Marin stables. The trails took you high up into the green hills. But she looked anxious, tired. She sat at the kitchen table braiding her hair, fingers moving nervously as she did and redid the tight plaits.

Could we go to Carmel again, she asked me? Could we put even the wet paintings into the rack in the van and go to Carmel, just run run run away from here?

"Sure, baby darling," I said. That was what the rack in the van was for. Long ago I'd rigged it to move the work in progress. But she had to help me get the Café Flore canvas downstairs without a smudge.

SHE seemed calmer as we drove out of the city. She was resting against my shoulder, her fingers curled around my arm.

After we'd been on the highway for a while, I asked:

"What's wrong, Belinda?"

"Nothing," she said in a low voice, her eyes on the road in front of us. Then after a while she said, "Nobody knows about the Carmel house, right?"

"Nobody."

"Not even your lawyers and accountants and those people?"

"I call my accountant and I tell him the amount of the property tax and he deducts it. I bought the house years and years ago. But why are you asking me all this? What's the matter?"

"Nothing." Dull, listless tone. "Just romantic, you know, that it's so secret. No phone, no mailbox."

She had laughed when I first told her that people in Carmel didn't have street numbers, that you went to the post office every day, if you wanted to, to get your mail. I had never collected anything at the post office that I could remember.

"Yeah, it's a hideaway," I said. "Yours and mine."

I felt her fingers tighten on my arm. Her lips brushed my cheek.

Did I ever think of maybe going back down to New Orleans, to my mother's old place, she asked.

I explained I really didn't want to do that, hadn't seen that house since 1961. Be a shock just to walk into it.

It would be so far away, she said.

"Who are we running from, Belinda?" I asked her. I tried to make it sound gentle.

"No one," she said, so softly it was like a sigh.

"Then we're not in danger of somebody just—"

"I wouldn't let anything like that happen," she said. Touch of annoyance, but with whom?

Then she was quiet, sleeping for a while against my shoulder. The heavy engine of the van made a dull roaring silence, the landscape barely visible in the darkness beyond the endless road.

"Jeremy," she said suddenly in an eerie dream voice, her body tensing, "I love you, you know that, don't you?"

"But something's wrong, isn't it?" I asked. "Something happened."

And what was I thinking? You keep your secrets from her and she's not supposed to keep hers from you? But your secrets come from her secrets. If she would only explain it all.

"Don't worry," she said in a whisper.

"But you're afraid of something. I can feel it."

"No, you don't understand," she said. Was there a catch in her voice or was it my imagination?

"Can't you trust me enough to tell me? I'm not breaking the rules, am I, just to ask why you're afraid?"

"It isn't fear," she said, and she was almost crying. "It's just sometimes . . . sometimes I feel really sad."

She was in wonderful spirits the next morning. All that week we made the local concerts, movies, plays in the evening. We dined at the little candlelight restaurants, walked on the clean white Carmel beach each morning at sunup. The house smelled of the wood fire that was always going on the hearth.

We did a lot of talking, too.

I told her all about the New Orleans house when she asked me, how I'd kept it like a museum or something, more out of paralysis than anything else. My wives had never seen it, neither had my friends, except my good friend, the actor Alex Clementine, who had known my mother all those long years ago.

And I almost told her the old secret, about the books I'd written under Mother's name.

But when it came to the crunch, I didn't. Just didn't. Alex had certainly been right about all that.

She said that the New Orleans house would be a wonderful place to hide.

"Someday," I said.

The Café Flore painting was done by the time we went back north.

〚 18 〛

"I DON'T understand," I said. "I thought you'd like to meet him. He isn't just famous, he's charming. And besides, he's my best friend."

"I'm sure he's terrific, I've seen him on television, I've seen him in the movies, but I don't want to go." Temper rising. "And I wanna make this concert, I told you I wanna make this concert, you won't go to rock concerts with me, you absolutely refuse, and so I have to go by myself."

"I don't like it. I don't want you going. And you've never done this before, besides!"

"But I wanted to! Look, I'm sixteen, aren't I?"

"Look, are you angry that I'm going to dinner with a friend?"

"Why would I be angry!"

"Look, you wouldn't go to the museum reception, you skipped out when Andy came to set up the sculpture, you disappear into your room if Sheila comes. You never pick up the phone when it rings. And here we're talking about Alex, one of the most famous stars in the history of the movies, and you don't even—"

"And what the hell are you going to tell all these people? I'm your niece from Kansas City who just came to visit? I mean, Christ, Jeremy, get some sense! You're hiding the best work you ever did in the god-damned attic, and at the same time you want to show me off to your friends?"

"But the point is Alex Clementine is the one person I don't have to explain anything to! Alex never tells the truth about anybody. He just wrote an entire book in which he didn't tell the nit-grit truth about a single person he knew."

But he'll tell everybody over dinner and cocktails forever, won't he? "You should have seen the little jailbait Jeremy had with him in S.F.—yes, Jeremy." No, not if I tell him not to.

"Go without me—"

"Look," I said. "All you care about is movies and—"

"Film, Jeremy, film, not movies and not movie stars either."

"OK, film. But he knows plenty about film. Not just gossip column stuff. He's worked with the best, you get him talking on—"

"I won't go, Jeremy!"

"Then stay home. But don't go to this damned rock thing. I don't want you going. I don't want you seeing the street kids, because if somebody *is* looking for you—"

"Jeremy, you're acting crazy. I'm going!" Bedroom door slammed.

I stomped downstairs. Sticky scent of hair spray in the air, clatter of junk jewelry as she went back and forth between her room and the bathroom.

"I don't want you taking the car to this thing alone," I called up to her.

"I can take a cab," she said with maddening politeness.

"I'll drive you."

"That's dumb. Go have dinner with your friend and forget about me."

"Ridiculous!"

She came to the bottom of the stairs wearing black jeans, flaming silk blouse, rhinestone heels, leather jacket. Hair a torrent of red and gold spikes, eyes black holes in space, mouth like a war wound.

"Where's my leopard coat, you seen it?"

"Good God," I said. "Not that coat."

"Jeremy, come on!" Flash of sweetness. She threw her arms around my neck. Musky perfume, rattle of beads. Unbearable softness of breasts under silk. Bra or no bra? Her hair felt like a century plant. Her mouth smelled like bubble gum.

"Suppose somebody's out there looking for you?"

"Who?" she asked. She went rummaging in the hall closet. "Here it is. God, you had it cleaned. You are the strangest person, Jeremy."

"Suppose there's some detective out there hired to find you." I could feel the hair rising on the back of my neck. Was I threatening her with it, or just warning her? She did have a right to know, didn't she? "There just might be somebody looking for you."

Flash of her glittering eye. False eyelashes? Probably just sticky gunk. She put on the coat, adjusted the collar, looked at herself in the mirror. High heels and jeans: kiddie tramp.

I swallowed, took a deep breath.

"A rock concert is a place he might look," I said. "If you were my kid, I'd have somebody looking for you."

"Jer, he would never recognize me under all this, now would he?"

WE were halfway to the auditorium before I said anything more. She was humming some little song to herself, tapping the dash with one hand.

"Would you be smart in there? Don't smoke any grass. Don't try to buy a beer. Don't do anything to get busted."

Laughter.

Slumped against the door, facing me, one knee up, arch of foot over impossible high heel shoe. Toenails polished bright red peeping through the lace stocking. Bracelets like armour on her wrists.

"I don't want them to find you, you know, whoever they are."

Did she sigh? Did she murmur something?

She moved forward with a new gust of perfume and put her arms around my neck.

"I've done all that—grass, acid, ecstasy, coke, you name it. All that's past."

I winced. Why weren't these clothes the past?

"Don't do anything to attract attention," I said.

In the flash of passing headlights she seemed to be burning up beside me. She popped her gum loudly when I glanced at her.

"I'll just fade into the woodwork," she said.

She caught me in another soft silky clinch, then she was out of the car while it was still moving.

Click of heels on the asphalt, throwing a kiss back over her shoulder. I watched her all the way through the crowd to the doors.

And what if we went some place where we could get legally married? Some southern state where she was old enough? And I could just say to everyone in the whole world—?

And it would be over right then and there, wouldn't it? CHILDREN'S AUTHOR TAKES TEENAGE BRIDE. You wouldn't even have to show the paintings. And her family, what would they do when they finally put it all together: kidnapping, coercion. Could they have it annulled and take her away to some private asylum where rich people stash their family troublemakers? Goddamn it all!

ALEX had a head start with the wine when I got there. He had been up in the Napa Valley all day shooting a champagne commercial. And we were dining alone, in his suite, which was just fine with me. The place was jammed with flowers, big showy red carnations in glass vases. And he had

on one of those glamorous full-length satin-lapeled robes I always asso-
ciate with English gentlemen or black-and-white forties pictures. Even a
white silk scarf tucked inside at the neck.

"You know, Jer," he said, as I took my place across from him, "we
could have shot this whole champagne thing in my backyard down south.
But if they want to fly me to San Francisco and take me on a tour of the
wine country and put me up in a nice little old-fashioned suite at the
Clift, who am I to object?"

The waiters had just set out the caviar and the lemon. Alex went to
work with the crackers at once.

"So what's happening?" I said. "You're locked in on 'Champagne
Flight' or what?"

*Try not to think of her in that mead hall full of barbarians. Why wouldn't
she come with me?*

"No, they wrote me out of the plot. Bonnie takes a young lover, some
punk, the masochistic angle you know, and I go off into the sunset ac-
cepting it philosophically. That way they can always bring me back. And
they might. But so what? This champagne commercial's just one of the
fringe benefits. We're shooting eight spots, and the figures are perfectly
ridiculous. There'll be magazine ads too. And there's talk of some auto-
mobile commercial. I tell you it's madness, the whole thing."

"Good for you," I said. "Take them for everything they're worth and
you're worth."

I tried the caviar. It was about as good as caviar ever is.

"You got it. Here, have some of this champagne, it's not bad for California," he said. A young waiter who'd been cleaving to the wall suddenly
sprang to life and filled my saucer glass. "And by the way, what's the big
secret you've been keeping from me?"

"What are you talking about?" I said. I think my face went red.

"Well, first off you're wearing a very expensive shaving lotion, which is
just the kind of thing you never bother with, and this is the first time in
my entire life that I've seen you in a decent suit. So who's the mystery
girl?"

"Oh, yeah, well, I wish there was some big secret I could tell you."
(And she did buy the suit and the shaving lotion.) "Fact is, all I want to
tell you is I'm right about what I said last time I saw you—about the
truth."

"What? Truth? We had a conversation about truth?"

"Come on, Alex, you weren't that drunk."

"You were. Did you ever read my book?"

"I'm telling you, the truth is the big pie in the sky. And it's time I used
all the lies I've told as the platform for it."

"You crazy kid. This kind of inanity is exactly what I come here for. Nobody down south talks like you. You mean, you're going to stop doing little kids in nightgowns?"

"Yes, I've kissed them good-bye, Alex. I've kissed them all good-bye. If I make it now, it will be strictly as a painter."

"So long as you've got the royalties coming in," he said. "But if it's all those horrible things, those roaches and rats you used to paint—"

"In a beautiful way," I said. "It's worse than that. My life's been taken over by something, Alex. And I'm glad the revelation happened now and not twenty years down the road when I'm—"

"As old as I am."

Yes, I'd been going to say that when I caught myself. But it was there suddenly that awful thought, what if I were lying there dying and all I saw when I looked back was Charlotte, Bettina, Angelica?

He gave me a big generous smile, even white teeth positively glistening.

"Jer, shut up about art, will you? You taste this champagne? I just said to a potential seventy-five million viewers that it was superb. What's it taste like to you?"

"I don't know and I don't care. Get me some Scotch, will you? And hey, there's something I want to know. Susan Jeremiah. Movie director. Does that name mean anything to you?"

"Yeah, up-and-coming if United Theatricals doesn't ruin her life with television movies. You can't learn anything in television. The standards are too low. These people are crazy. They go out to shoot so many pages a day and they do, no matter what happens."

"Any dish on Jeremiah that nobody else would know?"

He shook his head. "That thing she did at Cannes, *Final Score,* whatever it was, was full of lesbian scenes, real steamy. But now that's all hush-hush. You know, your bit about truth versus what the public wants? Well, nobody straightened out faster than Jeremiah did for a contract at United Theatricals. Right out of the art house class into prime time. Why are you asking me about her?"

"I don't know, just thinking about her. Saw her picture in a magazine somewhere."

"Oh, the press loves her. It's the hat and the cowboy boots and she really wears them. Quite a swagger, too."

"And they love you right now, don't they?"

He nodded. "In a real way, Jer, things were never better. Now let's really get down on this subject of truth for a second. My book's right up there in the fifth slot, you know that? And after this champagne commercial, two teleplays in the works, one a three-hour Sunday night special. I play a priest who's lost his faith and gets it back when his sister dies of leukemia. Now can you look me in the eye and tell me I should have told all in my book? What would it have done for me?"

I thought about it for a minute.

"Alex," I said, "if you had told all, I mean all, maybe they'd be feature films and not teleplays."

"You upstart kid!"

"And they'd want you for a French champagne instead of an American one that tastes like soda pop."

"You never give up."

The caviar was being removed now, and the main course was being served from those heavy silver dishes that the old hotels still use. Roasted chicken, Alex's favorite. It would do fine, but I wasn't really hungry. I kept thinking of her in that punk garb, rushing through the doors of the auditorium.

Sense of foreboding. I realized I was looking at us in the mirror. In the cream-colored satin robe Alex looked wonderfully decadent. No salt-and-pepper gray at *his* temples. He had never looked more like a wax museum monument to himself.

"Hey, Jer, come back," he said. Unobtrusive little snap of the fingers. "You look like somebody walked on your grave."

"No, just thinking. It doesn't make a damn bit of difference whether or not the truth sells. The truth just is the truth, that's all, even if it brings you right down to the bottom."

He laughed and laughed. "You're a scream," he said. "Yeah, the truth, and God and the Tooth Fairy and Santa Claus."

"Alex, tell me, do you know any of the top execs at United Theatricals?"

I mean, almost any teenager in America would want to meet Alex Clementine. And she wouldn't even hear of it, wouldn't even . . . something about the expression on her face when I said his name.

"What the hell has that got to do with truth, Jeremy?"

"Do you?"

"Know all of them. Assholes. They come out of TV. I am telling you, TV stinks, Jer. That Moreschi, the producer of 'Champagne Flight,' that kid might have really been something in life if it hadn't been for TV."

"Any dish on anybody . . . family problems, kids missing, runaways, that kind of thing."

He stared at me. "Jer, what is this about?"

"Seriously, Alex. Have you heard anything? You know, any stories about teenage kids vanishing, that kind of thing?"

He shook his head. "Ash Levine's got three boys, all good kids, as far as I ever heard. Sidney Templeton doesn't have any kids. He's got a stepson he plays golf with. Why?"

"What about Moreschi?"

Shook his head. "Just his stepdaughter, Bonnie's kid, she's socked away somewhere in a Swiss school. I heard about that enough from Susan Jeremiah."

"What do you mean?"

"Oh, Susan used that kid in a movie at Cannes. She was pretty crazy about her, wanted her for a new TV thing, but the kid's bricked up in a Swiss convent, nobody can get to her. Jeremiah threw a fit."

I leaned forward. An alarm bell had just gone off inside my head.

"This is the kid you told me about, the one with the hairdresser father—"

"Yeah, beautiful little girl. Blond hair and baby face, like her daddy, George Gallagher—now you talk about somebody irresistible, that's George Gallagher. Hmmmmmp. Can't stand it. Eat something, Jer, your food's getting cold."

"How old is she?"

"Who?"

"The kid! What's her name."

"Teenager, fifteen, sixteen, something like that. I don't think I ever heard her name."

"Are you sure she's in a Swiss school?"

"Yeah, everybody's been wanting that kid since Cannes, and the name and address is top secret. Marty even threw Jeremiah out of his office for bugging him about it. But he didn't fire her, and I can tell you that means the lady is hot."

I could feel my heart racing. I tried to keep my voice normal.

"You didn't see the movie at Cannes?"

"Nah, I can take a little Fellini or Bergman if I'm drunk enough, but . . . what's the matter with you, Jer? You look positively sick."

"Do you know anyone who does know the kid's name, somebody you could call right now, somebody—"

"Well, I could call Marty or Bonnie, of course, but that wouldn't be cool. I mean, with agents bugging them about that kid—"

"What about Gallagher or Jeremiah?"

"Hmm, I could maybe do it tomorrow. Let's see, Gallagher's in New York somewhere, living with some Broadway director, Ollie Boon, I believe it is, yeah, Ollie—"

New York. *My oldest buddy . . . It's raining in New York City.*

"Jeremiah's in Paris, could probably find out where. Hey, Jer, snap out of it, this is Alex, remember?"

"I have to make a phone call," I said. I almost upset the table as I stood up.

Alex shrugged and gestured towards the bedroom. "Help yourself. And if it's your girlfriend you're calling, give her my thanks for getting you to a decent barber. I never could."

I rang the Beverly Wilshire. Dan was out but would be back at nine. "Give him this message," I told the operator. " 'Champagne Flight' Bonnie—check out her daughter's name, age, pic, and whereabouts right away. Sign it J."

I hung up. My heart was skipping. I stood in the doorway for a moment just trying to get straight. It wasn't Belinda—of course, it wasn't. The Swiss school, I mean this little girl whoever she is . . . why were my legs shaking like this? What the hell damn difference did it make?

"Do me a favor, son," Alex was saying to one of the waiters, a very cute one of the waiters, "go into the refrigerator there and take out all those bottles of champagne. Keep'm, give'm away, I don't care what you do with them, but get me a nice cold bottle of Dom Pérignon right away, OK? That stuff's trash."

[19]

I'LL leave if you mention my parents again . . . it's the easiest way to get rid of me. No hard feelings. I will just go.

I chained the front door after me and went straight up to her room. Same posters, mags, empty purses, old suitcase. Susan Jeremiah squinting under the brim of her cowboy hat. Susan Jeremiah standing with one foot inside her mile-long Cadillac, same hat, same boots, same squint, beautiful smile.

Tapes under the sweaters. One of you has got to be *Final Score!*

I gathered them all up, though my hands were shaking (I mean, these are her things, buddy!) went downstairs to my office and locked myself in.

The television on my desk was small but new, and the video tape player there was as good as any of the others in the house.

I hated this, hated it, but there was no turning back now. I had to know the answer, no matter what I did or did not ever say to her. I had to know for myself.

I slipped the first tape into the machine, then sat back with the remote control in hand.

Old movie. Half the credits were gone, and the quality was dreadful. Almost certainly a pirate or a film recorded off television.

Director Leonardo Gallo. Ancient Roman streets, full of half-clad muscle men and cheesecake beauties. Melodramatic music. Most certainly this was one of those ugly badly dubbed Franco–Italian productions.

I touched the scanner and started to move through rapidly. Claudia Scartino, OK, I recognized her, and a Swedish starlet whose name I couldn't remember. And Bonnie, yes, there was Bonnie, of course!

I felt a tightening in my chest. It was true, I knew it was true, no matter what Alex had said about the Swiss school, and suspecting was one thing, knowing was another. Bonnie right there. And why else would Belinda own this piece of trash? I took it out, tried the next one.

Another mess. Leonardo Gallo. Claudia Scartino again, two old Hollywood stars, the Swedish cutie—whose name was Eve Eckling—and Bonnie again. But what else did these tapes mean to her? Did she care that much about her mother's old films?

Scan a little. OK. Lots of international breasts. Good lesbian scene between Bonnie and Claudia in a Roman bed. Some other time I'd have a hard-on.

Scan again.

Barbarians overrun the villa. Square-jawed American actor in animal skins and horned helmet grabs tender upper arm of Claudia Scartino, fresh from bath, clad only in towel. Slaves scatter, scream. Vase bounces on the floor. Clearly made of rubber. Little girl in flimsy Roman gown drops stick doll and puts hands to her head. Arm comes down around her waist, lifts her out of the picture.

Little girl. *Little girl!* I backed it up until she was there again, more, close-up, freeze-frame. No, not—yes, Belinda.

I sent it back another frame, then another, bigger close-up, froze it again. Belinda at six, maybe seven. Hair parted in the middle as now. Oh, yes, the eyebrows, the poochy little mouth, definitely Belinda.

For a moment I was too stunned to do anything but look at the blurred grainy image on the screen.

If there had been the slightest doubt, it was gone now.

I pressed down on the button and watched in silence as the thing rolled to its finish. She didn't appear again. There was no name in the credits. I had a strange taste in my mouth.

I got up mechanically, poured myself a glass of Scotch, came back and sat down again.

I felt like I had to do something, but what? Call Alex? Call Dan? It was true, I knew that now for certain. But I couldn't think what it meant to me or to her. I just couldn't think.

For a long time I didn't move, not even to drink the Scotch, and then I slipped the next cassette into the machine and started to scan.

OK, the same international gang. And this time in Renaissance drag and the Swedish woman is really putting on weight. But it's all right if you're playing a Medici. All right, come on. Where is Belinda?

And finally there she was again for a precious few moments, one of two little children brought in to be kissed good night. Ah, the roundness of her little arms, the sight of her dimpled hand clutching the doll.

I cannot stand this. The rest of the film rolled out in silver fast forward without her. Go to the next.

More junk. A Western this time, with a different director, Franco Manzoni, but Claudia was there again and Bonnie, too, and the same old American boys. I was tempted to skip it. But I wanted to find out everything I could. And it looked newer, the color sharper. I didn't have to wait long. Ranch house living room scene, girl of ten or eleven with braids, embroidery in hand, yes, Belinda. Simply lovely Belinda. Neck longer, waist very small. But hands still have dimples. Claudia Scartino sits beside her on couch, embraces her. Belinda speaks. I slowed it down. Not her voice, dubbed in Italian. Awful.

I indulged myself for a couple of minutes just drinking in one freeze-frame close-up after another. Breasts already, yes, and with those baby hands. Irresistible. Fingers positively pudgy still, and her eyes enormous because the face is thinner, slightly longer.

Scan again.

Belinda is in the dirt street during the shoot-out. She grabs Claudia, stops her from running to stop the duel. Bonnie appears in black hat, black boots, very de Sade, shoots Claudia. Men stopped in their tracks. Belinda goes into hysterics.

Is this acting? I couldn't calm down long enough to come to any opinion. She looked too much like a little bonbon in her gingham dress with the big sash, arms up, thick veil of hair flying. As she went down on her knees, I saw the pooch of her breasts again.

Again no credit.

But the fact is, this little girl, my little girl, my Belinda, has been *in* movies all her life. The teenybopper with the posters on the walls has been a starlet herself.

Next two Franco–Italian Westerns, lousy, she about the same age, same kind of part, Claudia and Bonnie again, but in the second of these she has a precious five minutes of being chased by a cowboy bent on rape whom she hits over the head with a water pitcher. If this isn't acting, it's something. Star quality, is that the vulgar phrase? Alex Clementine would know if he saw all this. Couldn't be objective. She was utterly adorable. Yet no credit, unless her real name is not Belinda at all.

Was seeing oil paintings of all this, of course. *Belinda in Franco–Italian Movie.*

But what am I thinking of? That we just go on from here?

Two more cassettes.

And suddenly everything changes. Grainy texture as before, but the color is brand-new, subtle. Extreme European look, but the title in English:

FINAL SCORE

All right!

American names I don't know are sliding gently down a backdrop of seaside cliffs, the unmistakable white buildings of a Greek island village.

AND INTRODUCING

BELINDA

I could hear my heart pounding in my head. The shock spread all through me like a chill. It is her name, all right, just that, Belinda, no last name, the same way they always used Bonnie. OK.

DIRECTED BY SUSAN JEREMIAH

Through a state of shock bordering on catatonia I kept watching. Let it roll at normal speed.

A Greek island. A gang of Texans, accents authentic, amateur cocaine smugglers, it seems, hiding out on the island until the right time to bring home the stash. Two men bitter and sophisticated, women same, but all bid for our sympathy with dreams of what they will do with the money. Arty, fast-paced, acting excellent, lots of talk. Extremely professional look. Texture awful, probably because it was shot originally in sixteen millimeter, or the videotape is just bad.

I can't stand it. Where is she? Scan:

Quarrels, sex. Relationships not quite what they seem. Red-haired woman fights with man, walks off alone at dawn. Beach. Sunrise. Exquisite. Stops, sees tiny figure riding towards her along the edge of the surf.

Yes, please come closer. Stop scan. Sound of surf. "And introducing Belinda." Yes. No mistake about it. There she is in one of those tiny white bikinis, which is infinitely more seductive than pure nakedness. Worse than the one she wears around here.

And she is riding the horse bareback.

She is *so* luscious as she comes smiling towards the redhead. The redhead is still pretty, very pretty. In fact, she is quite beautiful. But now she is utterly eclipsed by my darling.

The redhead talks to her in English. Belinda only shakes her head. The redhead asks her if she lives here. Again, Belinda shakes her head. Then she says something to the redhead in Greek. Lovely accent, the language soft as Italian yet somehow even more sensual. Touch of the East in it. It is the redhead's turn to shake her head now. But some sort of friendship is being struck.

Belinda points to a little house up on the cliff, extends an unmistakable invitation. Then she helps the redhead to climb up on the horse behind her. Gracefully the horse picks its way up the steep path.

Hair blowing in the wind, smiles, attempts at speech that fail. Unbearable, the easy sway of Belinda's hips as she moves with the horse, the light on her belly. Her hair is longer than it is now, almost covers her bottom.

In a small white house Belinda puts food on the table. Bread, oranges. Everything has the starkness and beauty of a Morandi painting. The sea is a rectangle of blue through the perfectly square window in the white wall. Camera on Belinda's face as it creates a skilled impression of naiveté and simplicity, which in real life Belinda simply never suggests. The red-haired woman is content for the first time in the film.

I don't think you have to be in love with Belinda to find her utterly captivating, to watch paralyzed as she points out things in the room, teaches the woman the words for them, as she laughs softly at the woman's miserable pronunciation, as she does the simple thing of pouring milk from a pitcher, buttering the bread.

Everything has become sensuous. The redhead wipes her hair back from her face and it is dance. Then the trouble comes back to her expression, the tension. She breaks down, and Belinda caresses her, strokes her red hair.

The fullness of Belinda's breasts beneath the childish face is too much. I can't stand it. Want to peel off the little triangles of white fabric, see the nipples in this new frame.

The redhead looks up, and then that shift happens that you see a thousand times between men and women in a film: intimacy alchemizes into passion. They are embracing, and now suddenly they are kissing. No intrusive music. Just the sound of the surf.

Why didn't I see this coming? Between a man and a woman it would have been a cliché. They rise from the table, go into the bedroom, off comes the bikini, the redhead's blouse, pants. They do not seem entirely sure what to do, only that they mean to do it.

And there is none of the urgency of the standard erotic film, and none of the fuzzy mysticism of the popular cinema either. The redhead is kissing Belinda's belly, kissing her thighs. Demure. Not very explicit at all. Close-up of Belinda's face gorgeously flushed. That's the X-rated part, that flush.

Cut. Back to the drug amateurs, and the redhead coming in. Man glad to see her, wants to make up, feels awful. She comforts him, no rancor. He's relieved. Distant expressions on her face.

I hit the freeze-frame and sat there for a moment trying to get my temperature to drop. I have been living with this girl, and this is her secret? She is an actress, and the audiences at Cannes applauded her, and the director wants her and the agents want her, and I take her out of a sleazy dump on Page Street, where the cops are questioning her, and I get on her case for going to a rock concert and I—

Scan again. Don't think.

Fights among the Texans, craziness, man beating woman, redhead intervening, getting smacked, smacking man back. Stop, scan again, stop. On and on it seems to roll, the true body of the film, with much smoking, drinking, and bickering. They don't really know what they want to do with the money from the cocaine. That's it. They are beyond being saved by the "final drug score."

The redhead appears dominant, taking charge as things deteriorate. Finally everybody is busy concealing the staggering abundance of cocaine in little white statuettes. The bottoms must be sealed with plaster, then covered with green felt. Peace at last with simple labor.

OK, makes good sense, good film probably, but right now all I want is Belinda.

Finally they are packing up. The tape has nearly run out.

Are they going to leave this island and Belinda?

No. Before dawn the redhead goes out, finds the little house, knocks. Belinda opens.

Sound up—the surf. Belinda gestures for silence. An old man is asleep in the other room. The women go down to the water together. I freeze-frame it a dozen times as they disrobe, embrace each other. And this time it goes on much longer, is greedier, more heated, their hips grinding together, mouths locked, but it is still demure. Faces as important as the anatomy. Belinda lies back on her elbows. This is the look of ecstasy I have seen countless times in my own shadow in bed.

Sunlight.

The ferry carries away the doomed quartet of Americans. Belinda unseen watches from the cliff. The redhead on the deck keeps her secret in weary silence, face going gradually dead.

THE phone rang.

Freeze it on THE END, copyright last year.

"Yeah." Why the hell didn't I let the machine answer it? But now I have it in my hand.

"Jeremy, listen to me!"

"Dan—"

"Bonnie's daughter *is* named Belinda! Sixteen, blond, the whole bit. All I need is the picture to be certain, but none of this makes sense."

"I know."

"Nobody's reported this kid missing! Agents all over this fucking town think she's in some fancy European school."

Blood pounding in my head. Can't talk. Talk.

"Jeremy, this is worse than anything I imagined. These people will kill you, Jer. Can't you see that? I mean Bonnie and Moreschi, they're front-page *National Enquirer* week in, week out!"

I wanted to say something, I really did. But I was just staring at the tapes, just staring back into time, into the first moment when I saw her in the bookstore. I was looking back over all of it. What had always been *my* worse fear? Not scandal or ruin, no, I'd been courting that from the beginning. It was that the truth would take her away from me, that the truth would mandate some action that would divide us forever, and she'd be lost, like a little girl I had painted out of the imagination, no more a warm and living being in my arms.

"Jeremy, this is a fucking bomb that can go off any minute in your face."

"Dan, find out where the fuck this Swiss school is and if they really think she's over there, goddamn it, if she's somehow pulled the wool over her mother's eyes."

"Of course, she hasn't. It's a cover-up, it has to be. Sampson's got to be working for Moreschi, and that's why he's sneaking around with these pix of the kid, and it's all so hush-hush in LA."

"Is that legal? Not even to report her missing? What kind of people are we talking about here? She splits and they don't even call the LAPD?"

"Man, you are in no position to throw stones!"

"Fuck it, we're talking about her mother."

"Do you *want* them to call the LAPD? Are you crazy?"

"You have to find out—"

"And you have to get rid of her, Jeremy, before Sampson tracks her to your door."

"No, Dan."

"Look, Jer. Remember I told you I thought I'd seen her before? It was probably the news magazines, Jer, could have even been on the tube. This girl is famous. The tabloids chase her mother all over this town.

They might blow the lid off before Sampson finds her, don't you see what this could mean?"

"Zero in on the parents. Find out when she disappeared. I have to know what went down."

I hung up before he could say anything more.

Seemed impossible to move then, to gather up the tapes, to carry them back upstairs.

But I did it.

And I stood there dazed, heart still overloading as I stared at the closet shelves.

The old film magazines were in a pile at the very bottom. And on the top of that pile was Bonnie smiling up at me from the cover of *Cahiers du Cinema.* And underneath that was Bonnie again on an old *Paris-Match.* And, yes, Bonnie on the cover of *Stern,* and Bonnie on the cover of *Cine-Revue.* And all those that didn't have Bonnie's face on the cover had her name somewhere there.

Yes, every single one of them had some connection to Bonnie.

And as I opened the most recent, the *Newsweek* that was over a year old, I found immediately the big color picture of the dark-eyed sex goddess with one arm around a gaunt black-haired man and the other around the radiant blond woman-child I loved:

"Bonnie with producer husband, Marty Moreschi, and daughter, Belinda, poolside in Beverly Hills as 'Champagne Flight' prepares for take-off."

⟦ 20 ⟧

Six a.m. Gray sky. Chill wind.

I was walking up Powell Street towards Union Square from the metro stop, not even sure where I was going, what I wanted to do. Looking for a place to rest, to think.

Left her sleeping in the four-poster, the old-fashioned quilts piled on top of her, her head to the side, her hair flowing over the pillow. Washed and scrubbed, all traces of the rock concert and the punk street kid gone.

And I had left a note by the bed.

"Gone downtown. Business. Back late afternoon."

Business. What business? Words calculated to hurt and confuse. Nothing was open except the bars and the dingy all-night restaurants. What was I going to do? What did I want to do?

One thing was for sure. After last night I couldn't go on until I came to some resolution.

Screaming fight when she walked in after the rock concert.

And I was the one drunk on Scotch by that time, and she sober and wary, glaring at me through the mask of punk makeup.

"What's the matter?"

"Sometimes I just can't stand it, that's all."

"Stand what?"

"Not knowing. Where you came from, what happened, why you ran away." Pacing the kitchen. Anger in my voice, boiling anger.

Goddamn it, you are a fucking movie star!

"You promised me you'd never ask me about all that again." Chewing gum. Eyes flashing like gaudy jewelry.

Stop playing Lolita.

"I'm not asking you. I'm just telling you that I can't stand it sometimes, that I feel sometimes like, like this is doomed, do you understand me?" Smash of glass into the sink.

She had stared at the broken glass.

"What's doomed, why are you acting like this?"

"You, me. Because it cannot be right. It just cannot be right."

"Why isn't it right? Do I hound you about your wives, your old girl-friends, the times you've been to bed with men? I go off to one rock concert by myself and you flip out and we're doomed suddenly."

"That has nothing to do with it. I'm going crazy, like you've taken over my life and yet I don't even know you, where you came from, how long you'll stay, where you're going—"

"I'm not going anywhere! Why should I go?" Hurt suddenly. Break in the voice. "You want me to leave, Jeremy? You want me to leave? I'll leave tonight."

"I don't want you to leave. I live in terror that you might leave. God-damn it, I'd do anything to stop you from leaving, but I'm just saying that sometimes—"

"Nobody *just* says anything. I'm here, you can take it or leave it, but those are the terms. For God's sakes we've been over and over this. This is us, Jeremy. This belongs to us!"

"Just like your body belongs to you?"

"For the love of God, yes!" California accent dried up, elegant clipped voice taking over, the real Belinda, Miss International-film-actress.

But she was really crying. She had bowed her head, rushed down the hall and up the stairs.

I had caught her at the bedroom door, taken her in my arms.

"I love you. I don't care then, I swear it—"

"You say it, but you don't mean it." Pulling away. "Go up and look at your damn paintings, that's what you feel guilty about, what you're doing, that they're a thousand times better than the goddamned illustrations you did before."

"To hell with the paintings, I know all that!"

"Let go of me!" Shoving me. I reached out. Her hand came up, but she did not slap me. Let her hand drop.

"Look, what do you want of me, that I make something up for you, to make it easy? I didn't belong to them, don't you understand? I'm not their fucking property, Jeremy!"

"I know." *And I know who them is, and goddamn it, how can you keep it secret? How can you stand it, Belinda?*

"No, you don't know! If you did, you'd believe when I tell you I am where *I* want to be! And you'd worry about the damned paintings and why they're better than all that slop you did before."

"Don't say that—"

"You always wanted to paint what was under the little girls' dresses—"

"Not true. I want to paint you!"

"Yes, well, that's genius up there now, isn't it? You tell me. You're the artist. I'm just the kid. It's genius, isn't it? For the first time in your fucking life it's not a book illustration. It's art!"

"I can handle that. I can handle what's happening to my life. What I can't handle is not knowing whether or not *you* can handle what's happening to *you!* I have no right—"

"No right!" She came closer, and I thought this time she would hit me, she was so furious. Her face was positively scarlet. "Who says you have no right! I gave you the right, goddamn it, what do you think I am!"

I couldn't endure it, the expression on her face, the pure malice.

"A child. A legal child. That's what you are."

She made some low sound as if she was going to scream. She shook her head.

"Get out of here," she whispered. "Get away from me, get away, get away!" She started shoving me, but I wouldn't go. I grabbed her wrists, and then I pulled her close to me and put my arms around her. She was kicking me, digging the toe of her shoe into my shin, stomping the heel into my foot.

"Let me go," she was growling. And then she did get her hand loose, and she slapped me hard over and over, hard stinging slaps that must have hurt her hand.

I pushed my face into her neck. My ears were ringing. Her hair was scratching me. Her hands were pulling at me. I just held her.

"Belinda," I said. "Belinda." I kept saying it until she stopped struggling.

And finally her body relaxed. The heat of her breasts was right against my chest.

The tears had made the mascara run down her cheeks in black streaks. She was trying to hold in her sobs.

"Jeremy . . ." she said, and her voice was small and fragile. It was positively pleading. "I love you," she said. "I really do. I love you. I want it to be forever. Why isn't that enough for you?"

* * *

Two o'clock. Must have been. I hadn't been looking at the clock however. I had been sitting at the kitchen table smoking her clove cigarettes. Sober by then, probably. Headache, that I remember. Bad headache. My throat had been sore.

Why had I looked at the damn films? Why had I called Dan? Why had I talked to Alex? Why hadn't I left it alone, done what I'd promised I would do?

And if I told her everything now, confessed the snooping, the prying, the investigation, what would she do? Oh God, to think of losing her, to think of her struggling to get away from me, to think of her going out the door.

And what about the other pieces of the puzzle? The damned Swiss school scam and the jackpot question, yes, why, why did she leave all that?

She had come downstairs in her nightgown. Not Charlotte's anymore, just hers. And she had sat down near me and reached out and touched my hand.

"I'm sorry, darling," I had said. "I'm sorry, I'm sorry, I'm sorry."

But you still won't tell me, will you? Not one fucking word about any of it —Bonnie, Susan Jeremiah, Final Score. *And I can't look you in the eye.*

Her hair had been loose and like foam over her shoulders in the light of the overhead lamp, all clean and sweet from the shower.

"Jeremy," she had said. "Listen to me. What if we were to go away, you know, really far away?"

No answer.

"Like what if we were to go to Europe, Jeremy? Maybe some place in Italy. Some place in the south of France."

"And you wanted so much to be in America," I whispered.

"I can wait for America, Jeremy. If we were in Europe, you wouldn't be worried about detectives or cops or whatever the hell it is you keep worrying about. We'd be safe and you could paint and we could just be alone."

"Darling, can't you just tell me who you are?"

"I'm me, Jeremy. I'm Belinda."

Our eyes had met and the heat had threatened, the awful, torturous heat of the fight again, and I had gathered her to me. No more of that. No, no more.

She had allowed the kisses. She had allowed the tenderness and even yielded to it for a moment.

But then she'd backed off. She had stood looking down at me, and her eyes had an icy ageless expression that had nothing to do with her tears.

"Jeremy, I am telling you now for the last time, make your decision. If you ask me one more time about the past, I will walk out the front door and you will never see me again."

SIX o'clock. Downtown.

Taxis in front of the Saint Francis. No cable cars sliding down the track.

And why are you so angry with her? Why do you stomp up Powell Street away from her as if she had done something to you? The first moment you ever saw her you knew she was no ordinary kid. You knew it. And that is why you love her. Nobody had to point that out.

And never, never has she lied about any of it! Not like you've lied, about Dan and about snooping in her room and watching her fucking videotapes. Her terms were always: Do not ask me about it. And you accepted them, didn't you?

And you know damn good and well you wouldn't have missed it for the world.

But everything is coming apart. That's the bottom line right now. You cannot continue until you resolve it. Make your decision, that is what she said.

I WENT up the steps of the Saint Francis, through the dark heavy revolving door into the gilded silence of the lobby. No night or day here. Enchanted stillness. Image of her the way she had looked standing there by the elevators that day, as coolly elegant as anything around her. Making movies since she was six, maybe even before that. And superstar Bonnie for a mother, imagine.

I went down the long right corridor past the shut-up flower stand, the dress shop windows. Like entering a little underground town, this. What did I want? The magazine store? Books, newspapers?

Oh, it was too easy.

There was the paperback bio of the goddess mother right there on the book rack, one of those mass market quickie jobs with no bibliography or index, and enormous print, all the information in it obviously gleaned from other people's interviews and articles. That's OK. Got to have it. No quibbles about that now.

Yes, grainy little black-and-white photos in the middle.

One, a grinning Bonnie in sunglasses on the terrace of her Greek island home.

Two, famous nude of Bonnie from *Playboy* of 1965. Yes, exceptional. What genes to be inherited.

Three, the famous picture of Bonnie in glasses and man's white shirt open down the front, advertising Saint Esprit perfume.

Four, Bonnie nude with dalmatians, by Eric Arlington, the poster that had ended up on a thousand dormitory walls.

Five, Bonnie's Beverly Hills wedding last year to Marty Moreschi, producer of "Champagne Flight," and guess who's there in a high-neck dress with filmy sleeves, looking as lovely as the bride? Belinda.

Six, that picture again of mother and daughter by the de rigueur pool.

All of this right here in just the kind of book she knew that I would never buy. She could have left it lying around the house! She could have read it right in front of me. I would never have even looked over her shoulder.

And oh yes, seven and eight, Bonnie in scenes from "Champagne Flight," of course, and with whom? Alex Clementine. My old friend.

I got out the three dollars to pay for this invaluable little piece of trash, then checked the magazines. I had seen Bonnie's face so often in the past year she was damn near invisible. *National Enquirer,* OK, big juicy cover story: BONNIE SAYS ITALIAN AMERICAN LOVERS ARE BEST. AND I'VE TRIED THEM ALL. Get that too. Can you believe this, you are buying the *National Enquirer?*

I also bought a toothbrush, a plastic razor, and some shaving cream and went to the front desk and rented the most inexpensive room they could give me. Luggage? "Painters redoing my house, fumes nearly killed me." Here are all the credit cards known in the Western world. I don't need luggage!

Just room service breakfast immediately. And a pot of coffee please.

I STRETCHED out on the bed and opened the stupid little bio. Just as I thought, lots of facts, quotes, and no attribution anywhere. Publishing houses who issue this sort of thing should be burnt down. But for the moment it gave me exactly what I wanted.

BORN Bonnie Blanchard in Dallas, Texas, in October 1942, Bonnie had grown up in Highland Park, daughter of a well-to-do plastic surgeon. Mother died when she was six. Went to live with brother, Daryl, on a ranch outside Denton after her father's unexpected death. Majored in philosophy at North Texas State.

"Everybody always thought Bonnie was just a big dumb pretty Dallas girl," said brother, Daryl Blanchard, Dallas lawyer and Bonnie's financial manager. "Nothing could be further from the truth. She was an A-student at Highland Park High. My sister always had her nose in a book. And she really can't see without the famous glasses."

It was the famous Music Department at North Texas State that changed the course of Bonnie's life.

"Here you have this dry college town," said her old Highland Park friend Mona Freeman, "I mean, you have to drive thirty miles north or south to buy a can of beer; yet here are these long-haired beatnik jazz musicians from New York City come all the way down here to play with the lab band, they called it, and don't you know they brought their beatnik poetry and their drugs with them?"

"It was after the lab band had won the award at the Newport Jazz Festival," said brother, Daryl. "North Texas was very hot. Stan Kenton used to come to recruit musicians for his band. The town was real proud of it. And, of course, Bonnie had never listened to jazz before and suddenly she was wearing black stockings and reading Kierkegaard and bringing home these writer characters and these musicians. Next thing you knew they were all jamming, as they called it, and then everybody was going to France."

"We were sitting in the Deux Magots when it happened," said sax player Paul Reisner. "Up comes this gang of Frenchmen carrying all their equipment on their shoulders. And it turns out it's this guy André Flambeaux and he takes one look at Bonnie and he goes down on one knee and he says in this thick French accent: 'Brigitte! Marilyn! Aphrodite! I want you in my movie.' "

Sweet Darkness was to make Bonnie the rage of the Paris Nouvelle Vague, along with Jean Seberg and later Jane Fonda.

"They were lined up all around the town square in Denton to see those first two films," said Mona Freeman. "But, you know, you expect that in your own hometown. It was when we heard about the billboard on Times Square that we knew she had really made it. And then came that sensational ad in *Vogue* for Midnight Mink."

"Bonnie really launched the Midnight Mink campaign," said Blair Sackwell, president of Midnight Mink. "And that first picture launched Eric Arlington's career as a photographer, whether Eric cares to admit it or not. We were running around frantically trying to decide which coat, and should we show her shoes, and what about her hair and all, and then somebody realized she was taking off all her clothes, and she had put on the full-length coat, and was letting it hang open all the way down, turned so you couldn't really see anything, you know, except of course that she was naked, and then she said, 'What's wrong with bare feet?' "

"Of course, people reprinted the advertisement everywhere," said Mona Freeman. "It was news, Bonnie barefoot in white fur. Midnight Mink was just the rage after that."

Ten films in five years had made her a household word in the United States and Europe. *The New York Times, Variety, Time, Newsweek,* they all loved her. Finally after the Italian *Mater Dolorosa,* an American box office smash, Hollywood finally did pay her enough to come home for two big-budget all-star disasters.

"Never again," Bonnie said, going back to France to make *Of Love and Sorrow* with Flambeaux, the last of her "artistic" films to be released in this country.

In 1976 Bonnie moved with six-year-old daughter Belinda to Spain, venturing out of her lavish suite at the Palace Hotel only to make Continental films for her sometime lover, director Leonardo Gallo.

"Why should a woman marry to have a child? I'll bring up Belinda to be as independent as I am."

Gallo's pictures, though never released in the United States, have made a fortune all over the Continent.

In 1980 Bonnie was hospitalized in London during the filming of a television movie with American star Alex Clementine.

"It was not a suicide attempt. I don't know how those rumors start. I would never do a thing like that. Never. You don't have to believe in God to believe in life."

She made a dozen more international films after that. She worked in England, Spain, Italy, Germany, even Sweden. Horror films, Westerns, costume adventures, murder mysteries. She played everything from a gun-toting saloon keeper to a vampire.

"No matter what you say about the films themselves," said United Theatricals publicist Liz Harper, "Bonnie was always terrific in them. And remember, even in the worst of times she was getting two hundred thousand to five hundred thousand dollars a picture."

"It was crazy," said Trish, Bonnie's oldest friend and longtime companion. "One time we visited her while she was making this picture in Vienna. We couldn't even tell what the story was, whether or not Bonnie was supposed to be sympathetic or somebody mean. But she always earned her money. She just did what the director told her."

After two more mysterious hospitalizations, one in Vienna and one in Rome, Bonnie finally retired for good to her private island paradise, Saint Esprit, which she'd purchased years before from a Greek shipping magnate.

"More pictures of me have been taken by the paparazzi off the coast of Saint Esprit in the last two years than in my entire life before that. I wake up and walk out on the terrace and it ends up in an Italian newspaper."

Bonnie's former European agent, Marcella Guitron, reported that she would not even look at scripts anymore.

"The quality erotic film she once made with Flambeaux is now dead. Hard-core porn had seen to that. And the great European directors she worked with were no longer making pictures. Of course, if Polanski or Fellini or Bergman had asked for her, that might have been different."

"Serious American directors had come into their own by that time," said New York film critic Rudy Meyer. "Altman, Coppola, Scorsese, Spielberg, and Lucas—those were the ones everybody was talking about."

"She was smart to quit when she did," said an actor who had worked with her in Hollywood. "On Saint Esprit she became a mystery with a new market value. That's when the big picture books on her started to appear in the chain stores all over the country. 'The Legend of Bonnie,' you know, all that. Course, she didn't get a nickel off it, but it kept her famous, especially with the college kids. They had a Bonnie Festival in New Haven and one in Berkeley and one in some little art house in LA."

Saint Esprit: a fifteen-room villa featured in *Architectural Digest* in 1982, two swimming pools, a private stable, a tennis court, a yacht, and two sail boats. Friends from Texas were flown in regularly for parties, dinners, reunions. Jill Fleming and Trish Cody, old Highland Park classmates, came to live there permanently in 1981.

Jill Fleming:

"You never saw anything like it. There we were in the middle of all that luxury, and Bonnie was just the same Texas girl we'd always known and loved, serving barbecue and beer on the terrace, making everybody feel at home. Her idea of a good time was being with old friends, watching the tube, reading a good book."

Texas friend Travis Buckner:

"Nothing could get Bonnie off that island. She had a closed system there. Every week Daryl shipped her crates of videotapes, books, magazines. Jill and Trish went to Paris or Rome to get Bonnie's clothes. The only way the perfume company ever got the endorsement from her was through Daryl. Daryl brought the company to her. Bonnie had her spot on that balcony, and she never moved from it except to go to the bathroom or to bed."

Trish Cody:

"Bonnie was the commodity and Daryl the brains behind it. No matter how much Bonnie ever made on a picture, half of it went to Daryl, and Daryl invested every penny in Texas land. She even sent half her expense checks back home. It was Daryl who had the foresight to buy the Beverly Hills house back in the sixties before property skyrocketed. Bonnie didn't want a house in California. And it was Daryl who rented it out to motion picture people all those years, getting them to foot the bill for the new pool and the new carpet and the new landscaping and the paint jobs, until it was a showcase when Bonnie finally came home."

Jill Fleming:

"Of course, it was Daryl who was behind the famous dalmatians picture. Eric Arlington could never have gotten Bonnie to pose if Daryl hadn't flown him in. These people had to go through Daryl."

Eric Arlington, photographer:

"I hadn't laid eyes on her since old Midnight Mink days. Frankly I had no idea what to expect. And there she was just lying there on the terrace, as lovely as ever, and these gorgeous black-and-white dogs were there beside her. And she said: 'Mr. Arlington, I'll pose for you if I don't have to move from here.'"

"'Just take off your clothes, ma chérie, the way you did last time,' I said to her. 'And let the dogs come into your arms.'"

Trish Cody:

"Of course, Bonnie just loved those dogs. She didn't see anything unnatural about letting them crawl all over her. Never occurred to her anybody would find it kinky."

Daryl:

"The college kids just loved it."

Eric Arlington:

"She is the most naturally exhibitionistic woman I have ever photographed. She adores the camera. And she trusts it completely. She lays down with the animals, stroking them and crooning to them, letting them lie naturally with her. It was done without the slightest contrivance. I never even asked her to brush her hair."

Hollywood columnist Lauren Dalton:

"Calling her the dark-haired Marilyn Monroe, that was all wrong. Bonnie was never used in her films as Monroe was used, to play a stupid woman who is unaware of her power over men. On the contrary, Bonnie knew and used her power. It was Rita Hayworth she admired and imitated. The sadness of Monroe has nothing to do with Bonnie and never did."

New York critic Samuel Davenport:

"When they put that scandalous billboard on Times Square in the sixties, Bonnie admitted that she had given approval. She didn't play games like the other sex goddesses in those days. When they were filming *La Joyeuse,* it was Bonnie who let the *Playboy* photographers onto the set. Even André Flambeaux was shocked. Bonnie said, 'We need the publicity, don't we?' "

Brother Daryl:

"Texas has always loved Bonnie. I think they made fun of Jane Mansfield. She embarrassed them. But my sister they absolutely adore."

Trish:

"Of course, she said she would never come back to Hollywood. You should have seen the scripts they sent her agent. Every now and then Jill and I would pick up a bundle of them in Paris and bring them back to Saint Esprit. They were those all-star disaster pictures, or the big Arthur Hailey *Airport*-style movies. They would have made her look like a fool."

Daryl:

"Hollywood never really knew how to use Bonnie. They were afraid of her—how shall we say?—her feminine charms. She just looked like a big doll in those pictures."

Joe Klein, Houston reporter:

"If it hadn't been for Susan Jeremiah, Bonnie would never never have gone to Cannes. Of course, young filmmakers were always after Bonnie to finance something, but here was a woman, and a woman from Houston, Texas, too, and the film was like the old Nouvelle Vague pictures that Bonnie had loved. No script, no plot. No lights even. And a handheld camera. A thousand kids have tried it, but Susan Jeremiah knew what she was doing. Always did."

Director Susan Jeremiah, from an interview at Cannes:

"When I came to see Bonnie on Saint Esprit, I fully expected to get thrown off the island within the hour. We'd filmed half of *Final Score* on Mykonos, and now we were flat broke and nobody would give us a dime. Of course, I'd seen Bonnie's French films. I knew she was an artist. I hoped she would understand what we were trying to do."

Cinematographer Barry Flint, Cannes interview:

"Well, for five days we were her guests, just eating and drinking anything we wanted. Swimming in the sea, swimming in her pool. And this gorgeous Texas woman, just sitting there in her lounger, drinking one beer after another and reading her book and telling everybody to do what they wanted to do. The crew was delirious. Then Bonnie agreed to put up the money to let us finish the picture right there. 'Half our color film is ruined, got ruined by the heat on Mykonos,' I told her. 'Well, here's some money,' she said. 'Go get some more film and this time keep it on ice.'"

Those who saw *Final Score* at Cannes say the scenes with Bonnie's fourteen-year-old daughter, Belinda, rival any explicit role ever played by her mother. For twenty-four hours at least Susan Jeremiah and Belinda were the talk of Cannes.

Houston producer Barry Fields
(who is no longer associated with Susan Jeremiah or the film):

"Well, first of all, we didn't know Belinda was fourteen when we shot that picture. She was just there and she was absolutely stunning and Susan wanted to use her. But anyone who calls it kiddie porn just hasn't seen that film. We got a standing ovation at Cannes."
Final Score to date has not been released in America—and may never be released.

United Theatricals executive Joe Holtzer:

"The legend of that film has really grown completely out of proportion. Calling it Susan Jeremiah's master's thesis might be more realistic. I think we can expect bigger and better things from Susan, certainly things that are more suitable for the American market as times goes on. Susan is presently doing some very good work for us in movies for television.

Bonnie in Beverly Hills:

"I just want Belinda to have a normal childhood, to go to school, to be protected from the bright lights and the frenzy of Hollywood. There is plenty of time for her to be an actress if that is really what she wants to be."

United Theatricals executive Joe Holtzer:

"The big news was the rediscovery of Bonnie. When word shot through the festival that Bonnie was at the Carlton, it was Bonnie they all wanted to see."

Bonnie in Beverly Hills:

"Of course, I wasn't expecting it. I'd met Marty Moreschi once before. He'd come to Saint Esprit to try to get me to do a cameo in an American picture. But I hadn't even heard of 'Champagne Flight.' He told me many of the big film stars were doing the nighttime soaps, as he called them. Joan Collins was world-famous as Alexis on 'Dynasty.' Jane Wyman was doing 'Falcon Crest.' Lana Turner, Mel Ferrer, Rock Hudson, Ali MacGraw—they were all back in business."

Marty Moreschi:
("tall, dark, hard-bitten but handsome with a heavy
New York street accent"):

"I called the studio, and I said, No way are you going to force Bonnie to do a screen test. Don't tell me anything. I am telling you! Bonnie is Bonnie. And she is on for 'Champagne Flight.' As soon as they had a glimpse of her getting off the plane at LAX, they knew just what I was talking about."

Director Leonardo Gallo:

"All the reports about booze, pills, it is absolutely the sad truth. Why deny it? Great actresses are often difficult, and Bonnie was touched with greatness. So she must have her American beer, it is true. But Bonnie is also the professional. For her the cocktail hour does not begin until work is completed. Bonnie is an artist. But yes, this beautiful woman had indeed tried to take her own life. More than once I alone stood between her and the angel of death."

Daryl:

"My sister never held up the production of a picture in her life. Ask anybody who ever worked with her. She was always on time, always knew her lines. She'd help the young actresses when they were scared. Show them little techniques to make it easier for them—how to hit their mark, that kind of thing. Her favorite people on the set of any picture were the young kids and the female members of the crew. She'd always have the hairdresser and the script girl and the makeup girl into her trailer after work for a glass of wine or beer with her."

Jill Fleming:

"She had pneumonia that time in Rome. She almost died of it. Soon as I saw the headlines, I told Trish we're getting on the next plane. We're going to take care of Bonnie. All the rest of the trash they write is to sell papers and magazines."

United Theatricals publicist Liz Harper:

"I'll tell you exactly what happened. We decided we'd do some re- search, find out how many people out there actually remembered Bonnie from the sixties. After all, 'Champagne Flight' was our big show for the coming season, and Bonnie had not been in a major picture for over ten years. Well, we sent our researchers into the field. We had them stop kids in shopping centers, talk to ladies outside supermarkets. We had them interview an organized sampling of viewers in our testing rooms here.

"At first, we could not believe the results. It turned out that *everybody* knew Bonnie. If they hadn't seen her old pictures on late-night television, they had seen the Saint Esprit perfume advertisements or the poster of her by Arlington with the dogs. Midnight Mink had just done a best- selling book of all their famous models. She was on the front page."

Trish Cody:

"It was Daryl's business sense absolutely. He said those ads had to read 'Bonnie for Saint Esprit.' And she had to have her glasses on, that was her trademark. Those ads have run in every Condé Nast publication for the last three years. And every poster from the Arlington picture had in the lower right-hand corner: 'Bonnie.' When she did the other ads, it was the same way. Daryl made her famous to a whole new generation of Americans."

Daryl:

"You can find that Arlington poster in some store in just about any shopping center in the country. Very tasteful. Very artistic. Of course, now the old Midnight Mink poster is out, too."

Jill Fleming:

"Bonnie knew what she was doing, telling them to name that perfume Saint Esprit after the island. She had *House Beautiful* over there immediately, and then *Architectural Digest*. Then *People* magazine came. It was the holy trinity of Bonnie, the perfume, the island. And then there was the *Vanity Fair* piece on her and *Harper's Bazaar* and that long feminist piece in *Redbook* about her retirement. I lost count of the Continental magazine crews that came trooping through. Seems somebody was always saying, 'Can we just put this little pink pillow here?' or 'May we just fluff up this little ruffle?' And all she did was sit there and drink her beer and read her books and watch her television. And Saint Esprit became powder and lotion and bath soap. She came home to the United States bigger than she had ever been."

Trish Cody:
(who has now returned to her thriving
clothing business in Dallas, Texas):

"She and Marty Moreschi are the perfect couple. She has single-handedly put 'Champagne Flight' at the top of the ratings."

Unidentified neighbor in Beverly Hills:

"If you're going to marry a man ten years younger than you, then why not a devastating Italian hunk from the streets of New York who is also a top television wheeler-dealer? The only thing Marty knows better than prime time is how to talk to a woman."

Gossip columnist Magda Elliott:

"The man's irresistible really. He's what you get when you ask Central Casting for the gangster with the heart of gold. It's only by choice that he is on the other side of the camera."

Jill Fleming
(in business with Trish Cody):

"I told her why not dress as a bride! It's your first wedding, isn't it? You wear white if you want."

Hollywood columnist Lauren Dalton:

"She spent three weeks at the Golden Door—diet, exercise, massage, the works, you know. And when she walked off that plane at LAX with Marty, they couldn't believe it."

Marty Moreschi:

"I fell in love with her the moment I saw her. And if I hadn't scooped her up at Cannes, you can be sure someone else would have done it. All those starlets all over the place standing on their heads to get attention. And there she was: Bonnie, the superstar."

Trish Cody:

"It was a real Hollywood wedding. And everybody knows Marty will take care of Bonnie, save her from the sharks in that town. Marty and Bonnie *are* 'Champagne Flight' now."

Blair Sackwell,
Midnight Mink president:

"Of course, we were disappointed that we couldn't get her to do the second Midnight Mink. And the idea we had for the wedding was gorgeous. We would have underwritten everything. Of course, I think Moreschi made a mistake there. He is her personal manager now, you know, never mind that Bonnie and I have been friends for years, that I visited her constantly on Saint Esprit before Marty was around."

Hollywood columnist Lauren Dalton:

"Blair Sackwell thought he could get her for the old price, of course, the free white mink. And he wanted her to wear it at the wedding, mind you. But everyone wants Bonnie. And sometimes old friends simply don't understand."

Marty Moreschi:

"My job is to protect Bonnie. She is besieged on all sides. After all, 'Champagne Flight' is launching its own line of products, and we've merged with Saint Esprit perfume, and Bonnie's privacy is precious at this point."

Blair Sackwell,
Midnight Mink president:

"If the show fails, and they all fail eventually, Bonnie will be calling us, you can be sure. No one has ever been asked to do Midnight Mink twice."

Jill:

"Marty is a natural guardian angel. One of those guys who thinks of absolutely everything."

Trish:

"We went home to Dallas with the assurance that Marty could handle everything. For the first time even Daryl was satisfied."

Jill:

"Well, the men in her life have always meant trouble. But Marty is a father, a brother, and a lover. He's the kind of husband who will end up being her best friend."

Trish:

"Ah, but those days on Saint Esprit were heaven."

Although United Theatricals will not confirm it, Bonnie is rumored to be making $75,000 a week for her role as Bonnie Sinclair, the émigré movie star come home to take over the family-owned airline on "Champagne Flight."

"Her comeback has not changed her a bit," says an unidentified actress friend. "She's the same sweet Dallas girl she always was, and Marty and she are truly in love. It's a second life for her."

Daryl:

"Thank the Lord they didn't try to make her a nasty person like Alexis on 'Dynasty' or J.R. on 'Dallas.' My sister never could have done it. In fact, it was genius to base the character of Bonnie Sinclair on her, to use the clips of her old movies in the series."

Liz Harper:

"The night Bonnie shot Marty was a comedy of errors. Here was this woman used to her own private island, and suddenly she is all alone in a big Beverly Hills house and Marty is supposed to be in New York—and, bang, in comes this man, and Bonnie doesn't have time to reach for her glasses."

Trish:

"Bonnie could not see a thing, not a thing without her glasses."

Marty Moreschi:

"I'd edited the scripts for her, gone over her lines with her, picked out her wardrobe for her. Even bought the damned gun for the bedside table so she'd feel safe in big bad crime-ridden America. But I didn't think to call that night before I came home."

The police were all over the house in five minutes. Bonnie was sobbing: "Marty, Marty, Marty."

"It's as if an angel was watching over those two," said 'Champagne

Flight' assistant producer Matt Rubin. "Five bullets and none of them did any real damage."

The rumor has it that he said: "Don't put me in that ambulance unless my wife comes with me."

Marty and Bonnie threw a big party within a week. "It was beluga caviar and Dom Pérignon all around," said Matt Rubin. "Marty still had his right arm in a sling."

Of course, Bonnie is open to the prospect of a feature film. Why not?

"Through Bonnie Sinclair I've discovered an entirely new dimension to myself. She is me, but she is not me. She can do things I never thought I was capable of."

A starring role in the new miniseries "Watch over Moscow" is more likely.

"But Marty handles all that," she said. "If Marty says do it, I will."

"She is ageless, she is enchanting, she is everything they say she is," said Alex Clementine, who recently starred as an old lover of Bonnie Sinclair in an episode of "Champagne Flight." "She is a goddess."

END OF BOOK

The *National Enquirer* said essentially that Bonnie does not eat a bite, smoke a cigarette, or drink a sip not approved first by husband Marty. "Italian men are not macho, they are guardian angels," said Bonnie. Bonnie's dress designers confer with Marty on color, cut, fabric. Bonnie is never out of Marty's sight.

No mention of Belinda or the school she was supposed to have gone to. She was obviously a bit player in this glitzy drama. But wouldn't somebody have noticed when she left the stage?

[22]

For a long time I lay on the bed thinking. There are stages to knowing, to absorbing. But the ugly thing was this: the answer to one question created another, and I was more mystified right now than I had been when I knew nothing about Belinda at all. I was more scared right now for her and for me than when I had known nothing at all.

If I was to save us, if I was to reach that decision she talked about, then I had to know and understand the whole thing. I couldn't go home right now and fake it. I couldn't just put my arms around her and pretend I didn't care why she'd walked off on Beverly Hills and United Theatricals and all that.

As for the Swiss school number, I was certain it was a cover-up.

But the essential thing was to know more.

I picked up the phone and called Dan Franklin at the Beverly Wilshire, gave him my number at the Saint Francis, and then, after thinking about it for exactly five minutes, I decided to see if I could lie over a telephone.

I mean, telephone liars are different in my book from those who can look you in the eye and do it. It was worth a try.

I called the New York publisher of the Bonnie biography and told them I was a San Francisco agent named Alex Flint who wanted to hire the author of the bio to do a celebrity book for one of my clients out here. It took about fifteen minutes and lots of bullshit, but I got the author's New York number and rang her at once. So far so good.

"Ah, yeah, that Bonnie bio was a piece of shit. I can do much better stuff than that, done work for *Vanity Fair, Vogue,* and *Rolling Stone.*"

"You underrate the book, it's pretty solid. Only flaw I see is where Bonnie's daughter, Belinda, is concerned. Whatever happened to that little girl? She's going to make more movies, isn't she?"

"They're crazy on the subject of protecting that kid, wouldn't give me five minutes with the goddess unless I agreed to downplay the kid totally, absolutely no stills from *Final Score.*"

"You're talking about United Theatricals."

"Yeah, and Big Mama herself, who is drugged out of her head by the way, at least she was when I saw her. It's a wonder she didn't walk right across her backyard pool."

"And you never saw the daughter."

"Nope, locked up at school in Europe they told me. But you should have seen the material I had to cut on that little girl."

"Yeah? What kind of thing?"

"Tons of stuff out of the European papers. Ever see the shampoo ads she did with her father when she was eight, both of them naked in the surf off Mykonos? I mean racy. But they wouldn't even let me mention G.G. That's her father. And then she had a two-week Christmas holiday affair in Paris with an Arab prince when she was thirteen. Photographers chased them all over the city. But the juicy stuff is before that. She was the one who'd haul Bonnie to emergency rooms all over Europe every time Bonnie overdosed. Talked her mother's way out of a drug bust in London when she was nine. And Bonnie tried to drive them both over a cliff the last summer they were on Saint Esprit."

"Some mother."

"Yeah, Belinda grabbed the wheel of the car and drove it into the side of the hill. A bunch of tourists nosing around in the Greek ruins saw the whole thing. Bonnie runs to the rail, tries to jump, screaming at the kid, 'Why did you stop me?' The tour guide restrains her. All over the Italian papers. After that no more tourists ever got to see the Greek ruins on Saint Esprit."

"No wonder they wanted it all covered up."

"Oh, yeah, real prime-time laundry job on Mama. But I shouldn't have played ball for a lousy five-minute interview with the zombie. She could have been reading her answers off cue cards. I got screwed."

"When did the kid go back to Switzerland?"

"No idea. What's this bio you want me to do? Who is your client?"

"Oh, yeah, right. Frankie Davis, an animal trainer from the silent film era, dying to tell his story, just a real sweet nostalgic story. He's willing to go five hundred dollars up front and one percent royalties—"

"You gotta be kidding. Catch you later."

She hung up.

This lying was easier than I had figured.

I put a call in at once to William Morris in Los Angeles and demanded to know did anybody there represent Belinda, Bonnie's daughter? Call Creative Artists Agency, they represent Bonnie. I did. I wanted Belinda for a big picture in New York, I said, all European money, this was important. The assistant to Bonnie's agent told me to forget it. Belinda was in school in Europe.

"But I spoke to Belinda at Cannes about this!" I said. "When did she decide to go back to school?"

"Last November. We're sorry, she has no plans to resume her career."

"But I have to reach her—"

"I'm sorry." Click.

I FLIPPED open the biography. Bonnie had shot Marty on November 5 of last year. There had to be a connection. Two events like that at the same time—the shooting and her dropping out of sight—just couldn't be unrelated.

I tried Dan again. No luck.

I rang Alex Clementine at the Clift. His line was busy. I left a message.

Then I ate a little breakfast, though I didn't much want it, tried Alex again, who was still busy, then I checked out.

IN the lobby the shops were just opening. Sunshine glared on the roofs of the cars lined up beyond the front doors. I went back to the newsstands, spotted a couple more pieces on Bonnie. Same old trash, and nothing about Belinda.

I WENT out and walked around Union Square.

Gorgeous white cocktail dress in the window of Saks—floor-length white silk trimmed in silver, sheer sleeves to the wrists, clinging skirt.

It was the kind of dress a girl could wear at Cannes, I imagined. Seemed to go with the atmosphere of the Carlton, champagne in glistening silver buckets, crystal glasses, suites crowded with pink and yellow roses, all that.

I felt empty and rotten. Everything was ruined. No matter that I could not fully understand why. It was all shot.

Intellectually I could remind myself that she had never lied to me. But what difference did that make now? It was too enormous what she had kept secret. So it was hers, and I had no right to be angry. It just did not work.

Yet I went into Saks, like somebody sleepwalking, and I bought the white gown for her, as if I could somehow recapture everything.

It was like wrapping up bright light when they smothered it in tissue and closed the box.

It was only eleven thirty when I left the store. And the Clift was less than five blocks away. I hailed a cab and went up there and took the elevator up to Alex's room.

He was all dressed up, even to an old-fashioned gray fedora, and a Burberry raincoat over his shoulders, when he answered the door.

"There you are, you rascal," he said. "I've been trying to reach you all morning. Just missed you at the Saint Francis. What in hell were you doing down there?"

Two bellhops were packing his clothes for him in the bedroom. And one of the handsomest young men I'd ever seen was sprawled on the couch in a pair of silk pajamas reading a magazine with Sylvester Stallone on the front.

"Look, I know you're mad at me for being so mysterious last night," I said. (The handsome kid didn't even look up.) "But is there some place we can talk?"

"You weren't exactly a barrel of laughs either," Alex said. "But come on downstairs with me, we'll have a little lunch, I want to talk to you, too."

He shut the door and guided me towards the elevators.

"Alex, I have to know something and you've got to keep it secret that I even asked."

"My God, more Raymond Chandler," he said. (The elevator was empty.) "OK, what?"

"Belinda," I said, "that's the name of Bonnie's daughter—"

"I know, I know. I got a hold of George Gallagher this morning in New York, but he's not the one who told me."

He took my arm as the elevator doors opened and ushered me across the lobby. I could feel people looking at him, feel them recognizing him. Or maybe it was just the romantic fedora and the pink cashmere scarf around his neck or the way he seemed to fill up the whole place with every step. Every passing bellhop or desk clerk nodded to him or gave him a quick respecting smile.

The Redwood Room was shadowy and inviting as always, with its dark wooden pillars and the small scattered tables each with its own muted light.

Alex's table was ready for him, and the coffee was poured into china cups at once. Alex seemed to glow in the dark as he looked at me.

As soon as the waiter left us, I asked:

"What did George Gallagher say to you about her? Tell me every word."

"Nothing much. But I'll tell you something very strange, Jeremy, I mean, stranger than stranger, unless the little boy is psychic."

"Which is what?"

He took a gulp of his coffee, then went on:

"Well, you know, I was telling him that a friend of mine and I were having dinner and we were trying to remember his daughter's name, you know, playing Trivia on the beautiful people and all that, yak, yak, would he take a load off my mind by just giving me the kid's name, you know, and G.G. asks, "Who's the friend. I say it's an author, old old friend of mine, children's author, matter-of-fact, and he asks, Jeremy Walker? Just like that."

Speechless.

"You still with me, kid?"

"Yeah. I want a drink, OK?"

He signaled the waiter.

"Bloody Mary," I said. "Go on."

"Well, I say, How did you ever guess Jeremy Walker, and he says, That's the only kid's author he's ever heard of who lives in San Francisco, but—guess what, Jeremy?—I never told him I was calling from San Francisco. I know I didn't."

Speechless.

"I know I just said, This is Clementine here, because I was trying to sound casual and all, you know. I've had a crush on G.G. for years. Anyway he says his little girl's name is Rumpelstiltskin, and he starts laughing. You gotta know G.G. to understand. G.G. is one of those little boys who will never grow up. He's Ollie Boon's lover, you know, the Broadway director, and he and Boon, well, they're like angels or something—I mean, both of them are sort of gentle good-hearted flakes. They're people who have actually made a bundle off being goodhearted. There's nothing bitchy or mean about them at all. So when he laughs, it's just sort of sweet. I say, Come on G.G., come straight with me. And then he says suddenly he's gotta go, he's really sorry, he loves me, loved my last bit on 'Champagne Flight,' give Bonnie hell and all! And he hangs up."

Speechless.

The Bloody Mary came and I drank it. And suddenly my eyes were watering.

"I mean this is weirder than weird, son. So I was sort of pissed. I mean, I wanna know her name! So I call my agent down at CAA and I ask him, which I should have done the first time round."

"Yeah."

"I mean, CAA handles Bonnie, you know. And he says Belinda. Her name's Belinda. He knows it right off. And the Swiss school thing is absolutely true by the way, she's been gone since November. Bonnie and Marty hustled her out of the limelight for her own good, he says. But what do you make of all that with G.G. in New York?"

"Can I have another drink?"

"Of course, you can!" He glanced towards the bar, pointed to my glass. "Now what do you make of it, that's what I want to know."

"Alex, my friend," I said. "Tell me anything else you know about this girl, anything at all. I mean, this is important, you can't know how much."

"But why, Jeremy? Now I mean it, why!"

"Alex, it's everything to me. I'm begging you—any dirt, anything—did you see her in LA? Did you hear anything about her? Even the craziest gossip. I know you're holding back. I knew you were the night of the dinner party when you were telling all the book people the stories, you were holding back something about Bonnie and Marty, we all knew it, something about that shooting, there had to be more to it, you know something, Alex, and you've got to tell me."

"Pipe down, will you? You're only talking about my boss."

The waiter set down the fresh drink.

"Alex, this is strictly confidential. I swear it."

"OK," he said, "this is the big one, the big one that could cost me a bankroll in Hollywood. Get me blackballed from every studio in town. Now can you keep your mouth shut? I mean, you never tell anyone where you got this! I mean, this is my career we're talking here, and I'm not going up against Moreschi for—"

"I swear."

"OK. The scuttlebutt down there—and I mean secret scuttlebutt—is that Marty Moreschi molested that kid. That's what happened. And Bonnie caught him and bang, bang, bang."

Silence.

"Next day they packed her off to Switzerland, poor baby. Bonnie was sedated, Marty was in intensive care. Bonnie's brother from Texas flew in, took the little girl to the airport, got her safely away from the whole circus."

"And Bonnie *made up* with Marty."

"She had to, son."

"You're putting me on."

"Jeremy, don't be too quick to judge these two. Take it from me. I've known this lady for years. She's one of these beautiful women who's just a nobody and a nothing, and when they make it big, they always fall apart. Money can't do anything for them. Fame only makes things worse. You might say Bonnie's been legally dead since the sixties. She believed all that Nouvelle Vague stuff in Paris; she really did go around carrying books by Jean-Paul Sartre under her arm. Flambeaux and those artistic types, they made her feel she was somebody, something was happening, taught her things a woman like that should probably never learn. Then ten years of making spaghetti Westerns and gladiator epics killed that girl. I mean, she is a perfectly ordinary person who is just beautiful enough to have been a doctor's wife living in a five-bedroom ranch-style suburban house.

"Now Moreschi pumps enough embalming fluid in her to keep her from rotting right on the spot. If she blows 'Champagne Flight,' she's finished. Pills, booze, a bullet, what difference does it make? Besides, she's burned her bridges. Even her old friends hate her now. Blair Sackwell, you know, Midnight Mink, he made her famous, and the actresses she knew in Europe, they can't even get her on the phone these days. So they sit around in the Polo Lounge crucifying her. The lady's on borrowed time."

"And what about Moreschi?"

"If you really want it straight, he's not so bad. He's network TV and he sucks and he doesn't know it, but he's not basically a vicious guy. In a real way he's better than just about everyone around him. That's why he's top of the heap at thirty-five years old. Story of his life most likely. He's done more with what he's got than anybody he knows. These people are not like you and me, Jeremy."

"What do you mean by that?"

"You've got your paintings, son. You've got this private universe of yours, these values you're always talking about. There's somebody looking back at me when I look into your eyes. And me, I'm happy. I'm always happy. I know how to be happy. Faye taught me that, and even after Faye died, I bounced back. But these people have never felt like you and me, not even for one moment of their entire lives."

"I know what you're talking about, but you don't know how ironic it is that you should say it now." I drank the fresh Bloody Mary, and it made my eyes water again. The Redwood Room seemed eerily quiet around us. Alex smiled sadly under the shadow of the fedora. When he lifted his cigarette, two waiters moved to light it.

"What I'm saying about Marty is this," he went on, "maybe it was like five minutes of kissy-face with the little darlin' and then she realizes, hey, this is a man, not some kid in the backseat of a car, and she can't turn him off that easily, so she screams for Mama, and, well, a man can wind up paying for something like that all his life."

"Him or somebody else," I said.

"Jer, I don't want to be stalled anymore. What has this got to do with you? I want to know now."

"Alex, you don't know how grateful I am for what you just told me," I said. "You've given me exactly what I need."

"Need for what? Jeremy, I'm talking to you. Answer me."

"Alex, I promise you, I'll tell you everything, but you have to give me a little time. And you wouldn't want to know right now, either, Alex, take my word for it. If anybody ever questions you about it, you have to be able to say you didn't know."

"What the hell—"

I stood up.

"Sit down, Walker," he said. "Sit down now."

I did.

"Now you listen to me. We've been friends for years, and you are dearer to me than just about anybody I know."

"Alex—"

"But there was one special time in my life, right after Faye died, when I needed you and you came through. For that alone, son, I'd do almost anything for you that I could."

"Alex, you never owed me anything for that," I said. It was true.

After Faye's funeral one of Alex's lovers, a young actor, had moved in on him, slipped Libriums into everything he was eating or drinking and sold off half his furniture and memorabilia before Alex caught on. In robe and pajamas Alex had walked to a neighbor's to call me, because all the phones in the house were locked up. I'd flown down at once, let myself in with my own set of keys, and gotten rid of the kid with a couple of threats.

It was nothing as hard as Alex had imagined. The kid was a schemer and a bully, but he was also a coward. And I was damned honored that I had been the one Alex called. But the incident hurt Alex, really hurt him. We'd gone to Europe immediately after that and stayed in his house near Portofino until he felt he was OK again and could go back to work.

"Alex, I enjoyed playing hero that time, if you must know, and in Portofino afterwards you treated me to the time of my life."

"You're in trouble, Walker, I know you are."

"No, I'm not, not at all."

"Then you tell me who the young lady was," he insisted, "the sweet young lady who answered the phone at your place this morning when I called."

I didn't answer.

"It couldn't be the kid, could it? The one everybody thinks is away at the Swiss school?"

"Yes, it was Belinda. And I promise you, one day I'll explain everything. But for now don't tell *anyone* about this. I promise, I'll call you soon."

I GOT a cab in front of the hotel.

All I wanted in the world right now was to be with her, to hold her, and to tell her I loved her. I was praying that George Gallagher hadn't called her and hadn't alarmed her, that she'd be there when I got home.

I'd confess the spying. I'd confess everything and then I'd tell her I'd made the decision, no more questions ever and this time I meant it. We were going to leave San Francisco and head south tonight.

If she could only understand the prying enough to let it go, we'd be all right.

Lovely to think about it suddenly, the van loaded, the long drive across the country together through desert and mountains and finally emerging in the sultry New Orleans heat.

Wouldn't matter, all the old memories associated with the house, Mother, the novels, all that. We'd make our memories in it, she and I, and we'd go far away from all of it. Nobody would ever find us down there.

As the cab moved up Market Street towards the Castro, I opened the Bonnie biography again and looked at the photograph of Marty Moreschi—the dark eyes shining behind the thick glasses, the thatch of black hair.

"Thank you, asshole," I said out loud. "You've given her back to me, you've made it OK for me to be with her, you're worse than me."

He seemed to be staring right back at me off the pulp page. And for an odd second I didn't hate him so much as I acknowledged we were brothers. We both found her irresistible, didn't we? Both took a risk for her. How he might have sneered at me.

Well, fuck him.

I was too elated and too relieved right now to care about him.

I thought about the things the biographer had said, about the suicide attempts and the car nearly going off the cliff on Saint Esprit.

Yes, it all made sense, it explained so much about her, the odd precocity, the strange almost-proletarian hardness, and the elegance and the sophistication, too.

She must have had a bellyful of it all before she even got to LA, and then they exile her to Switzerland, she takes the fall after he molests her so "Champagne Flight" can stay on the air. Damn them. And thank God for them and their madness.

Because we have our madness, don't we, she and I.

Just be there, darling, when I get there, just don't have run off on me, because of anything George Gallagher might have told you. Just give me a chance.

SHE wasn't there when I got home.

I went upstairs and into her room.

All her luggage was stacked on the bed—the new brown leather suitcases I had bought her and also the old battered case she had brought with her from the Haight.

One glance into the closet told me she had packed everything. Nothing left but the fancy satin hangers and the smell of jasmine sachet.

But the luggage was still here! Even the overnight case was still here. And everything was locked.

What a strangely affecting sight it was.

Made me think of another sight years and years ago—the bare mattress on my mother's bed the afternoon of her death.

I'd just come in from classes at Tulane and hurried up the stairs to see her. I guess I thought she'd be sick forever. And the minute I saw that bare mattress I knew, of course, that she had died while I was gone.

As it turned out, they'd had to take her to the funeral parlor. It was too hot that summer for them to leave her till I came home.

"Walk over to Magazine Street and see her," the nurse had said when she finally caught up with me at the bedroom door. "They're waiting for you."

Five blocks through the flat quiet tree-lined streets of the Garden District. Then Mother in a refrigerated room. Good-bye, my darling Cynthia Walker. I love you.

Well, Belinda wasn't going anywhere. Not yet!

I brought up the box I'd brought from Saks, and I unfolded the white and silver dress and hung it carefully in the closet on one of the padded hangers.

Then I went up to the attic, leaving the door open so I could hear her if she came in.

I took stock.

There were now twelve completed paintings of her, done over this the strangest summer of my adult life.

The last picture completed was another *Artist and Model,* from the series of timer photographs of us making love. I did better by this one than the first, though I loathed painting my own naked body on top of Belinda. But the work itself was terrific, I knew it, and I saw now, as I looked at it, the resemblance of her profile here to the profile of her beneath the caresses of the woman in *Final Score.*

Was she a woman or a child in this picture? Because you could not see her baby face well, it was pure woman with the hair of a fairy princess, or so it seemed.

Unfinished was another "grown woman" study, *Belinda in the Opera Bar,* nude as always against the backdrop of gilded mirrors and cocktail tables, except that she wore high-heel shoes and a pair of black kid gloves.

Macabre, the deeply detailed figure, the mouth almost pouting, the unwavering gaze.

Ah, it gave me shivers to look at it. And when that happens, I know everything, absolutely everything, is going to be fine.

But no time to lose.

I started carrying the canvases down to the basement, first the dry ones, then the moist ones, then the wet ones, and slipping them one by one into the metal rack inside the van.

Some smudging to the very edges was inevitable, but no more than a half inch on either side.

I could mend that when we got to New Orleans. The rack would keep them safe, like so many sheets of glass, until we got all the way home.

And then I'd know the next step in the series. It would come to me when we were in Mother's house. I knew it would.

Just come home, Belinda. Walk in the door now and let me hold you and talk to you. Let us begin again.

After all the canvases and supplies were loaded, I packed up all my own clothes.

I wanted to put her suitcases in the van, too, but I knew that was going too far.

And she wouldn't just bolt without those things, she wouldn't do that. I mean, she had left her own little sorry suitcase, too, and the overnight case and—

But the grandfather clock was chiming three when I finished and she was still not there.

Where to look for her? Where to call?

I sat staring at the phone on the kitchen wall. What if I called George Gallagher, what if I asked—? And what if he wasn't the "oldest buddy in the world" and hadn't told her anything? What if she was merely unhappy over last night's argument, what if, what if?

No, he was the "oldest buddy," and he had put things together. Damn it, Belinda, come home!

I went to the front windows to see if the MG-TD was parked out there. Why hadn't I thought of that before? If she had the car with her, I'd know for sure she was coming back, she wouldn't steal the MG, would she? But there it was, damn it, parked where she frequently parked it, right across the street—and not too far from a big long black stretch limousine, of all things.

Big black stretch limousine.

For a second I panicked. Had I forgotten some damned book signing or something? Was that limousine here to pick up me? Frankly that was the only time I ever saw a limo in this neighborhood, when they came lumbering into my driveway to pick up me.

But, no, that was all over, Splendor in the Grass in Berkeley had been the last one, the farewell one. And the driver of this limo was just sitting in it, smoking a cigarette. Tinted glass in the back of course. Couldn't see who was or was not there.

OK. Belinda's not driving the MG. That means she may be somewhere near and she'll come walking in soon.

When the phone finally rang at three thirty, it was Dan.

"Jeremy, I'm going to say it again before you stop me. Get the fuck away from her now."

"I'm way ahead of you. We're dropping out of sight for a while. You won't get any mail from me, but you'll hear from me by phone."

"Look, stupid. Saint Margaret's in Gstaad was asked on November 5 to accept Belinda Blanchard though the semester had already started, and on November 11 they were told that she would not be coming as planned. She is not now and has never been at Saint Margaret's. However, they have been asked to forward all her mail back to a law firm in the States. It is a cover-up."

"Good work, but I knew it was."

"And the shooting took place the night before the call to Saint Margaret's."

"Right. What else?"

"What do you mean, what else?"

"The connection between the shooting and Saint Margaret's, do you have it? Why did they send Belinda away?"

"Don't wait for the connection. The point is, if I could get all this simply by calling a friend in Gstaad and wining and dining a United Theatricals secretary, the *Enquirer* will eventually get it, too. Run for cover now."

"I am, I just told you."

"I mean without her. Jer, go to Europe. Go to Asia!"

"Dan—"

"OK, OK. Now listen to this. There are more detectives in this besides Sampson's people."

"Fill me in."

"Daryl Blanchard, Bonnie's brother, he's got his own men on the case, working just like Sampson. The mail goes from Saint Margaret's to his firm in Dallas. The girl from United Theatricals says he's a real pain. He and Marty scream at each other a lot long-distance."

"Not surprising."

"But, Jeremy, think again. The reason for this cover-up, what is it?"

"I can guess what it is. Something happened that night between her and this stepfather of hers."

"Very likely."

"So they don't want the slightest hint of that to get to the papers, and it's also what we figured in the beginning, she could be kidnapped. She's just a kid."

"Maybe. But study the pattern here. Jer, Saint Margaret's deals directly with Texas Uncle Daryl. Daryl deals with Moreschi. There is no evidence that Bonnie even knows her daughter is not in school."

"Wait a minute." I was stunned. I had thought I was ready for anything at this point, but that was too much.

"Bonnie may be the reason for the cover-up. They want to keep her working, they don't want her to know the little girl took off."

"That would be too ugly!"

"But don't you see what this means? These guys stink to high heaven, Jeremy. If they do get on to you and they do try anything, we can poleax them both."

What had she said to me that night? Even if they did find out about us, they wouldn't dare do anything? Yes, that had been exactly what she said.

"Bonnie is absolutely the legal guardian," Dan said. "I checked that out. She's been in court fighting the kid's natural father for years."

"Yeah, George Gallagher, the New York hairdresser."

"Exactly, and he's crazy about the little girl by the way. These guys Moreschi and Blanchard will have to get busy covering up their asses with him, too, if this gets out."

"You're keeping records of everything—"

"You better believe it. But I'm telling you, old buddy, these guys aren't the enemy. What I'm really scared of is the press. This woman's in *every* tabloid this week—"

"I know it."

"—and the story's too juicy. It's just lying there waiting to be discovered, daughter of superstar on the run, holes up with children's author who paints little girls. I mean, 'Champagne Flight' will keep you on the front pages for two weeks."

"But how dumb is this Bonnie? Wouldn't she even call Belinda at school?"

"Dumb's got nothing to do with it. Let me tell you what you're dealing with here. This is a woman who for years has not answered a telephone, opened a piece of mail, hired or fired a servant, even written a check. She does not know what it means to handle a rude salesclerk or bank teller, to have to pick out a pair of shoes for herself, to hail a cab. Her house has been adding live-in personnel steadily for the last twelve months. She now has a hairdresser, a masseuse, a maid, a cook, a personal secretary. She goes to the studio every day of her life in a chauffeured limousine. And Marty Moreschi is never out of sight. He sits and talks to her when she's in the bathtub. She probably doesn't know who's in the White House. And this is not a new condition for this woman. On Saint Esprit her brother, her agents, and her Texas cronies maintained her in the same protective cocoon. And your Belinda was no small part of that. By all reports she took her turn at sentry duty whenever Mother was feeling panicky, right along with the rest. And there was a roadside attempt at suicide that nearly killed Belinda—"

"Yeah, I know about that one. But it's illegal what they're doing—"

"Oh, you said it. And I'll tell you something funny, Jer, something real funny. You know, if I just happened on this whole story without knowing the kid was safe with you, I'd think she was dead."

"What are you talking about?"

"It's like the cover-up of a murder, Jer. She could be buried in the garden or something. I mean the school scam, all that. What would happen if Susan Jeremiah went to the LAPD and demanded an investigation? These guys could wind up indicted for killing this kid."

I laughed in spite of myself. "Beautiful!"

"But, back to the matter at hand. We've got a counter-strategy if these guys find you. With the press we do not."

And I've got a new problem, I was thinking. A stunning one.

"What if you're right," I said, "and they are keeping it from Bonnie but Belinda doesn't know?"

"It's possible."

"Bonnie would call the cops, wouldn't she? Bonnie would call the goddamned FBI to find her daughter, wouldn't she? I mean, there must be a bond between mother and daughter here that's closer than just about anything else in this woman's life."

"Could be."

"And what if Belinda thinks her mother doesn't even care? I am telling you that would explain a lot of things, Dan. It really would. I mean, here is this kid and something bad happens with this guy Marty and what do they do—they try to pack her off to Switzerland and she runs. And then she realizes her mother isn't even looking for her. No police, no nothing. I mean, this is bad. Here she makes her big gesture, and these guys write her out of the script."

"Maybe. Maybe not. She may know everything, Jeremy. I mean, the girl can put two quarters in a telephone, can't she? She could call this Bonnie."

Didn't she call George in the middle of the night?

"Could she get to Bonnie?"

"Hell, she could call Jeremiah. She could call the next door neighbors in Beverly Hills, if she wanted to. She could call somebody! No. If you want my guess, your Belinda's hip to everything that is going down. And just decided she'd had it, that's all."

"OK, look. As I told you, I'm splitting tonight. I'm going far away from here, and when you hear from me again, it will be by phone—"

"For God's sakes, be careful. You know how the *Enquirer* operates. They'll give you some bogus reason for the interview, then run upstairs and photograph her clothes in the damn closet."

"Nobody's interviewing me these days for any reason, believe me. I'll be in touch. Oh, and Dan. Thank you. I really mean it, you've been great."

"And you're being stupid. They'll crucify you if this hits the papers, I mean it, they'll make Texas Uncle Daryl and Stepdaddy Moreschi look like saints who found her in the Child Molester's Den."

"Good-bye Dan."

"They'll come to court with the canceled checks to prove what they paid the detectives, they'll say the cover-up was for her own good."

"Take it easy—"

"And you'll get fifteen years for molesting her, goddamn it."

"And what about Moreschi?"

"What about him? There's nothing on record says he touched her. She's living with you!"

"Bye, Dan, I'll call you."

I CHECKED and double-checked the house. Everything locked up tight, windows, doors to the upstairs deck, dead bolt on the attic, dead bolt on the darkroom downstairs.

All paintings, photographs, cameras, clothes loaded in the van.

Except her suitcases sitting there on the white counterpane of the brass bed.

Please come home, my darling, please.

I'll tell her everything at once. All I know, even about Bonnie maybe not knowing. Then I'd say: Look, you don't ever have to talk about it, it doesn't make any difference, but I want you to know I'm on your side, I'm here to protect you, I'll protect you from them if it comes to that, we're in this together, finally, don't you see?

She'd see. She'd have to. Or would she just gather up those suitcases and carry them downstairs to the cab she had waiting for her, saying as she went past me: You betrayed me, you lied to me, you lied all along.

If only she were a child, if only she were a "little girl," "just a kid," a "minor." Then it would be so much easier.

But she's not a child. And you've known that from the start.

FOUR thirty.

I sat in the living room, smoking one cigarette after another. I looked at all the toys, the carousel horse, all the trash we were leaving behind.

Should call Dan and tell him to sell this stuff—better yet, donate it to some orphanage or school. Didn't need it anymore, this lovely rubbish.

What I'd been feeling with her for the last three months was what people call happiness, pure and sweet.

And it struck me suddenly that the misery I'd felt last night was almost equal in intensity to the happiness I'd known before. These feelings had a searing heat to them that was like the desire I felt for her. And these were extremes I hadn't known for years before she came.

In my mind they were connected with youth really—the awful storms before success and loneliness became routine. I had not known how much I missed this.

Yes, it was like being young again, just that bad and just that magical. And for one moment I found myself thinking of it all from an unexpected distance and I wondered if I would miss this in the years to come, this second chance at joy and misery. I was so alive at this moment, so alive with love and foreboding, so alive with terror.

Belinda, come back.

When the grandfather clock struck five, she had still not come home. I was getting more and more frightened. The house was dark and cold, yet I couldn't bring myself to turn the lights on.

I looked outside, hoping, praying to see her coming up the street from the metro.

No Belinda.

But the limo was still there. The driver was standing beside it, smoking a cigarette as if he had all the time in the world.

Now what would that thing be doing here?

Rather ominous it seemed suddenly. Downright sinister. Maybe those cars always are.

Throughout my childhood they carried me to funerals, sometimes two and three times a year. They had meant death then exclusively. And it had always seemed an irony that these same luxurious black monsters carried me to television and radio stations, to newspaper offices and literary luncheons and bookstores, to all the inevitable ordeals of the standard publicity tour.

Didn't like the look of them, their heaviness, their darkness. Rather like coffins or jewel boxes they seemed, all padded and silent.

A chill came over me. Well, that was stupid. Detectives didn't stake you out in limousines.

Six o'clock came and went. California daylight outside.

I was going to give it one more hour, then track down George Gallagher somehow. George was the only one who could have tipped her off.

Nothing respectable in the refrigerator to eat. Get some steaks. One last meal together before the road. No. Stay here. Don't leave this house till she comes.

The phone rang.

"Jeremy?"

"Belinda! I've been out of my mind. Where are you, baby darling?"

"I'm OK, Jeremy." Shaky voice. And noise surrounding her as if she were in an outdoor phone booth somewhere, a dim rolling sound like the ocean behind it all.

"Belinda, I'll come get you now."

"No, Jeremy, don't do it."

"Belinda—"

"Jeremy, I know you went into my closet." Voice breaking. "I know you looked at my tapes. You didn't even rewind them—"

"Yes, it's true, I'm not going to deny it, honey."

"You knocked my things all over the floor. And—"

"I know, darling, I did, I did. It's true. And I did other things, too, to find out about you. I asked questions, I investigated. I admit it, Belinda, but I love you. I love you and you have to understand—"

"I never told you any lies about me, Jeremy—"

"I know you didn't, sweetheart. I was the one who told the lies. But please try to listen to me. We are OK now. We can leave tonight for New Orleans, the way you wanted to, honey, and we will get far away from the people who are looking for you, and they are looking, Belinda, they are."

Silence. And a sound that I thought was her crying.

"Belinda, look. My things are all packed, all the pictures are loaded in the van. Just give me the word and I'll load your suitcases. I'll come and get you. We'll get right on the road now."

"You have to think it over, Jeremy." She was crying. "You have to be sure because—"

"I am sure, baby darling. I love you. You are the only thing that matters to me, Belinda—"

"—I'm never going to talk about them, Jeremy. I don't want to ever explain it or drag it all out or answer questions, I won't. I just won't."

"No, and I don't expect you to. I swear it. But please, honey, realize, on account of what I did, the mystery can't divide us anymore."

"You still have to make your decision, Jeremy. You have to forget about them. You have to believe in me!"

"I have made it, baby darling. I believe in both of us, just the way you wanted me to. And we're going where this guy Moreschi and this uncle of yours, this Daryl, will never track us down. If New Orleans isn't far enough, we'll leave the country, we'll go to the Caribbean. We'll go as far as we have to go."

Crying.

"Where are you, honey? Tell me."

"Jeremy, think it over. Be real sure."

"Where are you? I want to come get you now."

"I will tell you, but I don't want you to come until morning. You have to promise me. I want you to really really be sure."

"You're in Carmel, aren't you?" That sound was the ocean. She was in one of the phone booths on the main street just a block from our house.

"Jeremy, promise me you'll wait until morning. Promise me you'll think it over that long."

"But honey—"

"No, not tonight. Promise me not tonight." Crying. Blowing her nose. Trying to get calm. "And if you still feel that way in the morning, well, then come and we'll go to New Orleans and everything will be OK. Just OK."

"Yes, honey. Yes. At the crack of dawn, I'll be at the door. And we'll be on the way to New Orleans before noon."

Crying still.

"I love you, Jeremy. I really really love you."

"I love you, Belinda."

"You'll keep your promise—"

"At the crack of dawn."

Cut off. Gone.

Probably already walking off from some phone booth on Ocean Avenue. Because the little hideaway had no phone.

Oh, ache for Belinda. But it was all going to be OK.

I sat down heavily at the kitchen table and for a long time didn't do anything except feel the relief course through me. It was really going to be OK.

WELL, the next few hours wouldn't be so hot, but the battle was over, and the goddamned war had been won.

I should stop sitting here, shaking with relief, and get up and go out and get something to eat now—that would kill a little time. I'd go to bed early, set the alarm for four o'clock, and be down there before six.

OK. It's OK, old buddy. It's really OK.

Finally I did get up, and I put on my tweed coat. I combed my hair.

THE air was bracing outside. Immediate slap of fresh wind.

The streetlamps had just come on, and the sky was fading from red to silver. Lights twinkling on the surrounding hills.

"Take a good look," I said to myself in a whisper, "because it might be years before you come back here." And that feels soooo good!

Limousine still there. Now that is really strange. I gave it the once over as I moved towards Noe. The driver was back inside.

Could it be someone watching for her?

Well, you are too late, you son of a bitch, because she's two hundred miles south and I'll shake you off on the highway within five minutes—Come on, Jeremy, this is pure paranoia. Nobody stakes out a house in a limo. Stop.

But just as I reached the corner of Noe, the engine of the limo started, and the big thing moved up to the corner and stopped.

I felt my heart tripping. This was mad. It was as if my staring at it had moved it.

I crossed Noe and walked towards Market, feeling a funny weakness around the knees. Wind stronger, cutting through the fatigue that had set in while I was waiting at home. Good.

The limo had also crossed Noe and was moving alongside me over in the right-hand lane. The sweat broke out under my shirt. What the hell is this?

Twice I glanced at the back windows, though I knew perfectly well I couldn't see through the tinted glass. How many times had I seen people on the sidewalk staring at my limo that way, trying to see in? Stupid.

It would go on at Market. It had to. It couldn't possibly turn left and follow me up Castro. That was illegal and perfectly absurd besides. A steak. Bring it home, throw it in the broiler. A little wine. Just enough to make you sleep.

But I had forgotten about Hartford, the little street that intersects Seventeenth just on one side. My side. The limo made a big awkward left turn and pulled into Hartford and stopped right in front of me as I reached the curb.

I stood still looking at it, at the blind glass again, and thinking, this makes no sense. Some dumb chauffeur is going to ask me directions. That's all.

And he's been waiting over three hours out there just to ask me personally?

The chauffeur was looking straight ahead.

There came the low electric hiss of the rear window being lowered. And in the light of the streetlamp I saw a dark-haired woman looking up at me. Big brown eyes behind enormous horn-rimmed glasses. In a dozen films I'd seen the same faintly imploring expression behind those lenses, same rich wavy hair brushed back from the forehead, same red mouth. Beyond familiar.

"Mr. Walker?" she asked. Unmistakable Texas voice.

I didn't answer. I was thinking in this strange hazy calm, with my pulse thudding in my eardrums, she really is beautiful, this lady, really beautiful. Looks just like a movie star.

"Mr. Walker, I'm Bonnie Blanchard," she said. "I'd like to talk to you, if you don't mind, before my daughter, Belinda, comes along."

The chauffeur was getting out. The lady slipped back into the shadows. The chauffeur opened the back door for me to get in.

[24]

I DIDN'T look directly at her. That was out of the question. I was too stunned for that.

But I'd glimpsed a soft clinging beige dress and a loose cape of the same color over her shoulders. Cashmere it probably was, and all her jewelry was gold—layers of it around the high-rolled neck of the dress and on her wrists. Out of the corner of my eye I saw her hair was loose. Scent of dark, faintly spiced perfume filled the car.

The limousine turned right onto Market and went back towards downtown.

"Could we go to my hotel, Mr. Walker?" she asked unobtrusively. Thick mellow Texas accent. "There everything would be very quiet."

"Sure, if that's what you want," I said. I couldn't hear any anxiety in my voice, just the sharp edge of suspicion and anger. But I could feel the fear in my head.

The limousine picked up speed, seemed to bore through the more sluggish traffic. The ugly car lots and characterless buildings of upper Market gradually gave way to the congestion of porno theaters, cafés, shop fronts crowded with army surplus, blaring stereos. The yellow streetlamps poured a merciless light on the trash-littered sidewalks.

"What is it exactly you want to talk about, Miss Blanchard?" Couldn't keep silent any longer. Panic rising. Had to keep it out of my voice.

"Well, my daughter, naturally, Mr. Walker," she said, the drawl not as pronounced as it had been years before in the pictures. "I hear she's been living with you now for three months or more."

So the mother doesn't know, Dan? And what would you advise me to do now? Ride this one out in silence? Or jump out of the car?

"Hear you've been taking very good care of her," she said in the same lusterless tone, her eyes obviously fixed on me, though I still didn't turn to look at her.

"Is that really what you've heard?" I asked.

"I know all about you, Mr. Walker," she said gently. "I *know* you've been taking good care of her. And I know all about who you are and what you do. I've read your books, used to read them to her."

Of course. When she was a little girl. And she's still a little girl, right?

"I always liked your work. I know you're a very nice man."

"I'm glad you think so, Miss Blanchard." The sweat was getting worse. I hated it. I wanted to open the window, but I didn't. I didn't move.

"Everybody thinks that about you, Mr. Walker." She went on with it. "Your publishing friends, your agents down south, all those business people. They all say the same thing."

The car was taking us all the way to the end of Market. I saw the gray tower of the Hyatt Regency rising on the left. Ahead the nighttime emptiness of Justin Herman Plaza. Cold, overcast down here.

"They say you're decent, all of them say that. You've never done harm to a living soul. Nobody says anything but that you're sane and you're sober and you're a nice man."

"Nice?"

Just slipped out, didn't it?

"So what is this about, Miss Blanchard? You're saying you're not going to call the police and have me arrested? You're not going to have your daughter picked up and brought home?"

"Do you think she'd come with me, Mr. Walker?" she asked. "Do you think she'd stay if I got her all the way back down there?"

"I don't know," I said. Try to sound as calm as she sounds.

The limousine was sliding into the shadowy covered driveway of the Hyatt. Cabs, limos all around us. Bumper to bumper we moved towards the curb. Flocks of people, porters hustling the luggage.

"I don't want my daughter back, Mr. Walker."

The car came to a halt. I found myself staring right at her.

"What do you mean?" I asked.

She had taken off her glasses and she looked at me with the vague, musing expression that the nearsighted often have. Then she put on a pair of dark glasses, and her full red mouth came into focus as if I were the one who had been blind.

"I don't want my daughter anywhere near me, Mr. Walker," she said quietly. "That's why I hope you and I can come to a little arrangement so that she'll be all right."

The chauffeur opened the door behind her and she turned away from me and raised a soft shapeless hood from the folds of wool over her shoulders and brought it down carefully around her face.

In shocked silence I followed her into the lobby and towards the glass elevators, heads turning everywhere as she made her way through the summertime tourist swarm. Just like walking with Alex through another lobby only hours earlier. And she had that same nearly preternatural gleam.

The cape flowed beautifully from her shoulders, and the layers of plaited gold at her wrist flashed in the dull light as she pressed the button to bring the elevator down.

Within seconds we were rising over the main lobby.

I stared numbly through the glass at the dazzling expanse of gray tiled floor below. Water shimmering in massive fountains, couples dancing sluggishly to the music of a small orchestra, concrete terraces climbing like the fabled gardens of Babylon to an unreachable enclosed sky above.

And this woman in the glass box with me, as glossy and unnatural as the world around us. The elevator stopped. She moved like a phantom past me.

"Come on, Mr. Walker," she said.

How like a goddess she was. And how petite and delicate Belinda was compared with her. Every detail of her—her long hands, her beautifully turned legs half hidden by the folds of the cloak, her long exquisitely shaped lips—seemed too vivid for real life.

"What the hell do you mean you don't want her near you?" I said suddenly. I was still standing in the empty elevator. "How can you say this to me about her?"

"Come on, Mr. Walker."

She reached for my arm, closed her fingers around my sleeve, and I followed her out and along the railing of the terrace.

"Tell me what the hell this is about."

"All right, Mr. Walker," she said, as she put the key in the lock.

She moved slowly in the large low-ceiling living room of the suite, with the cloak flaring gracefully around her. The hood had slipped down, and her voluminous hair was frozen in the illusion of free-fall. Not a strand was out of place.

Expensive emptiness. Formless new hotel furniture, rough new hotel carpet. Beyond the floor-to-ceiling window an overgrown thicket of downtown buildings without grace or design.

She let the cloak drop on a chair. Breasts beneath the pale-beige wool truly unbelievable, not just in size but in proportion to the tiny waist. Hips that swung from side to side with almost arrogant glamour under the plain narrow skirt.

What must it be like to live night and day with this much woman? How could there by any room for anyone else? Ah, but Belinda's was such a different brand of beauty. How to explain it? Comparisons of nymph to goddess, bud to rose, just did not come close.

She had taken off the dark glasses, and for a moment her eyes swept the room slowly, as if they wanted to drink in the muted light before the assault of sharp edges. Then the clear glasses came up again. And as she looked at me, I was startled to see the resemblance to her daughter. Same cheekbones, yes, same spacing of the large eyes, something vaguely similar even in the expression. But age would never give Belinda this chiseled nose and mouth, this Technicolor lushness.

"I can see why she likes you, Mr. Walker," she said with the same maddening politeness. Almost sweetness. "You're not just nice, you're a real good-looking man."

She took a cigarette from her purse, and instinctively I picked up the hotel matchbook from the table and offered her a light.

Ever see Belinda's match trick? I thought. *It's priceless.*

"You're much nicer looking than you are in your pictures," she said exhaling. "Kind of old-fashioned sort of man."

"I know," I said coldly.

She had the same flawless tan skin I'd noticed that first moment in Belinda, positively shining white teeth. Not a line to indicate either age or the character that often comes with it. Now that, Alex did have.

"Come on, Miss Blanchard. I love your daughter, and you know it. Now tell me what this is all about?"

"I love her, too, Mr. Walker. Or I wouldn't have come. And I want you to take care of her till she's old enough to take care of herself."

She sat down on the small red sofa and I took the chair opposite. I lit a cigarette of my own, and then realized it was one of Belinda's. Must have picked up the pack instinctively when I left the house.

"You want me to take care of her," I repeated dully.

I was getting over the shock, and the panic was going with it. But the anger was getting worse.

She looked tired suddenly. Something played at the edges of her eyes revealing strain. I might never have seen it without the magnification of the glasses. No laugh lines there. Positively unearthly. But again I was struck by her irrepressible voluptuousness. The wool dress was positively spartan, the gold jewelry as severe as it was brilliant, yet she was almost monstrous. To make love to her, what would it—?

"You want a drink, Mr. Walker?"

Bottles on the tray on the nameless piece of trash furniture, that might have been a sideboard.

"No. I'd like to get this straight. What you want, what you're talking about. You're playing some kind of strange game."

"Mr. Walker, I'm one of the bluntest people I know. I just told you everything. I don't want my daughter near me. I can't live with her anymore. And as long as you keep her and take care of her and see that she's safe and not out somewhere on the streets, I'll leave you alone."

"And what if I don't?" I asked. "What if I hurt her? Or she decides to walk out?"

She studied me for a moment, her eyes absolutely without expression, and then she looked down. Her head dipped just a little. And then she remained that way, so still that it was slightly unnerving. For a moment I thought she might actually be sick.

"Then I'll go to the police," she said, her voice more hushed than before. "And I'll give them the pictures you've taken of her, of you and her in bed together, the pictures I have from your house."

Artist and Model. The pictures taken with the timer.

"That you have from *my* house!"

Her head remained lowered, but she was looking up at me now, and it created a suggestion of timidity, which maddened me as much as her subdued voice.

"You had somebody break into *my* house?"

It seemed she swallowed, took a deep breath.

"Only the negatives were taken, Mr. Walker. And there are thirty-three of them to be exact. None of your paintings of her has been touched. What are you so mad about, Mr. Walker? You have my little girl in your house."

"The little girl you don't want back, Miss Blanchard. And it is *my* house."

"I'll give you three of the negatives now. And then another batch when she's eighteen. I believe that is a year and a couple of months from now. I haven't figured it with a pencil. But you get the idea. You keep her till she's nineteen, I'll give you more of them. If you can take care of her till she's twenty-one, you can have the rest. Course, you can't show those paintings of her either. But then you'd be cutting your own throat if you did that."

"And suppose I tell you to go to hell, Miss Blanchard."

"You won't do that, Mr. Walker. Not with the pictures I've got." Her eyes moved off again, the lower lids puckering slightly. "And all the other information I have about you, too."

"I don't believe you have those negatives. If someone had broken into my house, I'd know it, I'd sense it. You're lying to me."

She didn't answer right away. She sat frighteningly still, as before, like a mechanical doll that had wound down, like some kind of beautiful computer processing the question.

Then she got up slowly and went to the chair where she had dropped her purse. She opened it and I could see the top edge of a manila envelope as she reached inside. My writing on it, I could see that, my notation in the upper right-hand corner. She was taking a little strip of negatives out.

"Three negatives, Mr. Walker," she said. She put them in my hand. "And, by the way, I'm real familiar with the subject matter of those paintings you've done. I know all those things the police would find if they came to get her. I know what the press would do with the story, too. But no one else will ever know, not if we make our little agreement, like I said."

I held the strip of negatives up to the lamp. They were the most incriminating ones, all right. Belinda and I embracing. Belinda and I in bed. Me on top of Belinda.

And a stranger had walked through my house to get these, a stranger had broken into the darkroom and into the attic, gone through my things. But when had this happened? What was the precise date of the violation? How long ago had we lived with this false sense of security, Belinda and I both, while this other watched her, waited for his chance to break in?

I put the negatives in my inside pocket. I sat back making all those nervous little gestures you make when you are about to blow. I was rubbing the fingers of my left hand together, rubbing my chin with the back of my hand.

I tried to remember everything Dan had told me. OK, they weren't covering it up for Bonnie. But they had covered it up nevertheless.

She had returned to the couch, and I was glad she wasn't close to me. I did not want her to touch me. I didn't like it that our hands might have touched when she gave me the negatives.

"Mr. Walker, you can have money from me in any reasonable amount that you need to take care of her—"

"I don't need money. If you investigated me, you know I don't need money."

"Yes, that's true. Nevertheless I want to give it to you, because she is my child and it's my wish to provide for her, of course."

"And what is the bottom line on time with this blackmail, this little sales arrangement, this—"

"It's not blackmail," she said, frowning slightly. But at once the few lines created by the frown disappeared. Her face was bland again, as devitalized as her voice. "And I told you, till she's twenty-one is best. Until she's eighteen, well, that is kind of imperative. She's a child till she's eighteen. No matter what she might think, she can't take care of herself."

"She's been with me three months, Miss Blanchard."

"Just a year and two months till she's eighteen, Mr. Walker. You can do that much. You can keep her and those paintings of yours where no one will find them, no one will make a big fuss about it all—"

She stopped. The inner switch had been thrown again. But something was different. I thought maybe she was going to cry. I had seen Belinda's face change suddenly, crumple almost magically into tears. But that didn't happen. Instead her face remained listless, blank. And her eyes appeared to fog over. She was looking at me, but I could have sworn she didn't see me. And the tears that did come were so slow that they were only a film. The light seemed to have gone out inside her.

"You're a sane man," she murmured, the words slower. "You're rich, you're steady, you're good. You'll never hurt her. You'll look out for her. And you don't want to hurt yourself."

"Three months, Miss Blanchard, that's how long I've known her. Anytime she gets tired of it, she can walk out."

"She won't do it. I don't know what she told you, but I'd bet every cent I have that it was hell for her before she met you. She's not going back to it. She has what she's always wanted. And so do you."

"And so you go back down to LA and you tell yourself everything's hunky-dory, is that it? That your daughter is safe in my hands?"

The film appeared to settle where it was, glimmering behind the lenses of the glasses, and her expression dulled even more. Her mouth was half open. Slowly she looked away from me, as if she'd forgotten me. She just stared beyond me at the sterile emptiness of the room.

"What happened?" I asked. "What made her run? And why the hell would you do something like this—virtually turn her over to a man you don't even know?"

No answer from her. No change in her.

"Miss Blanchard, since the moment I laid eyes on your daughter, I've been asking those kinds of questions. They've obsessed me night and day. Just last night I went behind her back into her private belongings. I found the movies she'd made with you. This morning I read your life story in one of those cheap paperbacks. I know about your marriage, the shooting, this television series—"

"And your lawyer," she said in the same dead voice. "Don't forget about your lawyer, Mr. Dan Franklin, asking all those questions in LA."

Beautiful! And didn't it figure?

"All right." I nodded. "I had my lawyer trying to find things out, too. But I still don't know what made Belinda leave the way she did. And if you think I'm leaving this room without the whole story—"

"Mr. Walker you can't really bargain with me. I've got the negatives, remember? All I have to do is pick up the phone and call the police."

"Do it," I said.

She didn't stir.

"Call the police just like you did when she left, Miss Blanchard. Call the papers, too."

Very slowly, impossibly slowly, she lifted the cigarette to her lips. The tears were caught in her long black eyelashes, flashing for an instant like crystal beads. And there was a faint flush to her delicately shaded oval face, a faint quivering to her lips.

"Why didn't you report it when it happened? You might have picked her up in a week if her picture had been in the papers. But you let her roam the streets for nine months."

She laid the cigarette down in the ashtray as carefully as if it were a bomb about to go off. Then her eyes drifted to me again and settled and the glaze of tears shimmered so that for one moment her eyes were nothing but light.

"We had our people looking for her all over," she said. "Night after night I went looking for her on my own. I went down myself on Hollywood Boulevard and I walked miles looking for her, and asking the kids about her, and showing them her picture. I went in flophouses and crash pads looking for her that you wouldn't believe."

"But you don't want her back now that you've found her."

"No. I don't. I never wanted her back. Before she left I tried to send her off to school. I had her packed and ready to leave, but, no, she wouldn't go. She was past all that. Nobody was going to lock her up in a school. When she was little, that's all she ever talked about, wanting to be like other kids. But now she wouldn't hear of it."

"Was that the unforgivable crime, Miss Blanchard, that she had grown up? Enough to unwittingly attract your husband into trying something he shouldn't have tried?"

"The unforgivable crime, if you must know, Mr. Walker, is that she seduced my new husband in my house. And I caught her with him. And I tried to kill her for it. I aimed a gun right at her, and my husband got in front of her. Five bullets he took. Or I might have killed her the way I planned."

My turn to stop moving as if a switch had been thrown.

Panic returning, the rapid heartbeat, the blood rushing to my head.

She was watching me. Her face was a little more deeply colored. The tears were gone. But everything else was locked inside.

"You don't know the relationship there was between her and me," she said, voice even as ever. "She wasn't just my daughter, she was my closest kin." She smiled bitterly. "Don't faint on me, Mr. Walker. She did it. Your Belinda. She'd been sleeping with him all along. I heard them talking to each other. I tell you, it was more that than the sight of it, the way they were talking. And I didn't even understand the words, Mr. Walker. I'm referring to the tone of their voices. I'm referring to those little sounds coming through that door. I got the gun out of the night table and I went in there and I emptied it into that bed."

I took out my handkerchief and slowly wiped the sweat from my forehead, my upper lip.

"Are you sure that she did it the way you—"

"Oh, she did it, Mr. Walker, and I know why she did it, too. It was all new to her, being a woman"—the smile became broader, more bitter—"you know, having the magic, the charm. Well, it's old as the hills to me, Mr. Walker. I've been selling it one way or another ever since I can remember. Before I was a movie star, I sold it for a date to the prom. When we came back from the hospital, I said: 'You get out of my house. You'll never lie under any roof with me again. You aren't my child, you're a stranger. And you're going.' And she said: 'I'm going, but I'm going where I please.' "

"Maybe it didn't happen the way you think."

"She did it." The smile faded. The voice slowed a little, though it had never been very rapid or loud. "And I know what she was thinking, what she was feeling, I remember being that young and that stupid. I remember doing things like that just to see what would happen, going after another woman's husband just to see if I had the power to get him, to make a fool out of her. She became a stranger to me, all right, but she became a stranger that I understood real well."

I shook my head. "Did you listen to her side of it?"

"She said if I tried to make her go off to school, she'd go to the police, she'd say he molested her. That's what she said to me. She said she'd send him to prison for the rest of his life. She was leaving and better nobody try to stop her. She said just get out of her way or she'd go to the papers with it. She'd ruin everything."

"And what if that's what happened? He did molest her?"

"Not a chance, Mr. Walker. Not my daughter, Belinda. She was on the pill when she was twelve years old."

"But you're living with him after his part in this? She has to go, but he can stay?"

"He's just a man," she said. "I didn't know him from Adam this time two years ago. All her life she lived with me. She came out of my body. He's nothing. Put him in the right place, push the right buttons—he's easy to forgive. Nothing to it."

"A moral idiot, you're talking about. A live-in animal."

"What are you, Mr. Walker?" she asked. "What were you thinking when you took her to bed?"

"I wasn't married to her mother," I said. "I wasn't living in her mother's house. I wasn't trying to make a mint off her mother in a television series. And that's the crux, isn't it, Miss Blanchard?"

No answer.

"It was either side with him," I said. "Or 'Champagne Flight' crashes on takeoff, right? It was a package deal the whole time, wasn't it?"

"You don't know anything, Mr. Walker," she said calmly. "There's a thousand lackeys like Marty Moreschi down there in Hollywood. But there's one Bonnie. And Bonnie has made 'Champagne Flight.' Your idea isn't even interesting."

I studied her, confused by her seeming honesty, the way to her it all made sense. There was no defensiveness or bravado in her words.

But her face softened as I watched, becoming even more listlessly beautiful, like a portrait shot taken with a filter, all loveliness with quiet fire. Then her dark eyes brightened slowly, and the imploring look I'd seen a thousand times in her old films was suddenly there.

"I didn't need to forgive Marty," she whispered intimately. "I *wanted* to forgive him. And it meant a whole lot more than just having him or 'Champagne Flight.' It meant keeping a way of looking at things, Mr. Walker. Of caring about them." She paused, and her expression became even more intense, more poignant. "It meant wanting to wake up again in the morning," she said, "wanting to take the next breath. It meant caring about being alive, Mr. Walker, just to be with Marty and be working on that show. Soon as he gave me any means to make it up, I took it. I grabbed it. It was real easy, like I said."

I saw the movement of her throat as she swallowed. I saw her eyes mist again. The full sculpted softness of her breasts and hips beneath the cashmere dress gave her a look of almost irresistible vulnerability.

"I don't care who started it between them," she said. "I don't care whose fault it was. I don't ever want to see her again."

She stared at the carpet in front of her. She had folded her arms and bowed her head as if someone had struck her.

I didn't answer her, and nothing could have made me answer. But I understood just what she was asking me to understand. I hated seeing it her way, but she had made me see it. And I couldn't have lied to her. I knew just what she meant.

When Alex had tried to explain it, I had not heard it. But she brought it all home.

I had the strong feeling, too, that I would understand even better as the years passed, as I got older, when more battles had been lost and there were fewer and fewer things that had any true importance.

Yet I watched her without conceding. And my loyalty to Belinda never wavered. Dear God, she was fifteen when it happened. How much could she have understood?

I didn't try to think it through. I just imagined myself on the highway driving south to Carmel and coming up to the little house at morning and Belinda being there.

And I felt a new terror for Belinda, that she seemed now more than ever alone. I ached for her. I ached to protect her from the hurt and the despair in this room. And maybe for the first time since I had laid eyes upon Belinda, I understood her, too. I did.

I knew now why she would never talk about any of it. And it really didn't matter whose fault it was or who started it, just as her mother said. It was a disaster, that is what it was, a disaster for mother and daughter, and maybe only the two of them would ever know how bad it had been.

But this was not over. Not by any means. It would have been too convenient for me to walk out the door. And I'd be damned before I'd play this lady's game. It was as dark and convoluted as everything about her.

"What if you talked to Belinda now?" I asked.

It was impossible to tell if she had even heard.

"I could go get her, bring her here," I said.

"I've seen all I want to see of her," she said.

The particular brand of silence in the room filled the void between us. Distant traffic. A faint music from the lobby of the hotel, which must have been there all along.

"Miss Blanchard, she's your daughter!"

"No, Mr. Walker. You take care of her." She looked up as if roused from a stupor, eyes red and sad.

"What if she needs you, really needs you?"

"Too late for that, Mr. Walker." She shook her head. "Too late." And her hushed voice had a chilling finality.

"Well, I can't do what you're asking me," I said with a little finality of my own. "I can't be a party to this little blackmail scheme. I won't cooperate with you."

Frozen again in her thoughts. Silent. Helpless.

"What's it matter, Mr. Walker?" she said, looking up. "Nobody's going to the police. You know that, don't you? If she runs away, you call me. You'll do that much, won't you?"

"What if you're wrong about all of it—"

"Take her away somewhere, Mr. Walker. Someplace where nobody will find her or those pictures you're painting of her. Keep her out of the bright lights. Two years, three, it won't matter. Then you can both do as you damn well please. I'd never use the negatives against you. Can't you see that?"

"Then I'll take them now, Miss Blanchard, if you don't mind."

I stood up. She did not move. She looked at me as if she didn't even know who I was, let alone what I meant to do.

"I'll get them myself," I said.

I went to her purse. I took out the envelope. Checked the contents. They were there, all right. I counted them. Then held one up to the light. *Artist and Model.* OK. I looked in the purse. Brush, wallet, credit cards, makeup. Nothing else of mine in there.

"You're some blackmailer, Miss Blanchard," I said. "Your thugs take anything else?"

She was staring at me. And I thought I saw her smile, but I couldn't be certain. So many little things, indescribable things, can happen in a still face. Then very slowly she stood up. But it seemed for a moment she couldn't remember her intention. She appeared lost.

I reached out to steady her. But she moved past me to the desk by the floor-length window and she sat down and bent over slightly, leaning on her left elbow, as she wrote something on the hotel message pad.

"That's my address and my private number," she said, as she turned to give it to me. "If anything goes wrong, anything bad happens, you call me there and I answer, not some studio employee or some brother of mine who doesn't think I can add two and two. You call me night or day if she ever runs away."

"Talk to her."

"And about that brother of mine—be careful."

"He doesn't know where she is?"

She shook her head. "He'll never give up on finding her. Wants her locked up till she's twenty-one."

"For her sake or yours?"

"Both, I imagine. He'd lock up Marty, too, if I let him."

"That's consoling," I said.

"Is it, Mr. Walker? What do you think he'd do to you?"

"But he wants it all kept quiet just the way you do, doesn't he? No police and, God forbid, any newspapers."

"Can't say he does," she said wearily. "He'd call in the French foreign legion and NBC and CBS if he could. But he does what I tell him to."

"Good old Brother Daryl," I said.

"Blood means a lot in my family, Mr. Walker. You don't betray your own. And he's my brother, not hers."

"Well, since you tracked her right to my door, what's to stop him from doing it?"

She didn't answer right away. Then she smiled the little bitter smile again.

"Well, let's just say I have connections that Daryl doesn't have," she said.

"Like what?"

Not Alex. Alex wouldn't have betrayed me for the world. And George Gallagher? He wouldn't betray Belinda, from all I'd heard.

"Daryl thinks she's in New York," she said. "He thinks she's headed for Europe, to try to hook up with a director named Susan Jeremiah to make a picture. But even if he does find out about you, he'll come to me before he does anything. If you don't show those paintings of yours, that is. You do that, you bring everybody down on you. I'd have to come after you myself."

"Even after this little meeting?" I asked. "Attempted blackmail's a crime, so's breaking and entering, didn't anyone ever tell you that?"

She gave me another one of those long slow takes. Then she said: "Mr. Walker, let me tell you something about this whole situation. The way it's set up, no one really has *anything* on anyone else."

"I'm not sure you're right, Miss Blanchard," I said. "Maybe we've all got the goods on one another at this point."

She appeared to think that over—or merely to drift.

"Take care of Belinda," she said finally. "And don't you show those paintings to a living soul."

I didn't want to hear any more. I didn't want to say any more either. I only knew I wanted to get down to Carmel before morning. I turned to go.

"Mr. Walker."

"Yes?"

"Call me if anything goes wrong. Night or day, if anything happens, if she leaves—"

"Of course, Miss Blanchard," I said. "Why wouldn't I? I'm a very nice man, right?"

[25]

I⊤ was just getting daylight when I climbed out of the van and went up the gravel walk to the little cottage in Carmel.

The air inside was warm and full of the smell of the smoldering logs on the hearth. The milky light grew brighter as I watched, illuminating the flagstone floor, the comfortable old chairs, the cottage table, and the high dark beams above me.

I climbed the wooden ladder to the loft bed. Smell of perfume, of Belinda.

She lay curled on her side in a snarl of cotton sheets, her naked shoulders golden brown against the whiteness. Strands of yellow hair were caught on her cheek and on her moist lip. I brushed them aside, and she turned over on her back, the sheet slipping off her naked breasts, her eyes moving beneath her smooth closed eyelids.

"Wake up, Sleeping Beauty," I said. I kissed her. Her mouth was lifeless at first and then it opened slowly and I felt her body quicken under me.

"Jeremy," she whispered, and her arms went around my neck, pulling me close almost desperately.

"Come on, little girl," I said. "I've got everything in the van. Last night I called my housekeeper in New Orleans. She'll have everything ready for us. If we start now and drive on through, we'll be in my mother's house day after tomorrow."

Her eyes were glazed. She blinked to drive away the layers of sleep.

"You love me?" she whispered.

"Adore you. Now come on down. I'll make us breakfast. There are one or two things I want you to know, and then we'll get on the road immediately."

I got the groceries out of the van, put on the eggs and bacon and the coffee, and when she came down to the table, I kissed her again. A lot of her long hair was gathered up in the barrette, flowing down her back like a shaft of light. And she had put on her white jeans and one of those baggy white cotton sweaters I especially loved. She looked like a long-stemmed white flower.

"Sit down," I said when she tried to help. I dished out the food, poured the coffee. "I'm never asking you anything again, like I told you," I said, as I sat down across from her. "But I want you to know what I've done. I read the paperback trash I could find on you and your mother. I read the mags I could find. I even had somebody snoop into it down south. I know all about it. I'm confessing that now, up front."

Her eyes were staring past me. She had a listless expression too much like her mother. But underneath there was the threat of tears.

I reached across the table and took her hand. No resistance.

She looked as defeated as she had ever looked.

"I want to close the book on all of it, just the way I promised we would," I said. "No questions. Not a one. But there are some things you have to know. Susan Jeremiah's been looking for you. She wants you to make a picture."

"I know that," she whispered. "It can wait."

"You're sure? You want to see her, I'll help you. But your uncle Daryl, he's watching her. He's figuring on catching you if you try."

"I know that, too."

"OK. This is the last thing. The biggie. And I don't want this to hurt you, and I don't want this to make you hate me. But I have to tell you. There can't be any more secrets or lies."

So much like the mother in her listlessness and silence, and I had not thought of it last night in that room, though I'd seen it in Belinda countless times.

I took a deep breath.

"Your mother came to see me," I said.

No response.

"I don't know how she found us—it may even be that my own lawyer snooping around actually tipped her off. But whatever the case, she came to see me, and she told me to take care of you. She's worried about you, and she doesn't want her brother to find you and make trouble for you. She just wants you to be all right."

She stared at me, as if she couldn't absorb it, couldn't respond.

"I know this is a shock, an ugly shock, and I wish I didn't have to talk about it, but you have to know. I told her I loved you, I told her I'd let her know from time to time that you were all right."

I could not read her expression. Had the sadness deepened? Was she on the verge of tears? She just remained the same, and she looked so old suddenly and tired and alone.

I took her by the shoulders. She was so soft she might have fallen. But her eyes were fixed on me.

"OK. That's it," I said. "And if you can forgive me for the snooping, Belinda, then you've got to see that the worst has already happened, and we're OK."

She frowned a little, and her lip quivered, and, yes, she was going to cry. But even that seemed to take more will than she had.

"Don't, honey, everything's fine, honest it is," I said. "There are no more secrets to hurt us, Belinda. It's going to be better than it ever was. We're really free."

"I love you, Jeremy," she whispered. "I would have never let them hurt you. I swear to God. It's true."

It cut to my heart the way she said it, as if I were the one to protect.

"Yes, honey," I said, "and I won't let them hurt you either. And we're going far far away from them."

[26]

I DON'T know when the doubts started. Certainly not in those first few weeks.

WE drove straight through, one of us sleeping while the other took the wheel, so that we came into New Orleans late in the morning on the second day after we left California.

I thought I was exhausted when I turned off the freeway onto Saint Charles Avenue, but the old landmarks—the giant sprawling oaks, even the rusted squalor of the dreary midtown stretch—brought me to life immediately.

As we passed Jackson Avenue and moved into the domain of the Garden District, I felt an extraordinary sense of peace. Even the smell of the warm air was working on me.

Then I saw the high iron fence of the old house stretching back the side street. I saw the garden growing wild as ever against the screen porches and the white Corinthian columns. I saw the old Rose of Montana vine lacing itself around the high shuttered windows. Home.

I was in a daze when Miss Annie came out to meet us and to put the keys in my hand. The sense of the familiar was magical. I was overwhelmed by a flood of small sensation I had utterly forgotten.

The enormous rooms were cool as we stepped inside. The overhead fans churned, the old window air conditioners grinding away in that sound which becomes in time a good substitute for silence. There was the awful old painting of Lafayette, which Alex had remembered, and the pirate's head at the foot of the stairs, the worn oriental rugs still scattered about.

I stood for a moment in the door of the library looking at the table where I'd studied, the shelves still full of the nineteenth-century books in which I'd first learned about the paintings and drawings of the masters.

Belinda was quietly and obviously enthralled.

I took her hand and led her to the second floor. We went into Mother's bedroom. The blinds were closed with their slats open on the surrounding trees, just as Alex had long ago seen them.

I opened the French doors to the screened porch. I explained how we'd watched the Mardi Gras here unseen from the street. These porches were now a thing of the past, people thought they looked ugly on the old antebellum facades, but there was nothing quite like them for that feeling of fresh air and veiled privacy.

She looked small and fragile as she drifted around, examining the old mahogany pieces, the giant four-poster.

"Ah, Jeremy, this is a dream place," she said. She flashed one of her exquisite smiles.

"You like it, baby?"

"Can we sleep in this bed?" she asked.

My mother's embroidered pillowcases were still there, and the crocheted bedspread, all the same.

"Of course, we can," I said. "Yes, this should be our room." In the cool of the night we'd shut off the air conditioners and open the doors to the porch. We could hear the streetcar passing.

She helped me unpack the van. We trudged back and forth down the flagstone path through the melting heat until we had brought all twelve paintings into the back porch studio where I'd worked for so many years.

The porch was now enclosed in glass instead of screens. But the old green bamboo blinds were still there and I remembered Alex Clementine in his white linen suit lowering them all around as he said, "I'll make love to you, you know."

My old easel was there, the stool, everything. Even the cot on which Alex and I had sat together that afternoon.

But the garden had grown so high and wild that the light was only dappled. The roses grew in menacing arcs above the thick clumps of banana tree and the white and the pink oleander.

Purple althaea on their stiff stems by the back steps. Morning glory climbing all the way to the roof.

Ah, nothing grows in California the way it grows here. Not even love probably. The pink Rose of Montana ran out along the telephone wires that cut through the branches of the pecan tree. The calla lilies threw up their giant blooms against the brick foundations. Even the purple flags had their layer of velvet green moss. And far out in the overgrown grass the old iron lawn furniture was now half overturned amid the towering weeds and bracken.

Home.

She helped me with the luggage until we had it all upstairs. Carpet soft, as if it were growing into the polished risers. Smell of dust, mothballs, cedar when I opened the old armoires.

An absolute silence fell suddenly. We were standing together on the edge of the Brussels carpet.

"Love you, darling—"

I shut the door and carried her to Mother's bed. She let her head fall back as I unbuttoned her blouse. There were ribbons threaded in her braids.

Her hand went down between the rise of her breasts and snapped the clip of the bra so that the cups fell open on either side of her like two white shells. Her hips rose slightly as I pulled the jeans off her, then the panties. I pulled the pink bows off the ends of the braids. I ran my fingers down the braids roughly, loosening them, so they fell apart, the hair in ripples.

She slipped her arms around me, her lips pressed against my shoulder, my neck.

On top of the counterpane we did it. I turned over after and fell into the deepest easiest sleep I'd ever known it seemed.

California just slipped away into darkness. Out of California Gothic we go into Southern Gothic, I thought.

I heard Alex at a crowded supper table: "And then who should show up in her black limousine right outside his house but Bonnie!" No. Stop it. Wake up. Shift gears. Down south. Drifting. Bonnie's soft Texas slur: "I don't care who started it. I don't care whose fault it was. I don't ever want to see her again."

Sounds of New Orleans outside.

Five o'clock.

The air-conditioning was off. And the katydids were going—great sweeping choruses of grinding song from the trees. Ah, I'm home. I'm safe. I'm in New Orleans. Chimes in the house from one place and another, and then another. Mother always said, Set the clocks thirty seconds apart and the music will continue. Miss Annie must have known the trick.

Belinda!

She was sitting out on the porch in the white rocker. Breeze carrying the scent of dust and rain. She was wearing only a white silk slip and her feet were bare.

"It's so gloriously warm," she said. Slight sheen on her face. Her hair was parted in the middle, sort of tangled over her shoulders, kink from the braids still there. "Ah, Jeremy, let's never leave here. If we go off for a while, let's come back. Let's let this be home."

"Yes, darling baby, forever."

I stood at the edge of the railing looking down through the mesh of oak limbs at the silver streak of car track on the avenue. At Mardi Gras time they always came and clipped the branches back so the big papier-mâché parade floats could go by safely underneath. It hurt me to think of it.

Now the deepening green of the grass melted into the green of the trees, and beyond there was no glare of sky, only the muted colors of the houses far across the way, flash of pink crepe myrtle glowing in the gloom, white magnolia, bits of shining glass, translucent blue, wrought iron. The world woven in a net. There was no end, no beginning. Sunset and cloud were no more than tiny burning pieces.

"We'll go out to the lake tonight," I said. "Some old place at West End out over the water. Or the French Quarter downtown. What do you say?"

"Anything you want." Glisten of moisture on her breasts, her naked thighs under the lace border of the slip. Beautiful thing, the slip, all sculpted to her flesh, and such thick lace, and her feet on the dusty floor naked.

But first the photographs.

I turned on the lamps.

"Lie on the bed," I said to her gently. "On the embroidered pillows. No, keep on the slip."

"Now that's a change," she answered drowsily.

No tripod unpacked but I could hold the camera steady enough. Very grainy these would be, light terrible, but good enough. The painting would come blazing out of them soon enough.

Her legs were spread apart, the left knee raised to one side, her pink nipples clearly visible under the silk cloth.

I saw her fall into the usual trance as the shutter clicked. I thought of all those films she'd made. And the last, those exquisite love scenes in the sand. But this was too *this* for thinking of that.

Out of her suitcase I got one of her bras, a pink satin one with lace, and a tiny pair of pink bikini panties.

"Put on these for me, would you?"

I watched her peel off the slip. The bra closed in the front like the other. Ah, my teeth clenched seeing her tighten the clasp, breasts gathered like that. Then she smoothed the flesh into the cups, lifted each breast, dropped it, her fingers casual, rough. I got hard watching it. Then the panties came up stretched sheer over her pubic hair. I could see the silk seal itself over her secret lips. Little crack. Hair a dark shadow underneath.

She sat down on the bed again, scooting back to the pillows, letting the counterpane catch under her heel.

"Perfect."

I stood back looking at her, loving her. Knowing who she was—it changed nothing and it changed everything. It made all the difference in the world.

THAT night we walked all over the French Quarter.

We caught the jazz at Preservation Hall, roamed the shops, the garish Bourbon Street clubs, drifted past the old historical places—Pirate's Alley, Jackson Square, the cathedral.

She talked softly about the things she missed about Europe. Not Saint Esprit. That had been a prison. She talked about Paris and Rome mostly. She had so loved Rome. She had ridden all over Rome on a Vespa with Susan Jeremiah when they were doing the postproduction work at Cinecittà on *Final Score*. Susan was six feet tall and always did wear her cowboy boots and her cowboy hat. The Italians had loved her.

This place had those colors, she said. Stained walls, stone streets, the dark smells of Rome. Not like any place in America that she had seen. New York, LA, San Francisco—that was America to her.

I listened to all this quietly, sensing the change, that she could have her past now, that her life could extend backwards in time as well as forward with dreams and plans. Everything was going to be fine. It was going to be all right.

But I didn't push her. When we had coffee later in the Café du Monde, I asked about making *Final Score*.

"Well, you know I'd made movies all my life," she said. "I was in them before I can remember. I've seen films in which I was just a baby. And then the ads, too. I did some kind of baby shampoo ad when I was fifteen months, something like that. The pictures are somewhere. I'll show you. But then we went to Saint Esprit and everything was over, dead. Well, no, that's not true, there was one other picture maybe. I don't remember. But it was like prison or something, Saint Esprit."

"But in *Final Score* you had a big part."

She nodded. Then she was uncomfortable. "There's time for all that," she said. "It's OK, having to wait."

Afterwards, when we were walking back to Canal Street, she brought it up again:

"You know, one thing I learned about actors and actresses—I mean the big stars. They can be the most ignorant people if they get caught up in it very young. Some of them are damn near illiterate. And emotionally they're like people who have grown up in the penal system. I mean, they cannot control their emotions at all. I want to make pictures—I know I'm going to do it—but it doesn't hurt to live a little more life of some other kind before it starts."

Seemed like she was arguing with herself, trying to make it acceptable. It wasn't clear.

"Two years, honey," I said. "Two years and nobody can do anything to either one of us then."

I thought of Bonnie threatening me with those negatives, I thought of some faceless creature making his way through my empty house. When had it happened? When we were in Carmel that last time, the stranger flashing his light on my paintings? Scalding anger. Let it go, Jeremy. She gave the negatives to you without the slightest resistance. The woman is tragic. "Leave her to heaven," as the old poetry goes.

By midnight she was asleep in Mother's bed—our bed—and I was painting downstairs in the old place again. I was racing, trying to finish the last rough spots in the old canvases. Tomorrow I'd get the darkroom supplies, use the servants' bathroom by the kitchen. Everything would be perfect.

When I finally knocked off, I went outside and felt that embrace of motionless night you never know in San Francisco.

The great hulk of the house seemed to list like a ship in the dark, its twin chimneys swallowed in ivy. And scents of the flowers rose—the thick dizzying perfume you encounter everywhere here. Oh, why did I ever leave? I just took it with me in all the work I did. Charlotte and Angelica, even Sleeping Beauty, yes, especially Sleeping Beauty under her gauze of spiderwebs. But now everything is different. The past is alive. I am alive.

I looked up. She'd come to the back screen door. She wore just the slip again. And the kitchen light behind her burned through her hair.

Not a child. A woman standing there.

By the weekend she was getting around just fine in the van, she knew the whole city. She went out to the shopping centers just to feel America down here—sometimes hard to do. And the Quarter she loved, of course. And there were several good movies in town we hadn't seen. We had to see those, she said. And from what she gathered, the list of restaurants was endless.

I had started *Belinda in Mother's Bed*—two canvases that I was working on simultaneously. One was silk slip, the other bra and panties. And these were clearly the most erotic works I'd done so far.

I'd known the new direction would present itself, just as it had when I did the Café Flore painting, but now the mystery deepened. I was a man in the middle of a waking dream.

I could hardly keep at it when I was painting in her breasts and the panties. I'd knock off, go out into the yard, and let the heat lay me out flat. September in New Orleans. Summer still.

BUT it was working out, oh, so fine. Continuation of the grown-woman series. And if I'd doubled my usual speed in California, well, I was at hurricane speed here. I was back to five hours sleep a night at the most. Sometimes only three.

But the afternoons were perfect for napping. Miss Annie slept then. Belinda went riding in Audubon Park, hung around Tulane catching a class or two. She started a diary and sometimes wrote in it for hours in the library. I dozed on Mother's bed.

SHE was busy and content just the way she'd been before. The books were piling up. The new television sets and the VCRs and the cassettes were proliferating. We were set up in the bedroom and her room down the hall and the library downstairs.

ON Wednesday night she watched "Champagne Flight." I was soaking in the bathtub. The door was open. She never said a word to me about it. She just sat on Mother's settee, in a pair of tight white shorts and a pink halter—the kind of casual clothing she had never worn in San Francisco —and stared at the screen. I heard Bonnie talking. Then Alex. Then Bonnie. This must have been Alex's big bow-out for the young punk lover. Bonnie crying. Loathed the sound of it. *I don't ever want to see her again.*

A FEW more days passed before I remembered Dan. I had to call Dan! Everything else was going splendidly. I'd checked with New York from a pay phone downtown.

Rainbow Productions had paid the $350,000 for the rights to Angelica. My accountant was already allocating taxes, investment. Rainbow wanted me to come to LA for lunch, but that was out. No phone calls either. Take her away, gentlemen, please.

And now Dan. And having to tell him the last chapter, the awful chapter, that woman in the sterile room at the Hyatt with the cigarette like a prop in her hand.

But Dan deserved a call. Probably going crazy.

I went to a phone booth up on Jackson and Saint Charles. And I got his personal answering machine in San Francisco. "Leave a message of any length." Well, for the first time in my life I could take advantage of that. I began recounting the whole thing in veiled terms. "Not two hours after I talked to you I look out the window and—"

I think that's when it started. The doubts.

That moment when I was telling it.

I was standing in the booth and I was watching nothing outside, just the long brown wooden streetcar gliding by, the domed top all wet from rain uptown that wasn't falling here.

And I heard myself saying: "—like I was being kidnapped in a black limo, if you can believe it—" and "somebody had broken into the house, got the negatives and—" It hit me right then that it sounded preposterous.

"Well, this is really the capper," I went on, "but I got them back from her, the negatives, and—" No, that didn't make a whole lot of sense either, did it?

And the dream came back, the one I'd had the first afternoon in Mother's bed, of Alex telling everybody the story. What had been the feeling in the dream? *I don't believe it.*

"Well, Dan—" Mumble mumble. I found myself recounting how I'd checked the locks when I got back home in San Francisco. I could not figure out how the bastard got those negatives, even knew how to sort them out of the rest and—"You know, these guys are professionals, crack professionals, I guess." Is that true? "And the lengths these people will go to."

Better wrap this up.

"But you see, whatever happened with her and the stepfather put the cards in little B's hands. I mean, they didn't dare have the police pick her up, naturally—"

Hmmmm!

"And that's what it's like, a house of cards. Because everything is so precariously balanced. They screw me. Little B screws them. We all go down. Nobody's going to do anything to us until I decide to show those paintings—"

Had I told Dan about the paintings? "Later on the paintings, old buddy. I'll call again."

*   *   *

GLAD to be finished with that. Very glad. I hadn't told him where I was. Nobody would know that.

Whenever the phone rang in the old house, it was Belinda calling me or it was for Miss Annie—her son, the drunken cab driver, or her brother Eddie, the wraith of an old man who hammered nails in rotting boards on the side of the house.

I WENT down to the bar of the Pontchartrain Hotel and bought a drink. Had to get out of this muggy green weather for a little while.

Disgusting to have to backtrack like that even for Dan. But I couldn't cut Dan loose without a word, that was unfair.

But the story. *It didn't make sense, did it?*

[27]

SHALLOW dreams. I checked the lock on the darkroom again. The negatives were in the metal file cabinet in the darkroom. That's where I put things when I'm finished. Don't want them to burn if the house burns. Did I put them there? Thousands of sets of negatives in white envelopes. Marked what? Don't remember.

I was trying to pry loose the dead bolt and the oak door wouldn't even splinter. Like chipping at stone. No marks on the door. None.

Wake up. Eyes wide. Heart racing. The dream gone totally. And Mother's bedroom with the gold wallpaper, stained from the dampness, stains gleaming like snail tracks in the moonlight.

The streetcar passed outside. Smell of the jasmine coming through the French doors. Flash of headlights from Saint Charles Avenue.

Where was she?

I went downstairs. Light in the kitchen. Sound of the ice box. She was sitting at the white metal table eating ice cream right out of the carton. Barefoot. Shorty baby-doll nightgown, V of violet panties underneath.

"Can't sleep?" She looked up at me.

"Rather paint for a while."

"It's four o'clock in the morning."

"You still feel that way, that when you're eighteen, I can show the paintings and you don't care?"

"I love you. You're insane. You never talk like other people. Other people sidle into their subjects. You just come right out with it. Like chalk strokes on a blackboard."

"I know. You said it before. My friends call it naiveté. I call it stupidity."

"Show the paintings when *you're* ready. And for your information, Jeremy, I care passionately because I love the paintings, and I can't bear to think of waiting two years if you want to know it. In November, however, on the seventh, to be exact, I will be seventeen. One year from then, Jeremy. Or sooner, if you decide to just take it on the chin—"

Big spoon of strawberry ice cream.

"Think I should?"

Eyes hard for a moment.

"What would they do?" she whispered. Then she shook her head, shuddered, closed her eyes for a second. "Leave them out of it. You do what's right for you."

Another spoon of strawberry ice cream. Teenage shrug. "I mean, you know, be careful and all." Pure teenager. "I mean, you know, down here—" She looked around the high-ceiling kitchen. "I mean, down here you think you've just got God to worry about or something. The world's just gone."

"Yeah, God and ghosts, and truth and art," I said.

"Chalk strokes again!" She giggled. Then serious. "Those two *In Mother's Bed* are going to drive them crazy."

"What's so good about them?"

"Come on! You want some ice cream?"

"No."

Talking with another mouthful: "You realize I grow up in the pictures, don't you? I go from Charlotte's nightgown and the First Communion and—"

"Yes, of course. But you're not the one who grows up. I am."

She broke up. Soft laughter. Shaking her head.

"I'm living with a madman. And he's the only sane person I ever met."

"That's got to be an exaggeration."

I went out onto the glassed porch. Turned on the overhead bulb. Good God, these canvases. Something—what? In the first few seconds I always see new things. What?

She was standing behind me. Shorty top so sheer and short it wasn't even a garment really. Violet panties trimmed in lace. Good thing nobody from the outside world could have ever seen through the domestic jungle around us.

"I don't look so innocent anymore, do I?" she asked, looking at the canvases.

"How do you mean?"

But I knew. It was in the shadows around the eyes, the subtle lines in the face. The young woman was ripe as a peach is ripe underneath the white slip, arm resting on naked knee. Even the toes looked sexual, pushed into the wrinkle of the spread. I felt a little tremor of fear. But the painter in me was ruthlessly delighted.

[28]

FOUR o'clock. It was getting regular. And the dream right before was getting longer.

I wasn't just examining the darkroom door anymore. I was trying to force the lock on the attic. Or was I trying to make it so nobody could get in? No, I was trying to prove that nobody could have gotten in without my knowing it. Hidden keys. Where had they been? In the spice jar on the rack in the kitchen. The one marked rosemary, that was made of white opaque glass.

One chance in a million the bastard would have found them. I counted the jars in the dream: rosemary, thyme, oregano, on and on it went. Most of them empty. One had the keys to the darkroom and the attic.

And I always locked the doors, didn't I? Always. The thieves could take the dolls, the toys, the trains, the crap. But not the paintings upstairs or the pictures in the basement.

And I had shown her the white spice jar. "Here are the spare keys. If there is ever a fire, don't use them. Call the fire department and give them the keys when they come."

"Well, I'd try to save them," she said.

"No, no. But I just want you to know where the keys are."

And she had laughed. "You're always here. When am I here that you're not here?"

Had that been true?

And when was the house empty? When we had gone to Carmel? I had locked up and double-checked. Always. Or had I? What about that last time, when she had been so anxious and we had hurried. No, I checked.

Four o'clock. I went downstairs. The old black phone was in the little room beneath the stairs. That was where you had to go to talk on it when I was a child. You had to sit at the little wicker table and hold the stem in your right hand and the earpiece in the left. And the little room smelled like phone. No smell now. Just one of those smooth white things with buttons.

I imagined myself calling California. She'd answer in that slow Texas voice. Too sophisticated to be called a drawl. I'd say, "I just want to know, how did your man get into my house? How did he find the negatives?"

At five o'clock I was sitting in the living room when she came down.

"What's happening?" she asked. "You can't sleep at all anymore?"

"Come here," I said. She sank down on the couch next to me. "When you're here with me, everything is OK," I said.

But she looked afraid. She started brushing my hair back from my face, sending little chills over me with the touch of her hand.

"You're not . . . worrying again."

"No . . . just a little adjustment," I said. "My clock's off. It's on Pacific time . . . something."

"Let's go out, go downtown. Find that coffee place on the river that stays open all night. Have breakfast down there."

"Sure. OK. We'll take the streetcar, OK?"

"Come on." She tugged my hand.

"Ever miss it, the movies? Susan?"

"No. Not right now. Come on. We're going downtown. I'm going to wear you out today, then you can sleep tonight."

"I'll tell you how you can do that," I said. I put my hand inside the elastic band of her panties. My knuckles grazed her pubic lips. Immediately hot.

"Right here in the parlor?"

"Why not?" I asked. I pressed her down on the velvet pillows. The light was seeping through the lace curtains, getting caught in the baubles on the glass shade of the lamp. "Artist and Model," I whispered.

Something changed in her face. Her eyes locked. All the expression went away. Then she lowered her lids.

My heart was pounding. I felt a tightening in my belly.

She was staring at me in this cold, listless sort of way. Much much resemblance to Bonnie. So much resemblance to the last moment in

Carmel, when I had told her everything, and she had broken my heart with her sadness.

"Kiss me," she said, her voice deep and beautiful. And there it was, the imploring look, so like her mother.

Am I losing my mind? I am.

I had pulled her up before I could stop myself.

"What is it?" she asked. Flash of anger, red cheeks. She jerked back away from me, glaring at her arm where my fingers had left white marks in her tan. The blue of her eyes went dark, the first sun making her squint as it came through the blinds.

"I don't know," I said. "I don't know. I'm sorry."

She had her mouth set in an angry way, lower lip jutting slightly. And the color pulsed in her face. Then she looked sad, hurt, as if she was going to cry. She looked desperate.

"What's wrong now?"

"I'm sorry, baby darling," I said. "I'm sorry."

"Is it this house, Jeremy?" So worried. So sweet. "Is it, maybe, all the old things—"

"No, darling. I'm OK."

THAT afternoon I took her walking in the old neighborhoods. We went through the quiet shady streets of the Garden District past the fantastical Greek Revival mansions and across Magazine Street to the barren crowded Irish-German waterfront neighborhood, where my mother had been born.

I took her to see the magnificent churches built by the immigrants— Saint Alphonsus in the Romanesque style with its gorgeous paintings and stained glass windows—this built by the Irish from whom my mother had been descended. And Saint Mary's, the more delicate Gothic church with its splendid wooden statues of the saints and its soaring arches. The high narrow steeple was of curved brick, a craft now lost—this built by the Germans right across the street from the great gray facade of Saint Alphonsus.

Like treasuries, these were in the narrow treeless street, doors opening on sanctums of astonishing beauty.

I told her about the rivalry of the two groups and how the same priests had tended both churches. And once there had even been a French church on Jackson Avenue only blocks away. But that was gone before my time.

"The old parish was really dying by the time I was a boy," I explained. "There was always a sense of things passing, of the moment of high vitality being only a memory."

Yet there had been the May processions, yes, and the splendid feast days and the liturgical Latin still, and the daily masses in both churches to which you could go early in the morning and sit alone and in quiet until time for communion.

You didn't have to speak to other Catholics then. Old ladies scattered throughout the giant nave said their rosaries with lips moving in silence. Far off at the white draped altar where the flowers stood in shimmering banks amid the candles, the tiny bell tinkled in the altar boy's hand when the priest raised the host. You came and went in blessed privacy without a word uttered.

Not the way it was now with Catholics shaking hands and giving the "kiss of peace" and singing saccharine English lyrics.

We walked together back the narrow streets towards the river.

I told her about the old aunts who had died one by one throughout my boyhood. Dim memories of narrow shotgun houses, as we called them, with their rooms opening one upon another, and the oilcloth on the kitchen table, and cabbage and ham cooking in a big pot. A small painted plaster holy water fount fixed to the doorframe. You dipped your fingers and made the sign of the cross. Faded napkins, many times mended, smelled still of the hot iron that had pressed them.

Always people dying, though. Funerals. An aunt sick in an enameled iron bed in a rented room. Stench unbearable. My mother washing the plates patiently in a corner basin. Sitting patiently beside an iron bed in the charity hospital ward.

Finally only Mother was left.

"But, you know, it died for us when Mother moved out. I mean, it was never more than obligation, her taking me to visit. She had left it all behind when she went to night school and got her degree, and then marrying a doctor with a house on Saint Charles Avenue, well, that was the stratosphere to her people. And the novels? They'd go downtown and just stand there looking at her books in Maison Blanche department store. They wanted her to use the name Cynthia O'Neill Walker. But she wouldn't. She didn't like the three names. Yet we didn't even know the Walker family, never knew them at all."

"And you felt you didn't belong to anyone."

"No. It was an invented life. Used to dream I was poor, if you could believe it, and that I lived back here in one of these little houses. At Christmastime the kids talked of giving King parties. You baked a cake, there was a ring in it; whoever got the ring gave the next party. I wanted to be part of all that. I told my mother I wished we were rich enough to live in the government housing project."

We were walking at sunset past rows of the double cottages, the front porch divided by a wood partition so that each family can sit in privacy and peace. The little gardens burst with four-o'clocks. And the cracked pavements were alive with grass and the green moss that grows over everything. And the sky above was shading to a deep magenta. The clouds were tinged with gold.

"Even this is beautiful here," she said with her arm around me. She pointed to the white gingerbread eaves on each house and the long green shutters that covered the front doors.

"You know, one of the things I wanted to do in painting was to create a narrative of it—the Irish—German life that had been here. You know how I believe in narrative painting," I said. "I don't mean the exhibits where people write up long diatribes about the photographs or the pictures. I mean where the narrative is in the work itself. I believed that realism—representationalism—could embrace all this. And yet there would be remarkable sophistication."

She nodded, squeezing my hand lightly.

"I mean, when I look at the realists of our times, the photorealists, for example, I see such disdain for the subject matter. Why did it have to take that path? Why did the exact rendering have to focus upon vulgarity and ugliness? With Hopper, of course, it is coldness, utter coldness."

She said, yes, you always felt that. And even with Hockney you felt it.

"American artists are so embarrassed by American life," I said. "So contemptuous of it."

"It's as if they're afraid," she said. "They have to be superior to what they represent. They are embarrassed even that they do it so well."

"Why?" I asked.

"It's like a dream, American life. It frightens you. You feel you have to make fun of it, no matter how much you secretly love it. I mean, here is everything you want. You have to say it's horrible."

"I want the freedom of the primitive painters," I said, "to focus with love on what I find inherently beautiful. I want it to be hot, disturbing. Yet gorgeous always."

"And that's why they call you baroque and romantic, like that church back there," she said gently. "When I looked at the murals on the ceiling, I saw your work in them, your colors and your skill. And your excess."

"Ahh! Well, I'll make them think of better words than that with the Belinda paintings."

She laughed the softest, most delighted laugh. Her arm tightened around me.

"Make me immortal, Jeremy."

"Yes, darling dear. But you have things to do yourself, you know, you have films to make, roles to play."

"When you show the pictures, you should be really sure, really sure—" she said, suddenly serious. "It's easy in a place like this to be carried away."

"Yes, you've told me that. But isn't it why we came here?" I asked. I stopped and took her face in my hands and kissed her.

"You know you'll do it now, don't you?" she asked. "No doubts at all anymore."

"Haven't been for a long time. But if we don't wait that full year until your eighteenth birthday—"

Her eyes clouded. She frowned, closed her eyes, opened her mouth to be kissed. Ah, heat and softness.

"You know, you've changed towards me," she said.

"No, honey, no, I haven't," I protested.

"No, I don't mean for the bad," she assured me. "I mean, you hardly ever talked to me like this before."

It was true. I didn't say so, but I knew it.

"Why did you leave here, Jeremy? Why did you let the house stay the way it was all these years?"

We went on walking hand in hand. And then I started to tell her. The Big Secret. The whole thing.

I told her about writing the last two books for Mother, I told her about those heady days the last spring of Mother's life when *Crimson Mardi Gras* was made into a movie and I had gone out to Hollywood in Mother's place for the premiere.

"It was so strange, you know, knowing I wrote it and no one else even guessing. And the party afterwards, I mean not the big one at Chasen's but the little one at Alex Clementine's house, with Alex taking me up to all those people and introducing me. They would look right through me, thinking just for one split second before they turned away, how nice, her son."

She was staring at me silently.

"Alex didn't know then. But she told him later, when he came down to visit her, and he's known all these years. But it wasn't *Crimson Mardi Gras* that drove me away. It was what happened after, when they read Mother's will. She'd left her name to me. She fully expected me to go on using it. She expected me to write Cynthia Walker novels forever. She did not see why her death should be made known. And in the event it did become public knowledge I was to say the novels had been found in filing cabinets, that they were all finished by her before the final illness, that kind of thing—"

"That's ugly," Belinda said.

I stopped, startled by her word.

"Oh, she meant it with the best intentions. She thought I could use the money. She wanted me to have it. She'd even made arrangements with the publisher, gotten me guarantees. Her editors knew all about it. She'd exacted promises. It was really for me she did it. She didn't know anything about painting. I guess she'd thought I'd be broke all my life."

"So that's what all the little girls in your paintings are running from," she whispered. "And we're in the old house they can never escape."

"Are we?" I asked her. "I don't think that's true now, do you?"

We had come to the riverfront, and we were walking slowly over the deserted railroad tracks to the empty wharf. Evening stillness. Thump of jukebox from a darkened barroom doorway. Smell of hemp.

My heart was tripping. I tightened my grip on her hand as we neared the edge of the wharf right over the river.

"I don't believe she meant well," Belinda said to me gently. She was watching me, almost with alarm. "I think she wanted to be immortal, no matter what it meant to you."

"No, honest. She just never thought I'd do much on my own. She was always frightened for me. And I was a dreamer, you know, one of those really absentminded kids."

"It was annihilating what she did." Touch of protective anger. Flame in her cheeks.

The breeze came strong across the broad expanse of brown water. It lifted the curling edges of her hair.

"You are so lovely," I said to her.

"You didn't write any more of the books, did you?"

"No, of course not," I said. "But, you know, it all happened because of her in the end really."

"How so?"

"Because when her editor came out to San Francisco to argue with me —you know, to get me to reconsider—well, she saw the Sleeping Beauty canvases. And she offered me a contract for a children's book on the spot. I'd never even thought about a children's book. I just wanted to be a painter, a weird, crazy, unclassifiable painter. And there it was in all the windows on Fifth Avenue by the end of the year."

Just a trace of a bitter smile crossed her face. Something fragile in her expression.

"We're well matched, aren't we?" she said. And the smile turned to full bitterness, the worst bitterness I'd ever seen in her until now.

She turned and looked off to the far side of the river, at the great steel gray ship that was gliding south, the wind carrying away all sound.

"How so, baby darling?" I asked her. I felt a strange intensity, as if a light had touched something deep within me.

"We keep their secrets," she said, watching the progress of the ship. "And we pay the price." Her eyes flashed on me with uncommon vibrancy. "I hope you show the paintings, Jeremy! But don't you let me push you into it. I'm warning you. Don't you let me hurt you. You do it when it's right for you."

I was watching her, and the feeling of closeness to her I knew at this moment was greater than any I'd ever known. It was everything. It was everything to live for and die for. And I found myself thinking, as if I had forever to do it, how truly beautiful she was. Youth itself had always seemed so irresistible in her that she could have been homely and still beautiful—but she wasn't homely; she was as beautiful as Bonnie in her own way.

[29]

I WORKED until four A.M. That's how to fool the nightmare—paint, not sleep, at the usual time that it comes. I sketched Belinda standing on the wharf, her back to the river. I got the wind in her hair. I got the white shoes she'd been wearing and the little seersucker jacket and skirt. I got the bit of cotton lace at her neck. I did not try to remember the details. I just looked up and made the photograph of her appear in the air. I told my hand "Do it!" And by four o'clock she was standing on the edge of the wharf looking at me, and the river was a great flood of dark brown behind her beneath the charcoal sky, and she was saying, "Don't you let me hurt you."

"Don't you let me hurt you."

I LAY back exhausted on the cot, Mother's clocks chiming, one after another. The insects circled the naked bulb beyond the screen door.

I saw it all clearly from the nightgown picture on the carousel horse to this figure standing on the edge of the river: twelve paintings from child to woman. The nudity was no longer important. She could have her clothes now.

Four thirty.

I got up, began working again, filling in the brown that was the river, the charcoal gray that was the sky.

When the sun came shafting through the green leaves, she was glowing against the river, and the great sweeps of darkness behind her seemed menacing in the way the dolls and the toys and the wallpaper and the Holy Communion veil had never never been.

Miss Annie brought me coffee. The traffic was roaring along the avenue.

"Turn on the cool air, Mr. Walker," said Miss Annie. She went round the room, reaching carefully behind each canvas, to shut the glass windows, and then the silence came in a flood of coldness. And I wiped the sweat off my forehead with the back of my hand.

Now that's one way to fox a nightmare, I thought, staring at the picture.

Outside in the tall grass Belinda sat in one of the wrought iron chairs writing in her new diary.

"Come here and see this," I said.

THE next night the nightmare came again. I found myself staring at the clock.

I was thinking I locked the attic and the darkroom doors instinctively when I knocked off work. I locked up everything.

"Since you tracked her to my doorstep, why shouldn't Daryl do it?"

"Well, let's just say I have connections Daryl doesn't have."

"Like what?"

What connections? How did he get in?

Had he jimmied a window? What window? I'd checked them all again before I left San Francisco. Every lock in place and no scratch marks.

Paintings in the attic, she said she knew. How? But the negatives in the darkroom, that was still the toughest. Good Lord, what did he do, examine everything with a magnifying glass?

"Where are you, baby darling?"

"In Carmel."

"I want to come get you."

"No, not tonight. Promise me not tonight."

In the white envelope marked A and M for *Artist and Model.* Nothing more on it than that. A and M. In the manila folder marked B. She'd been standing there with me in the darkroom. I'd been showing her how I did it. Filed everything. A for the Angelica photographs. B for Belinda. How did *he* find it? I mean her detective, whoever it was, whoever the stranger was who came into my house.

She was a stranger.

"Promise me you'll wait until morning."

Black limousine out there at the curb, one, two, three hours.

"—before my daughter comes along."

Her face across the breakfast table in Carmel, her eyes when I said, Your mother came to see me. Her eyes. Not a flicker.

I got up, half asleep, went down to the back porch studio and started to work. Her face was perfect.

"Don't you let me hurt you."

"I would have never let them hurt you, Jeremy." Was that what she had said to me in Carmel?

I'm not that drunken woman, honey, that grand overblown Hollywood cliché of a woman, you don't have to take care of me, I will take care of us both.

THE next night it came sooner. Three a.m.

Saint Charles Avenue like a stage set down three. Streetlamps in the heavy lace of the tree branches. Rain turning the flagstones out front purple under the light.

"I want to talk to you before my daughter comes along."

The limo was parked right in front of the damned house for three hours. Belinda would have seen it if Belinda had not—

"—stranger."

I WENT down to the library and turned on the TV. Not a chance she could hear it upstairs over the air conditioner. Some old black-and-white film was what I needed. And there was a good one, too, with Cary Grant talking very fast and saying wonderfully clever things. Lovely patterns of light and shadow.

Before I'd left the house in San Francisco, I'd checked the spare keys. Still in the spice jar. Jar dusty. How clever was the son of a bitch?

Early in the morning before I'd left to go downtown and read that paperback bio of Bonnie in the Saint Francis Hotel, she had come down and asked me to run away, no, begged me.

"Promise me you won't come down to Carmel tonight."

Nobody broke into that house! You know it! Nobody picked that dead bolt on the darkroom door!

My head was pounding. The people on the television screen were chattering. Slick black hair of Cary Grant like the slick black hair of Alex Clementine. *"People don't want the truth, they want lies. They think they want the truth but they want lies."*

I shut off the TV.

I went upstairs.

She was sound asleep. Light from the hall on her face. I shook her. Shook her again. Her eyes opened.

"You did it, didn't you?"

"What?"

"You called her! You gave her the negatives!"

"What?"

She sat up, shrank back against the pillow. The sheet was covering her breasts, as if she was hiding from me.

"It had to be you," I said. "Nobody could have found them but you, gotten into the darkroom but you. The keys were in the spice jar, and nobody knew they were there but you. You did it!"

She was shaking. Her mouth was open. Not a sound coming out. She moved across the bed away from me.

"You did it. You told your mother where you were!"

Her face was white with fear. My voice was rising over the air conditioner.

"You did it. Answer me."

"I did it for you, Jeremy!" Her lips were quivering. Tears, yes, tears, of course, streaming down her face, her arms thrown up to cover her breasts under the pajama top.

"For me! Oh, my God!"

"You wouldn't stop worrying! You wouldn't stop asking! You wouldn't stop feeling guilty, damn it! You wouldn't just trust me!" Pillows falling off the bed, her heels dug into the rumpled counterpane. "You went into my things and found out who I was!"

"Oh, my God, you really did it. You really did. You called her and you got her to come up there and do this to me!"

She was sobbing as she got out of the bed and backed into the French door.

"Goddamn you, how could you do that!" I came around the bed towards her.

She screamed when I grabbed her arm.

"Jeremy, let me go!"

"I didn't care about you and that man, her husband. I didn't care about anything she said. I just wanted to protect you! And you pulled this one on me—that woman in that room and those negatives, you did this to me!"

"Stop it!" She was screaming loud enough for them to hear her outside. She was shrieking. She was scratching at my fingers, trying to get loose.

"How could you do it!" I was shaking her, shaking her.

"Stop it, stop it!"

"Get away from me then," I said. I shoved her against the dresser. Clatter of bottles. Something spilled, something broken on the marble. She stumbled, as if she was going to fall. Her hair was covering her face and a low choking sound was coming out of her, as if she couldn't breathe.

"Get away from me!"

She ran around the foot of the bed and past me into the hallway.

Then she stopped at the head of the stairs. She was crying uncontrollably. I watched her slide down till she was sitting on the top step. She went to the side, curling up against the wall. Her crying echoed down the long hall, like a ghost crying in a haunted house.

I stood there helpless looking at her. The sound of the air conditioner was like a whine, an ugly grating whine. My body felt hot and shaky and the inevitable headache had started pounding inside my skull. I wanted to move, to say something. I could feel my mouth working, nothing coming out.

She was crying and crying.

I saw her getting up, steadying herself, her shoulders bent, hair fallen away from the nape of her neck.

"No, don't come back in here, don't come near me!"

"Oh, God," she said, the tears just spilling off her cheeks.

"I don't care who started it . . . whose fault it was, I don't ever want to see her again."

"Keep away from me!"

But she kept coming towards me.

"Jeremy," she whispered. "Jeremy, please!"

I saw my hand go out, heard it hit the side of her face, saw her swing towards the doorframe.

"Damn you, damn you, damn you!" I slapped her again. She was screaming. She almost fell, and I grabbed her arm with my left hand, hit her again with my right. "How could you lie to me like that, how could you! How could you play a trick like that on me, how could you!"

Miss Annie's voice came from the stairwell, "Mr. Walker!"

Belinda tried to pull away. The back of her head hit the wallpaper in the hallway. She turned around as if she were trying to go through the wall itself.

"Look at me!" I was screaming. "Answer me!"

She turned and kicked at me with her bare foot.

"Let me go," she sobbed.

"Liar, liar. To do that to me. I would have done anything for you, gone to the ends of the earth for you, all I asked you was to tell me the truth!"

I had slapped her again. She was going down on her knees, and Miss Annie had a hold of my right arm.

"Mr. Walker, stop it." This tiny bit of a woman in a white bathrobe trying to hold onto my fist.

"Let go of me!"

"Mr. Walker, you'll kill her. Mr. Walker, she's just a child!"

I turned and doubled my fist and slammed it into the doorframe. I slammed it into the plaster. Saw the plaster give under the wallpaper. A great gaping hole broke in the pattern of leaves and roses. Stench of rottenness. Of rain and rats and rottenness.

Miss Annie was saying, "Come on, dear, come on," to her. I could hear their footsteps. Belinda gasping.

I hit the doorframe again. Saw the smear of blood on the lacquer. Then, thank God, I heard the lock on her door turn.

[30]

FIVE days after she left, the notebook came in the mail.

I had tried to talk to her after the fight. But it had been ghastly, going into that room, trying to tell her I was sorry, so sorry, and the words sticking in my throat. There had been bruises on her face, on her shoulders, and her tender naked arms. I had said: "We'll work it out somehow, we'll talk about it. This can not be the end of it, not for us." And from her nothing but silence. The same old silence and her eyes like the eyes of a dead person staring past me, at the leaves of the trees against the glass.

IN the middle of the night she had left.

I had stayed awake as long as I could, pacing back and forth, with only Miss Annie now and then coming to say, yes, she was all right. The truth was, I'd been afraid that if she started to leave, I wouldn't be able to stop her, that I would watch her go, unable to bring myself to say or do anything at all.

But I had stayed awake as long as I could.

I did not even remember lying down on the bed, only that when I awoke at three, it was no nightmare that woke me. And she was gone. The closets were empty, all of her things gone. The rain was coming in the open windows onto the floor of her room.

Through the entire house I searched for some note from her, but there was nothing. And only later that morning did I find the tape of *Final Score* on the marbletop bedside table in my room.

She must have come in while I was sleeping and put it right beside me. If only I had awakened then.

THEN five days later, after I had called Bonnie and called that damned son of a bitch Moreschi and called Alex and called George Gallagher in New York, the notebook came in the mail.

I WAS sitting on the settee in Mother's room and I was thinking how hideously old everything was, how beyond restoration. The rain was blowing right into the room through the French doors to the porch. Bonnie's private number was now disconnected. What the hell did I want of him? Moreschi had said, she was on her own, she'd always been. No, no detectives anymore. George had promised to call me if he heard from her. Alex kept begging me to tell him where I was and I wouldn't. Didn't want anyone to come now. Just wanted to sit here in the ruined room in the ruined house and listen to the rain fall.

Cold the breeze already in late September. And why had she left me *Final Score*? What had been the meaning? How had she looked at me when she laid the tape on the bedside table? Had there been hatred in her eyes then, too?

Three dozen times I'd watched the tape. I knew every movement, every word of dialogue, every angle of her face.

That and the rain falling were my only interests. And now and then the Scotch in the glass.

Then Miss Annie came up the stairs with a flat brown package. A messenger service had brought it. She had signed the receipt.

There was no return address on it, no name to indicate the sender. But I knew her writing instantly from those old notes: "Came, went—Belinda."

And I had torn it open to find the notebook with its fifty ruled pages full of that small, careful writing. And on the front label the words that struck the deepest pain:

FOR JEREMY, THE WHOLE STORY, WITH LOVE.

II

AND
INTRODUCING
BELINDA

II

Well, first off this is no sob story about Mother. I mean, about growing up with her drinking and her pill taking and her general craziness and all the things she did or did not do. I am not ready to lie down on a shrink's couch and say this was all bad.

The truth was, I had a ball. I traveled all over Europe with Mom, I was doing bits in her pictures even before I can remember. And I'm glad that it was the Dorchester in London or the Bristol in Vienna, or the Grande Bretagne in Athens rather than a tract home in Orinda, California. I can't say that I am not.

And I'm glad it wasn't Hockaday private school or Hollywood High instead of the college kids that traveled with us too. I loved those kids, and they came from all over the world and they had terrific energy. And they gave me more than any school ever could.

I mean, it was no picnic cleaning up vomit off the floor or calling a hotel doctor at four in the morning or getting in between Mom and Leonardo Gallo when he was pouring whiskey down her throat trying to make her go from crazy drunk to passed out. It was no fun dealing with her moods and her rages. But Mom, for all her problems, is a generous person. She gave me everything I ever asked for, everything I could ever use.

But to understand what happened here, Jeremy, you have to understand something about Mom. For Mom there really isn't anybody else but Mom.

She tried to kill herself at least five times that I know of, and two of those times, if she had succeeded, she would have killed me, too. The first time was when she turned on the gas in the guest house on the ranch in Texas. I was playing on the floor. She came in and sort of passed out on the bed.

The second time was when she tried to drive us over a cliff in Saint Esprit.

The first time I didn't react much. I was too little. My uncle Daryl came, turned off the stove, and got us out of there. I understood what happened because I heard what everybody said afterwards, about her being depressed and about her having to be watched. And several times Uncle Daryl said: "And Belinda, Belinda was in there, too." I guess I filed it away somewhere to understand later.

But on Saint Esprit I got furious after it happened. I mean, Mother would have driven us both over the cliff.

But Mother never saw that aspect of it. She never said one word about me being in danger. She even asked me later, "Why did you stop me? Why did you grab the wheel?"

When you see that side of Mother, you see craziness. I have seen it many times.

When she broke up with Leonardo Gallo, I had been in school, in Switzerland, for maybe a couple of weeks. They called from the hospital. Mom had taken an overdose but she was OK, and she wanted me to come. It was four o'clock in the morning and she had them wake me up and take me to the airport. And when I got to Rome, she was gone. She had checked out that morning and gone on to Florence because her old Texas friend Trish had come to get her. I didn't even know where they had gone for two days.

I was going crazy, all alone in the flat in Rome, with Gallo calling every hour and the reporters banging on the door.

But most of all I was embarrassed. I was embarrassed when the school called and the neighbors came over. I was embarrassed that I was there all alone.

When Mom finally called, all she kept saying was, "Belinda, it was important that I not see Leonardo, you know the way I feel."

I never forgot that, being embarrassed and bullshitting all those grown-ups, trying to make them think somebody was taking care of me.

And I remember Mother said: "Belinda, I feel so much better. Trish and Jill are taking care of me. Everything's fine, don't you see?"

Well, I could see all right. And even by that age, really, I knew not to argue with Mom. Arguing only confused her. It hurt her. If you pushed Mom hard enough on any subject, she would start crying uncontrollably and talking about her own mother's death, how when she was seven, she had buried her mother, and she should have died, too, right then. Her mother had died of an alcoholic seizure, alone in a big mansion in Highland Park. Once Mom started on that, there was no arguing or talking or anything. You just had to hold her hand and wait it out.

Yet there were times when I lost my temper. I screamed at Mom about things. But she would just stare at me with her large brown eyes, as if I were the crazy one. And afterwards, well, I'd feel stupid for forgetting that Mom couldn't ever really see what was going on herself.

She wouldn't hear of me going back to school after that. So my one and only two-week try at school was over.

But from that day on, I made sure I always had money. I had a couple of grand in traveler's checks always in my purse. I'd hide cash in places, too. I never wanted to be broke and alone again like that.

When I finally ran away last year, I had maybe six grand with me. And I still have some of that money, as well as money my Dad gave me later and money you gave me, too. I hoard money. In the night I go to look and see if it's there. Clothes, jewelry, the things money can buy, they don't mean that much to me, I think you know that. But the money itself, "just in case," I have to have.

But I don't want to jump ahead. And I want to say again that I wasn't miserable as a kid. I guess there was just too much excitement, too many good things happened, and during the early years Mom was always a very physically affectionate person, very warm. Later her warmth came to seem rather impersonal to me and even grasping. But not when I was little. Guess I needed it too much.

Even when we settled on Saint Esprit, things were good. Lots of people came to visit—Blair Sackwell of Midnight Mink, who is an absolutely wonderful friend of mine, and Gallo, and Flambeaux, Mom's first real lover, and actors and actresses from all over Europe.

And I was always taking off on shopping trips to Athens and Rome and Paris with either Trish or Jill. Mom had the stables especially built for the horses she bought me. She had a riding instructor come to live there, and I had this very good English girl as a teacher and companion, the one who really got me into reading. And I went on ski trips and tours to Egypt and Israel and a couple of students from Southern Methodist came over to tutor for a while. We had a ball on Saint Esprit. Pretty good for a prison, I have to admit.

When Trish found out I was going to bed with this Arab kid in Paris, this Saudi prince, I guess he was, the first affair I ever really had, she didn't get angry or upset. She just took me to a doctor to get the pill and told me to be really careful, and our talk about sex after that was just pure Texas and pure Trish.

"You know, be careful and all, I mean not just about getting pregnant, but, you know, sort of, you should like the boy and all (giggle, giggle). You know, just don't (giggle) hop right in the sack."

Then she told me all about when she and Mom were thirteen and they went to bed with these boys from Texas A&M, and they didn't have any birth control, so afterwards they ran to the drugstore and got hot Seven Ups and shook them and then squirted them inside to wash everything away. What a mess! We almost died laughing. "But, honey, don't get pregnant," she said.

I think you have to know Texas women to understand this, I mean girls who grew up like my Mom and Trish and Jill. Somewhere way back in the family there had been hard-shell Bible-reading Baptists, but by the time of Mom's parents the code was a very simple one of work hard, make money, don't get caught going too far with the boyfriend, and keep everything looking nice. I mean the Dallasites I met were never weighed down by any tradition. They were materialistic and practical, and how things looked—well, you cannot overemphasize the importance of this. It is Texas religion.

I mean Trish and Jill and Mom were all wild in high school, as they called it, but they dressed beautifully and they talked nice and they had loads of money and they drank only in private so that was all fine. Even Mom's mom had never taken a drink outside her own home. She died in a silk negligee and silk slippers. Mom was always saying things like, "She was not a flousy, you understand, she never went to barrooms, not my mother, none of that kind of thing." Appearances mattered, not sin.

And this, you see, is the freedom that I inherited, the way that I grew up, too. And Mom was a superstar before I was born. So the ordinary rules never applied to her. And I did not learn guilt about my body at all.

But to get back to the record, on Saint Esprit Trish and Jill took care of everything, but they could put the beer away as well as Mother, and sometimes it seemed I never went to sleep without hearing those drunken Texas voices and the laughing and the carrying-on.

But underneath it all there was a sense of Mother deteriorating. Of Mother getting further and further away from what Mother really wanted, which was to be a big star again.

The advertisements she did made her feel better. And then there was that fantastic Eric Arlington poster that sold all over the world. That was something, OK, but there was a lot of Trish and Jill catering to Mom, to her vanity and her fear. Of them sneering at the new movies they watched that didn't have Mom in them, of proving to themselves over and over by watching this or that new actress that nobody was as good as Mom. I mean, they acted like something big was going on if they watched a movie by a director that Mom had once turned down. I mean, nothing was happening but talk and drinking and laughing, that's all.

And though they did watch Mom and make her eat and go to bed early, they never told Mom the truth about a single thing. They were allies, that's what they were right up till the end. And Mom needed something more than that if she was ever to make her comeback, as you'll see.

Sometimes I got unnerved by it, the sense of Mom sinking, and I had to do something. I bought a Vespa on Rhodes when I was twelve and brought it home on the boat with me. And I rode all over the island at fifty-five miles an hour on that little thing, thinking mad thoughts about the craziness of it, that we were all trapped on Saint Esprit like in a French play.

When Blair Sackwell came to visit, he was really worried about me and he jumped on the Vespa with me, complete with his Midnight Mink lined coat, and we drove off together to the ruins of the temple of Athena, which is all overgrown with grass now and neglected, and Blair tried to comfort me and tell me I was just young and Saint Esprit couldn't last forever. Some day I'd get away. Blair was a real buddy, but I was getting very sick of Saint Esprit, feeling almost like running away.

Well, all this ended the day that Susan Jeremiah came. I know you know all about her now, because you told me you did in Carmel. And I'm sure you noticed the posters of her in my room.

Well, Susan and her film crew made an unauthorized landing on Saint Esprit, which hundreds of people have done. But when Susan said she was from Texas, Mom said, Come right in.

Susan wasn't like any other woman I'd ever met before, and understand I'd known actresses from all over the place since I was born.

Susan took my breath away. When I first saw her, I figured the cowboy boots and the hat had to be an affectation. After all, we came from Dallas. I was born in Dallas. We went back to Uncle Daryl's ranch all the time. And we never dressed like that.

But it became obvious within twenty-four hours that these *were* Susan's clothes. Susan went through sand and surf and high grass and up mountain paths in her boots. She wore jeans and shirts only. She didn't even have a dress.

When we finally went to Cannes months later, I kept thinking now Susan has to get in female drag. But it didn't happen. Susan wore a rodeo outfit, I mean strictly "Rhinestone Cowboy," with the satin shirt and pants and piping all over, and she was a smash. Susan is not what you call conventionally beautiful. But she is very good-looking in her own way.

I mean, she is tall and narrow, and she has something of what I would call a Texas country look to her, with her cheekbones close together and her eyes deepset. Her hair is short, but it's curly and full and it looks like somebody worked on it getting it nicely shaped, but nobody ever did.

Susan leaves other people breathless, too. And she has a way with the press which I found sensational. She looks right at the reporters and says, "I know what you're driving at," like she is on their side and then she sticks up for herself.

OK. That was the looks and the manner. But what was inside was even more surprising. Susan believed she could do anything. Nothing could stop Susan. There was maybe a second and a half between her deciding that she wanted something and reaching out her hand to get it for herself.

As soon as she got to Saint Esprit she just sat down opposite Mom on the terrace and she started describing her movie to Mom and what she needed to finish it—and was Mom interested, and did Mom want to help a woman director from Texas and all that?

She was going to make a big picture in Brazil afterwards, and she was going to make a picture after that somewhere in Appalachia, and all these films she was writing and directing herself.

She had plenty of money from her daddy in Texas, but she was over budget. Her dad had sunk eight hundred thou into the flick and he wouldn't give her a nickel more.

Well, Mother, as you probably know if you read the magazines, gave Susan a blank check. Mother took on *Final Score* for a percentage, and Mother got the film invited to Cannes.

And even before we left the terrace that first morning, Mother got me in the picture just by pointing me out to Susan and saying, "Hey, put Belinda in it somewhere if you can. Isn't she pretty? She is just real pretty, don't you think?"

Mom had gotten me into movies all over Europe in just that way. "Hey, put Belinda in this scene," she'd say, right when we were shooting. And I had always loved it. But it never occurred to Mom to ask anybody to give me a credit on a movie. So I'm in twenty-two films with no credit. And in some of them I talk and I act, and in one I even get shot to death. No credit.

That is, until *Final Score*.

Susan took one look at me and decided she would use me. And overnight the part started to grow in Susan's head.

She woke me up at four in the morning to ask me if I could speak Greek. Yes, I could, I told her, but I had an accent. OK. Few words. Then the next morning we started shooting on the beach.

Now understand I'd worked with all kinds of film crews but Susan's working methods were a revelation to me. The entire crew was five people and Susan herself got behind the camera. And she edited in her head as we shot so that not much would have to be cut away. I mean, it was very deliberate, everything that she did. And nobody had a script either. Susan just explained things to us before every take.

When we got to the little house and Sandy Miller and I got into bed together, I think the love scene really upset Sandy. She and Susan were lovers though I didn't know it then. But Sandy wants to be a great actress, and Susan said this was an important scene and Sandy had to play it and there couldn't be any cheating, and Sandy did what Susan said.

I didn't actually make love to Sandy, I don't know if you noticed that. It was Sandy making love to me. And Sandy is gorgeous, if you didn't notice. Sandy makes you understand why men used to call women tomatoes. She is like a big tomato. And frankly not a whole lot like anything else.

Later in Rome, however, I did make love to a woman, and it was Susan, of course. And that was pretty wild for me. But Sandy and Susan turned out to be inseparable really. And Susan had a hard time making Sandy overlook what happened. And, of course, I hadn't known at all that they were lovers and I was mad at Susan for a while.

But Susan and I only did it once. If you can call an entire afternoon once. Susan was in bed in the flat in Rome smoking a cigarette and I came in and sat on the bed by her. And then I saw that she was undressed. She kicked the sheet off her and she sat there smoking her cigarette and just looking at me. And I came closer and closer and then I reached out to touch her and she didn't do anything and I slipped my hand down between her legs.

This was like touching a flame and not being burned. And I did it. And then I kissed her breasts. I think it was very important to me to do it, after just lying there with Sandy, and the truth was, I could have been Susan's lover, at least for a while.

But it never happened after that on account of Sandy, and the truth is, I didn't have to sleep with Susan to love her. We stayed the best of friends. We got a Vespa, like the one I'd left at home, and we went everywhere on it together. We went as far south as Pompeii riding all night.

Sandy is not the kind of woman to take off on a Vespa. I mean, Sandy would not want to get her hair messed up. But she accepted me as long as there was no sex anymore.

Sandy is like Mother actually. She is not only passive, she has almost no language of her own. I could see that Susan not only did all the talking, she did the expressing of ideas for Sandy. Sandy was one of those people like Mother who can not think well on her own. I don't mean Sandy is dumb. She is not. But I have met many Sandys. Susan was the new thing to me.

But it really didn't dawn on me until the picture was entered at Cannes that Susan regarded me as something new, too. She saw me as her personal discovery, and she wanted me for other pictures. Frankly I was so enthralled with Susan that I didn't think much about how Susan saw me. There was always that feeling of lightness and speed with Susan, like we had put on the five-league boots of the fairy tales when we were together.

Next time I had that feeling it was with you. When you are painting, you are like Susan was in the editing room, you are just focused on that and no one can distract you, but when you stop painting, there is a light feeling about you as if you are very young and you don't care what anybody thinks of you, and we could just walk and talk on the beach or go anywhere and it didn't matter, just as long as you got back to the canvas at some point.

Now Mother is the very opposite. Mother is as professional an actress or movie person as I have ever seen. I mean, everybody who has ever worked with Mother loves her because she is just really perfect on the set and nothing stops her from doing her job. She can repeat lines perfectly on cue, she can find her mark always, she can go into a retake in exactly the right attitude each time. She may be drunk and crazy by seven in the evening, but somehow she manages to shut down before midnight. She is always on time.

But Mother has always been somebody's ticket to ride. Mother is as helpless as she is valuable. You have to write the part for her, shine the light on her, tell her what to do. She's no good without somebody else's energy at all.

Well, Susan wasn't just a director. She was the producer, the writer, the financier. She edited in twelve-hour stretches at Cinecittà with me watching her, she set up places for us to shoot more footage and blend it in. Then she was on top of the cinematographer in the lab getting the prints just perfect. She put her own money into making four terrific prints. And the sound track, that was almost entirely Susan, because we did not have a good sound engineer.

When we talked about the next film, the Brazilian film, she wanted input. She didn't need the total passivity of Sandy either. She could use you no matter what way you were. She is sort of omnivorous. She consumes everything. And I never made up my mind about the degree of ego in Susan. Is it possible to have so much faith in yourself that you have no ego at all?

When I came back from Rome to Saint Esprit, I told Mother all about the Brazil picture Susan wanted to make, and Mother said all that was just fine but somebody ought to go to Brazil with me to look after me but sure it was OK with her. She also said with a little bit of a sneer that if Susan didn't find a distributor at Cannes, Susan was dead.

OK. Susan understood that, of course. That is what Cannes was about. It wasn't just winning the awards or having fun at the Carlton, it was getting the distributors to take the picture both in Europe and the United States. And Mother said she would go to Cannes and she would hold a press conference with Susan and she'd do what she could to launch the film.

Well, Mother had not been off Saint Esprit since I was twelve years old. I was thrilled. This meant everything to Susan, and maybe with Mother backing us and me being Mother's daughter we could at least get an independent distributor in the States. Susan didn't think the film had enough conventional impact for the studios to touch it, but an independent distributor, that would be just fine.

The Brazil picture, that would be the big time. Sandy would play an American journalist in Brazil sent there to write travel articles about the beaches and the bikinis, and I'd be a prostitute that Sandy met, a white slave shipped there by a big-time crime ring, and Sandy would be determined to save me and get me out of Brazil. Of course, my pimp would be this big-time gangster and Susan had a guy to die for to play the part, I'm telling you, and he would really love me and all, sort of, I mean, Susan wanted things complicated the way they are in *Final Score.*

Susan can not stand to have things black and white. Susan feels that if you have a villain in a movie, then you have failed somewhere.

Anyway *Final Score* would be the debut film and then *Of Will and Shame* would be the breakout film. And Susan started writing press releases about us and about Cannes and sending them back to the United States.

My happiest memories of Saint Esprit are those last few days. Well, while we were shooting the movie earlier, that too, I guess. But for some reason those last few days are more vivid, things are better in focus for me, and I really knew Susan and Sandy by then.

Nothing yet had changed with Mother and Jill and Trish. They were still having the never-ending sorority girl beer bust on the terrace, and Susan was in her room with the door open and all the lights on typing away on her portable computer making up these press releases and then printing them out on her little thermal-paper printer and sticking them into envelopes and sealing them up.

I don't know what I was doing. Maybe brushing my hair and trying to

be a white slave prostitute in the mirror, trying to figure out how to
project the sensuality Susan wanted, I don't know. Just grooving on the
energy in the house, the sense of people having a good time, of there
being these areas of light and happiness between which I could navigate.
And, above all, the sense that we were going, we were leaving Saint
Esprit for Cannes and then Brazil after that—and me on my own down
there with Susan and Sandy. Oh, I couldn't wait to get to Brazil.

Well, let me tell you, Jeremy. I never got to Brazil.

OK. So Mother was going to get the cameras on us at Cannes. But
Mother was three sheets to the wind when she said all this. And about
two weeks before we were to leave for the festival, things began to happen, and it began to hit Mother that she was going to Cannes.

First off Gallo, her old lover and most-admiring director, sent a telegram, then her old European agent wrote, then Blair Sackwell, who'd
started his whole Midnight Mink campaign years ago with Mother, sent
his usual white roses and a note saying, "See you at Cannes." (By the way
Blair knows that white roses meant funerals to most people, but Blair
just doesn't care; white flowers are his signature and they are just fine.)
Then a couple of Paris magazines called to confirm that Mom was going,
and finally the festival people themselves called, wanting to know, was it
true Bonnie was coming out of hiding? Would she make an appearance?
There were strong indications they wanted to give Mother some special
tribute, show one of her old Nouvelle Vague films.

And somehow or other it got through to Mother: she was supposed to
go to Cannes.

I mean, one minute we had Mom snoozing and boozing as usual. And
the next we were pouring all the booze down the drain. Mother had to
have vitamin shots, a masseuse had to be flown in, there couldn't be
anything but protein on the table, Mother was going swimming three
times a day.

Next a hairdresser had to be found and sent to the Carlton ahead of
time. Now my dad used to be my mother's hairdresser, because that is
what he is by profession, a very famous hairdresser, known to all the
world as G.G., but they had had a fight two years before I went to Saint
Esprit, for which I blamed myself. It is a long story, but the important
thing is that Mom did not now have a hairdresser and this is a very big
thing to an actress like Mom. I will tell you more about my dad later, but
for now let me say this was a crisis. And also Mom had to have new
clothes.

When we finally checked into the hotel in Paris, she wanted me with
her every minute. Trish and Jill just weren't enough. She wasn't eating
anything now. She was half crazy. She'd wake me up at three and make

me sit with her so she wouldn't call room service for a drink. She'd talk about her mother dying and how, when she was seven and her mother died, all the lights in the world went out. I'd try to get her off that, talk to her, read to her even. And meantime we couldn't find a decent hair-dresser. As for the clothes, there was no time to have anything specially made.

Well, all this worked out for Mother finally, but what happened to me basically is that I couldn't get away from her long enough to get what I might need. And finally Trish said, "Look, Bonnie, she's got to buy some things, really," and while Mother was crying and saying she couldn't have me wandering off now, Trish just shoved me out the door.

And there I was, running all over Paris in one rainy afternoon trying to find some clothes for Cannes.

I honestly think that by the time we got on the plane Mother had forgotten why we were going. I don't think she even remembered Susan or *Final Score*. She kept telling me over and over that the big American directors would be there and they were the ones who were important now.

We had booked a big suite on the front of the Carlton with a wonderful view of the sea and the Croisette. Uncle Daryl, my mom's brother, whom you know of, had it filled with flowers, but he needn't have worried because Gallo sent four-dozen roses and Blair Sackwell sent more white roses and then there were a dozen arrangements easily from a Marty Moreschi at United Theatricals, I mean, flowers everywhere that you looked.

I don't think Mother expected all this. Even with the talk of the tribute I think she had expected to be patted on the head and no more. But as always happens with Mom, the attention only made her more afraid. Trish and Jill had to make her eat something and then she couldn't hold it down. The vomiting started, and I had to be in the bathroom with her till it was over. Then she tried again.

Finally I told her I had to find Susan. And she told me straight out that she didn't know how I could think of things like that at a time like this.

I tried to explain Susan was expecting to hear from us, but she was crying by this time, and that meant her makeup was ruined, and she told Jill that I was changing towards her, that I wasn't my old self, and Jill said that was her imagination and that I was not going anywhere, was I?

I didn't know what I would have done then, but Susan came at that moment, knocking on the door. She looked terrific in her silver satin tasseled shirt and silver pants, but Mother did not even look at her, she was sick again, and I took Susan into the bedroom and found out from her that our showing was tomorrow morning and we'd have a press conference right after and that is when Mother had to be there.

I told Susan that everything was just going to be fine. Mother was sick right now, but she'd be OK in the morning, that's how it was with Mother. She was always on time. As for me, I'd meet her before the screening, but I couldn't leave right now.

Meantime Trish had taken Mom into her room for her nap. And Uncle Daryl and a new Hollywood agent named Sally Tracy were having a drink in the parlor of the suite, and I brought Susan in to meet them.

They smiled at Susan but almost immediately told her very tactfully that they didn't think Mother would be doing the press conference after all. Lots of people wanted to see Mother. And the press conference about Susan's movie just wasn't the kind of exposure that Mother should have. Surely Susan understood that they have to orchestrate things.

Well, boy, did Susan not understand. Her face went dark as she looked at these two. And then she turned and looked at me. I said immediately that whatever the case I'd be at the screening and the press conference as Bonnie's daughter, and we could get some mileage out of that.

Susan nodded, then she got up, said, Real nice meeting you, Texas-style, to Daryl and Sally Tracy and she split. As for me, I was in a state of shock, but not so much that I didn't snap out of it and light into Uncle Daryl. Didn't he realize why we were here?

But he and Sally Tracy smoothly and almost cheerfully explained to me that the sort of films that Susan did were not going to find an audience in America and the smart thing to do was not get any deeper in. I said, Mom owes Susan, you know that. There isn't any ethical way to back out on Susan. But I could feel my face getting red.

What I was thinking basically was, this is my film, too, goddamn it, I'm in it and, damn it, we came here to support it. But what stopped me from arguing was realizing that this might make me sound just like Mother, as self-centered as she always was. I was just silent thinking about that, not wanting to sound like Mother, and then Uncle Daryl took me aside and told me all kinds of people had been contacting him about Mother. He was sure I understood.

Then Sally Tracy asked me about Susan's film, if there was a love scene with me in it and what kind of scene. I told her it was tasteful and it was sort of revolutionary because it was between two women, and she just shook her head and said, "I think we have a problem."

I said, "What's the problem?" And then Daryl said I wouldn't be at that press conference in the morning, no sir.

"Like hell," I said.

I was just about to light out for Susan's room when out of the other room of the suite there came this man. Now this is Marty Moreschi I'm talking about, but at the time, of course, I didn't know him at all. And let me explain how he came across.

Marty is not handsome, the way you are. He doesn't have your poise and cool, and even when he is as old as you are, he will never have your charm. Marty is self-made and what you call a loud, vulgar New York kid in a lot of ways. He has rather ordinary features and plain straight black hair. Nothing particular about him except everything seems particular, especially his deep, kind of purring voice, coming out of his chest, and his eyes, very brilliant and feverish eyes.

But like Susan, Marty is very impressive and very sexual, too. He is sinewy and hard all over, one of those wiry guys who is incredibly strong. And he is always suntanned black and is always in motion and always talking. So you respond as much to the way he glides up and takes your hand and to the way he laughs and says: "Belinda, honey! Bonnie's daughter, well, isn't this sensational, this is Bonnie's daughter, come here, honey, let me look at you!"—you respond as much to this as to his looks.

He is very hot. I mean, you feel it with everything. It isn't just sexuality with Marty, though Marty is practically compulsive on that score, it is that Marty just takes charge.

He was wearing an exquisite silver gray three-piece suit, and he had gold all over him—gold watchband, gold rings, gold cuff links, and I have to say that he looked very good to me, very good. He really has a fine body, really fine. I mean, the chest and the way the pants fit him, he looked very good right off.

Anyway, he came gliding out of Mother's room, and he said just what I just said, and he gave me his immediate lock-on attention, which usually means attraction, though, of course, it could have been flattery, just flattery. Of course, Marty swore later that it was not. Whatever the case, he said my mother was sensational, unbelievable, incredible, unreal, and all that and it was the thrill of his life to meet her and she was the dream star, the superstar, the star like they didn't make stars anymore and all that.

And by the time we were sitting on the couch together, and he was asking me how I'd like to come to LA and see my mother be big again, bigger than anybody. And he was throwing in all that crap like, "Hey, what's your sign, no don't tell me, you're a Scorpio, aren't you honey, yes, I knew it, terrific, you're a Scorpio, honey, and so am I. I am a double Scorpio. And I knew you were a Scorpio the minute I saw you because you are independent." And so forth and so on.

It sounds sleazy when I try to describe it, but there was this immense conviction behind Marty as he poured this on. And he was holding my hand and I could feel something coming through his hand. I mean, I felt a sort of overwhelming physical thing for him, and I wondered how many other women felt this, instantly, just from the touch, the way that I did.

I mean, I looked down at his hand and the way the dark hair was on his wrist, coming out of the white cuff, and the way the gold watchband was there with the dark hair. I mean, just this little thing was attractive to me. It was driving me wild.

I could tell you things about you that made me feel the same way, the way that you let your hair just grow loose and kind of wild, and the expression on your face when you look down at me, and the way it feels to sleep against your chest.

But the thing I am trying to describe here is the way that the attraction got to me, and short-circuited me, and how unprepared I was for all that.

Marty was meantime tuning in to everybody in the room, saying: "Can't you see that independence in her, can't you see that, Sally?" and the truth is, he hardly knew Sally, he had just met her. And: "You don't mind if I smoke, do you, ladies? Daryl, how about that Scotch now? You think the lady"—and that was Mother—"would mind if we had a little, what do you think, Daryl? Sensational!" And then he had his arm around Daryl and Daryl brought over the glass.

"Listen, honey, you and I have to be good friends," he was saying. "And you've got to let me make your mother big again in America, I mean big, sweetheart. Belinda, Belinda, is it? Sensational! Daryl, where'd your sister get that name for her? Talk to me, sweetheart. What can I do for you while you're at Cannes? What do you and the lady need? You call me. This is my number—" Blah, blah, blah and all the time his eyes narrow and brilliant like this is all earthshaking what is happening, then he says he has to blast off.

"So do I," I said. And I headed out the door, and before they could stop me, I was gone to find Susan while he was still kissing Sally Tracy and shaking hands and all that.

I thought Susan would be hysterical about Mother backing out. But she wasn't. We got right into rehearsing for the press conference. And she had already talked to two Continental distributors. It was a sure thing they'd take the film in Germany and Holland. And United Theatricals was very interested and, of course, United Theatricals was one of the biggest distributors worldwide. That would be dream stuff to get United Theatricals. But she had the inside track that they wanted it. They had heard the rumor that the film had a good narrative line.

When I got back to the room, I found out they had sedated Mother because she couldn't sleep. She was out cold. I went into her room and she was lying there with all those flowers around her and, I tell you, it looked like a funeral, this perfect statue of a lady lying there on the satin cover and the flowers all over the room. She seemed to be scarcely breathing. And it always scared me to see her drugged like that.

But they were going to show her most famous film at the Palais des Festivals, and there would be a supper and the tribute afterwards, and United Theatricals was somehow involved.

Well, that's it, I thought, and Susan's right. We might get United Theatricals to distribute after all.

The screening of *Final Score* the next morning was one experience I'll remember forever, in spite of everything else that went on. I mean, we really had the audience. You could feel it. And when those scenes came on and I saw the brand-new me up there—not the kid who had been in Mom's films years and years ago—well, what can I say? I had never seen the final cut either. And I was really stunned and grateful for how good Susan had made us all look.

When we got the standing ovation, Susan was holding my hand and Sandy's hand. And she was squeezing my hand so hard it hurt, and it felt just great at the same time.

The press conference was in the lobby at the Carlton and right off Susan got into the sexual issue, that this was a picture by a woman about women and the sex was clean. The idea was that the woman in the film had a private experience and it made her see the shallowness of the life in the fast lane and all that. The Texas band of dope smugglers had risked everything for the cocaine score. And yet, as they hid out on the island, they realized that they had no idea what to do with the money. The final dope scene wouldn't change their lives at all. But the interlude between the two women, that had made for a change in the heroine. And to say it was a gay film would have limited it. It was about a new kind of woman, who tries a variety of experiences in life, a woman who had the pressures and freedoms of a man.

From there it went right on to women in film, did women get a fair shake? And did Susan see herself as an American filmmaker, which of course she did. Her dope smugglers were Texan Americans. And then Susan threw in the fact that Bonnie had helped produce the film, and this was one woman helping another, the way Coppola had once helped his friend Ballard to make the *Black Stallion,* and so forth and so on.

That threw the focus right to me. And then the questions started about Mother's financing. And I tried to keep my voice steady while I explained how much Mother believed in the film of integrity, like the ones she had made in the past.

Then it was: Did I feel the love scenes in the film were tasteful and in the tradition of Mother's films?—and, of course, I said yes. Did I want to make more films? Yes, definitely. How did I feel about playing in a film that maybe I wasn't old enough to see in the United States? And Susan stepped in immediately and explained that no way would the film be X-rated. Had the reporters just been to the screening? What did they see? *Final Score* would get an R-rating, of course. And then she talked about me and Sandy as two of the most exciting actresses on the current scene.

Then came Sandy's moment, and she probably got as much mileage out of monosyllabic answers as any beautiful woman ever did. Susan rescued her a couple of times, and there was a lot more about America and Europe and Texas, but by that time it was repeating itself.

I'd say even now that it went wonderfully well. Susan was natural and convincing, and the reporters were never hostile to us. After all, we were the underdogs at Cannes. Nobody expected us to win anything. Nobody was out to get us. It was our moment of glory, and everyone was on our side.

Rumors were all over about United Theatricals distributing. But Susan wasn't going to lose her Continental people. She holed up in the room with the phones as the talk about United Theatricals brought more and more offers in.

Reporters attacked us when we went out for drinks. We were mobbed with questions. Did I have any new offers? Would Susan work in Hollywood? We told everybody about *Of Will and Shame,* the Brazilian film.

I was floating when I got back to the suite, but something was brewing in me, too. I was hurt by Mother in a way that I had never been hurt in the past. I could look back on many terrible things, but no matter what Mother had ever done to me, Mother had always suffered worse.

But this time Mother had hurt me, and it didn't involve her self-destructiveness or her carelessness. It involved something else. She hadn't come to the showing! And that hurt me as bad as her not coming to the press conference. Mother had not seen my film.

Yet again, when I came into the suite, I didn't flip over it. I couldn't. I was blocked again by the thought that I would be acting like Mother if I flipped over it. I'd be drawing attention to myself as Mother always did.

When I walked in, nobody even noticed me. Nobody even knew I was there. The whole place was in confusion. The showing of Mom's film had turned into a special evening of clips from all Mom's best. And Leonardo Gallo, who by the way had made a lot of garbage with Mom, was going to make the address. Well, he needed that all right. And maybe everyone would remember his younger days and not the garbage that killed Mom's career.

Anyway Mother was on the couch with Marty, and Marty was making her eat some cold cuts and some cold fish from a china plate. Mom looked wonderful, she really did. She looked fragile and just about ageless. And Marty was absolutely feeding her, putting the bites right into her mouth. And he was telling her in a hushed voice that television was easier than film. They had to shoot so many pages in so many days and you never got involved in extensive rehearsals or retakes. Her kind of professionalism would be perfect.

Mother was trying to eat. She kept saying that she didn't know if she could do this television thing, and, of course, I had seen this routine a thousand times before. I had seen her do it with Gallo on every picture and in Germany and in Denmark, and each time the director would take over, inspired by her vulnerability and humility and all that.

So this sexy guy, Marty, is some kind of director, I thought, and it is television of all things. Well, for a major role in an American film Mom would have done anything. But for TV? I almost laughed. Poor Marty what-ever-your-name-is. You better wipe your hands on a napkin and give up.

I went in to shower and change for dinner, and I tried not to think about the screening, that nobody, not Mom or Uncle Daryl or Trish or Jill had come. Don't think about it, Belinda, I kept thinking. You had all those strangers cheering for you. So what if these guys didn't even care? But I was getting more and more upset and finally crying, and I just let the shower run and run.

Then Trish was banging on the door. "Hurry, Belinda!" she said. "There's a press conference in the lobby right now."

Well, the crowd down there was easily five times what it had been for our conference. There was no comparison at all. Mother had really brought them out. And the whole thing was to announce that she'd be going back to the States to work for United Theatricals on a nighttime soap called "Champagne Flight."

Now if you know anything about movie people, Jeremy, you know that they really look down on television. You ask Alex Clementine. They disdain it utterly. So why the hell was this happening at Cannes?

Within seconds the answer was clear. Mom was the American Brigitte Bardot, Marty was saying, and the American Brigitte Bardot was coming home. On "Champagne Flight" she would play herself as Bonnie Sinclair, the émigré actress returning to take over the Florida airline empire of her father, and Mom's old films would be used in episodes of "Champagne Flight." Clips from Gallo, Flambeaux, all Mom's Nouvelle Vague successes would be used in this brand-new concept series, that would have the thrust of "Dynasty" and the style of Mom's old films.

In sum, Marty had made television news into film news and he had used the moment, on the moment, maybe better than anyone else could have done.

Now we were off to the special tribute and the dinner. I had to find Susan and Sandy. Surely they had been invited. Then somebody took my arm. It was this handsome young man from United Theatricals, I don't even remember his name if I ever knew it, and he said he was my escort, I was to go with him. We made a triumphal march out of the lobby, and, of course, somewhere under the noise and the glare of the lights and all the madness there was this little voice saying, "Not one word was said in Mom's press conference about *Final Score.*"

But frankly, as we left the lobby, I was pretty damned horrified not by their not mentioning us but by the idea of TV. I mean, what the hell was Mom doing in a nighttime soap?

But I didn't understand then what big business these nighttime soaps were. My mind really was on films. I didn't know that people all over the world watched "Dallas" and "Dynasty," that the stars of these shows even have their voices recognized by the overseas operators when they make long-distance calls. I didn't understand the immediate fame and money that this sort of thing conveyed.

I just thought, OK, if Mom wants to do this, this means we're going to the States and that's terrific, and what kid my age doesn't want to be in the States right now? And then Mom can make United Theatricals distribute *Final Score.* We are really doing just fine.

Like hell we were doing just fine.

Susan was not at dinner. No Sandy, no Susan at all. It was eleven o'clock before I finally found Susan in the bar. I never saw anything like the change in her. It was worse than the change in you when you hit me, because that was really the other side of the same coin.

Susan said, "Do you know what your mother has done? She's killed our picture. United Theatricals dropped us. We've got nothing. It's all over Cannes that the film's unmarketable. Everybody has backed off."

I said that couldn't be true. Mother was all wrapped up in herself, of course, but she would never have gone that far to hurt somebody else. But in my heart I knew Mom could let something like this happen. I had to find out what was going on.

I ran upstairs. I said I had to talk to Mother, and I practically shoved Uncle Daryl out of the way. But it turned out Mother's door was locked. She was in there with Sally Tracy, the American agent, and Trish, and they wouldn't answer when I knocked. They were talking over all the details, it seemed, little things that had to be worked out. Uncle Daryl told me there was really no problem, of course, with "Champagne Flight." The money part was done.

Then I started screaming. What about Susan? What about our film? Susan and Sandy and I had gotten a standing ovation out there.

"Now you calm down, Belinda," he said. "You know perfectly well if I had been there you would never have been in any such film."

"What are you talking about?" I asked him. "Mom made all her money off 'such films' and you know it."

"She wasn't fourteen when she did it," he told me.

"Well, I was playing bit parts in them when I was four," I said.

He yelled back, "That's got nothing to do with it. We are making the deal of the century in there, Belinda, and this is as much for you as for your mother, and I cannot believe that you would come here at this moment and—" You get the drift.

I don't know what I would have said next. I could see already I was against a wall. Uncle Daryl is forever loyal to Mom, and no matter what anyone has ever told him, Mom is his only concern. When she nearly drove me off the cliff on Saint Esprit, Uncle Daryl said to me long-distance, "And why did you let her drive, Belinda? Good Lord, on the ranch you'd have been driving at twelve years old. Don't you know how to drive a car?" That is Uncle Daryl. There is but one cause for Uncle Daryl and that cause is Bonnie, and, of course, Bonnie and Uncle Daryl have made Bonnie and Uncle Daryl very rich.

But to get back to the story, I didn't have a chance to say anything to him, because Marty Moreschi appeared right behind him. And when I saw this big mogul from United Theatricals, I just shut up.

I went into my room and slammed the door.

I am telling you that at this moment I felt alone. I couldn't reach Mom, I didn't really want to, and I had lost Susan. Susan had looked at me with coldness in her eye.

Then comes a knock on the door. Marty Moreschi. Can he come in? I said, "Later," but he begged me, "Please, sweetheart, let me come in."

OK, suit yourself, buster, I was thinking. But if you start that bullshit again, I'm going to scream.

But this was where Marty's intelligence came into play.

The look on his face was very serious when he walked into the room. "I did it, kid," he said. "I killed your film."

I looked at him for a minute, I guess. Then I burst into tears.

"I understand how you feel, kid. I really do. But you gotta believe me. That film would have done nothing in the U.S. And this, what I am doing now with your mother, is for you, too."

Now, as I am telling you this, I know I am not able to get across the way this was done. The sincerity of it and the way that he looked. Like he was going to cry suddenly, too. Like he really felt rotten about what was happening, too.

And I know what you think, Jeremy, that I probably fell for this, that it was just crap. But I think I will believe to my dying day that Marty was the only one there who really understood. I mean, he knew I was disappointed, at least he knew.

So this is how it happened that Marty and I were sitting on the bed and he was telling me in this emotional way that I had to trust in him, that there would be big deals for me in America, too.

Of course, I hated the way he said it. But that is movie talk, deals. You may mean art and beauty, but when you're talking the bottom line, you say deals.

There would be deals for Susan, he was telling me now, yes, Susan, he hadn't forgotten Susan. Susan was sensational. But *Final Score* had to be sacrificed. It wasn't the way to introduce me to the American public, and it wasn't the way to introduce Susan either. United Theatricals could do better making a deal with Susan to do a picture, just on the basis of how *Final Score* did at Cannes, without it ever being seen at home.

"But will you do that deal with Susan?" I asked him. He said he had it very much on his mind. He said, "That Susan, she is the real thing. And you are the real thing."

He said that once we got "Champagne Flight" underway, I'd be in a position to do whatever I wanted. Just wait and see.

"You've got to trust me, Belinda," he said. And there was a kind of frankness to all this. He had his arms around me and he was very close to me, and I guess about halfway through I realized that his physical presence was sort of confusing me. I mean, he was very attractive and I wasn't so sure he knew it or was even attempting to be.

Well, whatever the case, I didn't let him off the hook. I just didn't say things that made it OK.

I went out looking for Susan. And this time she was back in the room and she was really knocked down. She was for leaving the festival that very night. Everything was finished, she said.

"Kiddie-porn, that's what they're calling it. They're saying everything is wrong politically now for our film."

"That's where you fucked up," Sandy said, "using her at her age and all."

But Susan shook her head. She said there was all kinds of stuff being shown in the teen exploitation flicks in the U.S. It was a matter of labels and word getting around and people being deliberately frightened off.

Even the smallest distributors had left her high and dry. Yet everybody said *Final Score* was a wonderful film.

I was crying. I was miserable. But she hadn't really turned against me, that was clear. She said she was going right on with the Brazilian film. "Are you for that, Belinda!" "You better believe it," I said. I told her then what Marty had said.

"Marty Moreschi's television," she said. "But I think I can get the backing I need, even with *Final Score* in the can, when I get to LA."

When I left Susan, I knew I was too angry and disappointed and confused to go back to the suite. I couldn't have gone to sleep.

I went back to the lobby and out to the Croisette. I didn't know where I was going exactly, but just being in the twenty-four hour crowd and the excitement of Cannes was helping me. I could not calm down.

I had money in my purse, I figured I'd get a sandwich or something or just walk around. People were looking at me. Somebody recognized me and came over and took my picture. Yeah, Bonnie's daughter, and suddenly out of the blue there was my dad. My adorable dad.

Now one of the worst parts of the secrecy between us, Jeremy, was that I could never tell you about my dad. His name is George Gallagher, but, as I said, he is known all over the world as G.G., and he is very big in New York, having one of the most exclusive salons. Before that, he had one in Paris, which is where he met my mom.

Now there had been a big fight between my mom and my dad, as I already mentioned, and this was before I went to school in Gstaad. I'd spent a lot of time with G.G.—G.G. had always been wonderful to me. G.G. would fly to a city and wait for hours just to see me for lunch or dinner or take me for a walk in the park. We'd done quite a few advertisements together when I was little—his blond hair and my blond hair, shampoo ads, that kind of thing. We even did one with both of us naked which was in magazines all over the Continent, though in America they only showed us from the shoulders up. Eric Arlington photographed us for that one, the same guy who does the Midnight Mink pictures exclusively and who later did the famous Bonnie-with-dalmatians poster of Mom.

Anyway, when I was nine, G.G. and I went to New York on vacation, promising Mom we'd be back in ten days. We did a lot of work for a line of hair products Dad was marketing, and we also had an absolutely wonderful time. One week stretched into two, then three, and pretty soon we were gone a month. I knew I should have called Mom to ask her if it was OK to stay, I should have known how insecure she could be, but I didn't call because I was afraid she'd say, Come home. Instead I just sent messages back by cable and ran around with G.G., going to musicals, plays, hitting Boston and Washington, D.C., for tourist weekends, that kind of thing.

The upshot was, Mom got terrified she was losing me to G.G. She got hysterical. She finally reached me at the Plaza in New York and told me I was her daughter, G.G. wasn't my legal father, that she had never even intended for me to know G.G., that G.G. was breaking their original agreement, talking about her mother's death and how nothing in life was worth it and how she'd kill herself if I didn't come home.

G.G. and I were terribly upset, but the worse was yet to come. When we got off the plane in Rome, G.G. was hit with all kinds of legal papers. Mom took him to court to force him to stay away from me. I felt horrible for G.G. I felt I should have known Mom would flip like this, and there was G.G., spending a fortune on Roman lawyers and not even understanding what was happening. I could have died. But I couldn't leave Mom for a minute. She was in a state of nervous collapse. Gallo was in the middle of a picture and furious on account of the delay—and so was Uncle Daryl. Blair Sackwell was there, but nothing he said helped. I always blamed myself.

After that, G.G. left Europe. And I had always feared that Mom had something to do with the closing of his Paris salon. But I was just turning ten when these things happened, and the subject couldn't be mentioned without Mom starting to cry.

Now, as the years passed on Saint Esprit, I became a little bitter about G.G. Of course, G.G. and I kept in touch. I knew G.G. had become lovers with Ollie Boon, the Broadway director, and that he was very happy in New York, and sometimes when I went to Paris, I tried to call G.G. from there, which was easier than calling from Saint Esprit. But I felt horribly guilty for what had happened. And I was scared to know how bad for G.G. it had really been. G.G. and I finally drifted apart.

I don't know if you ever saw the shampoo commercials he did or the big magazine pictures we did together that time. If you did, then I think you will agree G.G. is very good-looking, and he will look young forever with his snub nose and little-boy mouth and blond curly hair. No matter what the style his hair is always cut real short with just the curls on top. He looks like the all-American boy actually. He is six feet four. He has the bluest eyes in the world.

Anyway there he was on the Croisette in Cannes. And Ollie Boon was with him—and so was Blair Sackwell of Midnight Mink, who has always been a real good friend of G.G.'s, too.

And G.G. was all dressed up in a black dinner jacket and a boiled shirt and so was Ollie Boon (I will describe Blair in a minute) and they were on their way to a party when we just collided on the Croisette.

Now I had never met Ollie Boon. He came across as very sweet like my dad. He is past seventy, but he is charming and goodlooking, too, with white hair and pretty teeth and silver-rimmed glasses and darkly tanned skin. As for Blair, well, he is what I would call divinely elegant, even though he is not over five feet one and has very little hair and a nose that is enormous and a voice so loud you would swear there is a mike in his chest. His dinner jacket and pants were lavender, his shirt silver, and, of course, he had a mink-lined cloak over his shoulders, which made him look absolutely insanely gorgeous at the moment that he screamed, "Belinda, darling!" and brought us all to a halt.

Anyway they just showered me with kisses, and Dad and I hugged and hugged, and Blair said that I should come with them, they were going to a party on the yacht of a Saudi Arabian and I would love the guy and do come right now. I was crying and Dad was crying. And we just hugged each other over and over till Ollie Boon and Blair decided to make fun of us and they started hugging each other and making false sobs, too.

"Come on to the party with us now!" Dad said.

But I was not about to dump all this misery on my dad. In a big rush I told him only the good things. About Susan and our standing ovation and that Mom was going to do "Champagne Flight."

Dad was so disappointed that he hadn't seen the film. "Daddy, I didn't know you'd be here," I told him.

"Belinda, I would have come to Cannes to see it," he said.

"Well, how do you think I feel that I didn't see it!" Blair yelled. "Your mother told me *she* was going to Cannes! She didn't say anything about this film!" It turned out Ollie had heard of it, heard it was terrific, and he congratulated me very formally while Blair fumed.

But then seriously Blair wanted to know why Mom hadn't told him when he had spoken to her long-distance in Paris, and a funny thing happened. I wanted to answer him, make some excuse, and I opened my mouth but nothing came out.

"Come on to the party with us, Belinda," G.G. said.

Then Blair got excited about Mom doing "Champagne Flight." What if she did Midnight Mink again? Did I think she would do it?

I didn't say anything, but secretly I thought, It's starting already, this "Champagne Flight" madness. Mom had been Blair's first Midnight Mink girl. But in all these years Blair had never never mentioned Mom doing Midnight Mink again.

Anyway Dad started pulling me towards the yacht.

"I'm not dressed up, Dad," I told him.

And he said, "Belinda, with that hair, you are always dressed up. Come on."

The yacht was posh all right. The Saudi women, the very same who wear veils when they get home to Arabia, were all walking around the low-ceiling ballroom in knockout fashions, and the men all had that deep burning look in their eye that meant they could carry you off to a tent. The food was fabulous and so was the champagne. But I felt too disheartened to enjoy it. I was just putting on a good face for Dad.

Blair wouldn't stop talking about Mother doing Midnight Mink again until Ollie Boon told him gently that he was talking shop and to shove it. And then Dad and I danced. The best part.

The band was playing Gershwin, and Dad and I just danced very slow together to some sad song. I almost cried again thinking about what happened and then, while we were dancing, I realized I was looking at this guy on the sidelines of the dance floor, another dark Arab I must have figured until I realized it was no Arab, it was Marty Moreschi of United Theatricals and he was watching me.

As soon as the song came to an end, he cut in on Dad and we were dancing before I could say no.

"What the hell are you doing here?" I asked.

"I could ask you that. Doesn't anybody care about you? Where you go, what you do?"

"Of course not," I said. "I'm fifteen years old. I take care of myself. Besides, the guy I was dancing with was my father, if you want to know."

"No kidding," he said. "You mean that's the famous G.G.? He looks like a high school kid."

"Yeah," I said, "and he's an awfully nice guy."

"What about me, you don't think I'm nice?" he asked me.

"You're OK, but what are you doing here? Booking a prime-time series called 'Sheiks on the Riviera' or what?"

"There's money here. Can't you smell it? But if you want the truth, nobody's taking tickets at the door and I just followed you in."

"Well, you don't have to follow me or worry about me," I said.

But the chemistry was started between us. I was feeling something so strong that it was embarrassing. I mean my face must have been sort of flushed.

"Come back to the hotel with me and have a drink," he said, "I want to talk to you."

"And leave my dad? Forget it." But I knew right at that very second that I was going. And when the number ended, I introduced Marty to Dad and Ollie Boon and Blair, and there was a lot of kissing and hugging again between me and Dad and swearing to see each other in LA.

Dad was pretty smashed. He whispered as we were hugging. "Don't tell Bonnie you saw me, OK?"

"Are things really that bad?" I asked.

"I don't want to tell you all of it, Belinda," he said, "but I'm coming to LA to see you this summer, of that much you can be sure."

Ollie was yawning and saying he wanted to go now, too. And Blair meantime had glommed on to Marty and was pitching the idea that Midnight Mink coats could be used on "Champagne Flight." Marty was doing a diplomatic number of noncommittal enthusiasm, which I was to see a thousand times in Hollywood later on.

I kissed Dad. "In LA," we said.

I was very nervous leaving with Marty. When I think about it now, I realize that the physical attraction you feel to a person can make you feel that something momentous is happening. It can create the illusion that nothing else matters at all.

It was the same thing I felt with you later on. But I was more prepared for it then, and that's why I did the disappearing act over and over in those first few days with you.

This time was the first time, and I didn't know what was happening, except I liked the touch of this man very much. And we did not even speak to each other as we went back to the Carlton and up to Marty's suite.

Now this was part of United Theatricals quarters at Cannes, and it was even more fancy than Mom's rooms. There was a buffet there, all kinds of wine, and the same clutter of flowers everywhere you looked. But except for a couple of waiters, the place was empty. And nobody saw Marty and I go into Marty's room.

Well, something is going to happen, and I do not know why I am letting it happen, I figured. I am as unimpressed with this guy's credentials as a girl could be. I mean, he killed my picture, didn't he? And I don't even know what or who he really is. Yet I was going into his bedroom with him and trying to be very cool to him and saying,

"OK, you wanted to talk?"

Well, what happened is, he started to talk. No big putting the make on me. He just talked. He lit a cigarette, poured me a drink, poured himself a drink, which he never drank by the way, successful producers almost never drink, and then he started asking me all about myself and life in Europe and what I thought about coming back to the States and saying how weird all this was for him, this Cannes number, and how he had grown up in a fifth-floor walk-up in Little Italy in New York. He looked around this fancy room with the damask wallpaper and the velvet couches and chairs, and he said, "I mean, like, where are the rats?"

I had to laugh, but he was fascinating me, really fascinating me, he was like a New York stand-up comedian, making his own connections one after another and talking about how Los Angeles was "Dedicated Surface" and how he felt like a gorilla in his five-hundred-dollar suits and he had to sneak off to get hot dogs after he left the fancy restaurants where the United Theatricals execs ate tiny portions for lunch.

"I mean, a plate of marinated mushrooms and a piece of dead fish at Saint Germain? This is lunch?"

I thought I would die of the giggles, absolutely die. I mean, I was utterly utterly hysterical listening to him.

"You can do anything, can't you?" he says to me. "I mean, I told you that junk out there on the buffet was squids in ink and you ate it. You just ate it. I saw them introducing you to some prince or something on that yacht and you just smiled. What's it like to be you?" he asked. "And that Blair Sackwell guy, all my life I've seen his ads in magazines, and you just put your arm around him and kiss him, just pals. What's it like to live the way you live?"

And when I started telling him a few things, I mean answering his questions, explaining how I'd always envied the school kids I saw in Europe and America, how I wanted to be part of something and all, he really listened. He did. His eyes got this gleam and he asked little questions that showed me he was responding to what I had actually said.

But I was also getting a pretty good fix on Marty during all this. He is not that untypical of LA at all. He does not believe that television is terrible. He lives with gradations of badness, and they are for him his standards. He defends TV by saying it is by the people, for the people, of the people and so was Charles Dickens. But he has never read one page of Charles Dickens. The pinnacle for Marty is what he calls hot. In hot everything comes together—money, talent, art, popularity. Marty has not sold his soul for hot—hot is his religion. He is the saint of hot.

Yet what gives Marty his force is New York street desperation and a sort of gangster style. He speaks in threats and ultimatums and pronouncements almost exclusively when he is not relaxed.

Like: "And I told them, 'Look you motherfuckers, you either give me that eight-o'clock slot or I walk,' and ten minutes after, the phone rings and they say, 'Marty, you've got it,' and I say, 'Damned right.'" It is forever like that.

But it has a naiveté to it. I mean, it is charmingly crude because Marty is so sincere about it. And Marty is a success at being this way.

Yet you only act like this when you are really afraid you are nobody, and that, too, is Marty all the way.

He will never forget where he came from, as he puts it, and it is not like being poor on the Coast, where the waitresses on Sunset Boulevard speak perfect English, where you drive through clean middle-class neighborhoods in San Francisco and they say this is the ghetto. Poor in New York is really poor.

I guess what I am trying to tell you, what I want you to understand, is that this was the beginning of a big affair, this conversation. That I talked for two hours to this guy before we went to bed, that bed wasn't the only thing he wanted. And to tell you the truth, I had been hating myself for the fact that going to bed was just about the only thing in my head.

Anyway it was pretty exciting. It did not and never did have the mystery that we had together, you and me. There wasn't the sense I had with you, that this is a once-in-a-lifetime great romance. It wasn't wonderful like that.

But I liked him, I really liked him. And then after about an hour of all this, something happened that really tipped the scales.

Marty had been to the screening of *Final Score*.

This I never expected. I mean, these people in Hollywood they don't have to see a picture to kill it. They'll buy a book for the movies when nobody has actually read the book.

But Marty had gone to see *Final Score*.

And when we got to talking about it, he said some amazing things. He said Susan had guts and vision. She was damned professional. And my part was dynamite, all right. I stole the picture from Sandy. No experienced actress would have let that happen. But what was wrong with the picture was that I looked more American than anybody in it. I had G.G.'s snub nose and little mouth and all that.

"So this chick goes to a Greek island and she finds a high school cheerleader?" he asked me. It did not work. The Texas dopers, they were terrific, the writing first-rate. But the Greek island and my looks? It was a fake foreign film. It didn't work.

Well, I don't know to this day whether or not this is true. But it surprised me coming from him, this kind of thought. But even more surprising was that he cared enough to think about the picture at all.

Anyway Susan was better off without this being her first release, he repeated. And this is when I jumped in and said, "OK, what are you going to do for her in the States?"

"I can't promise anything earthshaking," he said. "But I'll give it my damnedest." And then he reached out and shook my hand. "Now that's that whether you stay or go," he said. "May I kiss you?"

"Yeah," I said. "It's about time."

The lovemaking was terrific. It was truck-driver bang, but it was great truck-driver bang, probably the best there ever was. And why do I tell you this? Because you have to know to understand everything that happened. You have to know that although this guy never had your skill or your timing, I did eventually love him very much. And, of course, I had only been to bed with boys at that point. I didn't know what timing was.

Meeting you ended that love for Marty. It really did. You were the dream man to me when I met you—you are serious like the people I knew in the old days when Mom was still making a few good films and I would fall asleep at the table listening to arguments about life and art. You are elegant and refined and you are beautiful in your own neglected and easy way. And the timing, there is that too, of course, the mix when we touched each other, those times in bed when you were more purely physical than any man I'd ever been with.

But you see, Jeremy, that's what it took to kill the love for Marty. The love for Marty was very strong.

That night at Cannes was serious stuff.

When he woke up in the morning, he was scared. Probably people were looking for me, he said. He didn't believe me when I told him to relax.

"Get on the thing with Susan," I said to him. "It isn't why I went to bed with you. I would have done that anyway, but Susan is what I'm worried about right now."

Now to tell the truth I didn't think he could influence United Theatricals where Susan was concerned. He was television. So why would anyone in movies listen to him? I mean, sure they killed a movie for his TV deal, but that was easy. How would he ever get a deal for the woman whose picture he killed?

But what I didn't realize was that United Theatricals, like all big studios, was owned by a conglomerate, in this case CompuFax. And CompuFax had appointed two studio heads, Ash Levine and Sidney Templeton, right out of daytime TV in New York. Daytime TV. Let that sink in. I mean, who would have thought people like that could run a movie studio?—but they were running it, and they were Marty's old New York buddies, they had put Marty where he was. Marty had worked for Sidney Templeton as an assistant producer, in New York City, and Ash Levine had grown up with Marty. Marty had actually hired Ash Levine for his first job.

Now let me say here that there is a Hollywood story about Marty and Ash Levine—that one time in New York they got into a real jam fighting some kids on a rooftop and, when the kids ganged up on Ash, it was Marty who grabbed one of them and literally threw him off the roof. The kid died when he hit the pavements, and the gang scattered, and that is the only reason Ash is alive right now—and maybe Marty, too. I don't know whether that is really true. Marty would only smile and wave it away when I asked him. But I heard it in several places in Hollywood, and it was always given as the reason why Marty could have asked anything he wanted of Ash Levine.

By noon Marty and Susan and I were in the United Theatricals suite with these guys, Templeton and Levine. And these three men in their impeccable three-button suits were giving Susan the great rolling LA soft soap about the talent she had as a director and what a miracle it was that even with Mom's backing she had brought in that film.

Now Susan was sitting there with her white cowboy hat on, in her silk shirt with the fringe on the sleeves, and the white jeans, just listening to these guys, and I thought, She knows, surely she knows they screwed her and Marty is the one who did it—I know she knows and she is going to blow. But then something happened, which gave me to know that Susan would make it in Hollywood.

And, by the way, Susan already has.

Susan said not one word about the past but went right into her pitch for the Brazilian film. She told them the whole thing first off in one line, you know, what these guys call "high concept," probably one of the worst terms to ever come down the pike. American teenager saved from Brazilian white slavers by courageous American female reporter. Then she went into detail, calmly handling every objection they raised no matter how dumb it was. I mean, she took this film we had worked out in a frenzy of creativity, and she was willing to spoon-feed it to these fools.

And take it from me, these guys are fools. They really are fools. I mean, they said things to Susan like, How are you going to make Rio interesting? And what made her think she could write the script herself?

But it was when they talked about avoiding the lesbian overtones that I really got scared. But Susan didn't bat an eye at that one. She said *Of Will and Shame* was completely different from *Final Score* in that it was puritanical basically. I'd play an exploited prostitute, not a free spirit. All the sex we'd show would be bad.

I almost fell over dead when Susan said this. But they understood exactly. The moral hook would be there. The American woman reporter would take me away from sex, not go to bed with me. No lesbian overtones at all.

They were nodding, saying, Sounds good, and when could she let them see the script? They wanted to talk when she got to LA.

Finally it was over and she and I went out together and I was scared to death that she was going to ask me if I'd gone to bed with Marty and I didn't know what to do if she did. But she just said: "They're assholes, but I think we sold them. Now I have to go and get *Final Score* shown wherever I can."

Susan left Cannes immediately. But she had really impressed everybody. That night Ash Levine asked me to tell him all about her. Sidney Templeton liked her. And Marty liked her, too.

And she did get *Final Score* shown in art houses and festivals all over Europe. It was penny-ante stuff. But she gave it a life. And months later, when I was on the run, I was able to get a tape cassette of it from some special mail order house because Susan had given it that life.

Anyway after the meeting I went back to the suite, and Mom grabbed me and kissed me and said, Wasn't it terrific that we were going to Hollywood and this time they really wanted us. Just pure Mom. She got me in the bedroom, and she started sobbing, saying how this was like some dream and she still wasn't sure it was happening, and she looked around at all the flowers and she said, "Is all this really for me?"

I didn't say anything to her. And she acted just as if I'd answered her. She just went on talking about how great it all was, as if I was saying, Yes, Mom, the whole time. I was not saying a word. I was watching her, and I thought she really doesn't know what happened with *Final Score*. She doesn't know at all. And something happened inside me. It was as if I lost interest in her in a way. I mean, the rage I'd felt earlier was gone. I thought she had lost her ability to hurt me, that maybe once and for all I had really learned. Mom would never change. I had to change. I had to expect nothing from Mom.

Of course, I was wrong. I hadn't learned. What had happened was that I had Marty, and that felt so good and so warm and so special that I was protected, that's all.

We went right from Cannes to the U.S. although Trish and Jill went back to close up the house on Saint Esprit. Marty had to start shooting with Mom almost immediately to have everything ready for the fall season. I mean, "Champagne Flight" had to be completely rethought and rewritten with Mom.

And Marty wanted Mom to go to the Golden Door in San Diego and take off more pounds right away. Mom was actually perfect, if you want my opinion, but not by the anorexic standards of today.

So anyway Uncle Daryl went on to Beverly Hills to get our house ready—we had owned this house for years but never lived in it—and Marty and I checked Mom into the Golden Door and five minutes later were making love in the limousine on the return drive to LA.

For the next three weeks Marty and I were together constantly, either at my room in the Beverly Wilshire or in his office at United Theatricals or in his penthouse apartment in Beverly Hills. Of course, he couldn't believe nobody was checking on me, that the only "supervision," as he kept calling it, was Uncle Daryl having breakfast with me each morning at the Bev Wilsh and saying, "Here, go buy yourself something pretty at Giorgio's." But that is exactly the way it was. And I did tricks to keep it cool, too, I have to admit that, like leaving messages for Uncle Daryl about hairdresser appointments and things that made it sound like I was checking in when I was not.

And in a way this was the best time for Marty and me.

He took me all through United Theatricals. He had a big corner office there, and I watched for hours while Marty was at work.

In April he had already shot a complete two-hour season opener for "Champagne Flight," and now he was scrapping it and doing a whole new thing with Mother, and he had to get the network to go along. As producer-director of the show, he had a huge hunk of it—it was his life, as you can imagine—and I watched him write the script for the first show while he ate lunch, talked on the phone, and screamed at his secretary all at the same time.

At absolutely any minute Marty would want to drop everything and make out.

If we weren't doing it on the leather couch in his office, we were doing it in the limo or in my room.

Even when Trish arrived, nothing changed. Though, of course, I never provoked anybody's attention. If Marty stayed over, he hid in the bathroom when Trish came in.

But it was strange the effect this freedom had on Marty. At first I thought he was just scared of being caught with me. After a while I saw he did not like it. He did not approve of it. He actually thought Uncle Daryl and Trish were negligent. I got a kick out of that.

"Leave well enough alone, OK?" I said.

And this affair was really love to us, I swear that it was. You understand, I didn't sit there and think, well, this guy really loves me and I love him. It was just happening very intensely all the time. We would talk a lot about my life in Europe. Marty was really stagestruck. He really wanted to hear my stories about meeting Dirk Bogarde or Charlotte Rampling when I was four years old. He wanted me to tell him what skiing felt like. He was very worried about his table manners. He wanted me to watch him when he ate and tell him what he did wrong.

He talked a lot too about his Italian family, how he hated school, how he'd wanted to be a priest when he was little, how he hated his return trips to New York. "Things aren't real out here," he'd say about California, "but God, they are too real back there."

What came clear was that Marty really wanted to analyze things and didn't know how. He'd never taken a college class or talked to a psychiatrist, but he had a terrific drive to figure things out.

Telling the woman in his life his inner feelings, well, that was a real trip for Marty. The dam broke for him in those days. Suddenly talk meant something for him it had never meant before. And I came to realize that although he was very uneducated, he was also very smart.

Susan had been to the University of Texas and film school in LA after that. You are a highly educated man. Mom had even taken college courses. Jill and Trish had done their four years at SMU. But Marty had quit in the junior year of public high school in New York. Every day Marty heard remarks, references to things, even jokes he didn't understand.

I mean, we would watch the old reruns of "Saturday Night Live" on TV and he would grab my arm and say, "Why are you laughing, what does that mean?" "Monty Python's Flying Circus" was totally unintelligible to Marty. Yet Marty could go to see a film like *Last Year at Marienbad* and pay close attention to everything and come out and tell you just what went on.

Well, all that is not important now. Except to say that I know Marty and I loved him, no matter how it might look to anyone else. Things happened between us, things that no one may ever understand.

But as soon as Mom checked out of the Golden Door and we got on the plane for LAX from San Diego, Marty pretty much had to be devoted to her. Mom took over just as she had taken over in Cannes.

And much as Mom loved Trish and Jill and wanted them to stay in the new Beverly Hills house, Marty pretty well pushed them out of the way. It wasn't deliberate on Marty's part. He was simply more forceful. Mom really listened to Marty. Jill and Trish were her sisters. I was her sister. But Marty was the boss.

Marty supervised everything from the start. And he moved into his own rooms in the Beverly Hills house five days after Mom came back.

Now let me describe this house. It is in the flatlands of Beverly Hills, and it is enormous and old with the screening room in the basement, and the billiard room and the forty-foot pool outside and the orange trees all around. Uncle Daryl had bought it in the sixties for Mom. And Mom had never wanted to live in it. And Uncle Daryl had rented it out all these years. He had gotten the tenants to carpet it, furnish it, redo the pool, as part of various rental deals. As a consequence, Mom now owns a three-million-dollar hunk of California real estate with an all-electric kitchen, wall-to-wall carpets, mirrored dressing rooms, automatic sprinklers to water the gardens, and electric eyes to turn on the outside lights at dusk.

But it is not a great house. It does not have the beauty of our apartment in Rome or our villa on Saint Esprit. It does not have the charm of your narrow cluttered Victorian in San Francisco. It is in fact a string of cubicles done in decorator colors with a special faucet in the kitchen that gives you boiling water for coffee night or day.

Yet we enjoyed it. We wallowed in padded luxury. We lay on the patio under the filthy blue sky in smog-ridden Los Angeles and told ourselves it was OK.

And those first few weeks we did have a damn good time.

Marty took Mom to work every morning and stayed with her every minute through the shooting, often rewriting lines for her on the spot. Then he sat with her through dinner, making her eat everything on her plate. Only at eight did Jill and Trish take over, making her get in bed to talk or watch television so she'd be sure to be asleep by nine.

That's when Marty and I were together, locked in his bedroom or mine. We sat in bed together, reading scripts for "Champagne Flight" and talking about them and what was good and bad and all that.

Marty had a guarantee for at least thirteen one-hour episodes, and he was determined to do as much as he could before the big premiere in September. He often entirely rewrote the scripts himself.

By July I was helping him with this. I was reading material out loud to him during lunch or while he was shaving, and sometimes rewriting scenes myself. I advised on little details about the movie star character that Mom was to play. I wrote a whole scene for the third show of the season. I don't know if you ever saw it, but it was OK.

Finally Marty would say, Hey, Belinda, knock this down to two pages, will you? And I would do it, and he would just pass the scene on.

I loved all this. I loved working and learning things and watching how the show was done. Marty had very clear ideas about how things were to look and sometimes he didn't have the vocabulary to explain it. I went through magazines, showed him things, until he said, "Yeah, that's what I want, that's it." And when he finally got the right designer, well, things really took off.

Sometimes we left the house right after Mom had dinner. We went to the studio together and worked till two or three. And nobody seemed to take much notice of what was happening between us, and I was so involved in it I didn't think much about doing any acting of my own.

Understand, only a couple of months had passed since the Cannes festival and we were so busy.

Then one afternoon when I came home, Blair Sackwell was there, dressed in a silver jumpsuit and silver tennis shoes, nothing out of the ordinary for Blair actually, and looking like an organ grinder's monkey, and he jumped up off the couch and asked me why I was turning down everything after my big smash debut at Cannes.

Trish and Jill just looked confused. But Trish and Jill were always looking confused now.

Blair said some producer had even called G.G. in New York, he was so desperate to get in touch with me, and didn't I think I could stop being Greta Garbo? I mean, I was only fifteen.

I told Blair nobody had offered me anything, at least not that I knew of, and he just scoffed at that. He said Dad sent his love to me. Ollie Boon had a musical opening in New York right now or Dad would have been here, too.

But Blair's main concern was getting Mother to do the Midnight Mink thing again. Would I kindly talk to her? She'd be the only one in the entire world, he said, to do Midnight Mink twice.

I went into the other room and called Marty at the studio. Did he know anything about me being asked to do any movie roles? He said, no, he certainly did not, but I knew, didn't I, that my uncle Daryl had said a flat-out no to my being in "Champagne Flight." But I knew that, didn't I? He thought I knew that. Was I unhappy? What was going on? Tell him right now.

"Calm down, Marty," I said, "I was just asking you." Then I called Uncle Daryl, who was back in Dallas at his law office and he told me right off that Mom's agent, Sally Tracy, had orders to keep producers away from me. He had given Sally strict instructions that Bonnie wasn't to be bothered by people calling for me. Bonnie had no time to be worried about this. And he wanted all that *Final Score* business to just wither and blow away.

I called Sally Tracy. "Belinda, sweetheart!"

"You're not my agent, are you?" I asked her. "Are you turning down parts for me?"

"Well, darling, Bonnie doesn't want you pestered by these people. Darling, do you know the kind of offers you're getting? Sweetheart, have you seen these teen exploitation pictures?"

"I would like to know if somebody calls for me. I would like to know if I have an agent. I would like to be told these things."

"Well, if you want, darling, I'll have my secretary let you know everything, of course."

I put down the phone and I had a very funny feeling in me, a cold feeling, but I didn't know what to do. The fact was, I was happy working with Marty. I had not wanted to be anyplace else. But they should have told me what they were doing. I felt mad, but I did not want to be mad.

But that night I told Marty about it. "Did you want me to do bits in the series?" I asked.

"Yeah, at first," he said, "but bear with me, Belinda. Just listen to what

I say. I'm building your Mother right now. And why waste you in the background while that's happening? The smart thing to do is bide our time, see how the show does, and then build an episode around you." I could see the wheels turning as he was talking. "Got a couple of ideas already. But we're talking deep into the season, say, November, and I think I know just what I want to do."

As I said, it was confusing, because I was really happy working on the production end of it and, besides, I didn't know about being in the series. I mean, I wanted to make movies. I felt funny about the whole thing.

Next day on the way to the studio I asked Mom if she minded if I did something in the series. We were in the studio limousine and Marty sat next to her with his arm around her as always and I was across from them on the little jump seat beside the TV that nobody ever turned on.

"Of course not, honey," she said in her sleepy morning voice. She was staring out the window at the tacky pastel stucco apartment houses of Los Angeles as if it was not one of the most ugly, boring sights in the world. "Marty, let Belinda be in the show, OK?" But then she said, "You know, honey, you could go to school for a while now. You always wanted to. You could meet boys your own age. You could go to Hollywood High now if you wanted to. Doesn't everybody want to go to that school?"

"I don't know, Mom, I think I'm past all that. When September comes, I'm not sure what to do. Maybe I want to be in movies, Mom, you know what I mean?"

But she had drifted off just looking out the window. It seemed to me none of it mattered to her. She would look sleepy like this till she stepped on the set of "Champagne Flight."

"You do what you want, honey," she said a moment later like the last message had just gotten through. "You be in 'Champagne Flight' if you want to, that's just fine."

I said, Thanks, Mom, and Marty leaned forward and put his hand on my leg as he kissed me. And maybe I never would have thought a thing about it except that, as he drew back, I got a glimpse of Mom's face.

Mom looked at me in a very steady way. It seemed all the drug haze cleared for a second. And when I smiled, she did not smile. She was just staring at me like she was going to say something, and then slowly she turned and looked at Marty, who did not even notice because he was looking at me. Then she looked out the window again.

Not too cool, I was thinking, like don't get everybody on your case, Belinda, for being lovers with Marty. Leave well enough alone. But Mom probably hadn't even noticed—she'd been thinking of something else most likely when she was staring. I mean, Mom noticed almost nothing where I was concerned. Right?

Well, let's just say it was what I thought at the time.

Susan hit town a couple of days later. She came roaring into the Beverly Hills driveway in a white Cadillac convertible, in which she'd driven all the way from Texas because she had to think, she said, and talk to herself out loud while she was driving, about the Brazilian film.

I was very confused about *Of Will and Shame.* I didn't want to leave Marty, but no sooner had I gotten in the car with Susan to drive down to Musso and Frank's than I got fired up again. I'd have to leave Marty for this picture, no question. If I didn't, what the hell was I? An actress or nothing. I didn't tell Susan about Marty naturally. And I didn't tell her that Uncle Daryl might try to stop me either. After all, Mom would let me go, I was sure.

All through lunch at noisy Musso and Frank's, Susan talked about this picture. It was going to be terrific. They'd go for me all right. It was the ingenue part and I was Bonnie's daughter. Her big problem was Sandy. They would want a bankable actress for Sandy's role.

"So will you give in on that?"

"I'll have to. Sandy will ride it out, and I'll make Sandy when I have the power to make Sandy. She knows."

That night Marty listened to Susan's pitch very patiently. He set her right up for a meeting at United Theatricals. And when the bedroom door closed, he said, "You gonna be faithful to me in Brazil?"

"Yes," I said. "And you're going to be faithful to me back here in Starletville, aren't you?"

"Do you ever have any doubts about that, honey?" He looked very sincere at that moment and very loving and I felt that he was really on my side and had always been.

But they turned down Susan at United Theatricals. It was too risky, this picture. And Susan was too young to produce and direct herself. But they had an offer for Susan, a contract to direct three movies for television and they had the scripts right there.

Susan was crushed as I'd expected. When I went over to the Beverly Hills Hotel to see her, she was reading the scripts in the bungalow, drinking ice tea and smoking and making notes.

"Strictly formula," she said, "but I'm taking it. I mean Spielberg did his TV movies for Universal. OK. I'll go this route. They've agreed to Sandy in one of them. So that's settled. But there's nothing here for you, Belinda, nothing decent, nothing like what I was planning at all."

"I'll wait for Brazil, Susan," I said. And she looked at me for a minute, like she was trying to figure something out or thinking of saying something. But then she just said, OK.

Later on the phone Marty told her she did the smart thing. "Everybody's watching her," he said to me. "When she's got a real commercial idea, they'll listen. She just needs to be careful, you know. Don't pitch anything till it's dynamite and those three films are done."

I was kind of speechless through it all but watching everything down to the last detail. Susan would make it all right with these people. And I had my time now with Marty and didn't have to tell Susan about that and the Brazilian film might yet be made.

"Don't forget about it, Belinda," Susan said to me before she left. "We'll do that thing." I told her she could count on me whenever it happened. If she wanted to go tearing off without any money, well, I had enough cash in traveler's checks to carry myself down there. She just smiled at that.

"But there's something else," she said, "that I want to tell you before I go. You watch yourself with Marty."

I just stared at her. I thought, I will die if she knows I am sleeping with the man who killed our picture. How can I ever explain?

"You had them screaming at Cannes," she said, "and now look what you're doing, you're making this guy's coffee for him and emptying his ashtrays and riding to and from work with him and hanging around to hand him a Kleenex to wipe his nose."

"Susan, I've only been here two months. And you don't understand—"

"Don't understand what?" she asked. "That you're hooked on this guy and you've been balling him since Cannes? I'm not putting you down for that, Belinda. I know this guy. He's straight with you, though he's scared shitless your mother or those two sorority sisters in there are going to catch on. But I'm just telling you, Belinda, to remember who you are! OK, you're just a kid and you've got time, but what do you want to do with your life, Belinda? You want to be somebody or somebody's girl?"

Then she roared off in her Cadillac digging the wheels into the gravel and barely missing the electric gateposts, and I was just standing there thinking, well, she knew all the time.

And I will tell you something. The next time anybody asked me what I wanted to do with my life, what I wanted to become, well, it was almost a year later and it was you, in San Francisco, when we were having that first dinner together at the Palace Hotel. You looked at me the way Susan had, and you asked me what I wanted for myself.

Anyway Susan was gone, Brazil was gone. And I was having a ball with Marty. And having a ball just being in America, too. And very frankly I was having a ball not having to take care of Mom anymore.

On Saint Esprit Jill and Trish had been wonderful, but there had been a million little decisions they could not make. It had taken the three of us to do the hiring, firing, managing of the household. One of us was always with Mom.

Now Marty was taking over. And as he relieved us of more and more responsibilities, one thing was coming clear. Marty was actually better for Mother than we had been. It wasn't that we meant to support Mom in her drinking. We just couldn't control it. Marty could. He had "Champagne Flight" as the reason for every rule he laid down.

And he made Mom beautiful and kept her on the wagon. And the more he babied her and controlled her, the more she blossomed. Mom was definitely what Mom had thought she always wanted to be.

Of course, a lot of this was California self-improvement crap, you know, the mania for exercise and health food and vegetarianism and meditating and God knows what other garbage that is supposed to make you live forever and feel like a good person while you're doing all that. But it turned Mom into an amazon queen who could handle all the pressure of a TV series, the interviews, the appearances, which was far worse than a movie, if you ask me.

By the week of the premiere Marty was dominating Mom's life. He was sitting by her while she bathed, and reading her to sleep. He was picking her nail polish for her and standing around to make sure the hairdresser didn't pull her hair. He dressed her in the morning. He undressed her in the evening. And Trish and Jill and I were of no use anymore at all.

I loved it, no matter how disloyal or guilty I felt. And I was very relieved that the school year had started without anybody even noticing. I was having a wonderful time.

I don't know if you saw the premiere of "Champagne Flight," so I will tell you what Marty did. This was a two-hour special, of course. And in it Bonnie Sinclair, émigré actress, comes home to Miami to take over the family airline after her dad's mysterious death. A young devastatingly handsome cousin tries to blackmail her about the old erotic European films she has made. She appears to take the bait; she goes to bed with him; lets him think he's got her; then after they have made out, she tells him to get dressed and come into the other room. There's a surprise for him. Well, it's a big party and the whole family is there. All the important people in international society, too.

Then Bonnie introduces the young hunk cousin to everyone, just as he wants, and then a screen comes down and the lights go out and everybody settles back to watch scenes from Bonnie's old erotic films. The cousin is dumbstruck. I mean, Bonnie shows the very scenes the kid thought he was blackmailing her with. And Bonnie just smiles and tells him it has been a real wonderful evening and he should come see her anytime. He leaves, feeling like a fool.

Mom played all this very sympathetically. She is sad and wounded and philosophical as always, and when the young guy takes off in shame and embarrassment, she looks at the screen where they are showing the love scenes from her old pictures, and we see tears in Mom's eyes. That was the heart of the plot. The show ends with her in control of the airline, getting rid of the bad guys, including this cousin, and trying to find out who killed her father, of course.

OK, TV, I know. But it was perfect for Mom, and, of course, the budget was outrageous, the sets sumptuous, the costumes great. Even the sound track was a cut above the usual thing.

The big hit "Miami Vice" had had a powerful influence on Marty. He was horribly jealous of it. And he had sworn to make "Champagne Flight" stylish, more sophisticated than the other nighttime soaps. He also wanted a cop-show pace. The old "Kojak" was his model in that regard. And to tell the truth, Marty did what he set out to do. "Champagne Flight" had a cop-show feel to it and a rock-video look.

Actually there is an old cinema term for what Marty did, though I don't think Marty would know it. The term is *film noir.* "Champagne Flight" is probably the only *film noir* prime-time soap.

Marty waited like a maniac for the ratings. And within hours we knew everybody in America had tuned in to see Mother. "Champagne Flight" was a hit. It even made the news all over the country: Bonnie and Bonnie's old films.

After that, the reporters were after us constantly. The tabloids hounded us. And suddenly Marty could not be out of Mom's sight. Mom insisted he sleep in the room next to hers, moving Jill out of it, and she kept waking up, in spite of the sleeping pills, and getting confused about where she was. At three o'clock in the morning he'd be feeding her a little breakfast and telling her how good things were going and how they were all going to mop up.

Even getting Mom a full-time nurse didn't help the situation. Marty had to be there. The masseuse, the hairdresser, the lady's maid who took care of Mom's room and nothing else—they all took directions from Marty. Then one night some reporter from a European paper got over the electric fence and started photographing Mom with a flashbulb through the glass doors of her room. She woke up screaming. And Uncle Daryl had to bring her a gun from Texas, though everybody told her, You are crazy, you can not shoot that gun. But she had to have it in the table by her bed.

Of course, they were still shooting all through these early weeks, revis-

ing future episodes as reactions came in to what was already done. And
Mom was OK when she was working. She was OK acting or even reading
a script. It was any other time that Mom got crazy. Mom is one woman
who has never minded working late.

Maybe three weeks into the season I realized I had not been alone
with Marty since the night of the premiere. Then I woke up early in the
morning and I saw Marty standing at the foot of my bed.

"Lock the door," I whispered. I knew damn good and well Mom might
get up and start wandering around in a drugged-out state.

"I have," he told me. But he just stood there in his robe and pajamas
and did not get in the bed. I think I knew even in the dark that something
was terribly wrong with him. Then he sat down beside me, and he turned
on the lamp. The look on his face was awful. He looked embarrassed and
cut up and crazy.

I said: "It's Mom, isn't it? You went to bed with Mom."

His mouth was all out of shape. He couldn't seem to talk. He said in
this very strained voice that when a woman like that wanted you to go to
bed, you just couldn't say no.

"What the hell are you talking about?" I asked.

"Honey, I can't turn her down. Nobody in my position ever turned her
down. Don't you see?"

I just stared at him. I couldn't say anything. My voice was absolutely
gone. And right before my eyes he started to choke up, to cry.

"Belinda, I don't just love you, I need you!" he said to me in this
choked whisper. And he reached out to put his arms around me. He
started to kiss me.

I couldn't do this. I didn't have to think about it. I knew it. And I had
gotten out of the bed and away from him before I even made up my mind
what to do. But he came after me, kissing me, and then I was kissing him,
and this chemical thing had taken over and, of course, the love, the real
strong love, that probably didn't even need the chemical thing anymore.

I did a lot of arguing and saying no, but we were already back in bed
together, and we did it, and I cried myself to sleep.

Of course, he wasn't there when I woke up. He was with Mom again.
And nobody even noticed me pack up and leave the house.

I went down to the Strip, to the Château Marmont, and I got a bungalow there, and I made a couple of calls. I told Trish to cover the bills, I
had to be there right now, and please don't ask my why.

"I know why," Trish said. "I've seen this coming. Just be careful, Belinda, will you?" She called the Château and took care of the credit. And
that evening she left the message that she had squared it with Mom, and
Mom had signed a nice check for my bank account.

And there I was, sitting on the side of the bed in the Château Marmont and everything was over with Marty, and Susan was in Europe shooting a TV movie, and my mom, of course, did not even care apparently that I had moved out of the house.

Well, I went wild in the next few weeks. I roamed the Strip at night, talking to the bikers and the crazies and the runaways. I called back all the Beverly Hills kids who had called me when I first got here. I went to their houses, their parties, even drove with them to Tijuana one afternoon. I hung around Hollywood High sometimes when school let out. I made the sights of the city, the studio tours and even Disneyland and Knott's Berry Farm. I just ran around. Anything not to be alone, not to be by the phone. But I made sure I checked in with Trish at least once every afternoon. And the report was Mom was just fine. Just fine.

Mom probably didn't even notice my absence. And I was being driven out of my mind trying not to think about Marty, telling myself that it had to be over with Marty, that I had to decide about my future right now.

Now when I look back on it, I wonder what would have happened if I had called G.G. in New York. Mom might not have cared at all then if I had gone to G.G. Mom did not need me the way she had years and years ago. But the truth was, I could not bear the thought of losing Marty. I was in pain, just terrible pain.

And so I just ran around town. And of course some rather irritating things were happening, too. I was finding out I was a legal child.

For example, I'd known how to drive since I was twelve, but I couldn't get a license in California until I was sixteen. I couldn't go into places that served alcohol even if all I wanted was a Coke and the right to sit at a table and listen to the comedian who was doing the show. And, of course, I couldn't really confide in the kids I met. I wasn't about to tell them about my affair with Marty.

And I wasn't like these kids. I didn't get their mixture of being grownup and childish, real hard little LA kids on the one hand and babies on the other. I could never figure it out.

Who had my friends been in the past? Trish, Jill, Blair Sackwell, my dad. That's who. Not kids.

Things stayed superficial, if not downright artificial. Nothing really worked.

Well, of course, Marty showed up at the Château Marmont.

If he hadn't, I think my faith in life would have been crushed. I mean, not even one visit to see what had happened to me? And I don't know what I wanted then except maybe to see him and tell him that I would not sleep with him while he was sleeping with Mom. But I tell you, I was not prepared for the scene that Marty threw.

This was Marty's first big Italian opera number on me.

It was the middle of the night when he came to the door of the bungalow. And he was in some state when he came in.

First off, he wanted to know what kind of family did I have? Didn't they care that I was living down here on Sunset in a place like the Château with absolutely no supervision? That word again. I laughed.

"Marty, don't give me this shit," I said. "Don't wake me up to tell me my family doesn't give a fucking damn what I do. I've known that since I was two years old."

What about school? he demanded. Didn't anybody in the whole family care that I wasn't going to school?

"You dare suggest such a thing and I will kill you, Marty," I said. "Now get out of my room and leave me alone."

Then he got very embarrassed and upset, and he was almost crying when he said that Bonnie was asking for me. Bonnie didn't understand why I was never there.

"You tell me that," I said. I was crying.

And without another word spoken we were in each other's arms. I said no, of course, I said no over and over, but I didn't mean it and Marty knew it. And we were in bed together and it was just as it had always been. I suppose in some bittersweet way it was better, and then Marty was lying there holding me and trying to tell me what a hell this had all been for him.

"You know, sweetheart, it makes me think of the old saying, 'Be careful what you ask for, 'cause you might get it.' Well, I did. I asked for Bonnie, I asked for a number-one show. And I've got both of them, sweetheart, and I've never been so miserable in my entire life."

I didn't answer him. I was crying into the pillow. I was thinking mad things, like what if we got married, ran away to Tijuana and did it and then came back and told them, what would happen then? But I knew such a thing would never never happen, and I felt this rage inside me, just burning up all the words I might have said.

Marty went on talking. Marty went on saying things, until I realized what was going on. He was telling me he needed me, that he couldn't do it without me, that he couldn't get through the season the way things were. "You've got to come back, Belinda, you've got to. You've got to think of this thing in a different light."

"Are you putting me on? You think I'd live there in the house with you and Mother and her not knowing that you were sleeping with me, too?"

"Belinda, a woman like your mother doesn't want to know things," he said. "Honest to God, she does not. She wants to be taken care of, lied to. She wants to be used and use everybody else at the same time. Belinda, I don't really think you know your mother, not the way I do. Belinda, don't do this to me, I'm begging you."

"Don't do this to you!"

If you think you ever saw me throw a fit, you should have seen me then. I got up out of the bed and I started hitting him and screaming at him and telling him to get out of there and go back to her. "Do this to you!" I kept screaming. And then he grabbed me and he shook me and he sounded like a madman.

"Belinda," he said, "goddamn it, I'm only human, that's all I am."

"What the hell's that supposed to mean?" I asked him.

He sat on the side of the bed with his elbows on his knees. He said that the pressure was building and building and if he blew, Mom would blow, too.

"Look, honey, we're all in this together, don't you understand? She's banking it hand over fist, and that's your money, and we're riding this wave. Just please don't turn against me now, honey, please."

I just shook my head. Banking it hand over fist. What could I say?

"Come back to the house," he said, taking my hand. "Stick this out with me, Belinda. I am telling you, honey, the time I have with you is all I've really got left."

"You really think I would do that, Marty?" I asked.

And then he just broke down. He cried and cried, and I was crying and then it was time, he had to go back. If he wasn't there when she opened her eyes at five A.M. all hell would break loose.

He got dressed, and then he said, "I know what you think of me. I know what I think of myself. But Jesus, I don't know what to do. All I know is, if you don't come back, I can't fake this much longer, I'm telling you the truth."

"So it's my job to hold it all together, is that what you're saying? Marty, how many times do you think I have held it together for her? How many times do you think I've just swallowed it all and did what had to be done to make it OK for Mom?"

"But it's all of us, honey, it's you and me and her. Don't you see? Listen, those Texas chicks, they're leaving soon, I know they are. And there'll be nobody in that house but all those creatures, the nurse and the masseuse and that crazy hairdresser—and her and me. I tell you, I'm going to take that gun out of her dresser drawer and blow my brains out or something. I'm going out of my head."

I didn't have any more to say. I expected him to go then. He was already late. And I was thinking about calling G.G., asking if it would be all right with Ollie Boon if I stayed with him and G.G., but I knew I didn't have the courage to do that just yet.

Then I realized Marty wasn't leaving. He was just standing by the door.

"Honey, she and I . . . we're getting married," he said.

"What?"

"Big outdoor wedding by the pool at the house. The publicity's going out today."

I did not say one word.

Then Marty made a speech. In a very quiet manner unlike himself he made a speech.

"I love you, Belinda," he said. "I love you like I never loved anybody before now. Maybe you are the pretty girl I never had in high school. Maybe you are the fancy rich kid I could never touch in New York. I only know I love you, and I have never been with anybody outside my own family back in New York that I loved and trusted so much. But life's played a filthy trick on both of us, Belinda. Because the lady has announced that she wants to get married. For the first time in her whole fucking life she wants to get married. And what the lady wants, the lady gets."

Then the door closed behind him. He was gone.

I think I was still lying there alone and in a state of shock, when Trish came. If she knew Marty had been there, she never said so to me. She told me the wedding was supposed to be Saturday, that Mom wanted to do it right away and Uncle Daryl had already left Dallas and would be at the house sometime this afternoon.

"I think you should go back to Europe," she said. "I think you should go to school."

"I don't want to go to Europe," I said. "And I don't want to go to school."

She nodded and then she said I had to come and get my dress for the wedding and it was best Uncle Daryl didn't know I'd been at the Château Marmont.

Well, I got through the wedding and the week before it. I smiled at everybody. I did my part. Uncle Daryl was much too busy to even ask what I'd been doing, and so was everybody else. But when I did find myself talking to people now and then in the living room or at the reception itself, I said I would be going to UCLA soon, that I thought I could pass the examinations and start early. It ought to be fun.

The wedding itself was the big ticket in Beverly Hills. The tabloids offered a flat $30,000 for any picture taken inside the grounds. And the police had a hell of a time keeping people from blocking the streets. Mom was clearly in love with Marty. I had not seen her this way since the days of Leonardo Gallo. She was not just leaning on Marty or clinging to him, she was focused on Marty completely. And they both looked wonderful that afternoon.

But I will tell you something, the wedding itself was a put-up job. The minister was an overgrown flower child from the sixties, you know, one of those long-haired fifty-year-olds who lives in Big Sur or someplace and got his minister credentials in the mail, and the whole ceremony was sort of dingy with shared wine cups and wreaths of flowers on everybody's heads and all that. I mean, in the woods it might have been OK. But with this crowd, whose vocabulary goes like "We're talking major package" and "What about the bottom line" roaming around in the smog and the orange trees, it was a scream. And Uncle Daryl took me aside right after and told me not to worry about the money part of it, Marty had signed an airtight premarital agreement, and this thing was, well, strictly for Mother to be happy, it wasn't scarcely legal at all. "She's just lost her head over this New York Italian guy, that's the truth of it," he told me. "But don't you worry. He'll be good to her, I'll see to that."

I was dying. When I went inside to be alone for a little while, I found Trish and Jill in my bedroom, just sort of hiding from everybody, and Trish told me that she and Jill were going back to Dallas at the end of the week.

"She doesn't have any more use for us," Jill told me. "We're tripping on our own feet around here."

"Time we did something on our own, too," Trish said. She went on to explain that Daryl was willing to help them get started with a boutique in Dallas. In fact, he was giving them plenty. And Mom was going to endorse the store, too.

I felt crushed that they were leaving. Saint Esprit had been over for a long time now, but when they left, it would all be really gone.

I remembered what Marty had said about being alone in this house without them. But I wasn't staying here. I couldn't. It was just out of the question. Only I couldn't think about it right now with the music pouring in from the patio and people moving through all the rooms, like zombies, making no sound on the wall-to-wall carpet. I had to get away somehow.

"Belinda, come with us to Dallas," Trish said.

"Bonnie would never let her go," Jill said.

"Oh, yes she would. She's happy with her new husband. Honey, come stay in Dallas awhile with us."

I knew I couldn't do that. What would I do fifteen hundred miles from the Coast? Go to shopping malls and video arcades or take some nice class in English poets at SMU?

The whole afternoon had been a nightmare, and yet the worst was yet to come.

After Trish and Jill went back out into the crowd, I decided to change and get out.

Then Marty came and closed the door. The thing was over, he told me, everybody was leaving. And he just fell into my arms.

"Hold me, Belinda, hold me, honey," he said. And for a moment that was just what I did.

"It's your wedding night, Marty," I said. "I can't stand this, I just can't stand it." But all the time I was feeling his arms around me and his chest against me and I was holding him as tight as he was holding me.

"Honey, please, just give me this moment," he said. And then it started again, him kissing me—and I just left in my long dress and all, and caught a ride with one of the limos going out the gate.

On the way to the Château I asked this nice handsome man next to me, one of Marty's staff, to run into a liquor store and get a bottle of Scotch for me. When I got back to the bungalow, I drank the whole thing.

I slept for twelve hours straight and was sick for twenty-four after that. The phone woke me up on Wednesday. It was Trish, saying Uncle Daryl kept asking where I was.

"Just get down here till he leaves," she told me. "Then you can go back up there on the hill."

I got to the house around four o'clock. And nobody was around. Nobody except Mother, who was just telling her exercise coach and masseuse that they could go for the rest of the day. She had been swimming and she looked all tan and natural with her hair loose. She had on a simple white dress. Suddenly these people were gone, and we were alone in the room.

It was so strange. I don't think Mom and I had been alone like this in ages and ages. She looked amazingly clear-eyed and rested, and her hair was very pretty because it had not been done.

"Hi, darlin'. Where you been?" she asked. Drugged-out voice, OK, very level, but not slurred.

"I don't know, no place," I said. I shrugged. I think I started to move away when I realized that she was really staring at me. Now for Mom this is not a usual thing. Mom usually has her head down. She is usually looking away when you talk to her. She is not ever very direct. But she was looking right at me, and then she said to me in a very steady voice;

"Darlin', he was too old for you."

For a second the words were just there and I didn't know what they meant. Then I really heard them and I realized we were still looking at each other, and then she did something with her eyes that I have seen her do to other people a thousand times. She looked me up and down slowly, and then she said in the same flat drugged voice: "You're a big girl, aren't you? But you're not that big."

I was numb. Something was happening between me and Mom in these few seconds that had never happened before. I went down the hall and into my room. I closed the door and I stood there against it, and my heart was pounding so loud I could hear it in my ears. She knew, she knew all along, I was thinking, she knew.

But what did she really know? Had she thought it was a crush, a little teenage thing, that Marty had never reciprocated? Or did she really understand what had gone down?

I was shaking when I came in for dinner. But she never once looked me in the eye. She was really drugged by that time, murmuring and looking at her plate and saying she was sleepy, and obviously she could not follow the conversation at the table at all.

We all kissed Daryl good-bye and then I told them I was going, too.

I saw the darkest look of bitterness on Marty's face. But he just smiled and he said: "OK, honey, good-bye."

I should have known it was too easy. Two hours later, when I was crying in my room at the Château, he arrived. He was crying and I was crying, real Marty-style Italian opera, and we did not even talk about it. We just made love. I felt like something was broken in me by that little encounter with Mom. It killed me. It killed me inside.

That wasn't the woman I had looked at in the Carlton and thought, Ah, well, she doesn't know what she's doing. She doesn't know at all.

Something else had come out and, to tell you the truth, I had seen it come out at other moments, much less important moments over the years.

After a long time I told Marty about it, what she had said, how she had looked.

"No, honey, she doesn't know," he said. "She may think it was kissy-face and crushes, but she doesn't know. She wouldn't want you to come back to the house if she did."

"Does she want that, Marty?"

He nodded. He was getting up to get dressed. He had told Mom's nurse that he was going out to an all-night drugstore. It was a cinch Mom would wake up sooner or later and ask for him.

"She keeps asking, 'Where's Belinda?' She just doesn't seem to under-stand why you're not at her right hand."

I didn't argue with him, but I had a deep dark suspicion that Mom did know, and still she wanted me to come back, because she thought sure she'd taken Marty away from me. I mean, she was Bonnie, wasn't she? And what had she said, "You're a big girl, but you're not that big"? Yeah, she thought she could have both of us, all right; she'd just rearranged things a little, hadn't she? Better to suit herself. Another one of those instances of "Everything's OK now, Belinda, cause I feel fine."

And as of this day I think I read the situation right.

After Marty left, I got really drunk. I'd taken several bottles with me back to the Château from the house, and I drank every drop over the next few days, just lying alone in that room, and crying over Marty and wondering how I could make this misery end.

I thought of Susan. I thought of G.G. But then I thought of Marty. And I didn't have the strength to go to G.G. And the thought of telling anyone the whole story, the thought of ever confiding to anyone what had happened was an agony. I didn't want G.G. to ever ask.

I felt terrible and alone and I felt like a fool. I felt like Mom was right, I should never have fallen for Marty, Marty belonged to Mom. But half the time it was the booze thinking and I just drifted in and out of sleep like I'd seen Mom do on Saint Esprit for years and years.

The only thing that broke the nightmare of those few days was a call from Blair Sackwell one afternoon in which he told me furiously how Mom had dumped him and Marty Moreschi had cut him off.

"I was willing to put three inches of white mink stole on every one of those Bonnie dolls! My label! And the son of a bitch told me to back off. They didn't invite me to the wedding, you realize that!"

"Oh, get off my case with it, Blair, goddamn it!" I shouted.

"Oooh, like mother like daughter!" he said.

I hung up. And then I was so sorry. I sat up and started calling around trying to find him. I called the Bev Wilsh and the Beverly Hills. No Blair. And Blair was my friend, my really true friend.

But an hour later I got a delivery, two dozen white roses in a vase with a note saying, "Sorry, darling, please forgive me, love you always, Blair."

When Jill called the next day to say she and Trish were leaving, I had a hell of a time even talking I was so drunk. But I slept it off, got through being sick hungover, and took a cab to the house for the last dinner with them.

Mom was dopey but all right. Our eyes never met. She said how she was going to miss Trish and Jill, but they'd be coming out for visits all the time. Most of the talk was about the Bonnie dolls and the Saint Esprit perfume campaign and the big fight with Blair Sackwell because Marty didn't think she should do anything but "Champagne Flight" products right now.

I tried to put in a word for Blair. I mean, Midnight Mink was Midnight Mink, for God's sakes, and Blair was our old friend.

Marty just dismissed it. Product identification was everything, blah,

blah, blah. This boutique of Trish and Jill's was going to be sensational, with a life-size mannequin of Mom in the window. But why not Beverly Hills? he kept asking. The whole world wanted to shop on Rodeo Drive, and he could start them there, didn't they realize? Dallas, who goes to Dallas?

I watched them, the looks on their faces. They couldn't wait to get out. And they had been buddies with Blair, too, after all. No, they wanted to go home all right.

"Look, we're Dallas girls," Trish said. Then she and Jill and Mom looked at each other, and then they all did some school cheer or something, and they laughed, but then Mom looked real sad.

Time for much hugging and kissing, time for all the farewells. And then Mom lost it. She really lost it. She was crying in that terrible way she does before she really tries to hurt herself or something. Awful sound. And Marty had to take her in the bedroom before Trish and Jill left. As soon as I kissed them, I went in there.

"You stay with her, while I take them to the airport, I just can't let them go like this," Marty said.

Mom was sitting on the bed crying. And the nurse was there in a white uniform and she was giving Mom a shot.

Now this thing of the shot scared me. Mom had always taken drugs, all kinds of drugs. But why an injection? I didn't like to see the needle going into Mom's arm.

"What are you doing?" I asked the woman, and she made a little patronizing sign to me like, Don't upset your mother. And Mom said in a real drowsy voice:

"Honey, it's just for the pain. But it's not really pain." She put her hands on her hips. "It's just like a burn there, you know, where they do it."

"Do what?" I asked.

"Doesn't your mom look beautiful?" the nurse asked.

"What did they do, Mom?" I asked her. But then I could see it for myself. Mom's body had been changed. Her hips and thighs were much much thinner. They were taking the fat off her, that's what they were doing. And then she explained to me it was done in the doctor's office and they called it liposuction and it wasn't dangerous at all.

I was horrified. I thought the world thought my mom was beautiful just the way she was! Nobody had to re-sculpt Mom! These people are crazy, Marty is crazy to let this happen. She cannot eat a full meal, she is doped constantly, and now they are draining her body away from her. This is mad.

But the nurse was gone, and here we were alone, me and Mom. I felt

this awful terror that something would happen, that she would say something like she did before. I didn't want to be in the room with her. I
didn't even want to be near her.

But she was too far gone to say anything. The shot was really taking
effect.

She looked sad and terrible suddenly, just sitting there in her nightgown, like she was lost. And I kept looking at her, and the strangest
thought came to me. I know every inch of this woman's body. I slept with
her a thousand nights when I was a little girl. She'd even leave Leonardo
Gallo to sneak into my bed and we would snuggle in the dark. I know
what she feels like all over, what it's like to curl up in her arms. I know
what her hair is like and what she smells like, and I know where they
took the fat off her. I'd know the places blindfolded by just feeling with
my hands.

"Mom, maybe Trish and Jill would stay if you asked them to," I said
suddenly. "Mom, they'd come back."

"I don't think so, Belinda," she said softly. "You can't really buy people forever. You can only buy them for a while."

"Mom, they love you," I said.

"And you have to go your way, too, don't you, darlin', you're never
here anymore at all."

She was staring forward and her words were coming so slow it was
frightening.

"Mom, tell me," I said. "Is this what you want?"

She turned towards the pillows, but she was groping, her hands just
stroking the sheets, like she was looking for something invisible.

I pushed her back gently and moved the sheets down for her, and
helped her to get under them and then I tucked her in.

"Give me your glasses," I said.

She didn't move. She was staring at the ceiling. I took the glasses and
put them on the bedside table right by her private phone.

"Where's Marty!" she said suddenly. She tried to sit up. She stared at
me, trying to see me, though she couldn't without her glasses on.

"He's gone to the airport. He'll be back right away."

"You won't leave till he gets back. You'll stay here with me?"

"Course. Just lie down."

She sank back, just like somebody had let the air out of her. She
reached out her hand for me to take it. She closed her eyes. I thought she
was gone, but then she reached out again, feeling for her glasses and
then for the phone.

"They're there, Mom," I said.

It was still California daylight outside. I sat with her until she was deep asleep. She felt cold. I looked around this bedroom, this long white chamber with all the satin and mirrors and white carpet, and her dressing gown and slippers made of the same things as the bedspread and the curtains, and it all seemed horrible to me, horrible. Nothing in it personal. But the worst part was her.

"Mom, are you happy?" I whispered. "Do you have what you want?"

On Saint Esprit she had dozed off day in and day out on the terrace with her books and her beer and her television. Four years she had been like that—or was it longer? Was that really so bad?

She hadn't heard me. She was sound asleep, and her hand felt icy now.

I went into my room and closed the door to the hall and I laid on the bed and looked out the patio doors and the whole house seemed quiet and still. I don't think I had ever been in it when it was so empty. The staff had disappeared into the back cottages. There was no gardener prowling outside. All Beverly Hills seemed empty. You would never have known the filth of LA was beyond these orange trees, these walls.

I was crying. And mad thoughts were running through my head. I had to do something! I had to leave Marty, no buts about it. I had to go to either Susan or G.G., no matter how hard it was. But the pain in me was the worst I'd ever felt.

I knew I was just a kid, a kid gets over these things, this isn't even supposed to be love, love is illegal for a kid, I knew all that, oh, yes. Until you're twenty-one nothing's supposed to be real. But God, this was awful. This was so awful I couldn't move or think or even want to get drunk.

And, of course, I knew Marty was coming. I knew I'd heard the car in the drive. I knew I'd heard a door open somewhere. I kept looking out over the patio, through the orange trees, and I saw the California twilight coming, and the only sound was me crying. Just that.

It got darker and darker, and then I realized that somebody was standing on the other side of the patio doors. It was Marty, and he was opening the doors.

I felt so defeated. I knew it was wrong to sit up and to put my arms around him and kiss him, but I did not care. Just for this moment I did not care.

And I also knew that if I did it now with him in this bed, not ten steps from Mother, that I would do it again and again. There'd be no going to G.G. There would be just what Marty wanted, the three of us under this roof.

But I kissed him and I let him kiss me. I let him start taking off my clothes.

"Oh, honey, don't leave me, please don't leave me," he said. "Don't leave her, honey, don't leave either of us. She means it when she says she wants you to come home."

"Don't talk," I said.

"We're all she's got now, honey, you and me. You realize that?"

"Don't talk about her anymore, please, Marty," I said.

And then we weren't talking, we were just together, and I thought no, I will never never be able to give this up.

Then I heard the loudest noise I have ever heard in my life.

I mean, it was positively deafening. And for a second I didn't have the faintest idea what it was. Well, it was a .38-caliber pistol fired in a room about fifteen by twenty feet. And Marty shoved me off the bed onto the floor and screamed:

"Bonnie, honey, don't!"

And then the gun went off what seemed like twenty times. Everything was breaking. The glass bottles on the dresser behind me, the mirror, the electric clock by the bed.

But actually it was only five shots, and Marty had her by the hand and had gotten the gun from her. She was screaming. He was bleeding. She struggled and broke the glass in the patio door.

"Get out, Belinda, go!" he shouted. "Get out!"

She was screaming, "Give it back to me, let me finish it, there's one more bullet, damn it, let me use it on myself."

I couldn't move. Then the nurse came rushing in and the cook was there, and some other people I did not even know. And Marty said:

"Get Belinda out of here, now! Get her away, go!"

Well, I went as far as the pool and I listened while they called the ambulance. I could see Marty was OK and that Mother was sitting on the side of the bed. Then the nurse came running towards me:

"Marty says to go to the Château and stay there till he calls."

She had the keys to Marty's Ferrari and she drove me, telling me to crouch down and stay down until we were out of Beverly Hills.

Well, that night was hell.

The nurse did call to tell me Marty was OK, he was in intensive care, but he'd be out by noon probably, and Mom was sedated, not to worry at all. But then the reporters started. They started on the phones first and then they were coming to the door itself.

I was frantic. I opened the door once and six flashbulbs went off. Then I heard somebody ordering them off the premises. But somebody was knocking on the windows only minutes after that. I looked up and saw this guy who works for the *National Enquirer,* a guy I brushed off constantly on the Strip. He was holding up a matchbook with a phone number inside it. He was always giving these to me, saying, Couldn't a kid like you use the spending money, that kind of thing. I could use the matches, I always said. I pulled down the shade.

Finally about eleven a.m. I heard Uncle Daryl's voice through the door. I let him in and two flunkies from United Theatricals came with him and they started to pack up everything I owned.

He said he had already checked me out, to come with him. There were reporters all over the drive, but we managed to get into the limousine and on our way to the house.

"I don't know what got into you, Belinda," he said, taking off his glasses and staring at me. "That you could hurt your mother so much. It's all the fault of that Susan Jeremiah, if you want my opinion, putting you in that X-rated movie and all."

I was too disgusted to say anything to him. I hated him.

"You listen to me, Belinda," he went on. "You say nothing to nobody about what happened. Bonnie mistook her husband for a prowler. You were not even there, you understand? Now Marty has been shot in the arm and in the shoulder, but he will be out Thursday and he will handle the reporters, you are not to utter one word to a living soul."

Then he took out a handful of papers and informed me he had closed my bank account and I had no more money and no more credit either at places like the Château Marmont.

When we reached the house, he held my arm so tight that he hurt me as we got out of the car.

"You're not going to hurt Bonnie anymore, Belinda," he told me. "No, sir, you will not. You are going to a school in Switzerland where you cannot hurt anybody anymore. You will stay there until I tell you that you can come home."

I didn't answer him. I just watched in silence while he picked up the phone to call Trish in Dallas and tell her that everything was OK.

"No, Belinda wasn't there, absolutely not," he kept saying.

I didn't say a word.

I turned around and I went into the den and I sat down and I wrapped my arms around my waist. I felt sick. And it seemed I was thinking about everything, I mean absolutely everything, that had ever happened between me and Mom. I was thinking of the time she left me in Rome and that time on Saint Esprit when she floored the gas pedal and headed for the edge of the cliff. I was thinking about the time she had a horrible fight with Gallo and he was trying to pour the whiskey down her throat to make her pass out. I had tried to stop him and he had turned and kicked me across the room. His foot caught me right in the stomach and the wind had been knocked out of me. I had been lying on the floor thinking, If I can't breathe, I can't be alive.

Well, it was how I felt now. I could not breathe. The wind was gone out of me. And if I couldn't breathe, I couldn't be alive. I could hear Uncle Daryl talking to somebody about a school called Saint Margaret's and about going to London on the five-o'clock polar flight.

This cannot happen, I was thinking, he can not make me go there, not without seeing Marty, not without talking to Susan, not without G.G. This cannot go down.

I stared at my purse for a moment before I opened it, and then all of a sudden I was feeling around in it, making sure I had my passport and my traveler's checks. I knew I had three or four thousand in checks at least. Maybe a lot more than that. I had been hoarding them for years after all. I'd saved them after every shopping spree in Europe, I'd bought them in Beverly Hills from the money Uncle Daryl gave me to spend.

I was just zipping up my bag when Mom came in.

She had just come from the hospital and she had on her coat. She looked at me and her eyes had the usual glazed drug look to them. And she spoke in the flat drugged voice:

"Belinda, your Uncle Daryl will take you to the airport. He will sit with you until it's time for the Pam Am flight."

I stood up and I looked at her, and through all the haze of drugs I saw the hardness of her face, and the look in her eyes seemed absolute hatred as she looked back. I mean, when someone you have loved looks at you with hate like this, it is like seeing a stranger in that person's body, an impersonator inside that person's skin.

So maybe I was talking to the stranger when I spoke up, because I don't know how I ever could have spoken this way to Mom.

"I'm not going to any school in Switzerland," I said. "I'm going to where I want."

"The hell you are," she said in the same fuzzy voice. "You're going where I tell you. You're no kin of mine anymore. And you won't live under any roof under which I live."

I couldn't answer for a minute. I couldn't do anything. I just swallowed and tried not to cry. I kept staring at her face and thinking, This is Mom talking. No, it can not be Mom.

"Look, I'm going," I said finally. "I'm leaving now. But I am going where I want to go. I'm going to meet Susan Jeremiah and I'll make a picture with her."

"You go near Susan Jeremiah," she said real slowly, "and I'll fix it so she never works for any studio in this town. I mean, nobody will touch her. Nobody will bank one nickel on her or on you." She looked just like a zombie, the way she stood there, the way her voice was coming in that slow almost slurred way. "No, believe me, you are not going to Susan

Jeremiah with any stories of what went on here. And don't you get any ideas about G.G. either. I ran G.G. out of Paris and he remembers it. And I can run G.G. right out of New York. You will not go to these people and tell them stories about Marty and me. You will go to this school in Switzerland just like I told you. That is exactly what you will do."

I could feel my mouth moving but nothing was coming out. Then I heard myself say to her:

"Mom, how can you do this! How can you do it to me!" Dear God, how many times had she said those words, to everybody—How can you do this to me!—and now I was saying them. Oh, God, this was awful.

She went on looking at me like a zombie, and her voice came really low like before:

"How can I do this to you?" she said. "Is that what you ask me, Belinda? Well, I'll tell you how. When I had you, I thought you were the one thing in all this world that was mine, my own baby, come out of my body. I thought, when I had you, you were the one person who would always be loyal to me. My own mother was dead before I was seven, nothing but a drunk, that's all she was. Big fancy house in Highland Park. Might as well have a beer joint far as she was concerned. Never gave a damn about me and Daryl, didn't care enough about us just to keep herself alive. But I loved her. Oh, how I loved her. If she had lived, I'd have given her everything, I'd have scrubbed floors for her, given her every penny I ever made, done anything to make her happy, just to keep her wanting to be alive. Just the same way I gave you everything, Belinda, everything you ever asked for, things you never even had to ask for. What did you ever want that you didn't get?"

Of course, Mom often talked about her mother, as I've mentioned. But this was taking a new turn.

"Well, you don't need your mother, do you?" she asked me. "You're real grown-up, aren't you? And blood and kin mean nothing to you. Well, I'll tell you what you are. You're a tramp, Belinda. That's what we would have called you in Highland Park. That's what we would have called you in Denton, Texas. You're a cheap little tramp. And it's got nothing to do with spreading your legs for every man you set your sights on, Belinda. A tramp is a woman who doesn't give a damn about her own friends or her own kin. That's you, Belinda. And you're getting on that plane now with Daryl or I will turn you over to the California Youth Authority, so help me God. I will pick up that phone and I will tell them that you cannot be controlled and they will take you into custody and they will put you in a jail, Belinda, and they will make you do what they say."

It was like Gallo's foot hitting me in the stomach again. I was not breathing, and yet I was feeling this rage inside me, like something filling me up right to the roots of my hair.

"You do that, lady," I said to her, "and I'll put your husband in San Quentin for statutory rape on account of what happened. I'll tell the juvenile authorities everything that went on between him and me. It was unlawful intercourse with a minor, in case you're interested, and if you think they drove Roman Polanski out of this town for it, you wait and see what happens to Marty. It'll bomb your fucking 'Champagne Flight' right out of the sky!"

I was dying inside. Dying. And yet I was saying these things to her. And she kept staring in the same cloudy way and then she said:

"You get out of my house, Belinda. You will never ever again live under the same roof with me."

"You got it!" I said to her.

But Uncle Daryl had come past her and he grabbed me by the arm. "Give me your passport, Belinda," he said. He was pulling me out of the room.

"The hell I will," I said to him. He shoved me into the back of the limousine. And I held my purse in both hands. "I mean it, don't you try to take it," I said to him. He didn't answer. But he didn't let go of my arm.

I looked back at the house as we were pulling out. I didn't know whether Mom was watching or not. Then I realized she would tell Marty the things I'd said to her. And Marty would never understand what had happened, that I was trying to fight her and Uncle Daryl and that I'd never hurt anybody like that.

I was crying again when we reached the airport. Uncle Daryl jerked me out onto the pavement. People were staring. Everything I owned in the world was being taken out of the trunk. I never saw so many suitcases. They must have packed up everything at the house as well as the Château.

"Go inside," he said to me. And I went with him, but I was still holding my purse tight. He is not going to do this, I was thinking. I am not getting on any plane for London with him. No, sir, as he always says.

People were staring at me because I was crying. And my arm where he was holding it had gone numb. The man who had driven the limo was checking my luggage. He said they wanted to see my passport. I looked at Uncle Daryl and I knew it was now or never.

"Let me go," I said. He dug his fingers in, and when I felt the pain through the numbness, something snapped in my head. I turned and with my arms tight around my purse I shoved my knee right into his groin with all I had.

I ran through the airport. I ran like I haven't run since I was a kid. I ran through one set of doors after another and down escalators, and back up them and finally out onto the pavement and right up to an open cab.

"Hurry please, mister," I was screaming, frantic. "I've got to get to the Greyhound Station in Los Angeles. My mom's leaving from there. If I miss her, I'll never see my mom again."

"Go ahead, take her," said this poor guy who'd been getting into the cab.

Just before we made the final turn, I saw Uncle Daryl come running out there at the cab stand, but he had not seen me. At the bus station I switched cabs. I did it again at the Union train station, and at the bus station one more time.

And then I went right back to LAX and took the next plane to New York.

It had been six years since I had seen New York City, and I arrived there tired, dirty, and very scared. I had on white jeans and a white pullover sweater, which had been OK for California in early November, but it was already freezing in New York.

I knew Dad's salon in Paris had been called simply G.G., but it had never been listed in any book. Well, the New York phone directory didn't have it either. As for going ahead to some big hotel, I didn't dare.

I bought some overnight things and a bag at the airport, and went to the Algonquin and checked in with the cash I had on hand so I didn't have to give them my right name. Then I tried to get some sleep.

But I kept waking up thinking somebody was breaking into the room. I was terrified that Uncle Daryl had traced me and the police would come. And, of course, I had no intention of ever carrying out my threat to testify against Marty. That had been pure bullshit.

Which is why I had to be damned careful about G.G. when I found him, too.

Well, it was five o'clock New York time when I finally gave up on sleep altogether. And I went out to look for Dad.

Everybody in New York had heard of G.G. naturally, but the doorman and cab drivers I talked to did not know the location of his famous salon. One said he worked strictly free-lance. Others that it was a private house.

Finally I took a cab to the Parker Meridien, just to cash some traveler's checks, went back to the Algonquin, and set out to find Ollie Boon.

Now Blair Sackwell had said Ollie's show had just opened, so I asked the hotel concierge what he knew. Yes, Ollie Boon's new Broadway opera, *Dolly Rose,* was playing on Forty-seventh Street, just around the corner from the hotel.

Forty-seventh Street was jammed with limos and taxis when I got there. Lots of people were giving up and going the last two blocks to the theaters on foot. I ran right up to the ticket taker at the door and said I had to see Ollie Boon, I was his niece from Cannes, and it was a pure emergency, they had to get word to him right away. I took one of the giveaway programs, tore a page out of it, and wrote: "It's Belinda. Top Secret. Have to find G.G. Top Secret. Help."

An usher came back almost immediately to take me down through the little theater and out the side door to backstage. Ollie was talking on the phone in a cramped little dressing room right under the stairs. He played some sort of master of ceremonies figure in the musical, so he was already dressed in top hat and tailcoat and completely made up.

He said: "G.G.'s at home, precious. Here, talk to him on the phone."

"Daddy, I have to see you," I blurted out at once. "It has to be top secret."

"I'll come to get you, Belinda. I'm so excited. Go down to Seventh Avenue in fifteen minutes. Watch for Ollie's car."

The limousine was there when I got there, and in a second I was safe with Daddy and holding on to him in the backseat. It took us fifteen minutes of nosing through New York traffic to get to Ollie's SoHo loft. And during that time I gave Dad the headlines, more or less, Mom's threat to ruin him if I came to him, her story that she'd driven him out of Paris and how I'd gotten myself into an awful mess.

"I'd like to see her do it again," he said. He was really fuming when we got to the apartment. And to see Dad mad is strange. He is so gentle and so kind, it is almost impossible to realize he is angry. He sounds like a child playing angry in a school play. "She did it in Paris, all right, because she owned the salon. She gave it to me, you know, but she never put it in my name. Well, G.G.'s in New York is my apartment. And my appointment book is the only thing that counts."

Then I knew it was true that she'd driven him out of Paris, and my heart sank. But Daddy was so wonderful, so excited to see me. We were hugging and kissing the way we had at Cannes. He looked perfectly wonderful to me, all six foot four of him, and maybe there is that special thing between us, too, because I see in Daddy's blue eyes and blond hair the genes that are in me.

But to tell you the honest truth, almost anybody would love G.G. G.G. is so sweet and so kind.

Ollie's place was out of a magazine, an old warehouse with a million pipes and ceiling braces all carefully gilded, and miles of hardwood floor

as shiny as glass. Rooms were arrangements of antiques on various carpets under spotlights. Bits and pieces of wall existed just to hold paintings or mirrors or both. We sat down on two brocade couches facing each
other near the fireplace.

"Now, tell me what really happened?" Dad said.

Now, as I mentioned before, I had not confided in anyone all these
months. I have by nature never been a confider. Mom's drinking, the pill
taking, the suicide attempts—these were my life and they were secrets to
be kept. But now I started talking and things just poured out.

And it was agony to tell it, to range back and forth over Cannes and
Beverly Hills and try to put it all together, but once I started I could not
stop.

And I began to see things in a different perspective, even with all the
halts and backtracking and crying and disclaimers. I mean, a big ugly
pattern started to come clear. But I cannot tell you enough how much
this hurt me to tell it, how against my nature it was to drag everything
out.

I mean, I was lying to hotel clerks and doctors and reporters before I
could remember. And, of course, we had all of us always lied to Mom.
"You go in there and tell her she looks pretty, that she's just fine"—that's
what Uncle Daryl would say before her press conferences in Dallas,
when she was shaking and she looked awful and the makeup could hardly
hide the hangover bruises under her eyes. "You tell your mom not to
worry, you don't want to go off to school anymore, you're going to stay
with her on Saint Esprit from now on." "Don't you talk about the acci-
dent, don't you talk about the drinking, don't you talk about the reporters, don't you talk about the movie, everything's going to be just fine, just
fine, just fine, just fine."

Lies, that's all it ever was. And in my head? Fragments, puzzle pieces
that were never fitted together. And this telling it even to my darling dad
was like the final betrayal, the final break from Mom.

What I am writing to you now is the second real telling, and it is not
any easier as I sit here thousands of miles away from you alone in this
empty room.

Anyway G.G. didn't ask many questions. He just listened, and when I
was finished, he said:

"I hate this guy, Marty, absolutely hate him."

"No, Dad, really you don't understand," I told him. And I pleaded
with him to believe me when I said that Marty loved me, that Marty had
never meant to let things go the way they did.

"I thought he was an Arab hijacker when I met him," G.G. said. "That
he was going to hijack that yacht at Cannes. I hate him. But OK, you say

he loves you. I can believe somebody like him could love you, but not because of him, because of you."

"But, Daddy, this is the thing. I can't do what I threatened. I'd never tell the police things about Marty. And I think Mom knows that. What I have to do is lie low."

"Maybe she knows it and maybe she doesn't. And maybe if she calls your bluff there are other things you can do. You've got a hell of a story here, Belinda. And she knows that. She always knows what's really going on."

I was puzzled by his words, hell of a story. And I was also scared of what Mom could do. Maybe she couldn't bust Daddy's business in New York City, but what about the question of custody? I was a minor here as well as in California. Could she charge Daddy with harboring a runaway or something like that?

Ollie got home at midnight, wearing only a pair of jeans and a pullover sweater, a real after-theater switch. Dad cooked us all some supper and we ate, sitting on cushions at a round table near the fire. And then G.G. insisted we tell Ollie the whole thing.

"I can't go through this," I told him. But he said he'd been with Ollie for five years, he loved Ollie, and Ollie would never tell a living soul.

Now Ollie is sweet and gentle like my dad. He is a tall wiry man. He used to be a dancer but, now in his seventies, he cannot dance anymore. But he is still graceful and very elegant with bushy gray hair, and he has never had the plastic surgeons work on him, so his face is full of patience and wisdom, too. At least it seemed that way to me. OK. Tell him, I finally said.

Dad started using some of my same language. Only thing was he started at the beginning, the way I have in this written account. He started with Susan coming to the island and then us going to Cannes.

"Some story isn't it?" G.G. said to Ollie. Ollie was sitting there with his glasses pushed up into his hair. He was looking at me really kindly. For a long while he didn't say anything, then he spoke in this very dramatic and kind of theatrical voice.

"So they cut your movie," he said, "and they cut your career and then they cut your love affair."

I didn't answer him. As I've already explained, it was so against my grain to talk about Mom that I was raw all over. Ollie's sympathy was confusing me. I don't think I will ever be much of a confider. I don't have enough faith in talking about things. The tension just builds.

"And then they wanted to cut you out completely," he continued. "The Swiss school was the final exit. And you refused to be written out of the script."

"Yeah, I guess that is what happened," I finally said.

"Sounds like Mother suddenly found out you were competition and Mother could not handle that at all."

"You can say that again," G.G. said. "Mother cannot stand competition."

I started arguing: "But it wasn't planned like that, Mr. Boon, really it wasn't. She loves Marty and that is all she can understand."

Then Ollie made a sort of speech. "You're being kind to her, darling," he said, "and please call me Ollie. And let me tell you something about your mother, though I've never had the pleasure. I know this kind of person. I've known them all my life. They get the sympathy of others with what passes for insecurity. But what really motivates them is a vanity so immense most of us can not conceive of it. Insecurity is simply a disguise. I don't think from what you've told me that men mean much to your mother. You, her friends Jill and Trish, a circle of dazzling acquaintances, I suspect this is what your mother always wanted. And she only found it necessary to seduce and marry Mr. Moreschi when she realized he was in love with you."

This rang true. Horribly true. Yet my loyalty to Mother made it hurt very deep. But I remembered that time in the limo when Marty had kissed me. I remembered the look on Mom's face. Had that been the death knell, that little kiss?

But I argued. I told Ollie that Marty had taken care of Mom the way no other man had ever done. I could still remember Mom's boyfriends in the early days, demanding supper, asking where their clothes were, wanting money from Mom for booze and cigarettes. Mom would cook for two hours for Leonardo Gallo, and then he'd get up and throw the plate at the wall. Marty was the first man who took care of Mom.

"Of course," Ollie said, "and the babying would have been enough for her until you became a threat."

I was agreeing, but it was too ugly and too complicated still.

Then Dad said it really didn't matter what made Bonnie tick, I was here now, and I could live in New York, near to him and Ollie and that he would handle whatever Bonnie tried to do.

Ollie didn't answer, and then he said in a real small voice:

"That's all very nice except for one factor, G.G. United Theatricals is my producer. They financed *Dolly Rose.*"

I saw the two of them exchange looks.

Then Ollie made another speech like this:

"Look, darling. I understand your position. When I was fifteen, I was waiting tables in Greenwich Village and playing bit parts on the stage every time I had the chance. You're a big girl, and I'm not going to try to sell you any bill of goods about going home and letting yourself be packed off to school. But I won't lie to you either. United Theatricals is the biggest break I've had in the last twenty years of putting it together with Scotch tape on Broadway. Not only have they financed this musical, which doesn't make them a whole hell of a lot of money by the way, they're talking about financing the picture. And I would direct that picture, an opportunity I badly want.

"Of course, they wouldn't shut down *Dolly Rose.* They couldn't, but the picture? And the picture after that? One word from your mother and her studio executive husband and their interest in Ollie Boon would dry up overnight. No cross words, no explanation, just, 'Thanks for calling, Ollie, we'll get back to you.' And I'd never get a direct line to Ash Levine or Sidney Templeton again."

And then something came up which seemed very small at that moment, but it was to mean a great deal later on. Ollie went on with his speech. *Dolly Rose* was a lavish antebellum New Orleans piece, real Broadway opera, but the property he dearly wanted to make into a movie musical was *Crimson Mardi Gras,* a book written by Cynthia Walker, the southern writer, and guess who owned the rights? United Theatricals, which had made the straight movie in the fifties with Alex Clementine, and the mini-series a few years back. *Dolly Rose* was good Broadway, but it would never travel. The movie was iffy. But *Crimson Mardi Gras?* It would run forever. And the movie would be a smash.

OK, I understood Ollie's position, I said. And I really did.

I had grown up on location in Europe. I knew what it meant to lose the backing. I could remember a thousand arguments, phone calls, struggles to get the food trucks and the wardrobe trucks and the cameras just to stay put. I started to get up from the table.

But Ollie said: "Sit down, darling, I'm not finished. I've been frank with you about my position. Now what about yours?"

"I'm leaving, Ollie, I'm going out on my own. I'll wait tables in Greenwich Village. I can do that, too, you know. And besides, I've got some money of my own."

"Do you really want to be running from the police or from your family's private detectives? Do you want that kind of thing right now?"

"Of course, she doesn't, Ollie!" Dad said suddenly, and for the first time I realized how angry he was with Ollie. He was glaring at Ollie.

But Ollie didn't seem to take this very seriously. He just took Dad's hand, like to calm him down. Then he said to me:

"Then what you've got to do, dearest, is bluff these people. Bluff them hard. Tell them you want your freedom here and now and you will use the story and, believe you me, it is a terrific story, and you can use it not only with the authorities but with the press. But you cannot be connected with me when you do it, dearest, because I might very well lose my backers, no matter who wins your little war."

This time when I stood up, he didn't tell me to sit down. And this is what I told him and Dad both:

"You keep calling it my story. You keep saying what a hell of a story it is. And you tell me to use my story. But it's not mine, you see, that's the awful part. It's Mom's story and Susan's story and Marty's story, and I can't hurt all those people. I mean, you can be sure that the press would bring *Final Score* into it, and then this studio, this great big power we're all cringing in front of, would cut Susan loose as well. I don't own the rights to my own story! The rights belong to the grownups involved."

Ollie was very quiet, and then he said that I was a strange case. What did he mean, I asked him.

"You don't really like having power over others, do you?"

"No, I guess not," I said. "I guess all my life I watched people play with power—Mom, Gallo, then Marty and other people I hardly remember now. I think power makes people act badly. I guess I like it when nobody much has power over anyone else."

"But situations like that don't exist, darling," he said. "And you are dealing with people who have used their power over you shamefully. They aborted your career, darling. And they did it at a pivotal moment, and for what—a prime time soap? If you do go out on your own, you had better toughen up. You had better be ready to use their tools against them right from the start."

Well, by that time I was too exhausted to say anymore. This night for me had been a terrible ordeal. Confiding in them left me feeling awful. I was drained.

But I think G.G. could see it. He went to get a jacket for me and to get his own coat.

Then he and Ollie had a sort of conference, but I could hear them because there were no rooms in this place. Ollie reminded G.G. what the last legal battle with Mom had cost him. He'd left Europe flat broke. G.G. said, So what, he'd been mobbed by offers to endorse products as soon as he hit New York.

"This woman could get the studio lawyers on retainer to handle this! Your costs could run you ten thousand a month."

"This is my daughter, Ollie!" Dad was saying. "And she's the only kid I will ever have."

Then Ollie really got mad. He told Dad that for the last five years he had done everything he could to make Dad happy. And Dad started to laugh.

In other words a real fight was coming on. Dad started sticking up for himself in his own mild-mannered way.

"Ollie, I can't even work anymore without your getting mad about it. If I'm not at the theater before the show and after the show, you throw a fit."

But understand, with these two men even this was highly civilized and mellow, like they did not know how to scream at each other, and never had.

"Look," Ollie said, "I want to help your daughter. She's a precious darling. But what do you expect me to do?"

Nice words, I thought to myself, and he means them, but he's smart, and he's right.

And they had forgotten all about Mom's brother, Uncle Daryl, who was himself a lawyer, for Crissakes.

Next thing I heard was Dad on the phone making a call. Then he came and he put a coat over my shoulders, a real fancy mink-lined trench coat that Blair Sackwell had given him, and he told me the plan.

"Now listen, Belinda. I've got a house on Fire Island," he told me. "And it's winter now and everybody is gone. But the house is insulated, it's got a big fireplace and a big freezer, and we can lay in everything that you need. It's going to be lonely over there. It's going to be spooky. But you can hide there till we find out just what Bonnie's doing, whether she has called the police, or what."

Ollie was very upset. He gave me a big kiss good-bye. And Dad and I left in Ollie's limousine immediately and we spent the rest of the night getting stuff together for me to take. We went to the all-night markets and bought the food we needed and then Dad wrote down all my measurements and promised to bring me clothes. Finally at about three A.M. we were cruising through the dismal dark Astoria section of Queens out of New York City towards the town where you take the ferry to Fire Island, and I remembered something and sat up with a start.

"What day is this, Daddy? Is it November 7?"

"Gee, Belinda, it's your birthday," he said.

"Yeah, but what good does it do me, Daddy? I'm still only sixteen."

We nearly froze on the early-morning ferry. And Fire Island was spooky with not a soul anywhere, except the workmen who had come over with us, and the wind howling off the Atlantic as we followed the boardwalks to Dad's house.

But once we were inside everything was all right. There was lots of stuff still in the freezer, all the wall heaters were working, there was a lot of wood for a fire. Even the television was OK. And there were books in the shelves and lots of records and tapes. There was also a copy of

Crimson Mardi Gras right by the fireplace, and it was full of Ollie Boon's notes.

I enjoyed that first day there. I really slept OK. And at evening I went out on the end of the pier. And I watched the moon over the black ocean and I felt kind of safe and glad to be alone. I mean, maybe it was like being on Saint Esprit or something.

But I tell you, this joy did not last.

I was entering one of the strangest periods of my life. G.G. brought back lots of supplies the following day, he brought some nice warm winter clothes for me, pants, sweaters, coats, that kind of thing. But he also brought the news that there was absolutely nothing in the papers about my disappearance, and he had not been contacted. Nobody was saying anything about my running away.

I got that cold feeling again when I heard it. I mean, I was happy they weren't looking for me, right? But it should have bothered me, shouldn't it, that they were not worried enough to look?

Ah, I was so mixed up. And then with all my doubts and fears about it, with the pain of missing Marty and wondering what Mom had told him, with the pain of wanting so bad to see Susan, with all those pains I settled into the Fire Island house for three months.

When the bay froze in December, Dad couldn't get there. And at times even the phones sometimes went out.

And in this strange world of ice-cold glass and falling snow and burning fires and loud tape-recorded music, I was more alone than I had ever been in my life.

In fact, I realized I had never been alone really. Even at the Château Marmont there was the hotel around me, the world of Sunset Boulevard down there any time of night or day. And before that, the world had been a womb or something with Mom and Trish and Jill and all that.

Well, no more. I could walk round this house talking out loud to myself for hours. I could stand on my head. I could scream. Of course, I read a lot, went through novels, histories, biographies, everything Dad had brought. I read the libretto of every Broadway play ever written, since they were all in the bookshelves, and I listened to so much Romberg, Rodgers and Hammerstein, and Stephen Sondheim that I could have answered the sixty-four-thousand-dollar quiz on Broadway musicals after that.

I read *Crimson Mardi Gras* twice. Then I read all your mother's other books that Ollie had, and—guess what?—some of your books were there, too. Lots of adults have your books, as I'm sure you realize, but I never realized it until I saw all of them at Ollie's place.

I drank a lot, too, on Fire Island. But I was careful. I didn't want Dad to call when I was drunk or, worse yet, to see me that way. So I kept it kind of level, but at the same time I put it away. I drank the bar Dad had on Fire Island. One week it was Scotch and the next few days gin and then rum after that. I had a real party on Fire Island, and, you know, the funny thing was, it made me think a lot of Mom. I understood Mom better when I was drinking and listening to music and dancing the way I had seen Mom so often do.

The earliest memory I ever had of Mom is that way—Mom in the flat in Rome dancing barefoot to a record of a Dixieland band playing "Midnight in Moscow" with a glass in her hand.

But to return to the story, I went through a kind of hell on Fire Island. I mean, when you are that alone, it is like solitary confinement and things happen in your head.

Meantime Dad reported that the columns said Mom and Marty were lovebirds, and no one, absolutely no one, had called him from the West Coast. "You think they'd at least ask if I had seen you," he told me. But then he shut up when he saw the look on my face. "Come on, we don't want them looking," I reminded him.

Then Dad got a furious call from Blair Sackwell. All Blair wanted to do, he said, was send me a Christmas present, for God's sakes, and he could not get through to Bonnie and that pig Moreschi would not give him the name of my school. "I mean, what is all this!" Blair raged. "Every year I send Belinda a little something, a fur hat, fur-lined gloves, that kind of thing. Are these people crazy? All they'll tell me is she isn't coming home for Christmas, and they won't give me an address."

"I think they are," Daddy told him, "because I can't get the name of the school myself."

By Christmas I was in a terrible way.

New York was under a terrible snowstorm, the bay had frozen, as I said, the phones were down. I hadn't heard from Dad in five days.

On Christmas Eve I made a big fire and lay there on the white bearskin rug beside it thinking of all the Christmases in Europe, midnight mass in Paris, the bells ringing in the village at the foot of the cliffs on Saint Esprit. I am telling you, this was my darkest hour. I didn't know what my life was supposed to mean.

But at eight o'clock who should come banging on the door but Dad— with his arms full of presents. He had hired a jeep to bring him onto the island at the far end, and he had walked all the way on the wooden boardwalk through the freezing wind to the house.

Till my dying day I will love Dad for getting to Fire Island that night. He looked so wonderful to me. He had on a white ski cap and his face was ruddy from the cold wind and he smelled so good when he took me in his arms.

We cooked a big Christmas feast together, with the ham he had brought and all the wonderful delicacies, and afterwards we listened to Christmas carols until midnight. And I guess it was one of the best Christmases I ever spent.

But I could tell something was going wrong for Dad with Ollie. Because when I asked if Ollie would miss him, Dad's face got dark and he said, To hell with Ollie. He was sick of spending every holiday backstage through a matinee and an evening performance just so he and Ollie could drink a glass of wine in his dressing room. He said his whole life had revolved around Ollie before my arrival and maybe I'd done him a big favor and I should know.

But this was bravado. Dad was miserable. He and Ollie were breaking apart.

By February I couldn't stay on Fire Island a day longer. There was still no word from Mom or Marty about me. When Dad had made a call around New Year's, they'd given him the Swiss school spiel.

I told Dad I had to start living again. I had to move into New York, get a place in the Village, get a job, something like that.

Of course, Dad helped me. He picked the place for me, paid the huge bribe you had to cough up just to get a New York apartment, and then he got me some furniture and plenty of clothes. And I was free all right, I could walk through the streets and all and go to movies and do things like a human being, but it was snowing in New York and I was scared to death of the city every moment. It was bigger, uglier, and more dangerous than any place I'd ever been.

I mean, Rome is dangerous, but I understand Rome. Paris I know very well. Maybe I'm kidding myself, but it seems I'm safe in those places. New York? I don't know the basic rules.

Even so, the first two weeks were OK. Dad picked me up all the time to take me to musicals. We made every show in town. He took me to see his apartment salon, which was really unbelievable, I mean, like another world inside.

Now in a very deep way Dad hates being a hairdresser. I mean, he hates it. And if you could see this salon in New York, you'd understand what he has done.

It looks like anything but a beauty salon. It is full of dark woodwork and faded oriental rugs. There are parrots and cockatoos in old brass cages, and there are even European tapestries and those old dusky landscapes from Europe by people no one even knows. I mean, it looks like a gentlemen's club, this place. It is Dad's defense, not only against being a hairdresser but being gay.

For all Dad's gentleness, for all his sweetness, Dad really hates being gay. All the men in Dad's life, even Ollie Boon with his kind of British theatrical voice, are like this place. Dad would smoke a pipe if he could stand it. Ollie does smoke a pipe.

Anyway, everything in the salon was authentic, except maybe the combination. The ladies get tea on old hotel china and silver, the kind you use in your New Orleans house. I mean, it is somber and beautiful, and the other hairdressers are European, and the ladies do book six months ahead of time.

But there is no place to sleep there. I mean, Dad had long ago squeezed himself out. And suddenly Dad was talking about getting another flat in the same building and he and I living there together, and I realized, when he started spending every night at my place, that Ollie Boon had thrown him out.

This was crashing news to me, absolutely crashing. I mean, was I poison? Did I destroy every adult I touched? Ollie loved Daddy. I knew he did. And Dad loved Ollie. But over me they had broken up. I was sick about it. I didn't know what to do. Dad kept pretending he was happy. But he wasn't happy. Just mad at Ollie, and being very stubborn, that's all.

Then it happened. Two men showed up at the salon and showed the other hairdressers a picture of me and asked if I'd been around. Dad was furious when he came in. These men had left a number and he called it. He told them he had recognized his daughter in the picture. What the hell was going on?

The way he described them they were very smooth. They were lawyers. They reminded him he had no rights over me. They said if he interfered with their private investigation, if he even dared to discuss it with anybody or make it public that I was missing, he was in for very expensive trouble indeed.

"Stay put in your apartment, Belinda," Dad said. "Don't you set foot out of the door till you hear from me."

But it didn't take long for the phone to ring. And this time it was Ollie. These lawyers had been to see him at the theater. They told him I was mentally disturbed, had run away, might hurt myself, and that G.G. couldn't be trusted to do what was right for me. If Ollie heard or saw anything of me, he was to call Marty Moreschi directly, and by the way Marty admired Ollie. He would fly out soon himself to discuss the upcoming *Crimson Mardi Gras* production. He did think it was a better prospect for a film deal than *Dolly Rose* had been.

What bullshit, as if Marty had time to fly to New York City over a movie deal! It was a threat and Ollie knew it and I knew it.

"Darling, listen to me," Ollie said in his most theatrical voice. "I love G.G. And if you want the bottom line I do not think I can live without G.G. My little experiment of late of no G.G. has not worked out. But we're in over our heads. These people are probably following G.G. They may already know he's seen you. For God's sakes, Belinda. Don't put me in this role. I've never played the villain in any play in my life."

Good-bye New York.

And where do you go when you're a kid on the run? Where do you go when you've had enough of the snow and the icy wind and the dirt of New York City? What was the place the kids on the street called paradise, where the cops didn't even want to bust you because the shelters were full?

I called the airlines immediately. There was a flight out of Kennedy in two hours for San Francisco. I packed one bag, counted up my money, canceled phone service and utilities on the apartment, and split.

I didn't call Dad until I was ready to board. He was horribly upset. The lawyers, or whoever they were, had been to Ollie's house in SoHo. They'd been questioning neighbors. But when I told him I was at the airport and I had only five minutes, he really came unglued.

I'd never heard Dad cry before, really cry I mean. But he did then.

He said he was coming. I was to wait for him. We'd go back to Europe together, he didn't give a damn. He would never forgive Ollie for calling me. He didn't care about the salon. He was really coming apart.

"Daddy, stop it," I told him. "I am going to be all right, and you've got more at stake here than Ollie Boon. Now I will call you, I promise, and I love you Daddy, I can never never thank you enough. Tell Ollie I'm gone, Daddy. Do that for me." Then I was crying. I couldn't talk. The plane was leaving. And there wasn't time to say anything except, "I love you, Dad."

San Francisco was beyond my wildest dreams.

Maybe it would have looked different had I come there direct from Europe, from the colorful streets of Paris or Rome. But after New York in the middle of winter it was the loveliest city I had ever seen.

One day I'd been in the snow and the wind and the next I was walking those warm and safe streets. Everywhere I looked there were brightly painted Victorians. I rode the cable car down to the bay. I walked through the misty woods of Golden Gate Park.

I had never known there were such cities in America. Compared with this, the smoggy stretches of Los Angeles seemed hideous; and Dallas with its towers and freeways was hard and cold.

Immediately I met kids who would help me. And I got the room in the Page Street commune the first night. I felt like nothing could hurt me in San Francisco, which of course was a delusion, and I set about cooking up my false identity and hanging out on Haight Street to meet other runaways and roaming Polk with two gay hustlers who became my best friends.

The first Saturday we got a jug of wine and walked across the Golden Gate to have a party at Vista Point. The sky was clear, and the blue water was full of tiny seemingly motionless sailboats, the city beyond looked pure white. Can you imagine how it looked to me? Even when the fog rolled in, it was like white steam pouring down over the bright towers of the Golden Gate.

But, you know, the happiness didn't last. I got mugged about three weeks after I arrived. Some guy hit me in the doorway on Page Street and tried to steal my purse. I held onto it with both hands, screaming and screaming and, thank God, he ran away. All my traveler's checks were in there. I was terrified, and after that, I hid them under the floorboards in my room.

Then there was the drug bust upstairs on Page Street when the narcs tore up every single thing that belonged to the kids who lived there, I mean ripping the stuffing out of the furniture, pulling the wires out of the TV set, tearing up the carpets, and leaving the doors with the locks broken as they dragged the occupants out in handcuffs never to be seen again.

But through it all I was learning, I was determined to make it on my own. And part of what I needed was some sense of who I had been before. It was for that reason that I went to the second-hand magazines stores and bought back issues of magazines with stories in them about Mother. I got the videotapes of her old movies at the same time. And then the real piece of luck, finding an ad in a video magazine that said they could get you any movie, even one not released in the States. I sent off for *Final Score* and I got it. But, you know, I never had a machine to see these tapes. But it didn't matter. I had them. I had part of my past with me, even if I did tear off all the labels so nobody else would ever guess.

And one of the things that came clear to me was that the girls on the street were very different from the boys. The girls went nowhere. They got pregnant, on drugs, maybe even became prostitutes. They were often fools for the guy they met. They'd cook and scrub for some broke rock musician and then get thrown in the street. But the boys were a little more smart. They got taken nice places by the gay men they hustled. The gay men kind of romanticized them. The boys could actually use these meetings to move up and out of the world of the street.

Well, I puzzled over this a lot. How did the streets wear out girls, while boys passed through them? Why did girls lose, while boys won? Of course, not all the boys were smart. They lived hand to mouth, too, and kidded themselves about the glamour of their adventures, but they had a kind of freedom that women just never seem to have.

Whatever the case, I decided to behave like one of the boys. To look upon myself as somebody pretty mysterious and special and expect other people to be interested, that kind of thing.

And I found out something else, too. If I put aside my street clothes and punk makeup and wore a Catholic school uniform—and you could get the skirts second-hand on Haight Street—I was really treated quite well wherever I went. I mean, sometimes I had to go to the big hotels. I had to splurge on breakfast at the Stanford Court or the Fairmont. I had to be around the places I'd left. I didn't do anything except eat a good meal and read *Variety* as I drank my coffee, but I felt good doing that, just sitting there in the restaurant off the lobby and feeling safe. I always wore the Catholic school clothes when I did this. I wore them when I went strolling through the big stores. Somebody's daughter, that was my disguise.

Then one afternoon I opened the paper and there was your picture and an ad for the big book party downtown. Now even without Ollie talking about *Crimson Mardi Gras* I probably would have noticed it. I'd read all your books when I was a child.

But there was the added thing of reading *Crimson Mardi Gras* and finding all the old picture books in the Fire Island house. I was really curious. I wanted to see you. And I decided to play it the way a gay boy would have played it, to just go there and make eye contact, as they were always doing it, you know, cruise.

When I saw how handsome you were and how you kept flirting with me, I decided to take this a step further. I heard them talking about the party at the Saint Francis. I bought a book and went ahead to wait for you there.

Of course, you know exactly what happened. But let me tell you that it was one of the strangest experiences I had ever had since I left home. You were like some storybook prince to me, real strong but gentle, a kind of mad lover who painted beautiful pictures, and your house full of toys, well, it bordered on the outright insane.

Hard to analyze and perhaps it is too soon to try. I think you were the most independent person I had ever come across. Nothing touched you, except you wanted me to touch you, that was clear from the start. And as I said before, you were the first older man I had ever made love to. I'd never come across that kind of patience before.

And whereas everybody I had ever known had used their good looks, you didn't even know you were a handsome man. Your clothes didn't fit. Your hair was always messed up. Later on, it was fun transforming you, making you buy new suits and decent jackets and sweaters. Getting you measured for those suits. And you know what happened. You didn't care at all, but you looked terrific. Everybody noticed you when we went out together.

But I'm jumping ahead. The first couple of nights I fell in love with you. I called Daddy from a phone booth in San Francisco and I told him about you, and I knew everything was going to be OK.

But it might have all died that day you showed me the first Belinda paintings and told me that they would never be seen by anyone, that it would wreck your career. I just went crazy when you told me that. You remember. And I really meant to run away from you then, and maybe it would have been better for you if I had. It wasn't that I didn't understand what you'd said about never showing the pictures. It was just too much like what had happened with *Final Score.*

"Here it goes again," I thought. "I am poison, poison!" And yet the rage in me, the rage against everything was tearing me apart.

But you know what happened, the murder on Page Street and my calling you and then we were together again, and it was like Marty all over again, because I knew I loved you and I wasn't going to leave you, and whatever you did with the paintings, well, that was your decision, or so I kept telling myself.

And I was so happy just to be with you, to be loved by you, that it seemed nothing else mattered in the world.

I called Dad collect from your house, and this time I told him who you were and gave him the number, though I warned him not to use it because you were always there. And Dad was real happy with what was happening.

It turned out he knew your wife Celia, the one who works in New York City; she had come into G.G.'s often, and he got her talking about you, and when I called him the next time, he said you were very much OK from what Celia had said. Celia said the marriage "failed" because you were always working. You wouldn't do anything but paint.

Well, that was fine by me.

But meantime things were not going well at all for Dad. He had not gone back to Ollie. He was sleeping on a couch in the salon instead.

Even the night of the Tony Awards, when *Dolly Rose* walked off with everything, Dad would not go back when Ollie called.

And these lawyer types were bothering him. They kept insisting I was in New York and Dad knew where. Then strange things had started to happen. The rumor went round that one of Dad's hairdressers was sick with AIDS.

Now you know what AIDS is—you can't get it through casual contact. But it's scary, and people are just crazy on the subject. Well Dad had a whole slew of cancellations. Even Blair Sackwell called to tell him about the rumors. And Blair had helped to quash the whole thing.

But Dad was optimistic. He was winning the fight. He had made his move, as he called it, the day before with the lawyers who had come to the salon again. "Look, if she's really missing, we should call the police in on this," he had said right in front of them, and then he had reached for the phone. He had even asked the operator to connect him with the police department before one of these lawyers took the receiver and hung it up. "I am telling you," Dad said to them, "if I see you again and you still haven't found her, I am calling the police without fail."

I had to laugh hearing Dad do this tough talk. But it was a terrible thing to think of him up against these unpleasant men. But Dad kept insisting he was happy:

"It's chess, I'm telling you, Belinda, you just have to make the right move at the right time. And Belinda, the best part is this, they don't have the faintest idea where you really are."

Now when I made these collect calls to G.G., when I gave him your number, it never occurred to me in a million years that anyone would find that number on the record of Dad's calls. But that is exactly what happened. And they traced me in this fashion directly to your house.

And in July, after we had been together for almost six weeks, Marty appeared on Castro Street, walking straight towards me in front of the Walgreen's drugstore, and asked me to come with him in his car.

I was shocked out. I nearly lost it. What if you had come along right then?

But within seconds we were speeding away downtown to the United Theatricals suite at the Hyatt Regency, the very one where Mother was later to meet you.

Well, Marty was trembling and throwing an Italian opera scene before we ever got there. But I was not prepared for his immediately trying to put the make on me as soon as the door of the suite closed. I had to fight him off and I mean fight. But Marty is not mean. Truly he is not. And when he realized that I would not go to bed with him, he kind of came apart Marty-style, as he had done so many times at the Château Marmont and in Beverly Hills, and he told me everything that had been going on.

Things had been terrible after I left, what with Uncle Daryl insisting on hiring his own detectives to find me and Marty pursuing his investigation on his own. Mom had been crazy with guilt in the weeks that followed, telling him on the one hand not to look for me, then waking up screaming that she knew I was in danger, that I was hurt.

Trish and Jill had come back, and they had to be let in on the secret that I was missing, and they were real hard to control. Jill was for calling the police, and she was angry with Bonnie. As for Daryl, he blamed everything on me and had laid the legal groundwork to have me committed to a mental institution in Texas as soon as I was found.

Marty kept insisting to all of them that it was a big mix-up, nothing had happened between him and me, Mom had imagined it. If we hadn't all gone off half-cocked before he came back from the hospital, everything would have been OK. But the three Texans, as he called them, all believed Mom's version that I had tried to seduce Marty, though Trish and Jill were very worried about me and really thought the police should be called.

It was hell, Marty said, hell, hell, hell. But the worst part was that Mom had now convinced herself that Marty was keeping me somewhere. He had tried to reason with her about it, but it was useless. She was sure I was in LA and Marty and I were still carrying on.

Last week her delusions had really gone into high gear. While he was in New York, checking out my connections with G.G., Mom had decided he was really with me. She had written a note telling Daryl everything and then slashed her wrists, nearly bleeding to death before she was found.

Fortunately Jill got the note and destroyed it. And Marty had been able to talk to Mother and get her trust back. But it was getting harder and harder to keep on an even keel. If he left her for an hour, she was convinced he was with me. Even this trip to San Francisco was risky. Trish believed him, so did Jill, and they accepted it when he said he was going on with the search. As for Daryl he could not be sure.

Of course, Marty had been frantic with worry about me. He'd been on pins and needles while his men checked out this artist guy, as he called you, and made sure I was truly OK.

"But the bottom line is, you have to come back, Belinda, you have to kiss this guy good-bye and come back to LA with me now. She's drowning, Belinda. And there are other problems down there as well. Susan Jeremiah's gone to Switzerland to locate you. She is really breathing down everybody's neck. Honey, I know how you feel about me, I know that. And I know you never meant for all this to happen, but, good Christ, Belinda, the lady's going to off herself, damn it. There is only one way out."

Now it was my turn for Italian opera. And the first thing I screamed was:

"How could you try to ruin G.G.? How could you start these rumors about his salon in New York?"

He was immediately innocent. He hadn't done that, no he hadn't. If anybody did that, it was Uncle Daryl, blah, blah, blah. Then he said he'd stop the rumors. He would see to it personally, he would kill all that. Especially, of course, if I would come back.

"Why the hell can't you leave me alone!" I said. "How can you tell me I have to come back and let my uncle Daryl lock me up? Do you hear yourself? What you're saying—that I have to come back for her sake and your sake, my God!"

Calm down, please, he said. He had a plan and I had to listen to him. He would have Trish and Jill meet us at the airport, and we would go back to the house together, and then he would lay down the law that there would be no mental institution in Texas or convent in Switzerland or whatever the hell it was. I was free to do what I pleased. I could go on location with Susan in Europe, just the way I had wanted before. Setting me and Susan up with a television film, that was no problem, Susan had something in the works now, well, change it, one call to Ash Levine and he could do that. I mean, what the hell were we talking about here, for Crissakes, wasn't he the goddamn producer and director of "Champagne flight"? Bonnie worked for him. He'd pull rank.

"You're losing your mind, Marty," I said. "Mom is the show and you know it. And what makes you think you could stop Uncle Daryl? For years he's bought land all over Dallas and Fort Worth with Mom's money. He's not scared of you and United Theatricals. And why would Mom let me go off to do what I want with Susan when Susan works for you?"

He stood up. He was breathing fire, like I'd seen him a hundred times at the studio, pointing to the speaker phone on his desk. Only this time he was pointing to me.

"Belinda, trust me! I will get you in and out, I am telling you. But things cannot go on as they are right now."

I got up to go.

Then he softened, he was the quick change artist. "Don't you see, honey, I will muscle this thing through. The tension's at the breaking point down there. And I am going to relieve it when I bring you back alive and OK. You can have whatever you want, a little apartment in Westwood, anything. I will take care of it, I will do it, honey I am telling you—"

"Marty, I am staying in San Francisco. I am where I want to be. And if you don't leave G.G. alone, so help me God, I'll do something, I don't know what but—" I never finished.

He was screaming again. He didn't want to hurt me, the last thing in the world he wanted to do was hurt me, but I just could not turn my back on what was going on.

I was just staring at him. And I realized what I should have realized the first time I laid eyes on him on Castro Street. I no longer loved him, and, more than that, I was no longer really in sympathy with him. And though I understood what was happening, I knew that I could not change it. I knew that as surely as I knew the world was round.

Imagine me back in LA and Mother accusing me again of living with Marty, imagine. Imagine Uncle Daryl getting doctors to just take me away. I didn't know what the laws were in Texas. But I knew the legal jargon I heard on the streets of New York and California. I was a minor in danger of living an immoral and dissolute life. I was a minor beyond the supervision of an adult. And the evidence went way way back.

"No, Marty," I said. "I love Mom. But something happened between us the day after the shooting, something you'd never understand. I'm not coming down there to see her or talk to her, or Uncle Daryl either. And if you want to know the frank truth, nothing could get me away from San Francisco right now. Not even Susan. Marty, you've got to handle this on your own."

He looked at me and I saw him toughen. I saw him get street mean. And then he made his move, as Dad had done with the lawyers in New York.

"Belinda, if you don't do it, I'll have the police pick you up at Jeremy Walker's house on Seventeenth Street, and I will have him arrested on every applicable morals charge in this state. He'll do time for the rest of his life, Belinda. I mean it, I don't want to hurt you, honey, but you either come with me now or Walker goes to jail tonight."

And now I made my move with no time to think it through.

"You do that, Marty, and you're making the worst mistake of your entire career. Because not only will I tell the police that you pursued me, seduced me, and molested me repeatedly, I will tell the press as well. I will tell them that Mom knew it, that Mom was jealous, that Mom tried to shoot me and never reported me missing, and I am talking everybody now, Marty, from the *National Enquirer* to *The New York Times*. I will fill them in on Mom's drugs, on her neglect of me, and your being in cahoots with it. Believe me, Marty, I will bring you all down. And let me tell you something else, Marty. You do not have one shred of evidence that I ever went to bed with Jeremy Walker, not one shred. But I will testify in a court of law about the times I slept with you."

He was staring at me, trying to be tough, really trying, but I could see the hurt inside him, and I couldn't stand it. It was almost as bad as the fight with Mom.

"Belinda, how can you say these things?" he asked. And he really meant it. I know. Because I felt the same way that time with Mom.

"Marty, you are threatening us! Me and Jeremy! And G.G.!" I screamed at him. "Marty, leave us alone."

"Daryl's going to find you, honey!" he said. "Don't you see, I'm giving you what Daryl won't give you! I'm giving you a choice."

"We'll see about that, Marty. Daryl isn't going to hurt Mom, of that you can be sure. You may find this hard to believe with all your wheeling and dealing, but Daryl loves Mom the way you never have."

Then I tried to split out of there right then. But he was not going to let that happen, and the scene that followed was a terrible thing. I mean, we had been lovers, me and this man. And we were shouting and crying and he was trying to hold me and I was fighting him and then I did get out and I ran all the way down all the flights of steps in the Hyatt and out onto Market Street.

But, you know, Jeremy, I was terrified. And all I could think was, Belinda, you have done it again! You are dragging Jeremy into the muck and mire with you, just as you dragged G.G. and Ollie Boon. And you don't know what these people will do.

It was that night I begged you to go to Carmel. And I begged you to go down to New Orleans and open up your mother's house again. I wanted to run to the ends of the earth with you.

We drove to Carmel at midnight, as I remember. And all the way I kept looking in the side mirror, trying to see if somebody was following us.

Next day I called Daddy from a phone booth on Ocean Avenue, using quarters of my own, instead of calling collect, so there would be no record of the call, and I told Dad how Marty had traced me through the collect calls to him.

Dad was very scared for me. "Don't go back, Belinda," he said. "Stand your ground. Daryl has been here, Belinda. He insists he knows you were in the city this spring. But I used the same damn bluff on him, you know the police bit, and boy, did he back off. He's ashamed, Belinda. Ashamed nobody's called the authorities, and you know what he finally did? He begged me to tell him just if I knew you were all right. I played dumb,

Belinda, but he's going to find you, just like Marty did. Checkmate, Belinda. Remember, you can do it. They will not do anything to hurt Bonnie. Bonnie's the one who matters to them, all of them."

"But what about the salon, G.G.?" I was still frantic.

"I can handle it, Belinda," he insisted.

I never did and do not know to this day how bad it really got. I am only hoping till this moment that Dad is really all right.

That final week in Carmel was the last peace I really had. It was wonderful, our walks on the beach, our talks together. I tried hard to keep us from going back. But in your nice agreeable way you insisted we return to San Francisco.

And I was looking over my shoulder from then on out. I knew people were spying on us. I knew it. And as it turned out, I was right.

Meantime Susan's record TV movie premiered in early September, and it got a thirty percent share of the ratings, and it was damned good. Then "Champagne Flight" had its season opener with your friend Alex Clementine, and I watched it while you were upstairs working. I don't think you even knew.

Mom was terrific. No matter what happens to her she is always there for the camera. And she seemed to be putting the pain in it all right. But there was a new aspect to her. For the first time Mom looked gorgeously gaunt. She was the ghost of herself on the screen and I mean she was a spellbinder. And so, frankly, was the whole show. And technically, well, it was even more into the rock-video dream mode, with hypnotic music and snappy camera work. *Film noir* again all the way.

Then not two days after that, you told me Alex Clementine was coming, he was your friend, and you wanted me to go to dinner, and you got very adamant about it, which was not like you at all. Of course, I knew Alex Clementine. I met him in London when Mom was working on a picture with him years ago. And worse, I had just seen him last year at the Cannes festival. And, of course, I'd almost run into him at that publishing party the very first afternoon we met.

No way could I go with you. And if you brought him back to the house to show him the paintings, it would be all over right then and there.

I was frantic. But I was hoping. If I couldn't get to New Orleans, maybe someplace else.

And then Marty showed up again. I had a very strong feeling someone was following me when I hit the Golden Gate Bridge to go to the Marin stables and then, when I was riding, I realized I'd been right.

Now you know what the riding meant to me. But I wonder if you ever realized what an escape from worry it was. When I was on my horse, I felt I was away from everything in the world. And one of my favorite roads to take out of the hills of Cronkite was the one down to the ocean beach at Kirby Cove. It was closed to traffic most of the time, and I would often be the only person down there, riding in the surf, and it was a truly magnificent spot.

You could see the bridge and the city to the left of you and the ocean to the far right.

Well, if I had known on this afternoon that it was the last time I'd ride at Kirby Cove, I wonder how I would have felt.

I was halfway down before I saw a Mercedes on the road behind me, and then I realized it was Marty and I took off, down one of the steep trails. Of course, he came all the way to the campgrounds at the bottom, and there I figured, well, OK, it's crazy to run away from him. He is not going to leave me alone till we talk.

He wanted me to go to the hotel with him. I said hell no to that. But I did tie up the horse and get in the car with him. The horse was scaring him. He had never ridden in his life.

He said he had something pretty heavy to tell me. He had a manila envelope with him, and he asked me if I could guess what was inside.

"What the hell are you talking about?" I said. "What is this?" If there had been any lingering love last time, there was very little now. The envelope scared me. He scared me. And I was afraid I was going to break down.

"Your boyfriend down there on Seventeenth Street, what kind of a man is he that he paints pictures of you naked all over the place?"

"What are you talking about?" I asked him.

"Honey, I've had a couple of dicks watching you. They went on the roof of the apartment house next door to you, strictly routine. They saw all this stuff through the attic windows. Then they checked it out again from the balcony of the house across the street. I've got photographs of the whole gallery—" He went to open the envelope.

I said: "You son of a bitch! Just stop it right here."

I knew he could see how scared I was. He got right to the point.

"Look, it doesn't give me kicks to stick my nose in other people's business. But Bonnie gave me no choice. Last week she said she knew for sure we were living together, and she tried it again, pills this time, and enough to kill a mule. OK, I figured, this lady's going to die if I don't stop it, and I'm the only one in the world who can. I told her about you and Jeremy Walker. I gave the name, the address, the whole works. I brought in the file on him, the clippings my secretaries at the studio had rounded up. Still she didn't believe it. Belinda in San Francisco living with an artist? Come on, did I think she was as stupid as everybody else thought she was? She said she knew I wouldn't let that happen, that I was keeping you someplace in Los Angeles and I had been from the start. It was the lies that drove her crazy. The lies that made her lie awake and all that. OK, I told her I'd prove it. I sent these dicks up here to prove it. Get some pictures of you together. Catch you on the street together, find a window, get you going through the front door. Well, this is what they got, Belinda, three-hundred-sixty-degree angles on the headquarters of Kiddie-porn West. This stuff makes Susan Jeremiah's film look like Disney. It could make Humbert Humbert rise from the dead."

I told him to stop. I told him you could never show those pictures. It was out of the question. It would be the end for your career. Those pictures were our secret and to keep his filthy men from looking in our windows.

"Don't put me on," he said. "The guy's using you, Belinda! He's got nude photographs up there with the paintings. He could sell that junk now to *Penthouse* for a bundle. But that's not what he's after. Bonnie pegged him immediately. She says he's got a nose for publicity that's better than that Andy Warhol screwball in New York. He's going to make his big splash with nude paintings of Bonnie's daughter and to hell with you after that.

I went crazy. I started screaming. "Marty, he doesn't even know who I am!" I said. "Did Mother even stop to think that maybe this wasn't connected to her!"

"She knows it's connected. And, honey, so do I. It's just like what happened to you with Susan Jeremiah, don't you see? These people use you because you're Bonnie's kid."

I was out of my head. I would have hit him, but I was too busy holding my hands over my ears. I was crying. And trying to tell him that it wasn't that way, it had nothing to do with Mother, goddamn it. "Don't you see what she's doing!" I said. "She's making herself the center of it! And Jeremy doesn't even know about her. Oh, God, what are you doing to me? What do you really want!"

"The hell he doesn't," Marty said. "He's had a lawyer name of Dan Franklin snooping all over Los Angeles, bugging my lawyers about a picture they handed out in a couple of places when they were trying to locate you. Says he just happened on the picture in the Haight-Ashbury, I mean, the guy is Walker's lawyer, known him for twenty years. And he's trying to reach Susan Jeremiah. He's been bugging people at United Theatricals night and day."

He went on talking. He went on and on and on. But I didn't hear what else he said. I knew Dan Franklin's name. I knew he was your lawyer. I'd seen the envelopes on your desk with his name on them. I'd heard his messages on the answering machine.

I sat there crushed. I couldn't say another thing. Yet I couldn't believe what Marty was saying. You couldn't be planning to use the whole thing for publicity, not you!

Dear God, you were going through a battle that none of these people could ever understand.

Yet all kinds of things were coming back. You yourself had said, "I'm using you," those very words. And what about that strange conversation we'd had the very first afternoon after I'd moved in with you when you had told me you wanted to destroy your own career?

But nobody could be that devious, nobody could. Least of all you.

Finally I said again that you couldn't know, that Marty had somehow gotten it all wrong. I told him you'd never show those pictures. You made thousands off your books, probably millions. Why would you show the pictures?

But I stopped suddenly. You did want to show them. I knew you did.

Marty started talking again.

"I've checked this guy from every angle. He's harmless but he's weird, real weird. He's got a house in New Orleans—did you know that?—and nobody but a housekeeper has lived in it for years. His mother's stuff is just like she left it in the bedroom. Brush, comb, perfume bottles,and all. It's like that novel, that Dickens thing, you know, the one William Holden talks about in the movie *Sunset Boulevard* with the old lady named Miss Havisham or something, just sitting there and nothing being touched year after year. And I'll tell you something else. Walker's rich, real rich. He never touches the money his mother left him. He lives off the income from the income from the capital he socked away himself, that kind of thing. Yeah, I think he would show these paintings. I think he'd do it. I've been reading all the interviews with him, the press file we made on him, he's a real art nut, he says peculiar things."

It was hell listening to this. It was like seeing our world, yours and mine, reflected in a carnival mirror. I couldn't stand it anymore. I told Marty he was crazy. I called him crazy every way that I knew.

"No, honey, he's using you. And you know what his lawyer is doing? He's getting the dirt on us. He's figuring out why you ran, what happened, you know, that kind of thing. Why else would he be looking for Susan Jeremiah? No, this artist guy is a fruitcake. And your mother's right. He'll show the pictures and he'll use the dirt on us to keep us off his case and, of course, you won't do a thing to him when it happens, will you? You won't accuse him of anything any more than you accused me.

And Bonnie and I will be left with all the questions—how did we let it happen and all that?"

I told him I wouldn't listen anymore. You didn't know. I was trying to get out of the car.

He pulled me back by the arm.

"Belinda, ask yourself, why am I telling you this? I'm trying to protect you, too. Bonnie is for busting this guy now. She says if the cops pick you up at his place, nobody will listen to anything you say about me. She's for calling Daryl. She's for moving in right now."

"You burn in hell, you son of a bitch!" I told him. "And you tell Bonnie this for me. I've got the number of a *National Enquirer* reporter in my pocket. I've always had it, got it from him on Sunset Strip. And you better believe he will listen to what I have to say about you both. Him and the social workers and the juvenile judge will listen. If you hurt Jeremy, you'll go to jail."

But by that time I was out the car and I was running down the road. But Marty came after me. He grabbed hold of me, and I turned around and hit him, but it didn't do any good.

Something really awful was happening. I had never seen Marty like he was now. He wasn't just angry, the way you were the night we had our terrible and last fight. Something else was happening that only happens to men, something I don't think any woman on earth can understand.

He pulled me down onto the ground under the pine trees and he was trying to pull off my clothes. I was screaming and kicking him, but there was not a soul for miles to see or hear. And he was crying and saying terrible things to me, he was calling me a little bitch and saying he couldn't take any more, he had had enough. And then I started roaring, making sounds I didn't know I could make. I scratched at him, I pulled his hair. And the simple fact was, he could not do what he meant to do. Not unless he slugged me or something that bad. It was just a brawl that was happening, and then at one point I got him off balance and I threw him over on his back. I got away from him and started running again, stopping only long enough to zip my jeans again before I got on my horse.

I rode out of there like something in the Western movies. In fact I did a bad bad thing. I went right up the trails on the sides of the hills, knowing it was dangerous for the horse. She could have fallen, broken her leg, worse.

But she made it. We made it. We got back to the stables before Marty ever did, if he was even following, and I just about stripped the gears on the MG-TD making for the Golden Gate.

When I got into the house, I went in the bathroom. I had bruises on my arms and on my back but none on my face. OK, you wouldn't notice in the dark.

Then I checked in your office. And sure enough, Dan Franklin's envelopes were there. No doubt that he was your lawyer, so that part was true, OK.

I sat there stunned, not knowing who or what to believe, and then I went up to my room. The tapes, the magazines, hadn't been touched as far as I could see. But what was all over the walls? Susan Jeremiah. Five posters of her by this time, from the pictures I had clipped out of magazines all year. Wasn't it only natural that you thought I was related to Susan? I mean, good God, you did want to know who I was.

About this time you came in. You'd been out shopping for dinner, and you had a big bouquet of yellow flowers and you came up and put them in my arms. I'll never forget the way you looked at that moment. I have a freeze-frame forever in my head. You were so handsome. And you looked so innocent and honest, too. You probably don't remember, but I asked you if you loved me, and you laughed so naturally and you said I knew you did.

I thought then, This is the most special and truly kind man that I have ever known. He has never hurt anyone. He is only trying to find out, and Marty has twisted the whole thing.

I went upstairs with you and then I looked out the windows at the roof of the apartment house next to us and then across Seventeenth at the balcony of the other on the top floor. No one was there now. But from the big hills between here and Twenty-fourth Street anybody could have photographed us through these windows. There was no hiding from a thousand points of light.

I wonder if you remember that evening. It was our last good time in that house. You looked so beautiful to me that evening, all distracted and lost in the paintings and forgetting completely about dinner, by the way, as usual, and no noise in the attic but the sound of your brush touching the palette and then the canvas and you now and then murmuring something to yourself.

It got darker and darker. Couldn't see anything through the glass. Just the paintings all around us. And it didn't seem possible that one man had made them, that he had spun out all this complicated and detailed work.

I knew you did not know who I was. I knew it with all my heart. And I had to protect you from Mom and Marty, even if that meant protecting you from myself.

Your world was so alien to them. What did they know of what these pictures meant?

One year and two months until I was eighteen, that's all we needed,

but we would never have it, not with Marty and Mom and Uncle Daryl—
and now you. Yes, you and Dan Franklin were our enemies now, too.

Well, the following night was the end of it.

I never went to the rock concert that caused us to fight. I went instead
to a phone booth and spent hours trying to get in touch with G.G. and
then finally reaching him and asking him what I should do. "Call Bonnie," he told me. "Call her and tell her, she hurts Jeremy Walker and you
hurt Marty. Tell her you'll call that *National Enquirer* number. Chess,
Belinda, and it's still your move."

But something during that dinner with Alex Clementine tipped you
off. Maybe he made the connection for you between me and Susan Jeremiah. One line or two about Susan's film at Cannes and the girl who
starred in it would have done that.

I don't know what happened. I only knew we fought that night as we
had never fought. And you were not the man Marty and Mom believed
you to be when we were fighting. You were my Jeremy, innocent and
tormented and trying to get me to explain it all so that everything would
be all right.

How the hell could I explain it all so everything would be all right? Just
at least let me make that call to Mom, I was thinking, let me try for the
final stalemate, and then maybe, just maybe I can think of some way to
tell you something at least.

But I didn't really understand how far things had gone till the next
morning, after you had left the house and I found my videotapes on the
closet floor. The magazines were all messed up and you had left the
Newsweek open. Yes, you had your answers, or at least you thought you
did, and you wanted me to know you had them.

There was no turning away in silence anymore.

For an hour after you had gone, I sat at the kitchen table trying to
figure what to do.

G.G. had said call Bonnie. Stalemate. Ollie Boon had said use my
power against them, the way they used it against me.

But even if I held them off, what about you? What about your destiny
with the paintings? What about you and me?

It was out of the question that I draw you into this as it was, the way I
had done to G.G. and Ollie Boon. G.G. and Ollie had lived together for
five years before I separated them. And to hear of G.G. battling these
lawyers of Marty's was excruciating. With you it would have been even
worse. After all, G.G. was my dad, wasn't he? You had come into this so
innocently, so unsuspecting, and you had never given me anything but

the purest love. If worse came to worse, you might tell me to go back to them, your lawyer would probably tell you to do exactly that.

And I have to admit, I felt pretty angry at you, too. I was angry that I wasn't enough for you, that you had to know about my past, that behind my back you'd sent your lawyer down south to check me out, that you would never let the whole subject alone.

What did you want to do? Decide for me whether I had a right to run away from home? Yeah, I was angry. I have to admit it. Scared and angry.

But I didn't want to lose you either. That we were once-in-a-lifetime, that is what kept going through my head. Someday, somehow, I wanted to do something like you had done with your paintings. *I wanted to be like you!*

Can you understand this? Do you know what it means not just to love a person but to want to be like that person? You were somebody worth loving. And I just could not think of life without you.

Well, I was going to get us both out of this somehow. There had to be a way.

A lot of things came back to me—jams I'd been in—my escape from Uncle Daryl, sneaking down hotel fire escapes in Europe when the film company had stuck us with everybody's bill. The drug bust in London when I stood in the door of the hotel room holding off the cops with every line I could think of while Mom flushed the grass. And then the time in Spain when she had passed out on the stairway of the Palace Hotel and I had to convince them not to call an ambulance, that she was just drowsy from her medicine and would they please just help me to get her upstairs. Yeah, there had to be a way out, there had to be, and what Ollie Boon had said about power kept running through my head.

But I didn't have the power, that was the problem. I had the stalemate, but not the power. Who had the power? Who could call off all the dogs now?

Well, there was only one person who could do it, and she had always been the center of the universe, hadn't she? Yes, she was the goddess, the superstar. She could make them all do what she said.

I picked up the phone and I called a number that I had had with me in my purse since the day I left. It was the number of the phone by Mom's bed.

Six thirty. Mom, be there. Don't have gotten up yet, don't have gone to the studio. And three rings and I heard her same old low slurred voice barely breathing the word, hello.

"Mom, this is Belinda," I said.

"Belinda," she whispered, like she was afraid someone else would hear.

"Mom, I need you," I said. "I need you the way I never have in my life."

She didn't answer me.

"Mom, I'm living with this man in San Francisco and I love him and he is a gentle and kind man and I need you, Mom. I need you to make it all right."

"Jeremy Walker, is that what you're telling me?" she said.

"Yes, Mom, that's the one." I took a deep breath. "But it's not the way Marty told you, Mom. Until yesterday, I swear to you, Mom, this man did not know who I am. He may have had his suspicions and all, but he didn't know for sure. Now he does know and he's terribly terribly unhappy, Mom. He's confused and he doesn't know what to do and I need your help."

"You're not . . . really living with Marty?"

"No, Mom, never, not since the day I left."

"And what about the pictures, Belinda, all the pictures this man has done?"

"They are very beautiful, Mom," I said.

And here was a long shot, but I had to try it. I said:

"They're like the movies Flambeaux made with you in Paris. They are art, Mom, really and truly that is what they are." I tried to hold steady in the silence. "It will be a long time before anyone ever sees them, Mom. They are not what is worrying me now."

Again she didn't answer. And then I took the biggest gamble of my whole life.

"Mom, you owe me this one," I said gently. "I am talking to you as Belinda to Bonnie. And, Mom, you owe me this one. You know you do."

I waited, but she still did not answer. I felt like I was on the very edge of the cliff. One mistake and I was over the edge.

"Mom, help me. Please help me. I need you, Mom."

And then I could hear her crying. And she said so softly in a broken-hearted voice:

"Belinda, what do you want me to do?"

"Mom, can you come to San Francisco now?"

At eleven A.M. the studio plane landed, and she looked like a corpse when she stepped out the door. She was slimmer than I'd ever seen her and her face was like a mask, every line smoothed out. But her head was down as always. She never looked me in the eye.

All the way into the city I told her about you, I told her about the paintings, I asked her if the snapshots she'd seen had given her any idea how good they were.

"I know Mr. Walker's work," she said. "I used to read his books to you, don't you remember? We had them all. We'd always look for his new books when we went to London. Or Trish would send them from back home."

A knife went into me when she said this. I could remember us lying together and her reading to me. The backdrop might shift from Paris to Madrid to Vienna. But there was always a double bed and a bedside lamp. And she was always the same with the book in her hands.

Now she was a stranger who looked like a nun all this time under the hood of her cloak with her head down.

"But you're lying," she said, "when you say you never told him about me."

"No, Mom, I never told him. I never told him anything at all."

"You told him awful things, didn't you? You told him things about me and Marty and what happened, I know you did."

Again I told her I hadn't. And then I told her just how it had been. How you'd asked me and I made you promise and how maybe you had sent your lawyer to check on Susan because I had those posters of Susan in my room.

I couldn't tell if she believed me. I went on to explain what I wanted her to do. Just talk to you, tell you it was OK if we were together and we would never bother her again. Just call off all the lawyers and the detectives. Call off Uncle Daryl and let us alone. Then she asked:

"How do I know you'll stay with this man?"

"Mom, I love him. It's the kind of thing that happens once to some people, and to other people never at all. I won't leave him unless he leaves me. But if you talk to him, Mom, he won't do that. He'll go on with his painting. He'll be happy. And we'll both be OK."

"And what will happen when he shows these pictures?"

"Mom, it will be a long time before he does that. A long long time. And the art world is a thousand light-years away from our world. Who would ever make the connection between the girl in those pictures and Bonnie's daughter? And even if they did, who would care? I'm not famous, Mom, the way you are. *Final Score* never got released in this country. Bonnie is the one who is famous, and what would it all matter to her?"

We had turned off on Seventeenth now, and we were passing the house, because she wanted to see it, and then we drove on up the hill. We parked up there at the lookout point on Sanchez Street, facing all the buildings of downtown.

Then she asked if I had seen Marty since the day I left LA. And I said only when he came here to check on me, and we had only talked together. Marty was her husband now.

She was silent a long time then. And then she said softly that she couldn't do it, just couldn't do what I asked.

"But why can't you?" I was pleading with her. "Why can't you just tell him it's OK."

"What would he think I was doing, just giving my daughter to him? And what if he decided to tell somebody I'd done it, just handed you over to him. Suppose you ran out on him tomorrow. Suppose he showed the paintings he's done. What if he told the world that I had come and just given him my teenage daughter, said take her, like I was turning her out like a pimp right on the street?"

"Mom, he would never do that!" I said.

"Oh, yes, he could do it. And he'd have something on me all my life. That lawyer of his probably already knows plenty. He knows nobody picked up the phone to the LAPD when you ran off. He knows something happened with you and Marty. Maybe you've told them both more than that."

I begged her to believe me, but I could see it was no use. And then it came to me. What if she thought she had something on you in return for what she was doing? What if she thought she had the upper hand? I thought of the *Artist and Model* pictures. I knew those pictures. I liked them. I'd been through all the prints a dozen times. And I also knew that not a single one of them proved a damn thing. You couldn't see who I was in them. And you could hardly make out who you were either. They were just a real mess. Really grainy, lousy light.

But would Mom know that? Mom could hardly see even with her glasses when she was doped up.

I decided it was the best shot I had. She listened while I described them to her. "You could tell him your detectives got them out of the house when they tracked me down. You're doing it for my safety, holding the pictures over him, you know, and that you'll send them all back to him when I'm eighteen. By that time it won't really matter, Mom, whether or not I'm with him or whether or not he shows the paintings. It will all be past. He'd never hate you for it, Mom. He'd just figure you were trying to protect me."

The car took me back down to Sanchez and Seventeenth and I went up to the house. I was hoping and praying I wouldn't find you there yet. The phone rang, and it was Dan Franklin of all people. I just about died.

I almost brought her the prints for *Artist and Model,* but then she might see that they proved nothing at all. So I got the negatives out of your file in the basement, and I was just leaving when the phone rang again. This time it was Alex Clementine. I thought my luck is really running low.

But I made my getaway then. And finally, after we went over and over it, Mom had the plan pretty well clear in her mind. I'd go on down to Carmel, she would wait for you and then use the argument we'd agreed on to get your promise to take care of me.

Then a slight change came over her. She lowered the hood of her cloak for the first time and she looked at me.

"You love this man, huh, Belinda? Yet you give me these pictures? You just put his neck in the noose like that for your own little schemes." She smiled when she said it, one of those real ugly bitter smiles that people do, that makes things so much worse.

I felt the breath go out of me. Back to square one, it seemed. Then I said real carefully, "Mom, you know you can't really use your pictures. Because if you did, I'd send Marty straight to jail."

"And you'd do that to my husband, wouldn't you?" she asked me, and she looked at me very intently, as if she was trying to see something very important to her.

And I thought for a moment before I answered, I thought about what she really wanted here, and I said:

"Yes, for Jeremy Walker I'd do that. I really would."

"You're some little bitch, Belinda," she said. "You have both these men by the balls, don't you? Back in Texas we would have called you slick."

I felt such a sense of injustice then, I started crying. But more important, I could see by her eyes that I had said the right thing. Marty had no part in what I was doing. I was in love with you. She was convinced at last.

Yet she was still looking at me, and I could feel the moment getting more and more dangerous. One of those speeches again, I thought, and I was right.

"Look at you," she said real low so I could hardly hear her. "All those nights I cried over you, wondering where you were, wondering if maybe I was wrong about your being with Marty, maybe you were off all alone out here. I think I kept accusing Marty of lying 'cause I couldn't face the other possibility, that you were really lost and maybe hurt. But that wasn't it at all, was it, Belinda? All the time you were in this fancy house with this rich Mr. Walker. Yeah, slick is the word for you."

I held steady. I thought, Belinda, if she says the sky is green, agree with her. You have to. That is what everyone else has always done.

"You don't even resemble me, do you?" she asked. Same flat voice. "You look like G.G. You sound like G.G. It's as if I had nothing to do with it at all. And here you are peddling your ass just the way G.G. always did since the time he was twelve years old."

I held steady. I was thinking I had heard this side of her before. It would come out in flashes when she talked to Gallo or when she told Trish or Jill about somebody that was mean to her. But she had only shown it to me once before now. Chilling it was to see her smiling and hear the vicious things she was saying. But again, I thought, Belinda, get the job done.

"G.G. ever tell you how he got started," she asked, "hustling the old queers for money on his way up? Ever tell you how he lies to those old ladies when he curls their hair? That's what you are, aren't you, a liar like G.G. And you're hustling Mr. Walker, aren't you? Got him tied up in ribbons and bows. I was a fool not to think that G.G.'s blood would come through."

I was boiling inside. I think I looked out the window. I'm not sure. My mind wandered, that much I remember. She was talking still and I could hardly follow what she said. I was thinking to myself how hopeless this is, all of it. The truth will never be known. And all my life I have lived with this kind of confusion, everything mixed up, just giving up over and over again that anything would ever be understood.

She and I might never see each other again after this. She'd go back to Hollywood and live on drugs and lies until she finally did do it with a gun or pills, and she'd never know what had driven us apart. Did she even remember Susan or the name of our movie? Would anyone ever get through to her about those times when she had almost killed me in trying to kill herself?

But then a terrible thought came to me. Had I ever tried to tell her the truth myself? Had I ever tried for her sake to reach her, to make her see things, just for a moment, in a different light? Everybody had lied to her ever since I could remember. Had I gone along for reasons of my own?

She was my mother. And we were going our separate ways in hatred. How could I let that happen without even making an effort to talk about what had gone on? Good God, how could I leave her like this? She was like a child really. Couldn't I even try?

I looked at her again. She was still looking at me. And that ugly smile was there just like before. Say something, Belinda. Say something, and yet if it goes wrong and you lose Jeremy—And then she spoke instead.

"What are you going to do, little bitch," she asked, "if I don't blackmail your friend, Mr. Walker? Tell me, what you're going to do to us all, G.G.'s daughter? Bring us all down?"

I was staring at her, kind of on hold, and stunned like she had hit me, and then I said:

"No, Mom. You're wrong about me, all wrong. All my life I've protected you, taken care of you. I'm still doing it. But, so help me God, you hurt me and Jeremy Walker, and I will look out for myself and him."

I got out of the car, but I stood there with the door open. And then after a long time I leaned back inside. I was crying. I said:

"Play this last role for me, Bonnie. I promise you, I'll never darken your door again."

The look on her face then was terrible. It was heartbroken. Just heartbroken. And in the most tired voice with no meanness at all she said:

"OK, honey. OK. I'll try."

I talked to her one time after that. It was close to midnight and I went out to the phone booth in Carmel and I called her private line, as we had planned.

She was the one crying then. She was stammering and repeating herself so badly I could hardly make out what she said. She told me something about how you took the negatives from her, that she hadn't pulled it off. But the awful thing was that she'd tried to turn you against me. She said she didn't mean it, really she didn't, but you kept asking her questions and she had said the meanest things about me and Marty and all that.

"Don't worry, Mom, it's OK," I said to her. "If he still wants me after all this, then I guess it's just really fine."

Then Marty came on the line. "The bottom line is this, honey. He knows we're on to him. He won't use those pictures if he's got a brain in his head."

I didn't even answer that one. I just said, "Tell my mom I love her. Tell her now so that I can hear it." And after he did, I heard him say, "She loves you, too, honey, she says to tell you she loves you." I hung up.

But, you know, after I left the phone booth, I went walking on the beach, letting the wind just sear me to the bone. And I kept seeing her when she said: "OK, honey, OK. I'll try." I wanted so to run the tape back and be in that moment again and just to hold her in my arms.

"Mom!" I wanted to say. "It's me, Belinda, I love you, Mama. I love you so much."

But that moment would never come again. I'd never touch her or hold her again ever. Maybe never even hear her voice speaking to me. And all the years in Europe and on Saint Esprit were gone away.

But there was you, Jeremy. And I loved you with my whole heart. I loved you so much you can not imagine. And I prayed and prayed for you to come. I prayed to God you would not ask me anything else ever, because if you did, I might spill everything and I could never never tell it and not hate you for making me tell.

Please, Jeremy, just come. That was my prayer. Because the truth was, I'd lost Mom a long time ago. But you and me—we were forever, Jeremy. We really were once-in-a-lifetime. And the paintings would live forever. Nobody could ever kill them the way they killed Susan's movie. They were yours, and someday you'd have the courage to show them to everyone else.

Well, now you have it, Jeremy. We have come to the finish. The story is finally told. For two days straight I have sat in this room writing in this notebook, filling every page both sides. I am tired and I feel the misery I knew I'd feel when all the secrets were finally revealed.

But you have now what you always wanted, all the facts of my life and past before you, and you can make the judgment for yourself that you never trusted me to make.

And what is your judgment? Did I betray Susan when I went to bed with Marty the very night after he killed her picture? Was I a fool to want his love? And what about Mother in those crucial weeks in Los Angeles? All my life I'd cared for her, but I was so in love with Marty that I stood by and did nothing as she starved herself, got hooked on the medications, the plastic surgery, and all the other things that turned her life into sleepless nights and bad dreams. Should I have gotten her out of it somehow to some place where she could have taken stock? And was I guilty all along of a worse betrayal of her, of never trying, for her sake and mine, to break through the games we all played?

You called me a liar that night when you hit me. You were right, that I am. But you can see now that I was lying before I could remember. Lie, keep secret, protect—that was life with Mom.

And what about Dad? Did I have a right to go to him, to come between him and Ollie Boon? Dad lost Ollie after five years of being with him. Dad loved Ollie. And Ollie loved Dad.

You decide. Have I harmed every grown-up who ever had any dealings with me, from the day that Susan set foot on Saint Esprit? Or was I the victim all along?

Maybe I had a right to be mad as hell about *Final Score*. And I did love Marty, that I will never deny. Did I have a right to expect Uncle Daryl and Mom to care about my life and what was happening? I was Mom's daughter, after all. When they didn't, was I right to run away from them, to say, "I will not be sent to Europe, I will strike out on my own"?

If I only knew the answers to these questions, maybe I would have told you the whole thing before now. But I don't know the answers. I never did. And that's why I hurt you with the stupid blackmail trick. And God knows, that was a mistake all right.

I knew it was long before you ever suspected what happened. I knew it when I called G.G. from New Orleans and I could not bring myself to tell him about it, to explain to him how things had worked out. I was too ashamed of what I'd done.

But then we were so happy together, Jeremy. Those New Orleans weeks were the best of all. Everything seemed worth it. I knew in our last weeks that you'd won your inner fight. And I told myself the blackmail trick had saved us both.

Well. It is a hell of a story, isn't it, just as G.G. and Ollie Boon said it was. But just as I said, it was not my story to tell. The rights really do belong to the grownups. And you are one of them now. There will never be a day in court for me where all this is concerned. Escape was my only choice before. Escape is my only choice now.

And you must understand this. You must forgive it. Because you know you had your own terrible secret, your own story, which belonged to someone else, which for so long you could never tell.

Don't resent me for saying it, but the secret was not that you wrote those last novels for your mother. It was the secret of the novels you wouldn't write after her death. She didn't just leave you her name in her will, Jeremy, she asked you for eternal life, and that you could not give. You know it's true.

And in guilt and fear you ran away from her and left her house like a tomb of olden times complete with every little thing that was hers. Yet you couldn't get away from it. You painted the house in every picture in every book. And you painted your own spirit running through it, trying to get free of your mother and her hands that reached out in death.

But if I'm right about all this, you are out of the old house now. You have painted a figure that finally broke free. With love and courage you opened the door of your secret world to me. You let me come not only into your heart but into your imagination and into your pictures, too.

You gave me more than I can ever give you. You made me the symbol of your battle, and you have to go on winning the battle, no matter what you now think of me.

But can't you forgive me for keeping my mother's secrets? Can't you forgive me for being lost in my own dark house, unable to get out? I have made no art that can be my ticket to freedom. Since the day *Final Score* was sold out, I have been a phantom, a shadow compared with the images you painted of me.

It won't always be so. I am two thousand miles away from you already, I am in a world I understand, and we may never see each other again.

But I will be OK. I won't make the mistakes I made in the past. I will not live on the fringe again. I will use the money I have and the many things you gave me, and I will bide my time until no one can hurt me or hurt the people I love through me anymore. And then I will be Belinda again. I will pick up the pieces and I will be somebody, not somebody's girl. I will try to be like you and Susan. I will do things, too.

But, Jeremy, this is the most important part of all. What will happen to the paintings now?

I want you so badly to show them for my sake that you must be wary of what I say. But listen just the same.

Be true to the paintings! No matter how you despise me, be true to the work you've done. They are yours to reveal when you are ready, and so is the truth of all that has happened to you with me.

What I am saying is you owe me no secrecy and no silence. When the time comes to make your decision, nothing and no one must stand in your way. Use your power then, just as Ollie Boon told me to do. You have made art out of what happened. And you have earned the right to use the truth in any way that you want.

No one will get me to hurt you, of that you can be sure. This year, next year, the year after—whenever you make your move—you can count on my loyalty. You know how good I am at keeping quiet.

When I left New Orleans, I told myself I didn't love you anymore. I had seen hatred in your eyes, and I thought I hated you, too. I thought I would end this letter by saying that I hate you now more than ever because you made me tell you the whole truth.

But you know I love you, Jeremy. And I always will. It was once-in-a-lifetime, it really was, and your paintings have made it forever. Holy Communion, Jeremy. You've given eternal life to you and me.

Intermezzo

intermezzo

RAIN falling. Great slanted sheets of rain. They hit the screens with such force the screens billowed, and the water swept the old floorboards, spraying off the legs of the rocking chair, spraying into the room. Dark puddle creeping into the flowers of the rug. Voices downstairs? No.

I was lying in bed with the Scotch on the table beside me. Next to the phone. Been drunk since Rhinegold's visit, since I'd finished the new *Artist and Model.* Would be drunk until Saturday. Then back to work again. Saturday deadline for this madness. Until then the Scotch. And the rain.

Now and then Miss Annie came with gumbo and biscuits. "Eat, Mr. Walker." Flash of lightning, and a deafening crack of thunder. Then the echo of the thunder, which was just the streetcar rolling by through the storm. Water was coming in under the wallpaper in the upper-left corner. But the paintings were all safe, Miss Annie had assured me of that.

Sound of people walking? Only the old boards creaking. Miss Annie wouldn't call a doctor. She wouldn't do that to me.

I'd done all right till I'd finished the new *Artist and Model:* she and I fighting, my slapping her, her falling back against the wall. Then I'd started deceiving myself, one drink, two, it wouldn't matter, just the background to finish. And the phone was not ringing. I was the only one calling: Marty, Susan, G.G., somebody find her! My ex-wife Celia had said, "This is awful, Jeremy, don't tell anyone!"

Bonnie's private line disconnected. "Leave me alone! I tell you I don't care, I don't care!"

I'd been drunk when Rhinegold left actually. He had wanted to start shipping the pictures immediately. "No," I said. I had to have them here with me until it was all finished. One week from Saturday he would be back. One week to do the last one, to write the program notes, to fight out the final arrangements. No later than Saturday, sober up, begin.

Call, Belinda, give it one more chance. Once-in-a-lifetime remember? *Already two thousand miles away from you.* Where? Across the Atlantic? *A place I understand.*

Belinda in Final Score was done. Her profile and Sandy's perfect. No cheating, as Susan Jeremiah would have said. And what a great voice that woman had, Texas hard and soft at the same time. On the phone from Paris she'd said, "Hang in there, old buddy, we'll find her. She's no nut case like Mama. She isn't going to do that to all of us."

Yeah, Sandy and Belinda finished. And the block print one, *Belinda, Come Back,* in the same somber colors as all the rest, also done. And *Artist and Model* only needed a little more shading, a little more deepening. Put yourself on automatic pilot, soul control, you ought to call it, and go ahead, old buddy, and finish your hand hitting the side of her face right before she went down to the floor.

"What more must you do?" Rhinegold demanded. *"Belinda, Come Back* is the finish. Can't you see this yourself?" Sitting there hunched over in his black suit, staring at me through Coke-bottle thick glasses, the specialist in understatement.

I'd grabbed his sleeve as he was leaving, "OK, you've agreed to everything, but you tell me, what do you really think!" They were all lined up in the hallway, up the staircase, in the living room.

"You know what you've done," he said. "You think I'd agree to this lunacy if it wasn't perfection?" Then he was gone. Flight to San Francisco to look for the warehouse on Folsom Street. Madness, he had been ranting. "San Francisco is a place where you buy mountain bicycles and running shoes. We should be on West-Fifty-seventh Street or in SoHo with an exhibit like this! You are destroying me!"

The Artist Grieves for Belinda. That's what remained to be done. Blank canvas. And hour by hour in this unforgivable stupor I painted it in my mind as I lay here, Scotch or no Scotch. The artist with torch in hand and the toys blazing—trains, dolls, tiny lace curtains on plastic windows. The end of the world.

OK. You can have your slothful misery until Saturday. You know the phone is not going to ring.

"Listen, asshole, you want my advice?" Marty had said, and she was so right about the sincerity. "Forget her! I did it. You do it. You got off light, asshole, don't you know it? Her mother was that close to hanging you up by the balls."

Thunder so low I could hardly hear it. The gods moving their wooden furniture around a giant kitchen up there. The oak scrapes the side of the house, everything in motion, leaves, branches, metallic light.

G.G. in that soft boyish voice over the phone from New York: "Jeremy, I know she wouldn't do anything crazy. She'd call me if she wasn't OK."

Time for hallucinations?

I could have sworn I'd just heard Alex Clementine's voice in this house! Alex talking to another man, and it couldn't be Rhinegold because Rhinegold had left days ago for San Francisco as planned. The other man spoke very softly. And Miss Annie was talking to them, too.

Got to be an hallucination. Had refused to give Alex my number, no matter how drunk I was. I'll see you in San Francisco, I told him. I'll be just fine, perfectly fine.

It was only to G.G. and to Alex and to Dan that I told the whole story: her letter, Bonnie and the blackmail attempt, and how I had hit her and hit her and hit her. And that Marty and Bonnie would no longer look for her.

Belinda, Come Back. This is not the end of our story. It can't be.

Dan had been so angry. "Where the hell are you! You're drunk, I'm coming to get you!" No, Dan. No, Alex.

Lightning again. Everything gorgeously visible for a fraction of a second. The settee and the petit point pillows. Framed cover of *Crimson Mardi Gras,* letters faded under spotted glass. this was the smoothest Scotch. After years of white wine or a beer now and then, it was like mainlining. I mean, the furniture was moving.

Then Miss Annie said very firmly: "Please let me tell Mr. Walker that you are here!"

Light spray of rain hitting my face and hands. Glistening on the arch of the telephone receiver. Call, Belinda. Please, honey. It's going to take so long. Two weeks before I can even leave here, and then taking them all back across country and everything else that has to be done. *I still love you. I always will.*

Goddamn it, that was Alex's voice.

The rain shook the screens. The wind was cold for only a moment, as though something else in the house had been blown open. The oak branches were really thrashing out there. Like the hurricanes I remembered, when the magnolia trees came up and the tin roofs flew off the garages or flapped in the wind like the covers of books. Paint the hurricane. Paint it! *You can paint anything you want to now, don't you know that?*

Seems I had had a freeze-frame of *Final Score* on the television set. But that was hours ago, wasn't it? And when you leave it on freeze-frame for more than five minutes, the machine cuts off.

"You just leave it to me, dear lady," Alex was saying. "He'll understand."

"Mr. Walker, this is Mr. Alex Clementine from Hollywood. He insisted on coming up here, and this is Mr. George Gallagher from New York."

And voilà Alex. Just like that. How marvelous he looked, mammoth and gleaming as always as he came striding into the cool damp gloom. And right behind him a tall boy-man with Belinda's eyes and Belinda's blond hair and Belinda's mouth.

"Good lord, you're both here," I said.

I tried to sit up. The glass was lying on its side on the table and the Scotch was spilling. Then G.G., this six-foot-four blond-haired boy-man, this god, this angel, whatever he was, came and picked up the glass and wiped at the spilled Scotch with his handkerchief. What an ingratiating smile.

"Hi, Jeremy, it's me, G.G. Guess this is kind of a surprise."

"You look just like her, really you do!" Dressed all in white, even the watchband was white leather, white leather shoes.

"Christ, Jeremy," Alex said. He was striding back and forth, looking at the walls and the ceiling, at the high wooden back of the bed. "Turn on the air-conditioning in this room and shut those damned doors."

"And miss this lovely breeze? How did you find me, Alex?"

Thunder again. It broke violently over the rooftop.

G.G. jumped. "I don't like that."

"It's nothing, doesn't mean a thing," I told him. "How the hell did you find—?"

"I can find anyone when I have a mind to, Jeremy," Alex said solemnly. "Do you remember the insane things you said to me over the phone? I called G.G., and G.G. said it's a 504 area code. I see you trust G.G. with things like your phone number, though you don't trust your older friends."

"I didn't want you to come, Alex. I gave him the number in case Belinda called, that was all. Belinda hasn't called, has she, G.G.?"

"Then we get to the airport, and I tell these cab drivers, no, I want an old guy, somebody who's been driving for a couple of decades, and finally they bring up this colored man, you know, the Creole quadroon kind with the caramel skin and gray hair and I said, 'You remember Cynthia Walker, the woman who wrote *Crimson Mardi Gras?* She used to have a house up on Saint Charles, peeling paint, closed shutters, course they might have changed it.' 'Take you right to it, not changed at all.' It was simple enough."

"You should have seen him in action," G.G. said softly. "We had a whole crowd around us."

"Jeremy, this is sick," Alex said. "This is worse than what happened after Faye died."

"No, Alex, looks deceive you. I've made a bargain with myself and everything is under control. I'm merely resting, storing of energy for the final picture."

Alex got out a cigarette. Flash of G.G.'s gold lighter.

"Thank you, son."

"Sure, Alex."

I reached for the glass, but couldn't reach it.

Alex was staring at me, as if I were wearing a blindfold and couldn't see it, the way he looked at my clothes, the Scotch, the bed. Dark spots from the rain all over his fedora and the cashmere scarf was white this time, hanging all the way down the front of the Burberry.

"Where is that little lady? Madam! Can you fix something for this gentleman to eat?"

"Not till Saturday, damn it, Alex, I told you this is planned."

"Of course, I can, but can you get him to eat it, Mr. Clementine? I can't get him to eat a thing."

"I'll feed him if I have to. And some coffee, madam, a pot of coffee, too."

I tried to reach the glass again. G.G. filled it for me.

"Thank you."

"Don't give him that, son," Alex said. "Jeremy, this place is exactly the way it was twenty-five years ago. There is an opened letter on the dresser, postmarked 1961, do you realize that? And a copy of *The New York Times* for the same year on this night table."

"Alex, you're getting excited over nothing. Did you see the paintings? Tell me what you think."

"They're beautiful," G.G. said. "Oh, I love them all."

"What did you think, Alex? Tell me."

"What did Rhinegold tell you? That you'd go to jail if you did this thing? Or is he just out to make a buck off it?"

"You're not really going to do it, are you?" G.G. asked.

"Jeremy, this is hara-kiri. What kind of a man is this Rhinegold? Get on this phone. Call it off."

"She hasn't called you, has she, G.G.? You would have told me the minute you walked in."

"Oh, yes, Jeremy, I would have. But don't worry. She's all right. She wouldn't let things get too bad without calling me. And the phones are covered night and day."

"Speaking of phones, do you realize you called Blair Sackwell two nights ago at two o'clock in the morning," Alex thundered, "and you told him the whole thing?"

"And there're people at my place if she comes," G.G. said. "They're waiting for her."

"Not the whole thing, Alex," I said. "Just who she was and who I was and that she was on the run and that I hurt her. I don't have to tell the whole thing. I don't have to hang anyone. But the truth's got to come out, Alex. Goddamn it, she exists, she has a name and a past and those paintings are of her, and I love her."

"Yes," G.G. said softly.

"And that's why I called Susan Jeremiah in Paris and Ollie Boon, too. I called that woman who wrote the Bonnie biography, I called my wives. I called Marty at United Theatricals after Bonnie disconnected her private line. I called my editor and my publicist and my Hollywood agent and I told them all what was going on. I called Andy Blatky, my sculptor friend, and my neighbor Sheila. And I called all my writer friends who work for the papers, too."

And I should have stuck it out, finished the last painting, done the program notes. I'd be out of here by now.

"Calling Blair Sackwell is like calling 'CBS News,' Walker!" Alex said. "What do you mean, friends who work for what papers, where? Do you think you can control what's going to happen?"

"Yes, that's true," G.G. murmured, shaking his head, "that's really true about Blair and he's in such a rage already."

"Why don't you just get a fucking thirty-eight, the way Bonnie did!" Alex yelled.

"You should have heard Blair on the subject of Marty," G.G. said. Look of distaste, like a baby tasting carrots for the first time. "Blair calls him the Gruesome Statistic and the Ugly Reality and the Awful Fact."

"Clementine, I'm going to find her, don't you get the message! I'm going all the way with it, and I'm getting her back and we're going to be together, that is, if she hasn't done something crazy out there."

"Blair's got this idea that he's going to find her," G.G. said. "He has this wild idea she'll do Midnight Mink for him. He'll pay her one hundred grand."

"What the hell did Moreschi say to you?" Alex demanded. He was towering over me now, his hair curling under the hat brim from the humidity, his eyes burning in the shadowy light. "Are these friends of yours on the papers really friends?"

"Blair's never paid anybody any money before," G.G. said. "He just gives you the mink coat."

"It doesn't matter what Marty said. I was giving Marty a gentleman's warning, that's all. It might get out of hand."

"Oh, terrific! That's like warning Dracula," Alex said.

"I'm not out to hang Marty or anybody! But this is for Belinda and me! Marty has to understand it, that it's Holy Communion. I was never using Belinda. Marty was so wrong about the whole thing."

"You using Belinda?" Alex demanded. "You're about to wreck your goddamned life just to find her and—?"

"Oh, no, nobody's wrecking anything, can't you see it?" I said. "But that's the beauty of it, there is no simple angle—"

"Jeremy, I am taking you back to California with me now," Alex said. "I'll get that Rhinegold character on the phone and get these pictures shipped to some safe place. Berlin, for example. Now that's a good safe place."

"Out of the question, Alex."

"Then you and I will go to Portofino, like we did before, ad we will talk this thing out. Maybe G.G. will come along."

"That's wonderful, but as of Saturday I start working again, and I've got two weeks to finish that last canvas. Now about the house in Portofino, I'll sure as hell take it for a honeymoon."

"Are you really going to get married?" G.G. asked. "That is so beautiful!"

"I should have asked her when we came down here," I said. "We could have gone to Mississippi and done it with the age limit there. Nobody could have touched us."

"Where is that woman with the food?" Alex demanded. "G.G., start him a bath, will you, son? There is hot and cold running water in this house, isn't there, Jeremy? Those clawed feet in there do belong to a bathtub!"

"I love her. Once-in-a-lifetime, that's how she put it."

"I can consent, you know," G.G. said. He went towards the bathroom. "My name's on her birth certificate. I know right where it is."

"Make the water good and hot," Alex said.

"Stop it, Alex, I bathe every night before I go to bed, just the way my mother taught me. And I'm not going anywhere till Rhinegold comes back and takes over. It's all set."

Steam was flooding out of the bathroom. Sound of running water rising under the roar of the rain.

"What makes you think she'll marry you after you beat the hell out of her?" Alex demanded. "You think the press will like that angle any better? With you forty-five and her sixteen?"

"You didn't read her story—"

"Well, you practically told me every word of it—"

"—she'll marry me, I know she will."

"They can't do anything to her if she's legally married," G.G. said.

"Jeremy, you're not responsible for your actions," said Alex. "You have got to be stopped. Isn't there an air conditioner in this room?"

He started closing the French doors.

"Don't do that, Alex," I said. "Leave the doors open. I'll have Miss Annie fix up the back bedrooms for you. Now calm down."

Miss Annie came in with a tray of steaming dishes. Smell of gumbo. The room was too quiet suddenly. The rain was dying out there. Silent glimmer of lightning. And G.G. like a ghost of the all-American boy in the bathroom door as the steam poured out around him. God, what a goodlooking man.

"I'll get you some fresh clothes, Mr. Walker," Miss Annie said. Drawers sliding out. Smell of camphor.

Alex was sitting beside me. "Jeremy, call Rhinegold. Tell him the whole thing's canceled."

"Do you want sugar in this coffee?" G.G. asked.

"Walker, we're talking felony, prison, maybe kidnap, and even libel."

"Alex, I pay my lawyer to say that stuff. I sure as hell don't want to hear it for free."

"This is what Marty was screaming," G.G. said. "Libel. Did you know that Blair called Ollie and told him everything?"

"I called Ollie myself and told him," I said. "I own the stage rights to *Crimson Mardi Gras.* United Theatricals doesn't own them, never did."

G.G. laughed. "Don't talk business when you're drunk, Jeremy, not even to Ollie," he said.

"It was just broadcasting, old boy," I said. "Just broadcasting. And as for *Crimson Mardi Gras,* he can have it."

"Yeah, well, you let your agents handle that," Alex said. "Now drink this stuff, this gumbo, what is it, you like this? Drink this coffee. Sit up. Where is your lawyer, by the way?"

"I am sitting up. And you're misunderstanding everything. Until Saturday, I told you, this is a planned interlude of drunkenness. And my lawyer is in San Francisco, where he belongs, thank you. Don't get any ideas about asking him to come here."

"Ollie said that in Sardi's everybody was talking about Belinda and Marty and Bonnie and the whole story," G.G. said.

"Good God," Alex said. He took out his handkerchief, mopped his forehead.

"I didn't say anything against Marty and Bonnie," I said. "Not even to Susan Jeremiah. But goddamn it, she is alone out there, and those people did something to *me,* they did it with their detectives and their cameras with the zoom lenses and their fucking pressure on her and, goddamn them, if they get hurt. We're coming out of the closet with it."

"G.G., turn off the bathwater. Jeremy, you will not make any more calls!"

"I'll get the bathwater," said Miss Annie. "Mr. Walker, please eat the gumbo. I'm putting these fresh clothes in the bathroom for you on the back of the door."

"Alex, I completed two whole canvases since I spoke to you. Now I have vowed to drink until Saturday, and on Saturday I shall rise and finish everything. It is all going as planned."

"Jeremy, this is going to hurt," Alex said gravely. "But it's time I said it. Today *is* Saturday! It has been since twelve o'clock last night."

"Oh, my God, you don't mean it."

"It's true, Mr. Walker," Miss Annie said.

"Yes, it is," said G.G. "It's Saturday. Two o'clock, in fact."

"Get out of my way, I've got work to do. I've got to clean up. Miss Annie, fix up the back bedrooms for my guests. What time is it? Two o'clock, you said?"

I got out of the bed and fell down immediately. The room just tipped. Alex caught me. Miss Annie had the other arm. I was about to throw up.

"G.G., I think this is going to be a long one," Alex said, as he steadied me. "Madam, I will not trouble you to fix up the back bedrooms. I'll just call the Pontchartrain Hotel down the street and arrange for a nice suite. Care to join me, G.G.?"

"Oh, I'd love to, Alex," G.G. answered immediately. "Jeremy, you don't mind if I hang around for a few days, do you? Just till you're really OK?"

"Not at all," I answered. I was upright again, walking. "Stay till I'm finished and we'll leave for the Coast together. You can keep me company while I'm painting." I had my hand on the knob. My head was throbbing. "I'm chartering a plane to take the paintings back. God, I hope it doesn't crash. Wouldn't that be horrible?"

"Not if you don't fly with them," Alex said.

Miss Annie was unbuttoning my shirt. The bathroom smelled of mint bath salts. I was not going to be sick, I was going to die.

Alex was looking at G.G. "One bedroom or two, G.G.?" He reached for the phone.

"Whatever you say, Alex," G.G. was beaming back. "I'll go the food, you go the lodgings. We'll take Jeremy to Antoine's for dinner and Brennan's for breakfast and the Court of Two Sisters for lunch. Then we'll make Arnaud's and Manale's and K-Paul's and—"

"Count me out, gentlemen," I said. The water was hot, real hot. "I'll be in my studio working when you come back for your brandy and coffee."

Miss Annie would have unzipped my pants for me if I hadn't stopped her.

Alex winked at me as I pushed her gently out the door.

"At least this part's working out well, isn't it?" he said, then he smiled at G.G. "I'll take care of everything, son, thank you, and let me say you certainly are a nice polite Yankee boy."

III

THE CHAMPAGNE FLIGHT

1

THE story broke in the *San Francisco Chronicle* the week before the exhibit opened.

Jeremy Walker, "beloved" children's author and the creator of the indomitable "Saturday Morning Charlotte," might soon shock his forty million loyal readers with a one-man show in San Francisco consisting entirely of nude studies of a young adolescent girl. Even stranger than Walker's reported shift from wholesome children's art to erotic portraiture were the rumors concerning his blond blue-eyed model, that she was none other than sixteen-year-old Belinda Blanchard, daughter of "Champagne Flight" superstar Bonnie, a teenage runaway missing from her mother's multimillion-dollar Beverly Hills home for over a year.

A separate feature article went on:

"Walker's catalog copy explains that Belinda came into his life as a mystery, that he did not learn her identity as Bonnie's runaway daughter until the paintings were almost completed, and that in a violent and regrettable argument he hurt Belinda and drove her out of his life. This exhibit is a tribute to Belinda as well as a declaration of Walker's 'artistic freedom.'

"Will the public find these canvases obscene? The five by seven color photographs in the handsome exhibit catalog leave nothing to the imagination. This is representational art at its most literal. No camera could reveal more of the girl's endowments. But one week from today, when the exhibit opens in two Folsom Street galleries, handsomely refurbished entirely for this event by New York art dealer Arthur Rhinegold, the public can judge for itself."

Dan was beside himself. Why the hell wouldn't I let him hire a criminal lawyer right now?

Alex threw up his hands and said: "Let's all go to dinner at Trader Vic's while we still can."

Only G.G. was smiling as we sat around the kitchen table drinking our coffee and reading the article.

"Soon as it hits the wire service," he said, "she'll see it and she'll call, Jeremy."

"Maybe, maybe not," I said. I had visions of her walking along wind-swept streets in Paris, never glancing at the papers on the stands. But my heart was thudding. It had begun!

Rhinegold called an hour later. The press was driving him insane to get early glimpses of the pictures. But nobody was getting through that door until the museum people had seen the work on Sunday night as planned. Ten thousand copies of the catalog had just arrived in the ware-house. The bookstore at the Museum of Modern Art had just called to place an order. We were going to sell the catalog, weren't we? Wouldn't I reconsider putting a price on it.

"It will help us to print more copies!" Rhinegold insisted. "Jeremy, be reasonable."

"All right," I said. "But you keep mailing them all over. You keep giving them away."

By noon we knew the LA papers had carried their versions of the story, with added material about the "suppression" of *Final Score*. I was called the Rembrandt of children's book illustration. "Saturday Morning Charlotte" was praised as an oasis in the desert of children's TV. Belinda was called "mesmerizing" in her first performance by the reviewer who had seen her debut at Cannes. Another story was devoted entirely to Marty and Bonnie and United Theatricals' decision at Cannes not to distribute *Final Score*.

"The fully illustrated exhibit catalog is every bit as hefty as any of Walker's children's books," said a feature writer in the *Los Angeles Her-ald-Examiner*, "and it is only when measured against the earlier adven-tures of Charlotte or Bettina that the obscenity here can be fully under-stood. Belinda appears to be Walker's heroine unclothed. Would Bonnie have ever permitted such exploitation of her daughter had she known of it? Where is Belinda now?"

The telephone started to ring.

From one o'clock to six I answered reporters' questions. Yes, I had lived with her, yes, I was trying desperately to find her, no, Bonnie and

Marty were not to my knowledge looking for her any longer. Yes, I knew the paintings might jeopardize my reputation, but I had to go with the paintings. The paintings were my most important work to date. No, my publishers had not commented. No, I was not worried about negative reactions. An artist has to follow his obsessions. That had always been my way.

Dan gave up and went back to his office to arrange for his secretary, Barbara, to come over and field these calls.

Alex was getting a little tired of the house, just as I knew he would, what with my cooking and the one Victorian bathroom. I wouldn't be offended, would I, if he went on up and got a suite at the Clift?

"Of course not, Alex, go ahead. I wouldn't blame you if you lit out of here altogether, I told you that, you and G.G. both."

"Undiscussable," Alex murmured. "I'll be five minutes away if you need me, and you call me and tell me what's happening. I'll never get through on that phone!"

G.G. was worried about the phone, too. It was ringing non-stop by seven. The operators were cutting in with "emergencies" when I was on the line.

"I'm going with Alex," G.G. said. "I'll call New York and give them the number of the hotel room, and that way she can reach me if she can't reach you."

My ex-wife Celia called from New York after dinner. She was hysterical. She'd been trying to get through for an hour and a half. It was in the columns: WALKER WALKS OFF ON YOUNG FANS.

"Celia, I told you, I wouldn't do another children's book if somebody chained me in a dungeon and said I had to do it or I'd never be let out."

"Jeremy, that sounds like a children's book! What's this girl got, to make you flip out like this over her? Jeremy, you need help."

"Celia, from the first moment I saw her, it was for me!"

The Dallas papers had it on Tuesday morning, concentrating on Bonnie, their hometown girl. She and Belinda had been photographed together five years ago at their last press conference in Dallas. Could a secret rift have separated mother and daughter for over a year?

As for Walker, who "claims" to have lived with teenage beauty Belinda as he painted her, his books were in every library in the metroplex. Walker's last appearance in Fort Worth in 1982 had been a mob scene with two thousand books sold.

Then the call came from Houston that the *Chronicle* and the *Post* there had also run it with the focus on Jeremiah saying, "There are hints of a Texas-size scandal here."

There was a picture of Susan in the de rigueur cowboy hat. "For a year

I tried to reach her for a part in a movie," Susan had told the paper long-distance from Los Angeles. "They kept telling me she was away at school. Now it turns out she was in San Francisco living with Jeremy. It's a damn good thing somebody was taking care of her."

No, Susan hadn't seen the catalog, though she'd try to be in San Francisco for the opening. "Look, he doesn't have to prove his integrity as an artist. Go in any bookstore. Open one of his books."

Her Dad was quoted as saying he was proud of her *Final Score*. They'd tried to get it shown at a film festival in Houston and run into the most suspicious difficulties. "I mean, I think United Theatricals killed this picture for highly personal reasons. I think we have a case of ego and temperament, and old-style Hollywood prima donna who didn't want any competition from an ingenue who just happened to be her little girl. But then there are a lot of things about it that puzzle us."

"I can tell you this much," Susan added. "If and when I find Belinda, I'm offering her the lead in my next picture. It's real nice and all that that she's the subject of eighteen paintings by Jeremy Walker, but her own career's been on ice a little too long."

Jeremiah had wrapped up her commitments to United Theatricals. Galaxy Pictures was bankrolling her new venture, *Of Will and Shame,* with Limelight to distribute worldwide.

OK, Susan, take it and run with it, honey. Everything was working out just fine.

Now those guys with the British accents were calling from the *National Enquirer.* They were so surprised when I agreed to talk to them.

"I love her. I quarreled with her because I didn't understand all the things that had happened to her. She had starred in this wonderful movie, and then it was never distributed. Ask Susan Jeremiah. And in Hollywood she'd had a tragic romance. She'd been in terrible shape when she ran away from home. She was in New York for a while when detectives started looking for her. Then she came to San Francisco where we met. But, you see, the important thing is that I find her. She's out there somewhere all alone."

Stringers from the *Globe* and the *Star* came right to the front door. In fact, when I went to answer the bell, I saw a number of people standing around out there. A flashbulb went off when I stepped onto the porch. My neighbor Sheila was talking to a man on the curb.

"Way to go, Jeremy!" Sheila shouted. She waved a copy of the catalog. The reporters tried to get in the door.

"Nobody inside," I said, "now what do you want to know?"

We were still talking when another stringer showed up from *People* magazine. Come on, if I just let her in, it meant she could sell her story.

She needed the money. I said no. I noticed there was a guy up on the balcony of the wooden apartment house on the corner, shooting pictures with a telephoto lens.

G.G. called from the Clift at eleven thirty. "The phone situation is almost impossible. How could Belinda possibly get through?"

"Dan's working on that. The phone company may be able to put in another line. But at the rate it's going, that won't help very much."

"Well, I just got a call from friends in Boston. It's in the papers there, and it was in the *Washington Post,* too."

"And Belinda has not called," I said dejectedly.

"Patience, Jeremy," G.G. said. "By the way, Alex is coming up in a while to have a nightcap with you."

"Who's going to bed after the nightcap?" I asked. "I'm sitting here by the phone."

"Yeah, me too."

But I was asleep on the studio floor with the answering machine up loud when G.G. shouted to me through it on Wednesday morning:

"Jeremy, wake up. *USA Today* just ran it. So did *The New York Times.* That's bound to reach her in Europe. The *Herald Tribune* over there must be carrying it by now."

By Wednesday noon the local news radio station was running items about us constantly. We were getting calls from friends in Aspen and Atlanta and even Portland, Maine.

Then Dan came in with the *Los Angeles Times.* Marty Moreschi and Bonnie had issued a statement denying all knowledge of Belinda's whereabouts or activities for a year. "Bonnie is shocked and horrified to learn of this bizarre exhibit of paintings in San Francisco. Through private agencies Bonnie has been searching night and day for Belinda since the girl's disappearance. Bonnie's first and only concern is for her daughter's welfare. Bonnie is on the verge of nervous collapse."

An hour later, the Cable News Network ran live footage of Bonnie and Marty mobbed by reporters outside the offices of a lawyer on Wilshire Boulevard. And there Marty in his tight three-piece suit, gold watchband flashing, stabbing his finger at the reporters:

"This is her daughter you're talking about! And now we find out she's been living with this screwball painter in San Francisco? How do you think she feels?"

Glimpse of Bonnie, dark glasses, head bowed as she passed through the glass doors of the building with Marty behind her.

Then suddenly "Saturday Morning Charlotte" was staring at me from the screen.

* * *

I GOT the first hate call about three that afternoon. The speaker was on, so Dan could also hear it.

"Child molester! You like painting little girls naked? Some children's author you are!" Click.

I got chills all over. Dan crushed out his cigarette and walked out of the room. After that, it was maybe one hate call to every five from friends or reporters.

AROUND four I decided it was time to check out the Carmel house. I dreaded going there, finding it cold and empty, but what if by some miracle Belinda was there?

I picked up G.G. at the Clift and we drove south in the MG-TD, with the top down. The wind felt good.

The radio told us that prominent Dallas attorney Daryl Blanchard, brother of "Champagne Flight" star Bonnie, was on his way to Hollywood to see his sister regarding Belinda's disappearance. Daryl refused to make a statement to the press.

I wasn't surprised to find everything in Carmel the way Belinda and I had left it—even the soft little bed still rumpled—and no evidence that she had ever returned on her own to the place.

Agony to come back to this little house.

I sat down and wrote a long note to her and put it on the kitchen table. G.G. wrote a note of his own, giving her the number at his hotel. Then I left her some money in the loft upstairs—several hundred dollars in a white envelope on the pillow. Then it was time to go.

The fog was rolling in. Carmel was ghostly. I felt a touch of fear. I stood in the door of the cottage for a long time, looking at the scattered primroses in the sandy garden, the great twisted limbs of the Monterey cypress reaching up to the gray sky. The fog was blowing up the street.

"God, I hope she's all right, G.G.," I whispered.

He put his arm around my shoulder. But he didn't say a word. All through the last week in New Orleans he had been so encouraging, so optimistic. But I knew he made it his business to cheer up others. I'd seen the same trait in Belinda. They smiled for others, said the right things for others. I wondered how deep you had to dig to find out what G.G. really felt.

When I looked at him now, he gave me one of his subtle protective smiles. "It's going to be fine, Jeremy. Honest. Just give her the time to find out."

"You say that like you really believe it," I said. "You're not just trying to make things OK?"

"Jeremy, when I saw the paintings," he said, "I knew everything was going to be OK. Come on, give me the keys, I'll drive back if you're tired."

WHEN we got back, we had dinner in the kitchen with Alex and Dan. Alex had brought a good bottle of Cabernet Sauvignon and some excellent steaks, the kind you can hardly find in a market, and some cold lobster for salad. G.G. and I were the cooks.

We ate in silence, with the machine on as the voices came one after another into the room:

"Jeremy, this is Andy Blatky. Have you see the *Berkeley Gazette!* I'll read it to you, man, listen: 'Though the final judgment can only be made from the canvases themselves, there is little doubt from the catalog that these paintings constitute Walker's most ambitious attempt to date.' "

"People like you should be prosecuted, do you know that? You think just because you call yourself an artist you can get away with painting filthy pictures of a young girl?"

"Listen, you don't know me. I loved your books, but how could you do it? How could you do something so dirty? How could you do that to us?"

"Turn it off!" Alex said.

THE New Orleans papers didn't run the story till Thursday and they were rather polite. IN THE SOUTHERN GOTHIC TRADITION? asked the headline over the grainy black-and-white newsprint photos of the top half of *Belinda with Doll House* and *Belinda with Communion Things.* "Children viewing these remarkably realistic rendered paintings of the nude Belinda should at least be accompanied by adults."

The Thursday *Miami Herald* said the exhibit would destroy my reputation forever. "This is smut, call it what you will, and the crassness with which these so-called catalogs were mailed to the press represents a cynicism which might leave even old-time big-city porn peddlers stunned."

A local commentator on one of the San Francisco television stations said pretty much the same thing.

Network news reports showed a big, hefty dark-suited Daryl Blanchard landing at LAX to a mob of microphones and questions. "We have been sick with worry over my niece since her disappearance. I know nothing about this man in San Francisco. Now, if you gentlemen will please excuse me—"

My ex-wife Andrea called late that night. She was both sarcastic and genuinely concerned. Had I seen the San Jose newspapers? I'd always wanted to destroy myself. Was I happy now? Did I know what I'd done to her and to Celia? The San Jose papers had printed photographs of three

of the Belinda pictures with headline: PICTURES AT AN EXHIBITION—AN EM-
BARRASSING CONFESSION. A local feminist, Charlotta Greenway, had blasted
the work as the "exploitation of teenage Belinda Blanchard," saying the
exhibit, which hadn't even opened yet, ought to be closed down.

Andy Blatky called again Friday from Berkeley to tell me that the story
in the *Oakland Trib* had featured a photograph of a book exhibit at
Splendor in the Grass on Solano Avenue, with the statement that my
autograph party there two months ago might be the last appearance as a
children's author that I would ever make. "Hang in there, man!" Andy
said.

But by the weekend it was the *New York Post* that had gone the far-
thest, quoting freely from Midnight Mink president Blair Sackwell, who
had been "ranting" about the "Belinda scandal" on every TV and radio
talk show that he could book. He had publicly blasted Marty Moreschi
and United Theatricals for covering up Belinda's disappearance and trying to ruin G.G.'s famous salon in New York.

"You don't get AIDS from a hairdresser," Blair was reported as saying, "and G.G.'s employees don't have it and never did." G.G. had closed
his doors officially three weeks ago. One loyal customer, Mrs. Harrison
Banks Philips, was quoted as saying it was perfectly atrocious what had
happened to G.G. She'd gotten four anonymous phone calls in one day
warning her not to use his services. G.G. should sue.

"Of course, United Theatricals won't comment," Blair had thundered
in a later telephone interview. "What the hell are they going to say? Isn't
anybody asking why this girl ran away from home in the first place?
When she ended up with Jeremy Walker, doesn't sound like she had any
place else to go!"

Blair had "waved" the catalog to television viewers on the David Let-
terman show. "Of course, they're gorgeous paintings. She's beautiful,
he's talented, what do you expect? And I'll tell you something else, too,
it's damned refreshing to see a picture that doesn't look like a two-year-
old threw a carton of eggs one by one at the canvas. I mean, the guy can
draw, for God's sakes."

On the Larry King show Blair had railed against Marty and Bonnie.
Belinda had disappeared the night after the shooting. Blair wanted to
know what had happened in that house. The pictures were not pornographic: "We're not talking *Penthouse* or *Playboy* here, are we? The
man's an artist. And speaking of pictures, I have a standing offer: one
hundred thou to Belinda if she'll do Midnight Mink. And if Eric Arlington won't take the picture, I'll take it. I've got a Hasselblad and a tripod,
for God's sakes. For years I've been telling Eric how to make those

photographs, I say, yeah, that's it, now do it. All he does is press the button on the camera. Well, hell, I can do that myself."

Syndicated columns were now carrying items about Blair and the exhibit all over the country. Jody, my publicist, called from New York to say there's been another big piece in the LA papers all about Susan Jeremiah and the film that was "censored" by United Theatricals.

My LA agent left two messages on the answering machine, but no comment. My New York editor did the same thing.

AT seven P.M. Sunday night I sat at the table with a glass of Scotch in front of me. That was dinner. I knew that the museum people were just arriving at the gallery on Folsom Street. Rhinegold had notified them of the special showing a month ahead of time. And then mailed the catalogs all over the world as instructed.

It was these people—from the Whitney, the Tate, the Pompidou Center, the Metropolitan, the Museum of Modern Art in New York, and a dozen other such places—who would have the first crack at the work.

But a good two dozen other people would be there tonight, the big rich art patrons, the millionaires from London and Paris and Milan whose purchases carried almost as much distinction as the museum purchases because their collections were "so important," the people whom every art dealer sought to impress.

These were the people who meant everything to Rhinegold. These were the people who meant everything to me. Though anyone could buy one of the Belinda paintings, these people were given first choice.

But would they come to a nameless gallery on Folsom Street in San Francisco even for Rhinegold, who had always wined them and dined them in the proper places in Berlin and New York?

I sat back with my arms folded, thinking about years and years ago in a studio in the Haight-Ashbury when I wanted to be a painter, just a painter. I hated these people, the gallery system, the museums. I hated them.

My mouth was dry, as if I were about to be shot by a firing squad. The clock ticked. Belinda didn't call. The operator didn't break in on the voices talking into the answering machine to say, "Emergency call from Belinda Blanchard, will you release the line?"

It was late when Rhinegold came in. He was scowling. He wiped his face with his handkerchief as though he was uncomfortably hot. Still he didn't take off his black overcoat. He hunkered over in the chair and glared at the glass of Scotch.

I didn't say anything. A wind outside was lashing the poplars against each other. The voice talking to the answering machine said so low I could hardly hear it: "—should call me in the morning, I was the one who hosted your tour in Minneapolis, and I'd like to ask you a few questions—"

I looked at Rhinegold. If he didn't say something soon, I was going to die, but I wasn't going to ask.

He made a face at the Scotch.

"You want something else?"

"How gracious of you," he sneered. It seemed he was trembling. With what, rage?

I got the white wine out of the refrigerator, filled a glass for him, and set it down.

"All my life," he said slowly, "I have struggled to get people to look at art dispassionately, to evaluate the accomplishment that is there. Not to talk previous sales and status buyers, not to talk fashion or fads. Look, that is what I say to my clients. Look at the painting itself."

I sat down opposite him and folded my hands on the table. He stared at the glass.

"I have loathed gimmicks, publicity tricks," he continued. "I have loathed the devices used by lesser artists to publicize their work."

"I don't blame you," I said quietly.

"And now I find myself in the midst of this scandal." His face reddened. He glared at me, his eyes behind the thick glasses impossibly huge. "Representatives from every museum in the world were there, I swear it! I've never seen such a turnout, not in New York or Berlin."

I could feel the hairs rising on the back of my neck.

He grabbed the glass of wine as if he was going to throw it at me.

"And what can we expect from such a situation?" he demanded, eyes flashing on me like goldfish bumping the aquarium glass. "I mean, do you realize the danger?"

"You've been warning me about it continuously since this started," I replied. "I'm surrounded by people who warn me about everything. Belinda used to warn me three times a week."

So what the fuck happened? Had they split at the canvases? Walked out scoffing? Told the reporters on the curb it was trash?

I let the Scotch warm me. I felt sad suddenly, immensely and awfully sad. Just for one second it was Belinda and I alone upstairs in the studio, the radio playing Vivaldi, and I was painting and she was lying on the floor, her head on a pillow, reading her *French Vogue* and the deadline for this pain was "someday."

"Someday." I'd been sitting in this room for five days. That's not very long. Not very long at all, and yet it seemed forever. And she was where?

A loud coarse voice broke through the lowered volume of the answering machine: "Jeremy, this is Blair Sackwell, I'm in San Francisco at the Stanford Court. I wanna meet you. Come down here now."

I lifted a pencil and wrote down Stanford Court. Rhinegold did not even seem to notice, to have heard. He continued to stare at the glass.

I looked at the blank television screen in the corner. On the eleven o'clock news would they say the experts had pronounced the work trash? I looked at Rhinegold. His lower lip was jutting, he was squinting as he studied the glass.

"They loved it," he said.

"Who?" I asked, unbelieving.

"All of them," he said. He looked up. Face reddening again. Heavy cheeks trembling. "It was electric in that room. The people from the Pompidou, who bought your last painting! The people from the Whitney, who would never even consider your work. Count Solosky from Vienna, who once told me you were an illustrator not a painter, don't talk to him of illustrators. He looks me in the eye and says, 'I want the *Holy Communion*. I want *The Carousel Trio*.' Just like that, he says it. Count Solosky, the most important collector in Europe!"

He was in a fury. His hand had curled into a fist beside the glass.

"And that's why you're unhappy?" I asked.

"I didn't say I was unhappy," he said. He sat up straight, adjusted the lapels of his coat, and narrowed his eyes. "I think I can safely say that in spite of all your efforts to destroy my integrity and my reputation, *this exhibit will be a triumph*. Now, if you will excuse me, I am going back to my hotel!"

2

BLAIR was surrounded by reporters in the lobby of the Stanford Court when I got there. Everybody was scribbling. The old-fashioned flashbulbs were really going off.

I was blinded for a second. Then I saw G.G. getting up out of the chair beside Blair. G.G. was all shiny in a white silk turtleneck and brown velvet blazer, but even at six foot four he didn't outshine Blair.

Belinda had not exaggerated when she described this man. He was maybe five feet two and had a very leathery tanned face with a big nose and huge horn-rimmed glasses and only a crown left of gray hair. He was dressed in a perfectly fitted suit covered all in silver sequins. Even his tie had sequins. And the raincoat hanging over his shoulders was lined in white mink. He was puffing on a George Burns-style cigar and socking down whiskey on the rocks as he told everyone in a harsh, booming voice that he couldn't verify that Belinda had had an affair with Marty, of course he couldn't, what did they think he was, a Peeping Tom, but they damn well ought to ask why Bonnie shot her husband and nobody called the LAPD when Belinda ran away.

I was stunned. So it had come to that—and so quickly. Oh, Belinda, I thought, I did try to keep it clean.

"Jeremy!" Cynthia Lawrence of the *Chronicle* was suddenly standing in front of me. "Did Belinda ever tell you there was something between her and Moreschi?"

"One hundred Gs!" Blair roared at me, as I tried to get around Cynthia, "for the wedding picture of you both in Midnight Mink."

Laughter and titters from the reporters, both the old friends and the strangers.

"Sure, if Belinda's willing," I said. "Married in Midnight Mink, why not? But why not two hundred Gs, if it's going to be two of us instead of one."

Another volley of laughter.

"When two people marry," Blair yelled, aiming the cigar right at me, "you're supposed to become one!"

Through the laughter the reporters were shouting out questions.

"Then you do intend to marry Belinda?"

"Is Bonnie on drugs!" Cynthia asked.

"We don't know that!" G.G. said impatiently. I could see he was finding this as unpleasant as I found it. In fact, he looked almost angry.

"The hell we don't!" Blair said, climbing to his feet and pulling the raincoat around him. He tapped his ashes onto the rug. "Just go down there, have a drink in the Polo Lounge, and listen to the gossip. She's so out of it she couldn't talk and chew a stick a gum at the same time, she'd strangle."

"Will you marry Belinda?"

"But it's just gossip!" G.G. said.

"Yes, I want to marry Belinda," I answered. "I should have asked her before."

I still couldn't see straight from the flash. More questions. I couldn't follow.

"Let's get out of here," G.G. whispered in my ear. "Belinda wouldn't want all this to happen. Blair's out of his mind."

"Jeremy, are you happy with the response to the paintings?" "Jeremy, were you at the preview?"

Blair seized me by the arm. Amazingly strong little man.

"Was it a long affair between Marty and Belinda?"

"They were like glue in Hollywood," Blair said. "I told you. Ask Marty about that."

"G.G., was it Bonnie and Marty that ruined your business?"

"Nobody ruined my business, I told you. I decided to leave New York."

"That's a fucking lie," Blair said. "They spread their rumors all over town."

"G.G., will you sue?"

"I don't sue people. Blair please—"

"Tell them what happened, damn it!" Blair roared. He had G.G. on one side and me on the other and he was shoving us across the lobby. I almost laughed it was so ridiculous. The reporters were following like bugs around a porch bulb.

"The rumors about the salon started when they came looking for her," G.G. explained with obvious difficulty. "But by the time I sold the business we had things well in hand. I did get quite a price for the business, you know—"

"They ran you out of New York!" Blair said.

"And what were the rumors?"

"Did you know she was living with Jeremy Walker?"

"I knew they were friends and he was good to her and he was painting her pictures. Yes, I knew."

"Jeremy," Cynthia almost tripped me. "Did Belinda ever tell you Marty had been carrying on with her?"

"Look," I said, "the important thing is the exhibit opens tomorrow. That is exactly what Belinda and I both want, and I hope, wherever she is, she will hear about it. Her movie *Final Score* was stopped, but no one will stop me from showing the paintings I did of her."

We had reached the elevators. G.G. pushed me inside after Blair. Then G.G. blocked the reporters as the doors closed.

"Ah ha!" Blair roared. He stuck the cigar between his teeth and rubbed his hands together.

"You're saying too much!" G.G. said. "You're going overboard. You really are." Even as upset as he was, he kept his soft tone, and his face showed worry as much as anger.

"Yeah, that's what my aunt Margaret told me when I bought out her little fur company and ran my first ad with Bonnie right smack in the middle of *Vogue!* Don't look pale, Walker. I'm going to crucify that Hollywood wop, that Gruesome Statistic, that Awful Fact."

Reporters were waiting when the doors opened.

"You guys get out of here," Blair said, leading us past them, "or I call the front desk." He was puffing cigar smoke ahead of us like a little locomotive.

"Jeremy, is it true the family knew she was with you? That Bonnie came here herself?"

What? Had I heard that right? I turned, tried to focus on the reporter. That part of the story I'd told to no one, no one—except those closest to us, G.G. and Alex and Susan. But they would never have told.

The reporter was a young man in a windbreaker and jeans, nondescript, steno pad, ballpoint, portable tape recorder clipped to his belt. He was scrutinizing me, must have seen the blood rushing to my face.

"Is it true," he asked, "that you met with Bonnie at the Hyatt Regency right here in San Francisco?"

"Look, leave us alone, please," G.G. said politely. Blair was watching me intently.

"That true?" Blair asked.

"Listen to this!" the reporter said, as he stood between me and the door to the room. He was flipping through the steno pad. I noticed the little tape recorder was running. The red light was on.

We were ringed in by inquisitive faces, but I couldn't see them. Nothing registered.

"I have a statement right here from a limousine driver who says he drove Bonnie *and* Belinda to the vicinity of your house on September 10, that, after Belinda got out of the car, Bonnie waited three hours in front of your Seventeenth Street house before you came out, and then he picked you up at—"

"No comment!" I said. "Blair, have you got the key to this damned door?"

"Then she knew you were living with Belinda!"

"Bonnie knew where Belinda was!"

"Why the hell no comment!" Blair shouted. "Answer his questions—tell him. Did Bonnie know the whole time?"

"Did Bonnie know about the paintings?"

"Open the door, Blair," G.G. said. He grabbed the key out of Blair's hand and unlocked the door.

I went inside behind Blair. G.G. shut the door. He looked as exhausted as I felt. But Blair sprang into life immediately.

He tossed off the mink-lined raincoat, stomped his foot, and rubbed his hands together again, the cigar between his teeth.

"Ah ha, perfect! And you didn't tell me she came here. Who's side are you on, Rembrandt?"

"You keep this up, Blair," G.G. said, "and they'll sue you. They'll ruin you, the way you keep telling people that they ruined me!"

"They did ruin you, what the fuck are you talking about?"

"No, they didn't!" G.G. was clearly exasperated. The blood was dancing in his cheeks. But still he wouldn't raise his voice. "I'm here because I want to be. New York was over for me, Blair, I left because it was over. The worst part is, Belinda doesn't know that. She may think it's all her fault. But they'll go after you with their big guns if you don't stop."

"So let them try. My money's in Swiss francs. They'll never get a cent of it. I can sell furs from Luxembourg just as easy as from the Big Apple. I'm seventy-two. I got cancer. I'm a widower. What can they do to me?"

"You know you can't live anywhere but New York," G.G. said patiently, "and the cancer's been in remission for ten years. Slow down, Blair, for God's sakes."

"Look, G.G., the thing's out of control," I said. "If they nailed down that limousine driver—"

"You said it," Blair said at once. He picked up the phone, punched in a single digit, and demanded in a loud voice that the hall outside his room be cleared immediately.

Then he shot past me into the bathroom, looked in the shower, came back out. "Look under the bed, you strapping nitwit!" he said to G.G.

"There is no one under the bed," G.G. said. "You're dramatizing everything as usual."

"Am I?" Blair went down on all fours and lifted the spread. "OK, nobody!" he said. He stood up. "Now you tell me about this meeting with Bonnie. What did she know?"

"Blair, I don't want to fight their dirt with more dirt," I said. "I have said everything that needs to be said."

"What a character! Didn't anybody ever tell you all great painters are pricks? Look at Caravaggio, a real bastid! And what about Gauguin, a prick, I tell you, a first-class prick."

"Blair, you're talking so loud, they'll hear you in the hallway," G.G. said.

"I hope so!" he screamed at the door. "OK. Forget about Bonnie for the moment. What did you do with the letter Belinda wrote you, the whole story?" Blair demanded.

"It's in a bank vault in New Orleans. The key is in another vault."

"And the photographs you took?" Blair asked.

"Burned all of them. My lawyer kind of insisted on that." Excruciating, burning all those prints. And yet I had known all along the moment would come. If the police got the photographs, the press would get them, and everything would change with the photographs. The paintings were something else.

Blair considered. "You're sure you vaporized every one of them."

"Yes, what didn't burn went down the garbage disposer. Not even the FBI could get their hands on that."

G.G. gave a sad little laugh and shook his head. He'd helped me with the burning and grinding, and he'd hated it, too.

"Oh, don't be too cocky, sonny boy!" Blair shouted at him. "Didn't anybody ever tell you transporting a minor over the state lines for illegal purposes is a federal crime?"

"You are a madman, Blair," G.G. said calmly.

"No, I'm not. Listen, Rembrandt, I'm on your side. But you were wise to torch that stuff. Ever hear of Bonnie's brother, Daryl? He'll be on your tail in no time. And United Theatricals is already getting calls from the Moral Majority—"

"You know that for sure?" I asked.

"Marty himself told me!" he answered. "In between gypsy curses and gangster threats. All through the Bible Belt they're calling the affiliate stations. What's this bullshit, they're asking, about Bonnie letting her daughter run away from home? You go home and make sure there's nothing to connect you with her but art and that romantic slop you wrote in the exhibit catalog."

"I've already done all that. But I think G.G. is right. You're not being very personally careful."

"Oh, you're a sweetheart, you really are." He started pacing, hands in his pockets, the cigar between his teeth again. Then he whipped it out of his mouth. "But let me tell you something, I love that little girl. No, don't look at me like that, and don't say what's on the tip of your tongue. You think I hate Bonnie 'cause she snubbed me. Your damned right, but hating her is like hating bad weather. I love that little girl. I watched her grow up. I held her when she was a baby. She's sweet and kind like her daddy, and she always was. None of that other bullshit ever touched her. And I'll tell you something else. There were times in my life when every single connection I had was bullshit, crap I'm talking, business, lies, major filth! And you know what I'd do? I'd get on the phone and call her. Yeah, Belinda. She was just a kid, but she was a person, a real person. At parties on Saint Esprit we would go off together, her and me, we'd ride her goddamn motorcycle. And we'd just talk to each other, her and me. She got screwed by those bums. And it was damned near inevitable. Somebody should have looked out for her!"

Blair took a long drag off his cigar, spewing all the smoke into the room, and then he sank down into a little chair by the window and put the heel of his silver tennis shoe up on the velvet seat in front of him. He was lost in his thoughts for a second.

I didn't say anything. The sadness came over me again, the sadness I'd felt so strongly back in the kitchen at the house and in the little cottage in Carmel. I missed her so much. I was so afraid for her. The exhibit was a triumph, that was the word the most cautious of men had used, a triumph, and where was she to share it with me? What the hell did all of this mean till she came home?

Blair was watching me through the cloud of smoke from his cigar.

"Now you gonna tell me what happened when Bonnie came up here?" he demanded. "You gonna give me all the dirt or not?"

There was a loud knock on the door suddenly. Then another knock and another, as if more than one person was out there.

"No, Jeremy," G.G. said, looking straight at me, "don't do it."

I looked into his eyes and I saw Belinda again. And I saw this over-grown sweet kid who meant just what he said.

The knocking got louder. Blair ignored it. He continued to stare at me.

"Blair, don't you see?" I asked. "We're past all that. I don't have to tell anybody anything else. And neither do you."

"G.G., open that fucking door, damn it!" Blair said.

The reporters, crowded into the corridor, were holding up the morning papers. They had the new editions of *The World This Week* in their hands, the early morning *Los Angeles Times,* and the New York tabloid *News Bulletin.*

"Have you seen these stories? Do you have any comment?"

NURSE TELLS ALL. BONNIE, DAUGHTER, AND HUSBAND IN LOVE TRIANGLE. KID-DIE PORN PAINTINGS OF BONNIE'S DAUGHTER, BONNIE'S DAUGHTER RUNS FROM STEPFATHER TO TRYST WITH SAN FRANCISCO PAINTER. BONNIE, STAR OF "CHAM-PAGNE FLIGHT," ABANDONS TEENAGE DAUGHTER FOR PRODUCER HUSBAND. BE-LINDA STILL ON THE RUN.

"Well, Rembrandt," Blair said over the noise. "I think you gotta point."

[3]

ALL morning long as people lined up for two blocks before the Folsom Street gallery, the news came in, through television, radio, telegrams at the front door, and calls from George and Alex on a private line that had just been installed.

Three more lines had been added to my regular number also, but, now that the tabloids had the story, the situation was worse than ever with the hate calls coming in from as far away as Nova Scotia. Dan's secretary, Barbara, was at the house now full-time, answering as fast as the machine.

It was all coming out. Nurses, paramedics, a chauffeur who had been fired by Marty, two of my neighbors who had seen Belinda with me—those and others had apparently peddled their stories. Film critics dragged out their old notes on the Cannes showing of *Final Score*. The TV and radio people were too cautious to use the tabloid accounts verbatim, but one medium fed upon another with ever-increasing confidence. News of fire, flood, political events—all this continued as before —but we were the scandal of the moment.

The morning network news showed live coverage in LA of United Theatricals executives disclaiming all knowledge of the alleged disappearance of Bonnie's daughter, Belinda, insisting that they knew nothing about the distribution of *Final Score*.

"Champagne Flight" would air this week as scheduled, said network spokesmen. They had no comment on reports that affiliates all through the South were dropping the program.

Again and again "modest" portions of the paintings were flashed across the screen: Belinda's head in the Communion veil, Belinda in punk makeup on the carousel horse. Belinda in braids dancing.

Television cameras stopped Uncle Daryl's car as he tried to leave the Beverly Hills Hotel. Through the open window he said: "I can tell you right now, as God is my witness, my sister, Bonnie, knew nothing about her daughter living with this man in San Francisco. I don't know why the exhibit has not been closed down."

The late edition of the morning *Chronicle* ran a picture of G.G. and me and Blair taken in the lobby of the Stanford Court. DID BONNIE KNOW OF WALKER'S PAINTINGS? Two kids in the Haight claimed to have known Belinda, they called her "wild, crazy, lots of fun, just a really beautiful spirit" and said she'd disappeared off the street in June.

When the noon news came on Channel 5, I saw my own house live on the screen, got up and went to the front windows and looked out at the video cameras. When I went back to the kitchen, they had switched locations to the Clift downtown and the reporter on the scene was talking about the closing of G.G.'s salon.

I flicked the channel. Live from LA the unmistakable face and voice of Marty Moreschi again. He was squinting in the southern California sun as he addressed reporters in what appeared to be a public parking lot.

I turned up the volume because the doorbell was ringing.

"Look, you want my comment!" he said in the equally unmistakable New York street voice, "I wanna know where she is, that's what I wanna know. We've got eighteen pictures of her naked up there, selling at half a million a pop, but where is Belinda? No, you don't tell me—I tell you!" The loaded .38-caliber finger again aimed at the reporter. "We've had detectives scouring this country for her. We've been worried sick about her. Bonnie had no idea where she was. And now this clown in San Francisco says she was living with him. And she consented to these pictures. Like hell!"

"I knew he'd take this tack," Dan said. He had just come into the kitchen. He was unshaven and his shirt was a mess. Both of us had slept in our clothes listening to the answering machine and the radio. But he wasn't angry anymore. He was concentrating on strategy instead.

"—come right out and say she was missing?" Marty yelled. "And have some guy kidnap her? And now we find out this world-famous children's artist was busy painting every detail of her anatomy? You think he didn't know who she was?"

"He is slick, he is real slick," Dan said.

"It's a dare," I said. "It's been a series of dares from the beginning."

Marty was getting in the car, the window was going up. The limousine was pushing through the flash of silver microphones and bowed heads.

I hit the remote control again; the anchorwoman on Channel 4: "—of the LAPD confirms that no missing persons report was ever filed on fifteen-year-old Belinda Blanchard. Belinda is seventeen now, by the way, and her whereabouts are still completely unknown. Her father, internationally known hairstylist George Gallagher, confirmed this morning that he does not know where she is and is eager to find her."

The door bell was now ringing incessantly. There was a knocking.

"How about not answering it?" Dan said.

"And suppose she's out there?" I asked.

I went to the lace curtains. Reporters on the steps, the video cameraman right behind them.

I opened the door. Cynthia Lawrence was holding an open copy of *Time,* which had hit the stands less than an hour ago. Had I seen the article?

I took it from her. Impossible to read it now. The questions were coming not only from her but from the others farther down on the steps and on the sidewalk. I scanned the scene, the crowd across the street, the teenagers on the corner, people on the balconies of the apartment house. There were a couple of men in suits next to the phone booth by the grocery store. Cops? Could be.

"No, she hasn't contacted me," I said in answer to a question I'd hardly heard. "No idea at all where she is," I said to another. "Yes, she would, I can say that with absolute conviction, she approved of the paintings and she loved them."

I shut the door. Cynthia could always buy herself another magazine. I ignored the ringing and pounding and started in on the *Time* article. They had run full-color pictures of *The Carousel Horse Trio* and the one I secretly loved most of all, Belinda in the summer suit, standing with her back to the river titled simply *Belinda, My Love.*

"Why would this man, who is a household word to millions, risk his reputation as a trusted and admired children's artist for such an exhibit?" asked the writer. "No less unsettling than the frank eroticism of these paintings, each one faithfully rendered in a five-by-seven color photograph in the expensive exhibit catalog, is a narrative of ever-deepening madness as we see Belinda subjected to the artist's bizarre fantasies—*Belinda with Dolls, Belinda in Riding Clothes, Belinda on the Carousel Horse*—before she is finally transformed into the most enticing of women —*Belinda in Mother's Bed*—only to be victim of stunning violence in the carefully rendered fight of *Artist and Model* in which the painter strikes his muse cruelly across the face, causing her to sink to the floor against a backdrop of stained and broken wallpaper. This is not merely a children's author's attempt to commit public suicide, it is not merely a tribute to a young woman's beauty, it is a self-indicting chronicle of a lurid and conceivably tragic affair. To learn that Belinda Blanchard was in fact a teenage runaway when these pictures were painted, to learn that she is again missing, is to arouse speculation that is perhaps best pursued by law enforcement officials rather than artistic critics."

I closed the magazine. Dan was coming down the hall. He had a steaming cup of coffee in his hand.

"That was Rhinegold on the phone, he said four guys from the SFPD just went through the exhibit."

"How does he know that's what they were? Surely they didn't show their badges to him—"

"That's exactly what they did. They didn't want to stand in line like everybody else."

"Holy shit," I said.

"Yeah, you can say that again," he said, "and I've called in a criminal lawyer name of David Alexander and he'll be here in two hours and I don't want to hear another word on that score."

I shrugged. I gave him the *Time* article.

"Does this say what I think it says?"

I went to the private line in the kitchen and dialed Alex:

"I want you to leave now. Go back to LA. This is too ugly already."

"The hell I will," he said. "I was just talking to the girls at 'Entertainment Tonight.' I told them I've known you since you were a kid. Look, George and I will bring you some supper around six o'clock. Don't try to go out. They'll ruin your digestion. G.G. is down in the lobby talking to them, by the way. One of Marty's lawyers came here personally this morning, but I'll tell you something about G.G., he's sweet, but he's not dumb, no, not at all, he just slipped around that guy like a feather in a draft. You never saw such beautiful evasion. Hey, hold on. OK, that was this nice boy who's been getting me cigarettes and things. He says he thinks the guys talking to G.G. down there are plainclothes policemen. My lawyer's on the way up from LA to give G.G. a hand."

The phone rang almost as soon as I put it down. Dan answered, and all I heard was mumbling and yes and no for about ten minutes.

The doorbell was ringing again. I went back to the curtains. Kids all over out there, some of them neighborhood teenagers I'd seen at the corner store or just walking around on Castro or Market. Couple of very wild punk types from the Café Flore a block away, one with pink hair, and the other with a mohawk. But no Belinda.

I saw my neighbor Sheila wave as she went by. Then someone approached her. She was trying to make a clean getaway, but other people were asking her questions. She was shrugging, backing off, almost stumbled off the curb. Then she sprinted towards Castro Street.

How would Belinda look if she tried to come to the door?

I went back into the kitchen. Dan was off the phone.

"Look, Uncle Daryl has just called the district attorney's office personally," he said. "The SFPD wants to talk to you and I'm trying to stall them till Alexander's on the case. Uncle Daryl is on his way up from LA by plane, and Bonnie has just been checked into a hospital."

"I'll talk to them anytime," I said. "I don't want a criminal lawyer, Dan, I told you that."

"I'm overruling you on that one," he said patiently. "We'll reconnoiter when Alexander gets here."

I went down the back steps and into the garage and had the car out and roaring up Seventeenth Street to Sanchez before the crowd on the street could make up its mind what was going on.

When I got to the Clift, the police had just left. G.G. was sitting on the couch in the suite with his elbows on his knees. He looked tired and puzzled, pretty much the way he'd looked last night. Alex was in that gorgeous satin robe of his, pouring drinks for both of us and having room service send up some lunch.

"I figured it this way," G.G. said quietly. "I wasn't under the oath, so it didn't have to be the whole truth, just the truth, if you know what I mean. So I told them about her coming to New York and about my hiding her on Fire Island and the mean way those Hollywood men acted, but I never told them the things that she said. I told them about her leaving for San Francisco, and I told them how happy she was when she called with the news about you. I told them she loved the paintings. She really did."

He stopped, took a little of the wine Alex had given him, and then he said:

"I'll tell you what worries me, Jeremy, they kept asking about the last time I'd heard from her, they kept saying 'Are you sure the call from New Orleans was the very last time?' It was as if they had some fixed idea in their minds. Do you think they know something about her whereabouts that we don't?"

THE crowd in front of the house was even bigger when I got back. I had to honk my way through the garage door. Then a couple of reporters came into the garage after me. I had to lead them out into the street and close the door and go up the front way, or they would have been all over the backyard.

"Jeremy, is it true you found Belinda in a hippie pad on Page Street?" someone shouted. "Did you tell a San Francisco policeman that you were her father?" "Hey, Jeremy, have you seen *Final Score* yourself?"

I shut the front door.

Dan came down the hall. He'd shaved and cleaned up, but the expression on his face unnerved me.

"The police are really putting the pressure on," he said. "Alexander is trying to stall them, but you're going to have to talk to them sooner or later, and Alexander thinks that voluntarily is the best way to go."

I wondered suddenly if you could paint in prison. Idiot thought. How the hell was I going to protect her from all this if I was in prison? No, things just wouldn't move that fast.

When I came into the back office, Barbara handed me an open telegram. There was a pile of them in front of her, they'd been coming almost nonstop. The phone machine was recording the incoming voices at low volume. I think I heard someone whisper: "Pervert!"

I took the telegram.

"CONGRATULATIONS ON THE NEW SHOW. SAW CATALOG. STUNNING. WOULD BE THERE IF I COULD. ON WAY TO ROME TO GET INTERPOSITIVE OF *FINAL SCORE*. WILL CALL ON RETURN IF I CAN GET THROUGH. SUSAN JEREMIAH."

"Ah, beautiful," I whispered. "That means she's making more prints of the movie. When did this come?"

"Probably yesterday," Barbara said, "there's fifty of them here. Twenty more were delivered this morning. I'm going through them as fast as I can."

"Well, they're the best line of communication at this point," I said, "so let the machine answer the phone while you check them out."

"Call the number this was phoned from," Dan said. "It's an LA number. See if we can reach Jeremiah there later on."

"I've got other news for you," Barbara said. "From Rhinegold. He was here while you were gone. A Fort Worth millionaire named Joe Travis Buckner is furious that the museums have first right to the paintings. He wants two paintings now. But the representative from the Dallas Museum has made the first solid and unequivocal offer: five hundred thou for *Belinda with Dolls*. Rhinegold has asked for two weeks in which to evaluate the offer. And oh yeah, this other guy," she stopped to glance at her note pad, "this Count Solosky? Is that it? Solosky? Well, anyway he's from Vienna, and he settled on four of the paintings, paid already. Do you know how much money that is? Rhinegold seems to think he's as important as a museum or something. Pretty terrific, right?"

She looked at me. And I knew I ought to say something, just to be polite to her, because she was so nice, and she was tired from working so hard. But I didn't say anything. I couldn't.

I went into the kitchen and sat down in my usual chair.

So Count Solosky had put his signature to the check. And he was only the collector Rhinegold had courted for three decades, the man he considered the premier art collector in the world today. And this right on top of the first sale of my work to any museum in America. It was "pretty terrific," all right. At least it was to the guy I'd been six months ago on the Memorial weekend day that I met her at the ABA convention, the guy who said, "If I don't go over the cliff, I'll never be anything." How she had smiled at that.

Impossible to put it in focus for anyone else. Impossible to sharpen the focus myself. It was all at a great remove, like a landscape done by an impressionist: color, line, symmetry, all indistinct, having more to do with light than what was solid.

"This isn't going to help, you know," Dan said.

[4]

THE police were due at nine thirty A.M. Tuesday morning. David Alexander arrived about two hours before that. He was a slender blond-haired man, perhaps fifty, rather delicate of build with ice-blue eyes behind gold-rimmed aviator glasses. He listened with his fingers together making a church steeple, and I vaguely remembered reading something about that particular mannerism, that it denoted feelings of superiority, but that didn't mean much to me.

I didn't want to talk to him. I thought about Belinda, what she said about telling her whole story to Ollie Boon. But Alexander was my lawyer, and Dan insisted I tell him everything. OK. Set your emotions on the table like an envelope of canceled checks.

The morning news was hellish. G.G. and Alex, who had come over for breakfast, refused to watch it. They were having their coffee in the living room alone.

Daryl in a somber charcoal gray suit had read a prepared statement last night to network reporters:

"My sister, Bonnie, is in a state of collapse. The year of searching and worrying has finally taken its toll. As for the paintings on exhibit in San Francisco, we are talking about a deeply disturbed man and a serious police problem as well as a missing girl, a girl who is underage and may be herself disturbed. These paintings may well have been done without her consent, possibly without her knowledge, and certainly they were done without the consent of her only legal guardian, my sister, Bonnie Blanchard, who knew nothing about them at all."

Then "feminist and antipornography spokesperson" Cheryl Wheeler, a young New York attorney, had been interviewed regarding the obscenity of my work. She stated her views without ever raising her voice.

"The exhibit is a rape, plain and simple. If Belinda Blanchard did live with Walker at all, which has not been established by the way, she is one of the increasing victims of child abuse in this country. The only thing we do know for certain at this moment is that her name and likeness have been ruthlessly exploited by Walker, perhaps without her knowledge."

"But if Belinda did approve the exhibit, if she consented, as Walker says—"

"For a girl of sixteen there can be no question of consent to this kind of exploitation any more than there can be consent to sexual intercourse. Belinda Blanchard will be a minor till the age of eighteen."

But the network program had closed with a capper: kids in the town of Reading, Alabama, led by a local deejay in a public burning of my books.

I'd watched that one in stunned amazement. Hadn't seen anything like it since the sixties, when they burned the Beatle records because John Lennon had said the Beatles were more famous than Jesus. And then, of course, the Nazis had burned books all during the Second World War. I don't know why it didn't upset me. I don't know why it seemed to be happening to someone else. All those books burning in the little plaza before the public library of Reading. Kids coming up and proudly dumping their books into the flames.

David Alexander showed not the slightest reaction. Dan didn't say, I told you so, for which I was more than grateful. He merely sat there making notes.

Then the doorbell was ringing, and G.G. came in from the living room to say the police had just come in.

There were two tall plainclothes gentlemen in dark suits and overcoats, and they made a very polite and nice fuss over Alex, saying they had seen all his movies and they'd seen him in "Champagne Flight," too. Everyone laughed at that, even Alexander and Dan smiled good-naturedly, though I could see Dan was miserable.

Then the older of the two men, Lieutenant Connery, asked Alex to sign an autograph for his wife. The other policeman was eyeing all the toys in the room as if he was inventorying them. He studied the dolls in particular, and then he picked up one of the dolls that was broken and he ran his finger over the broken porcelain cheek.

I invited them into the kitchen. Dan filled the coffee mugs for everybody. Connery said he'd rather talk to me alone without the two lawyers, but then Alexander smiled and shook his head and everybody laughed politely again.

Connery was a heavyset man with a square face and white hair and gray eyes, nondescript except for a rather naturally appealing smile and pleasant voice. He had what we call in San Francisco a south of Market accent, which is similar to the Irish-German city street accents in Boston or New York. The other man sort of faded into the background as we started to talk.

"Now you are speaking to me of your own free will, Jeremy," said Connery, pushing the tape recorder towards me. I said yes. "And you know that you are not being charged with anything." I said yes. "But that you might be charged at a later date. And that if we do decide to charge you, we will read you your rights."

"You don't have to, I know my rights."

Alexander had his fingers together in a steeple again. Dan's face was absolutely white.

"You can tell us to leave any time you wish," Connery assured me. I smiled. He reminded me of all the cops and firemen in my family back in New Orleans, all big men like this with the same kind of Spencer Tracy white hair.

"Yes, I understand all of that, relax, Lieutenant," I said. "This whole thing must look pretty weird from your point of view."

"Jeremy, why don't you just answer the questions?' Dan said in a kind of cranky voice. He was having a terrible time with this. Alexander looked like a wax dummy.

"Well, Jeremy, I'll tell you," Connery said, taking a pack of Raleighs out of his coat pocket. "You don't mind if I smoke, do you? Oh, thank you, you never know these days whether people will let you smoke. You're supposed to go out on the back deck to smoke. I go to my favorite restaurant, I try to have my usual cigarette after dinner, they say no. Well, what concerns us more than anything right now, Jeremy, is finding Belinda Blanchard. So my first question, Jeremy, is do you know where she is?"

"Absolutely not. No idea. She said in her letter to me in New Orleans that she was two thousand miles away from there and that could mean Europe or the West Coast or even New York. She was seventeen years old just about four weeks ago, by the way, on the seventh. And she had a great deal of money with her when she left and lots of nice clothes. If I knew where she was, I'd go to her, I'd ask her to marry me because I love her and I think that's what we should do right now."

"Do you think she would marry you, Jeremy?"

The words came with a strange evenness and slowness.

"I don't know. I hope so," I said.

"Why don't you tell us the whole thing?"

I thought for a moment about what G.G. had said, about them seeming to have some fixed idea about Belinda. And then I thought about all Dan's advice.

I started with meeting her, the big mess on Page Street, her coming home with me. Yes, the statement of the cop was correct, I did say she was my daughter. I wanted to help her. I brought her back here. But I didn't know who she was, and one of the conditions was that I didn't ask. I went on about the paintings. Three months we lived together. Everything peaceful . . .

"And then Bonnie came here," Connery said simply. "She arrived at SF International in a private plane at eleven forty-five A.M. on September 10 and her daughter met her there, right?"

I said I didn't know that for certain. I explained how I'd found out who Belinda was from the tape of *Final Score* and all that. I described Bonnie's coming here, and how we'd gone to the Hyatt and she'd asked me to look after Belinda.

"Tried to blackmail you, to be exact, didn't she?"

"What makes you say that?"

"The statement of the limousine driver, who overheard her planning this with her daughter. The car was parked. He says that the glass was not all the way up between him and the backseat and he heard everything they said."

"Then you know it was all a sham. Besides, before I left the Hyatt, I had the pictures back." But I felt relief all over. He knew the worst part. I didn't have to tell him. And now for the first time I could explain with some degree of clear conscience why Belinda and I had fought.

I told him about the fight, about Belinda leaving, and about the letter that came five days later and why I decided to go public with the paintings right away.

"It was a moment of synchronization," I said. "My needs and her needs became the same. I'd always wanted to show the paintings. I wasn't kidding myself about that anymore by the time we went south. And now it was in her interest to show them, to get out the truth about her identity, because it was the only way she could stop running and hiding—and maybe forgive me for hitting her like that, for driving her off."

Connery was studying me. The Raleigh had gone out in the ashtray.

"Would you let me see the document Belinda sent you?"

"No. It's Belinda's and it's not here. It's someplace where nobody can get it. I can't make it public because it's hers."

He reflected for a moment. Then he began to ask questions about all kinds of things—the bookstore where I'd first seen Belinda, the age of my mother's house in New Orleans, about Miss Annie and the neighbors, about restaurants where we'd dined in San Francisco and down south, about what Belinda wore when we were in New Orleans, about how many suitcases she owned.

But gradually I realized he was repeating certain questions over and over—in particular about the night Belinda had left and whether or not she'd taken all her belongings, all those suitcases, and whether or not I'd heard anything, and then back to Did she pose for the photographs willingly and why had I destroyed them all.

"Look, we've been over and over all this," I said. "What do you really want? Of course, I destroyed the photos, I've explained that. Wouldn't you have done it if you were me?"

Connery became immediately conciliatory.

"Look, Jeremy, we appreciate your cooperation in all this," he said. "But you see, the family is very concerned about this girl."

"So am I."

"Her uncle Daryl is here now. He believes that Belinda may have taken drugs on the street, that she may be deeply disturbed and not really capable of taking care of herself."

"What did her father say about that?"

"Tell me again, you went to sleep at about seven o'clock. She was in her room until then? And the housekeeper, Miss Annie, had taken her some supper?"

I nodded. "And when I woke up, she was gone. The tape of *Final Score* was on the night table like I told you. And I knew she meant for me to keep it and it meant something, but I was never sure what. Maybe she was saying, 'Show the pictures.' That is what she said in her letter five days later—"

"And the letter."

"—is in a vault!"

Connery glanced at the other detective. Then he looked at his watch.

"Jeremy, listen, I do appreciate your cooperation, and we'll try not to take too much more of your time, but if you'll excuse Lieutenant Berger—"

Berger got up and went to the front door, and I saw Alexander gesture for Dan to go with him. Connery continued:

"And you're saying, Jeremy, that Miss Annie did not see Belinda leave the house."

"Right." I heard the front door open.

Dan had come in and gestured to Alexander. They went out.

"What's going on?" I asked.

They were standing in the hallway reading what looked like a couple of papers stapled together, and then Connery got up and joined them and Dan came back in to me. He said:

"They've got a perfectly legal and extremely detailed warrant to search this house."

"So let them," I said. I stood up. "They didn't have to get a warrant." Dan was worried.

"With the way that thing's worded, they could rip up the damn floorboards," he said under his breath.

"Look, I'll go upstairs with you," I said to Connery. But he said, no, that wasn't necessary and he'd see to it that the men were very careful. I said, "Go on then, the attic is unlocked."

The look on David Alexander's face was secretive as he looked at Dan, and I frankly resented it. If I was going to pay this guy, I wanted him to convey his secrets to me.

But the house was now teeming with detectives. There were two men in the living room, where G.G. and Alex were standing by somewhat awkwardly amid the dollhouse and the carousel horse and the trains and things, and I could hear them above stomping up the uncarpeted attic steps.

Connery was just coming down when I went to the foot of the stairs. Another detective had a couple of plastic sacks, and one of these had a sweater in it, a sweater of Belinda's that I had not even known was still here.

"Please don't take that," I said.

"But why, Jeremy?" Connery asked.

"Because it's Belinda's," I said. I pushed past the man and went up to see what was really going on.

They were going over everything. I heard cameras snapping in the attic, saw the silver explosion of the flash on the walls. They had found a hairbrush of hers under the brass bed, and they were taking that, too. I couldn't watch this, people opening my closet, and turning down the bed covers.

I went back down. Connery was looking at the dollhouse. Alex was seated on the sofa, watching him calmly. G.G. stood behind Connery at the window.

"Look, Connery, this doesn't make any sense," I said. "I told you she was here. Why do you need evidence of that?"

The doorbell rang, and one of the detectives answered it. There were two huge shaggy brown German shepherd dogs sitting obediently in front of two uniformed policemen on the porch.

"Jeremy," Connery said in the same friendly manner, slipping his arm around my shoulder just as Alex might do it. "Would you mind if we took the dogs through the house?"

I heard Dan mutter that it was in the fucking warrant, wasn't it?

G.G. was staring at the dogs as if they were dangerous, and Alex was just smoking his cigarette and saying nothing with a deceptively serene expression on his face.

"But what in God's name are the dogs looking for?" I asked. "Belinda isn't here."

I could feel myself getting unnerved. The whole thing was getting crazy. And there was a crowd outside so large, apparently, that I could hear it. I didn't want to look through the curtains to be sure.

I stood back watching the dogs tiptoe over the old Lionel train cars. I watched them sniffing at the French and German dolls heaped beside Alex on the couch. When they went to sniff Alex's shoes, he only smiled, and the officer led them away immediately.

I watched in silence as they went through all the lower rooms and then up the stairs. I saw Alexander follow them up.

Another plainclothesman had come down with another plastic sack. And I saw suddenly that he had the Communion veil and wreath in it, and also Mother's rosary and pearl-covered prayer book.

"Wait, you can't take that," I told Connery. "That book and rosary belonged to my mother. What are you doing? Will somebody please explain?"

Connery put his arm around me again: "We'll take good care of everything, Jeremy."

Then I saw that the two men coming down the hall from the kitchen had my entire photograph file from the basement below.

"But there are no pictures of her in there," I said. "That's old material, what's going on?"

Connery was studying me. He hadn't answered. Dan only watched as these things were carried out of the house and down the front steps.

Barbara came into the hall from the back kitchen and said the phone was for Connery, would he come this way?

"Dan, what the fuck are they doing?" I whispered.

Dan was obviously in a silent rage. "Look, don't say anything more to them," he whispered.

G.G. had gone to the window and was looking out. I stood beside him. The policeman with the Communion wreath and veil was talking to the newsmen out there. The Channel 5 truck was taping the whole thing. I felt like punching the guy. Then I saw the guy had another plastic sack too with something in it. It was Belinda's black riding crop and her leather boots.

Connery came in from the kitchen.

"Well, Jeremy, I want to let you know that the police in New Orleans have just completed a legal search of your mother's house there. It was all done proper, through the courts and all, as it had to be, but I just wanted to let you know."

He glanced at the stairs as the dogs were being led out. I saw him look at the uniformed man who was leading the animals, and then Connery went over to the man and they whispered together for a minute, as Alexander slipped past them and into the living room.

Connery came back.

"Well, let's talk a little bit more, Jeremy," he said. But neither of us made a move to sit down. And Alex and G.G. did not move to leave. Connery glanced around, smiled at everybody. "Want to talk in private, Jeremy?"

"Not really, what more is there to say?"

"All right, Jeremy," he said patiently. "Do you know of any reason why Belinda would not contact you at this time?"

Alexander was watching all this most attentively, but I saw that Dan was being called into the kitchen, probably for the phone.

"Well, she may not know what's happening. She may be too far away to have heard. She may be scared of her family. And who knows? Maybe she doesn't want to come back."

Connery weighed this for a few seconds.

"But is there any reason why she might not know at all what's happening, or not be able to come back?"

"I don't follow you," I said.

Alexander closed in without a sound.

"Look, my client has been as cooperative as can be expected," he said in a low cold voice. "Now you do not want us to get an injunction on the grounds of harassment, and that is just what—"

"And you guys," Connery said equally politely, "do not want us to convene a grand jury and move for an immediate indictment either, do you?"

"And on what grounds would you do that?" Alexander asked icily. "You have nothing. The dogs did not give the signal, am I right?"

"What signal?" I asked.

Dan was now back in the living room, behind Alexander.

Alexander moistened his lips reflexively before he answered, his voice as low and steady as before.

"These dogs had Belinda's scent before they came in here," he explained. "They got it by clothing provided by her uncle. And if Belinda had met with foul play on the premises, the dogs would have assumed a certain position over any spot where the body might have been placed. The dogs can smell death."

"Good God! You think I killed her!" I stared at Connery. And I realized he was studying me as clinically as before.

"Now the dogs in New Orleans did not give the signal either, did they?" Alexander continued. "So you have no proof of foul play at all."

"Oh, Christ, this is awful!" I whispered. I went to the armchair and sat down. I looked up and, without meaning to, looked right at Alex, who was sitting back on the couch just watching everything, his face a perfectly pleasant mask of his feelings. He gave me the smallest "Take it easy" gesture with his hand.

"If you tell this to the press," I said, "it will destroy everything. It will ruin everything that I've done."

"And why is that, Jeremy?" Connery asked me.

"Oh, good God, man, don't you see?" I said. "The pictures were supposed to be a celebration. They were supposed to be wholesome and beautiful. They were a tribute to her sexuality and to the love between us and how it saved me. This girl was my muse. She woke me up from all this, damn it!" I glared at the toys. I kicked at the train on the floor as I stood up. "She brought life into this place, this very room. She wasn't a doll, she wasn't a cartoon character, she was a young woman, damn it."

"That must have been very frightening, Jeremy," Connery said softly.

"No, no, it wasn't. And if you let it out that you think I killed her, then you make it all kinky and dirty and like a thousand other aberrant stories —as if people couldn't break the rules and love each other—without there being something ugly and violent and bad! There was nothing ugly or violent or bad!"

I could feel Alexander studying me as intently as Connery. Dan was monitoring everything, but he was also nodding just a little, as if this part of it was OK. I was so grateful for that little nod. I wished I could tell him, would remember to tell him.

"The exhibit was supposed to be the perfect ending and the perfect beginning!" I said. I walked past them all into the dining room. I glared at the dolls on the back of the piano. I felt like smashing them. Smashing all this garbage. "Don't you see? The end of hiding for her. The end of hiding for me." I turned around to look at Connery. "We were coming out of the closet as people, don't you see?"

"Lieutenant," Alexander said under his breath. "I really must ask you to leave."

"I didn't kill her, Lieutenant," I said, coming towards him. "You can't go out there and say that I did. You can't make it ugly like that, you hear me? You can't turn me into a freak like that."

Connery reached into his overcoat pocket and drew out a folded copy of the exhibit catalog.

"Jeremy, look, you did paint this, didn't you?" He showed me the riding picture—boots, crop, hat.

"Yes, but what's that got to do with murder, for Chrissakes."

Alexander tried to intervene again. G.G. and Alex continued to watch in silence, though G.G. had slipped way back into the bay window, and I could see the fear in his eyes. No, G.G., don't believe this!

"Well, wouldn't you say that was pretty kinky, Jeremy?"

"Yeah, kind of, so what!" I said.

"But this, Jeremy, the title of this picture is *The Artist Grieves for Belinda*. That is the word you used, isn't it, Jeremy, 'grieves'?"

"Oh Christ."

"Jeremy, I must warn you that you are under surveillance and that, if you try to leave San Francisco, you will be arrested on the spot."

"Don't make me laugh!" I said. "Just get the hell out of my house. Go out there and tell your filthy suspicions to the reporters. Tell them that an artist who loves a young girl has to kill her, that you won't settle for anything between a man and a girl her age that was just plain wholesome and good!"

"I wouldn't do that if I were you, Lieutenant," said Dan. "In fact, I wouldn't say anything about suspected homicide to anybody until you talk to Daryl Blanchard, if I were you."

"What's this about now, Dan?" Connery asked patiently.

"Daryl's heard from her?" I asked.

"Call just came in back there," Dan said. "Daryl now has official custody of his niece and the LAPD has issued a warrant for her arrest on the grounds that she is a minor without proper supervision, leading an immoral and dissolute life."

Connery could not hide his annoyance.

"Oh, that's just great," I said. "If she tries to come to me, she gets busted. You bastards, you want to put her in jail, too."

"I mean, you and I both know, Lieutenant," Dan said, "that if you go for that indictment, well, a warrant out for the arrest of the murdered person, it's kind of a—"

Alexander finished the sentence: "—exculpatory," he said.

"Right, exactly," Dan said, "and I mean you can hardly indict a man for murder when you're trying to arrest the—"

"I get your drift, counselor," said Connery with a weary nod. He turned, as if he was going to take his leave, but then he looked back to me.

"Jeremy," he said sincerely, "why don't you just tell us what happened to the girl?"

"Jesus, man, I told you. She left that night in New Orleans. Now you tell me something—"

"That's all, Lieutenant," Alexander said.

"No, I want to know!" I said. "Do you really think I could do something like that to her!"

Connery opened the catalog again. He held *Artist and Model* in front of me. Me slapping Belinda.

"Maybe you'd feel better, Jeremy, if you just came clean on the whole thing."

"Listen, you son of a bitch," I answered. "Belinda's alive. And she'll come when she knows about all this, if your goddamn warrant doesn't scare her off. Now arrest me or get the hell out of my house."

He drew himself up, put the catalog back in his pocket and, with the same sympathetic expression he'd had all along, he said:

"Jeremy, you are suspected of foul play in connection with the disappearance of Belinda Blanchard, and I should remind you that you have the right to remain silent, the right to have an attorney present whenever you are questioned, and anything that you say may be used against you if you continue to talk."

For the next few minutes little if anything registered, except that Connery had left, Dan and Alexander had gone into the kitchen and wanted me to follow, and that I had sunk down into the armchair again.

I looked up. Alex was gone and so was G.G., and for a moment I felt as near to panic as I ever had in my entire life.

But then G.G. appeared at the arm of the chair with a cup of coffee in his hand. He gave it to me.

And I heard Alex's clear voice from the front porch. He was talking to the reporters: "Ah, yes, we go way back together. Jeremy's one of my oldest and dearest friends in the world. Known him since he was a boy in New Orleans. One of the nicest men I've ever known."

I got up and went to the back office and cut off the answering machine to put in the new message.

"This is Jeremy Walker. Belinda, if you are calling, honey, let me tell you that I love you, and you are in danger. There is a warrant out for your arrest, and my house is being watched. This line may be tapped. Stay on, honey, but be careful. I'll recognize your voice."

[5]

By eleven Tuesday evening every TV station in the country was flashing her picture. And warrants had been issued for her in New York and Texas as well as California. A big beautiful photo taken of her at the press conference in Cannes was on the front page of the evening papers from New York to San Diego. And Uncle Daryl had even offered a $50,000 reward for any information leading directly to her arrest.

And it was no secret to the reporters who covered the story that Daryl himself might not even be granted custody of Belinda if or when she was picked up. The authorities could jail Belinda. In other words, to get Belinda, Daryl had been willing to put her fate in the hands of the courts.

And once the courts had her, they could, if they chose, incarcerate her not merely until she was eighteen, but until she was twenty-one.

Daryl had done this. Daryl had turned Belinda into a criminal. And he continued to vilify her to anyone who would listen, with information he had received from "various private investigative agents," insisting that Belinda "had consorted with immoral and dissolute persons," "had no visible means of support," "is known to have abused drugs and alcohol," and "might have suffered extensive and/or permanent damage from the drugs she might have ingested in New York's Greenwich Village and San Francisco's infamous Haight."

Meanwhile the "torrid scenes" of *Final Score* were getting more word of mouth. An LA underground paper had run stills from the picture as well as photos of my paintings. The television stations picked them up.

Final Score was scheduled to open tomorrow at the Westwood in LA for a guaranteed two-week run.

The phone situation worsened. The private number had apparently been leaked to the public. It too was now ringing nonstop. And during the long hours of Tuesday night I got as many hate calls now for Belinda as I did for myself. "The little bitch, who does she think she is?" a female voice would hiss into the phone. "I hope they make her wear clothes when they find her." It ran like that.

But burning just as brightly in the public imagination as the image of "Belinda, Teen Temptress," was the image of Belinda, victim, murdered by me.

The SFPD had given the press, as well as Marty Moreschi, everything it needed to put Belinda in an early grave dug by the "weirdo artist" in San Francisco.

IS BELINDA DEAD OR ALIVE? The late edition of the *San Francisco Examiner* had asked. The S.F. Police had indicated there was a "secret collection of hideous and horrible paintings" in my attic, works full of "insects and rodents and clearly the creation of a disturbed mind." The house was described as a "madman's playground." And aside from the photographs of *The Artist Grieves for Belinda* and *Artist and Model,* there were pictures of the items police had taken with them—the Holy Communion "paraphernalia" and the leather boots and whip.

On the Wednesday morning news, Marty broke down as he greeted reporters outside the offices of the LAPD, where he had been interrogated about Belinda:

"Bonnie is afraid she may never see her daughter alive again."

As for his sudden leave of absence from his two-million-a-year job as vice president in charge of television production at the studio, it had nothing to do with the cancellation of "Champagne Flight," which had in fact been announced the night before. On the contrary, he had asked for time off to devote himself completely to Bonnie.

"In the beginning we only wanted to find Belinda," he continued, "now we are afraid of what we will find out." Then he turned his back to the cameras and wept.

The press continued, however, to vilify all of us. Bonnie had abandoned her child. Marty was the suspected cause of it. The superstar of "Champagne Flight" had become the evil Queen from *Snow White.* No matter how often they tried to throw the spotlight on me, it always came back to them for another bow.

And though Dan kept insisting that the warrants for Belinda made it hard for the Grand Jury to indict me, I could see by the morning papers on Wednesday that something insidious was happening.

The two concepts of Belinda—criminal on the run and murder victim—were not at odds with each other. On the contrary, they were merging with each other, and the whole was gaining new strength.

Belinda was a bad girl who got killed for it. Belinda was a little sex queen who got exactly what she deserved.

Even a long dignified feature in the national edition of *The New York Times* took this approach. Child actress Belinda Blanchard, only daughter of superstar Bonnie and famous hairdresser G.G., may have earned her first real star billing in an erotic role that climaxed in her death. The LA *Times* made the same connection: Had the sensuous baby-mouthed beauty of *Final Score* seduced death as easily as she had seduced the audience at Cannes?

I was horrified as I watched the process. Dan was clearly more worried than he would admit. Even G.G. seemed crushed.

But Alex was neither surprised nor upset.

He was keeping up his loyalty campaign valiantly, calling press people all over the nation to volunteer statements about our friendship, and he was pleased to be making his own news stories: ALEX CLEMENTINE STANDS BY OLD FRIEND in the LA papers, and CLEMENTINE DEFENDS WALKER in the *Chronicle* here.

But when he came for dinner Wednesday night—when he brought the dinner, in fact, of pasta and veal and other goodies—we finally sat down to talking, and he told me calmly that he was not surprised by the "bad girl gets it" angle at all.

He reminded me tactfully and gently of that discussion we'd had outside the Stanford Court so many months ago, in which he'd warned me that people were no more tolerant of scandal now than they had ever been.

"Got to be the right dirt in the right measure," he said again. "And I don't care how many teen sex flicks they crank out every day down there in Tinseltown, you're forty-five and you fucked a teenager and you won't say you're sorry, and your goddamn paintings are selling, that's what's making them mad. They've got to believe somebody's sorry, somebody's going to pay, so they just love the idea that she's dead."

"The hell with them," I said. "And I want to tell you something else, Clementine, all the votes aren't in yet."

"Jeremy, listen, you've got to take this more calmly is what I'm saying. This link between sex and death, well, hell, it's as American as apple pie. For years every movie they ever made about gay sex—or any kind of weird sex for that matter—always ended with suicide or somebody getting killed. Look at *Lolita*. Humbert Humbert shoots Quilty, then he and

Lolita both end up dead. America makes you pay that way when you break the rules. It's a formula. The cop shows do it all the time."

"You wait, Alex," I interrupted. "When everything is said and done, we'll see who was right about sex and scandal and money and death!"

"Death, please stop talking about death," G.G. said. "She's all right and she'll get through."

"Yes," Dan agreed, "but how?"

Alex nodded. "Look what's going on out there," he said. "Those plainclothes fellas are questioning every teenage girl that passes the house. They're stopping them, demanding their identification. I saw them doing it when I came in. Can't you push those fellas back a bit? And I'll tell you something else I heard. United Theatricals said it's been getting crank calls from girls saying they're Belinda. My agent told me that this morning. Now how the hell would the secretaries down there know the real Belinda if she called?"

"What about Susan Jeremiah?" G.G. asked. "Anybody heard from her? Maybe Belinda can get through to her!"

Dan shook his head. "She's renting some house on Benedict Canyon Drive in LA, but the guy who answered the phone there this afternoon said she's still en route from Rome. She was supposed to land in New York this morning, then go on later to Chicago before she headed home."

"How about trying the number again?" I asked.

"Just did. Got the answering machine. The guy's out for dinner. I'll try him again later on."

Well, Susan was busy, and who could blame her?

Final Score had opened at noon at the Westwood in Los Angeles to sellout crowds. Posters of a bikini-clad Belinda on horseback were suddenly on sale all over Sunset Boulevard.

I wasn't even finished eating when my LA agent got through on the private line to tell that, if and when Belinda showed, she had a career waiting without even lifting her hand.

"You're kidding, Clair, you had the operator cut in on the line to tell me this!" I was furious.

"You bet, and it took me a fucking thirty minutes to persuade the phone company to do it. I had to convince the supervisor it was life or death. Does everybody in the continental U.S. have your number? Now listen, about Belinda, you tell her for me I'm getting calls two a minute on her. Have you seen that movie? Look, all I'm saying is, Jer, you find her, you marry her, and you give her my message, OK? I'll represent her, I can cut a million-dollar deal with her in two seconds with Century International Pictures. That is, if—well, if—"

"If what!"

"If she doesn't end up in jail!"

"Gotta go, Clair."

"Jeremy, don't be hasty. Ever hear of the concept of public pressure? 'Free Belinda and Jeremy, the San Francisco Two!' and all that."

"Put it on a bumper sticker, Clair. We might need it. You gotta point."

"Hey, you know your publishers are just sick, don't you? The bookstores are shipping back your books! Let me make a deal for that exhibit catalog, Jeremy, that's one of the hottest irons in the fire you've got."

"Good-bye, Clair. I love you. You're the most optimistic person I've spoken to all day." I hung up.

I was dying to tell Alex about all of that, that maybe *both* of us had been right in that old argument about sex, death, and money. But that would have been premature. Later, Clementine, I kept thinking. Because I know she's OK, and she's coming, I know she is, she's OK. And let them send back my books!

Meantime "Entertainment Tonight" was already on the air, announcing the permanent cancellation of "Champagne Flight." Marty Moreschi was again being questioned by the LAPD regarding his relationship with the missing teenager, Belinda Blanchard.

As for Jeremy Walker, the New York Museum of Modern Art had just announced it would make an offer to purchase *Belinda in Brass Bed,* a ten-by-twelve canvas divided into six panels. The board of directors of the museum would make no statement on the scandal surrounding the work.

As for "Saturday Morning Charlotte," the network was still denying rumors that it would cancel, though the program had lost its major sponsor, Crackerpot Cereal. "Millions of kids watch Charlotte," said the network spokesman, "who have never heard of Jeremy Walker." Charlotte now had a life independent of her creator, and they could not disappoint the millions who expect to see her every Saturday morning at the regular time of nine o'clock.

Rainbow Productions was also going ahead with its development of Jeremy Walker's *Angelica,* though children all through the Bible Belt were burning their copies of the Angelica books. Rainbow fully expected the storm to blow over. But there was some talk now of doing Angelica with live actors rather than as a cartoon film. "We think we might have a very eerie story here," said the vice president of Rainbow, "a sort of *Secret Garden* type of story about an adolescent girl living in an old house. We have bought a story and theme here as well as drawings, you realize."

And speaking of live actors, "Entertainment Tonight" was on the spot outside the Westwood to garner reactions to *Final Score*. The film was rated excellent by just about everybody. And Belinda? "Charming." "Just beautiful." "You can kind of see what all the fuss is about."

"Soon audiences in the Big Apple will have their opportunity to view the controversial film," said a rather attractive female commentator. *"Final Score* opens tomorrow at New York's Cinema I."

"Good for Susan. Good for Belinda," I said.

Around eight thirty David Alexander arrived. He had been with the DA all afternoon.

"Look, they have nothing on you essentially," he assured me. "They found not one shred of evidence in this house that proved either sexual contact or foul play. Some blood on a sheet turned out to be menses. So she lived here. This they already knew. But the police pressure is mounting. The pressure from Daryl Blanchard is mounting.

"This is the deal they are offering as of now. If you will plead guilty to several lesser charges—unlawful sexual intercourse and contributing to the delinquency of a minor—they agreed to send you to Chino for sixty days for psychological testing and then the public will be satisfied. We have a little room to negotiate on these charges, but frankly there is no guarantee as to what the eventual sentence may be."

"I don't like it," Dan said. "Those psychologists are crazy! You draw a picture of her with a black crayon, they'll say the black crayon means death. They don't know anything about what they're doing. We may never be able to get you out."

"This is the alternative," David Alexander explained coldly. "They will convene the grand jury and ask for an indictment on charges of murder, and the grand jury will subpoena Belinda's letter. And when you refuse to turn this over, you will be arrested for contempt of court."

"I'd destroy the letter before I gave it over to anyone."

"Don't even think of that. The letter is crucial. If your little girl is never found alive—"

"Don't say it."

"Besides," Dan said, "you can't destroy the letter. The letter's in a vault in New Orleans, right? You can't leave California. You try and they'll bust you on the contributing thing, and they'll use the testimony of that cop you lied to when you brought Belinda home from Page Street that night."

"That is unfortunately true," Alexander said. "And then they'll pile on charges. They've got a sworn statement from your housekeeper in New Orleans that Belinda did sleep in your bed. And a former waiter at the Café Flore insists he saw you giving her wine to drink, though she was underage. Then there's the kiddie-porn law in connection with the sale of the catalog in local bookstores, the catalog, you follow me, not the paintings. Well! The list is endless. But the fact remains, and I can not emphasize this sufficiently, without Belinda to testify against you or without her body to conclusively prove murder, they have nothing major that will stick!"

"When do you have to give them an answer?" I asked.

"By noon tomorrow. They want you in custody by six P.M. But the pressure is mounting. They're getting national media attention. They have to act."

"Stall them," Dan said. "They won't make a move to arrest Jeremy without warning—"

"No. Our communication lines are good. Unless, of course, something changes dramatically."

"What the hell could change dramatically?" I asked.

"Well, they could find her body, of course."

I stared at him for a moment. "She's not dead," I said.

AT eleven a delivery man from Western Union was there again, this time with a dozen or more telegrams. I went through them hastily. There was one from Susan that had come from New York.

"TRYING LIKE CRAZY TO REACH YOU, WALKER. IMPORTANT NEWS. OPERATORS WON'T CUT IN. CALL THIS NUMBER IN LA. HEADED FOR FRISCO TOMORROW NIGHT. BE CAREFUL. SUSAN."

I went to the phone. It must have rung ten times before a sleepy Texas voice answered in Los Angeles.

"Yeah, man, she called from Kennedy a couple of hours ago. Says she's got good news for you, and it's getting better and better. And she also told me to tell you she tried every trick in the book to get through to you up there."

"But what news, what else did she say?"

"Be careful, man, she says your wire is undoubtedly tapped."

"I'll call from the phone booth in five minutes—"

"Not necessary. All I know is what I just said. She's going on to Chicago to set up *Final Score*. Then she'll be headed back here. She really tried to get through to you, man, and so did I."

"Listen, you give her these names and numbers," I said. "Blair Sackwell, Stanford Court Hotel, San Francisco, and G.G.—that's Belinda's father, George Gallagher—at the Clift. She can get through to them and they can bring the message to me."

I was excited when I hung up. Alex and G.G. were just coming in from the Clift with G.G.'s suitcases. G.G. was taking Belinda's old room upstairs, because he was certain now that the police had him under surveillance and would pick up Belinda if she showed up at the Clift. In fact, they'd been stopping young women and asking to see their identification, until the hotel complained about that.

I knew Alex wasn't going to last long outside a five-star hotel, but he was here for a couple of drinks and a little visit, and there was a nice fellow back at the hotel instructed to take a cab up here immediately if Belinda called.

"Don't get too excited about all this," Alex said when I told him about Susan. "She's probably talking about her picture, remember she's the director, she's got a shot at national distribution or she wouldn't have gone to Rome and all that."

"Hell, she said news. Good news," I said. As soon as I got some extra quilts for G.G., I called Blair at the Stanford Court and told him. He was excited. He said he'd stay right by the phone.

Around midnight my neighbor Sheila rang the bell to tell me that my little telephone answering machine message to Belinda was being broadcast by rock stations all over the Bay Area. Somebody had even given it a little background musical score.

"Here, Jer," she said, "when there's a funeral in my hometown or some big tragedy or something, people bring things. Well, I know this is no funeral and it's no picnic either, but I thought you could use a nice batch of cookies, I baked these myself."

"Sheila, you'll visit me in jail, won't you?" I asked.

I watched the cops stopping her on the corner. I told Dan.

"Fucking harassment," he said. "They can't box you in like this. But we'll wait to use that when it's best."

AT three A.M. Thursday morning I lay on the floor of the attic studio, my head on a pillow, the city lights my only illumination and the lights of the radio at my side.

I smoked a cigarette, one of hers actually, from an unopened pack I'd found in her bathroom when I came home. Her perfume had been in her closet still. Yellow hairs on the pillow slip beneath the quilt.

The telephone gave its brief muffled ring. Out of the speaker came the sound of the machine clicking on:

"My name is Rita Mendleson, I am, well never mind what I am. I believe I may help you to find the missing girl. I see a field full of flowers. I see a hair ribbon. I see some one falling, blood. . . . If you want further information, you can contact me at this number. I do not charge for my services, but a modest donation, whatever your conscience dictates—"

I touched the volume button. Soon came the inevitable click, the inevitable ring in the bowels of the house below, where a young stenographer hired by Barbara sat at my desk listing each caller and each message on a yellow legal pad.

The radio talked in the dark. A CBS commentator, coming from somewhere on the East Coast:

"Do they chronicle the deterioration of a mind and a conscience as well as a love affair gone wrong? Belinda begins innocently enough, in spite of her nudity, as she gazes at us from setting after setting all too familiar to the readers of Walker's books. But what happened to the children's artist when his model matured before his very eyes, when his considerable talent—and make no mistake these are masterpieces we speak of, these are paintings that will survive even the most cruel of revelations here—but what happened when that considerable talent could no longer confine her to the playroom and she emerges the young woman in bra and panties lounging lasciviously on the artist's bed? Do the last two pictures of this haunting and undeniably beautiful exhibit chronicle Walker's panic and his eventual grief for the irrepressible young woman whom he felt compelled to destroy?"

I fell asleep and I dreamed.

I was in a grand house that was familiar to me. It was Mother's house and my house in San Francisco or some beautiful amalgam of the two. I knew all the hallways and the rooms. Yet I saw a door I had never seen before. And when I opened it, I found myself in a large exquisitely decorated corridor. One door after another opened on rooms I had never visited. I felt such happiness to find this. "And it is all mine," I said. Indescribable happiness. A feeling of such buoyancy as I moved from room to room.

When I spoke, it was five thirty and there was a pale rosy light burning through the textureless gray membrane of the sky. Smell of San Francisco in the morning, the cold fresh air from the ocean. All impurities washed away.

The dream lingered; the happiness lingered. Ah, too lovely, all those new rooms. This was the third time in my life I had dreamed this dream.

And I remembered coming down to breakfast years and years ago in New Orleans when I was a boy and telling Mother, who wasn't sick then, about just such a dream.

"It's a dream of new discoveries," she'd said, "of new possibilities. A very wonderful dream."

The night before I'd left New Orleans with all the Belinda paintings, the last night I had spent in Mother's bedroom before coming back to San Francisco, I had dreamed for the second time in my life this dream.

I'd woken to the rain lashing at the screens. And I'd felt Mother was close to me, Mother was telling me again that it was a very wonderful dream. That was the only time I really felt Mother since I had come home.

Paintings had come into my mind then, whole and complete paintings that I would do when Belinda and I were together again. How private and wonderful it had been, a whole new series springing to life so naturally, as if it could not be stopped.

The canvases were huge and grand like the rooms in the dream. They were of the landscape and the people of my childhood, and they had the power and scope of history paintings, but they were not that. "Memory paintings," I had said to myself that last night in New Orleans, going out on the porch and letting the rain wash me. The atmosphere of the old Irish Channel streets came back to me, Belinda and I walking, the giant breadth of the river suddenly at my feet.

I saw the old parish churches in these paintings, I saw the people who lived in the old streets. *The May Procession,* that was to be the first of these paintings, surely, with all the children in their white clothes and the women, in flowered dresses and black straw hats, on the sidewalks, with their rosaries, and the little shotgun cottages behind them with their gingerbread eaves. Mother could be in this picture, too. A great thronged incandescent painting, awesome as it was grotesque, the faces of the common people I had known stamped with their sometime brutality, the whole gawdy and squalid, and tender with the details of the little girls' hands and their pearl rosaries and their lace. Mother with her black gloves and her rosary, too. The bloodred sky, yes, as it was so often over the river, and maybe the untimely rain falling at a silver slant from lowering clouds.

The second painting would be *The Mardi Gras.* And I saw it as clearly now in San Francisco, lying as I was on the attic floor, as I had seen it that last stormy night back home. The great glittering papier-mâché floats shivering as they were pulled beneath the branches of the trees, and the drunken black flambeaux carriers dancing to the beat of the drums as they drank from their pocket flasks. One of the torches has fallen into a float crowded with satin-costumed revelers. Fire and smoke rise upwards like the graphic depiction of an open-mouthed roar.

The morning light was brighter now over San Francisco, but the fog was still solid, and the gray walled the windows of the studio. Everything was bathed in a cold luminous light. The old rat and roach paintings looked like dark windows into another world.

My soul ached. My heart ached. And yet I felt this happiness, the happiness of the paintings yet to be done. I wanted so badly to begin. I looked down at my hands. No paint left on them after so many days of being away from it. And the brushes there waiting, and this light pouring in.

"But what does it all mean without you, Belinda?" I whispered. "Where are you, darling? Are you trying to get through, or is anger the cause of your silence, anger and the unwillingness to forgive? Holy Communion, Belinda. Come back to me."

[6]

ON the morning cable news we saw the noon lines outside the theater in New York that was showing *Final Score*. *The New York Times* had already given the picture a rave.

"As for the ingenue herself, she is irrepressibly appealing. The distasteful publicity surrounding her is simply forgotten once she appears. But one can not help but wonder at the contradictions and ironies of a legal system that is absolutely compelled to brand this well-endowed and obviously sophisticated young actress a delinquent child."

Cable News Network at noon carried a spokesman from the Museum of Modern Art in New York. A very private gentleman, he seemed, bald, myopic, reading through thick glasses a prepared statement. When he paused for breath, he would look at some distant point high above, as though trying to pick out a certain star. Regarding the acquisition of the Belinda paintings, the museum recognizes no obligation to judge the personal or public morals of the artist. The museum judges the paintings as worthy of acquisition. The trustees are in concurrence as to the unmistakable merits of the work.

Then the New York critic Garrick Samuels, a man I personally loathed. "We seldom see an artist break out like this with such heat and force," he said. "Walker demonstrates the craft of what we call the old masters, and yet the pictures are distinctly modern. This is a unique wedding of competence and inspiration. You see this how often? Maybe once in a hundred years?"

Thank you, Samuels, I still loathe you. Conscience in order on all counts.

I walked down the hall, looked out the windows. Same crowd, same faces. But something was different. The tour bus which usually passed without pausing on its way up to Castro, to show the gays to the tourists, had come to a halt. Were those people inside looking at my house?

ABOUT one, Barbara awakened me from an uneasy nap on the living room couch.

"A kid just came to the door with a message from Blair Sackwell. Please call him at this number from a phone booth at once."

I was still groggy when I went out the front door. And when the reporters swamped me, I could hardly even be polite. I saw the two plainsclothes guys get out of their gray Oldsmobile. I looked at them for a second, then I waved and pointed to the phone booth by the corner store.

Immediately they nodded and slowed their pace.

"Who are those guys, Jeremy?" "Jeremy, has Belinda called you?" The reporters followed me across Noe and Seventeenth.

"Just my bodyguards, gang," I said. "Any of you guys got a quarter?"

Immediately I saw five quarters in five hands. I took two of them, said, Thanks, and closed the phone booth door.

"Well, that sure as hell took you long enough!" Blair said as soon as he answered. "Where's G.G.?"

"Asleep, he was helping with the phones most of the night."

"Jeremiah's man in LA just got through to me. Said Susan caught him on her way out of Chicago an hour ago. He wouldn't even talk to me on the Stanford Court line, said to go call him from someplace down the street. That's where you're talking to me now. Now listen. Susan says she knows for certain that Belinda was at the Savoy Hotel in Florence until two days ago."

"Christ, is she sure?"

"When Jeremiah got to Rome, friends told her Belinda had been doing extra work at Cinecittà. They had lunch with her less than two weeks ago in the Via Veneto. She was just fine."

"Thank God!"

"Now don't come apart on me. Listen. These people said Belinda had been living in Florence and coming down to work a few days a week. Jeremiah put her dad's confidential secretary on it in Houston. The woman called everybody Susan knew in Florence, friends of Belinda's, Bonnie's, the works. She hit pay dirt yesterday afternoon. Turned out Belinda had checked out of the Savoy on Tuesday, same day Susan left

Rome. She'd been there under her own name, paid her bill in full in traveler's checks, and told the concierge she was headed for the Pisa airport, she was going back to the States."

I slumped against the side of the phone booth. I was going to start bawling like a child if I didn't get a grip on myself.

"Rembrandt? You still there?"

"Blair, I think I was beginning to believe it myself," I said. I took out my handkerchief and wiped my face. "I swear to God, I mean, I think I was beginning to believe she was dead."

There was a pause, but I didn't care what he was thinking. I shut my eyes for a minute. I was still too relieved to think straight. I felt a crazy impulse to open the damned door of the phone booth and yell to the reporters:

"Belinda's alive! She's alive!" Then the reporters would jump up and down and scream "She's alive," too.

But I didn't do it. I stood there, caught someplace between laughing and weeping, and then I tried to reason things out.

"Now, we can't call TWA or Pan Am for the passenger list," Blair said. "It's too risky. But she couldn't have gotten through Kennedy or LAX until yesterday. And it was already front page news."

"Blair, thousands of people go through customs. Maybe she went through Dallas or Miami or someplace where it wasn't—"

"And maybe she went to the moon, who knows? But the point is, she is probably in California already, and she's probably given up on the damn phones. I mean, if I can't get through to you and Jeremiah couldn't get through to you, then nobody can get through. And I suppose you caught Moreschi this morning when he picked up Bonnie at the hospital, telling everybody about the cruel crank calls she'd been getting from kids claiming to be Belinda?"

"Oh, shit."

"Yeah, you said it, but Marty thinks of everything. He says the studio and the local radio stations have been getting the crank calls, too."

"Christ, he's locking her out, does he realize that?"

"So what would you do if you were her? Come straight here?"

"Look, Blair, I have a house in Carmel. Nobody, I mean nobody knows about it except G.G. and Belinda and me. G.G. and I were down there last week. We left money and a note for Belinda. She might have gone there. If I were her, I would have gone there, at least to get some sleep and make a plan. Now if either G.G. or I try to drive down, we take these plainclothes suckers with us—"

"Give me the address," Blair said.

Quickly I described the place, the street, the turnoff, how the houses didn't have any numbers, all that.

"You leave it to me, Rembrandt. Midnight Mink is a heavy item in Carmel. I know just the guy to send over there, and he doesn't even have to know why he's doing it. He owes me one for a full-length coat I delivered to him personally just in time for Christmas for a beat-up old movie queen who lives in a falling-down hermitage just north of there at Pebble Beach. I spent Christmas Eve of 1984 at thirty-eight thousand feet thanks to that SOB. He'll do what I say. What time is it, one fifteen? Call me at this number at four, if you haven't heard from me before that."

DAN and David Alexander were just getting out of a cab in front of the house when I got back. We went inside together.

"They want you to surrender at six P.M.," Alexander said. "Daryl Blanchard has just issued a statement to the press in New Orleans. After speaking to your housekeeper there and the officers who interrogated her, he says he now believes his niece to be dead. Bonnie made a similar statement in Los Angeles when she was discharged from the hospital. But we can still make a deal on the minor charges. The public won't know the difference once you are in custody. That is all they want."

"You gotta listen to me. She may be on her way here." I told him everything that Blair had reported. I told them about the hideaway in Carmel. I also told him about the "crank calls."

David Alexander sat down at the dining table and made that steeple out of his fingers just under his pursed lips. The dust swirled in the rays of sun breaking through the lace curtains behind him. He looked as if he were in prayer.

"I say, call their bluff," Dan said soberly. "It will take them time to convene the grand jury, it will take time to subpoena her letter."

"And then we lose our bargaining power as to the lesser charges," Alexander said.

"You've got to keep me out of jail until I make contact with her," I said.

"But how do you propose to make contact and what do you expect—?"

"Look," Dan said, "Jeremy is asking us to keep him out of jail as long as we can."

"Thank you, Dan," I said.

Alexander's face was rigid, completely concealing whatever were his true thoughts. Then he made some little shift in expression that indicated perhaps he'd made up his mind.

"All right," he said. "We'll inform the deputy district attorney that we have new information as to Belinda's whereabouts. We need time to investigate. We will argue that the warrant for Belinda may be frightening and intimidating her, which is highly detrimental to our client's position. We will push the date of surrender back as far as we can."

AT three o'clock a bellhop from the Stanford Court rang the bell and gave me a new number for Blair. Please call him from a booth as soon as I could.

"Look, she's been in the Carmel house. Today!"

"How can you tell?"

"Ironclad evidence. The newspapers open all over the breakfast table with today's date. And a half-drunk cup of coffee and an ashtray full of half-smoked fancy foreign cigarettes."

"That's it. That's Belinda!"

"But no luggage and no clothes. And guess what my man found in the bathroom? Two empty bottles of Clairol Loving Care."

"What the hell is Clairol Loving Care?"

"A hair rinse, Rembrandt, a hair rinse. And the color was chestnut brown."

"Way to go, Belinda! That's wonderful!" The reporters on the corner heard me yelling. They started running towards me. I gestured for them to be quiet.

"You bet it is, Rembrandt! 'Cause Loving Care washes out. How the hell could I do the wedding photo of you in Midnight Mink if her beautiful hair was permanently dyed brown?"

I laughed in spite of myself. I was too happy not to laugh. Blair went on talking.

"Look, my man left notes for her all over. But she's already cleared out. And my line's tapped. And so is G.G.'s at the Clift. And what's to stop her from ringing your doorbell and getting stopped by the cops no matter what color hair she's got?"

"She's not that dumb, not Belinda, you know she isn't. Listen, speaking of G.G. and Alex, I gotta get word to them about this. They went up to Ryan's Café two blocks from here. I'll call you at the hotel when I get back."

I hung up and shoved my way through the reporters. Couldn't say why I yelled, why I was smiling, really, guys, get off my back, not now! I gave a friendly wave to the plainclothes guys, then started walking fast up to Castro Street.

I didn't realize till I crossed Hartford that the reporters were following me, about six of them at a distance of less than three feet. Then there were the plainclothes guys behind them.

I really started to get crazy. "You guys leave me alone," I started yelling at the reporters. They just clumped together and looked at me, as if to say, Nobody here but us chickens. I thought I'd go nuts. Somebody took my picture with a little automatic camera. Finally I just threw up my hands and stalked up the hill.

When I turned the corner, there was Alex in his fedora and raincoat and G.G. in a denim blazer, standing like two male models out of *Esquire* magazine in front of the Castro Theater looking at the playbills.

"Jeremy!" G.G. shouted when he saw me. He waved for me to come to them quick.

But I had already seen the marquee above them. The man on the long ladder was still putting the black letters in place:

MIDNIGHT SHOW TONIGHT—DIRECTOR ON STAGE IN PERSON
BELINDA IN "FINAL SCORE"

"Jeremy, break out your black dinner jacket and if you don't have one, I'll buy you one," G.G. said, as he took my arm. "I mean, we're going, all of us, first-class, goddamn it, even if we have to take the gentlemen with their nightsticks with us. I am not missing my daughter's debut this time around."

"You just may see your daughter in the flesh!" I said.

I made sure my back was to the little crowd of cops and reporters as I huddled there with Alex and G.G. and told them everything Blair's man had found out.

"Now all I have to do," I said, "is stay out of the slammer for another twenty-four hours. I know she's coming. She's less than two hundred miles away."

"Yes," Alex sighed, "that's all, unless she turned around and went the other direction, as far as she could from here."

He beckoned to the reporters. "Come on, ladies and gentlemen," he said, "let's all go into the Twin Peaks bar now and I'll treat you to a round of drinks."

[7]

At eleven forty-five p.m., Susan Jeremiah's white Cadillac stretch limousine lodged itself uneasily in the narrow driveway, and the reporters mobbed it, cameras flashing, as Susan stepped out of the rear door, smiling under the brim of her scarlet cowboy hat, and waved to us at the living room windows just above.

G.G., Alex, and I pushed our way down the steps. We were all turned out in black dinner jackets and boiled shirts, cummerbunds, patent leather shoes, the whole bit.

"You're going to miss the film, ladies and gentlemen, if you don't hurry!" Alex said genially. "Now everybody has a press pass? Who does not have a pass?"

Dan went across the street to the plainclothesmen in the Oldsmobile. No need for anyone to get crazy. He had four passes for them compliments of Susan, and we were now leaving to go up to Sanchez, turn right, then go down Eighteenth to Castro then right again and down to the theater, which was actually only one block from here.

It seemed to be going amicably enough, but then Dan gave me the signal that he was going on with the cops.

"Can you believe it!" G.G. muttered. "Are they holding him hostage? Will they beat him with a rubber hose if we make a mad dash?"

"Just move on, son, and keep smiling," Alex said.

As we slid one by one into the blue-velvet-lined car, I saw Blair, cigar in hand, opposite Susan, in the little jump seat, wearing the lavender tuxedo Belinda had described in her letter, and the inevitable white mink-lined cloak. The car was already full of smoke.

Susan put her arm around me immediately and gave me a quick press of her smooth cheek.

"Son of a bitch, you sure as hell know how to launch a picture, Walker," she said in her slow Texas drawl. Her red silk rodeo shirt had three inch fringe on it, and a crust of multi-colored embroidery set off with rhinestones and pearls. The pants appeared to be red satin, her boots too were red. Her cowboy hat was resting on her right knee.

But the woman herself obscured the brilliance of the clothing. She had a sleek dark-skinned radiance to her, a cleanness of bone and line that suggested a perfect admixture of Indian blood. Her black hair was luxuriant even though it was clipped short and brushed back from her face. And if Belinda had gotten all that right in her letter, she'd left out a few things. The woman was sexy. I mean conventionally sexy. She had big breasts and an extremely sensuous mouth.

"Blair's told you everything?" I asked. We were still doing a bit of kissing and handshaking but the limo was backing out.

Susan nodded: "You've got until six in the morning to give yourself up."

"Exactly. That's the max we could get. Might have been better if Bonnie and Marty hadn't joined brother Daryl in New Orleans this evening to personally prevail upon the New Orleans police to dig up the garden surrounding my mother's house."

"The lying shits," Susan said. "Why the hell don't you give them both barrels, Walker? Release Belinda's letter not to the police but right to the press."

"Can't do it, Susan. Belinda wouldn't want it," I said.

The limousine was turning on Sanchez. I could see one car of plain-clothesmen in front of us, and the other right behind.

"So what's our strategy?" Blair said. "No one's heard from her, but that is hardly surprising under the circumstances. Her best bet may be to show up at the premiere tonight."

"That's exactly what I'm hoping she'll do," I said. "The announcement was in the evening *Examiner.*"

"Yes, and we ran time on the rock stations," Susan said, "and did handbills on Castro and Haight, too."

"All right, suppose she shows up," G.G. asked. "Then what do we do?"

We were slowing down now that we had turned on Eighteenth. In fact, there was a heavy traffic jam as we approached Castro. Typical late-night party atmosphere all around. Music pumping from the bars and from the speakers of the tramp electric guitarist on the corner and out of the window of the upstairs record shop.

"The question is, what are you willing to do?" Blair asked, leaning forward and fixing me with his eyes.

"Yeah, that's what me and this guy here have been talking about," Susan said gesturing to Blair. "Like we're down to the wire now, you're facing jail in the morning. Now, are you willing to make a run for it, Walker, if it comes to that?"

"Look, I've been sitting in the living room of my house for the last five hours thinking about nothing but that very question. And the answer is simple. It's just like the exhibit. My needs and Belinda's needs are in total synchronization. We've got to get ahold of each other and get out. If she wants a divorce later she can have it, but right now she needs me just about as much as I need her."

I could see Susan and Blair exchanging glances.

Alex, who had taken the other jump seat opposite, was watching them, too.

And strangely enough I was getting nervous, upset. I could feel my hand shaking. I could feel my heart accelerating. I wasn't sure why this was happening just now.

"You have anything to say, Alex?" G.G. asked a little timidly. "I've got her birth certificate in my pocket. It's got my name on it, and I'm ready to do whatever Jeremy wants me to do."

"No, son," Alex said. He looked at me. "I realized in New Orleans that Jeremy was going down the line with this thing. As I see it, his getting away somewhere long enough to marry Belinda is the only chance he's got. I think those lawyers would admit that, too, if one of them wasn't so cold-blooded and the other one wasn't so scared. I just don't see how you're going to do it. You need anything from me, you can have it. I'll be all right no matter what happens. At this point I'm just about the most famous innocent bystander involved."

"Alex, if any of this winds up hurting you—" I started.

"It hasn't," said Susan offhandedly. "Everybody in Tinseltown's talking about Alex. He's coming out of it a hero, and real clean. You know the old saying, 'Just so long as they spell his name right . . .' "

Alex nodded, unruffled, but I wondered if it was that simple.

"I love you, Alex," I said softly. I was really on the edge of losing it suddenly, and I wasn't sure why.

"Jeremy, stop talking like we're going to a funeral," Alex said. He reached over and gave my shoulder a nudge. "We're on our way to a premiere."

"Listen, man," Susan said, "I know what he's feeling. He's going into the slammer at six A.M." She looked at me. "How do you feel about splitting out of here tonight whether Belinda shows or not?"

"I'd do anything to get to Belinda," I said.

Blair sat back, crossed his legs, folded his arms, and looked at Susan in that clever knowing way again. Susan was sitting back, her long legs stretched out as far as they could go in the limo in front of her, and she just smiled back and shrugged.

"Now all we need is Belinda," she said.

"Yeah, and we've got cops to the left of us and cops to the right of us," Alex said casually. "And at the theater cops in front and back."

We had rounded the corner onto Castro, and now I could see the line, three and four deep, all the way back from the theater to Eighteenth.

Two enormous klieg lights set out in front of the theater were sweeping the sky with their pale-blue beams. I read the marquee again, saw those lights flickering all the way up on the giant sign that read Castro, and I thought, If she isn't here, somewhere, just to see this, my heart is going to break.

The limo was crawling towards the theater entrance, where a roped walkway had been made, to the left of the box office, leading to the front doors.

It might damn well have been an opening at Grauman's Chinese Theater, the crowd was so thick and making so much noise. The limousine was turning heads. People were obviously trying to see through the tinted glass. G.G. was searching the crowd, I could see that. But Susan was sitting there like someone had said, "Freeze."

"Oh, Belinda," I whispered. "Just be here for your own sake, honey. I want you to see this."

I was really losing it. I was coming apart inside. Up till now the whole thing had been endurable moment by moment, but after so many days shut up in the cocoon of the house, this spectacle worked on me like sentimental music. Yes, really, coming unglued.

Susan picked up the phone and spoke to the driver:

"Listen, you stay out front till we come out. Double-park, take the ticket, whatever—OK, OK, just so long as you're there when we come out the doors." She hung up. "This is a fucking mob scene all right."

"Worse than New York?"

"You better believe it, look."

I saw what she meant. The side of Castro Street opposite the theater was packed. The oncoming traffic wasn't moving at all. A couple of cops were trying to loosen up the jam ahead of us. Another pair were trying to keep the intersection clear. Everywhere I saw familiar faces, waiters who worked in the local diners, the salespeople from the local shops, neighbors who always said hello when they passed. Somewhere out there was Andy Blatky and Sheila and lots of old friends I'd called this afternoon. Everybody I knew would be there actually.

We were moving closer inch by inch. There was no air in the limousine. I felt like I was going to start bawling on the spot. But I knew the worst hadn't come yet. It would when Belinda appeared up there on the screen. That is, unless Belinda appeared right here first.

And it was happening at the Castro, of all places, our neighborhood show, the elegant old-fashioned theater where she and I had seen so many films together, where we'd snuggled up together in the dark on quiet week nights, anonymous and safe.

The limo had angled to the curb. The crowd was really pushing on the red velvet ropes. The box office had a big sign saying SOLD OUT. The local television stations had been allowed to set up their video cameras just beyond it. And a little group of people were arguing at the far right door, where a hand-lettered sign read PRESS ONLY. And somebody was shouting. It looked like a woman in spike heels and an awful leopard skin coat was getting turned away, but not without a noisy fight.

People looked bewildered as the plainclothesmen got out of the car in front of us and went straight towards the lobby door. Dan was right behind them. He turned when he got to the video cameras and watched as our driver got out of the limo and came around to open the door.

"You go first, darlin', this is your audience," Alex said to Susan. Susan put on her red cowboy hat. Then we helped her to climb over us and get out.

A roar went up from the young people on either side of the ropes. Then cheers went up from everywhere, in the intersection up ahead and across the street. Camera flashes were going off all around.

Susan stood in the brilliant light under the marquee waving to everybody, then she gestured for me to get out of the car. The flashes were blinding me a little. Another cheer went up. Kids were clapping on either side of us.

I heard a chorus of voices shout: "Jeremy, we're for you!" "Hang in there, Jeremy!" And I gave a little silent prayer of thanks for all the liberals and crazies, the gentle freaks, and the plain ordinary tolerant San Franciscans here. They weren't burning my books in this town.

There were screams and whistles coming from everywhere. G.G. got his big round of applause as he stepped out.

Then I heard a shrill voice:

"Signora Jeremiah! Eeeh, Signora Jeremiah!" It was coming from our right. In a thick Italian accent it continued: "Remember, Cinecittà, Roma! You promise me a pass!"

Then an explosion went off inside my head. Cinecittà, Roma. I turned from right to left trying to locate the voice. The coat, the awful leopard coat I just saw, it was Belinda's! Those spike heels, they were Belinda's. Italian accent or no Italian accent, that was Belinda's voice!

Then I felt G.G.'s hand clamp down on my arm.

"Don't make a move, Jeremy!" he whispered in my ear.

But where is she!

"Signora Jeremiah! They won't let me into the theater!"

At the press door! She was staring right at me through big black-rimmed Bonnie-style glasses, the dark-brown dyed hair slicked straight back from her face. And it *was* that ghastly leopard coat. Two men were trying to stop her from coming forward. She was cursing at them in Italian. They were pushing her back towards the ropes.

"Hold on there, just a minute there," Susan called out. "I know that gal, everything's OK, just calm down, it's OK."

The crowd erupted suddenly with a new explosion of cheers and shrieks. Blair had gotten out of the limousine and was throwing up both his arms. Whistles, howls.

Susan was striding towards the men who were shoving Belinda.

G.G. held me tighter. "Don't look, Jeremy!" he whispered.

"Don't move, Jeremy!" Blair said under his breath. He was turning from right to left to give the crowd a good view of the lavender tuxedo. They were really eating it up.

Susan had reached the scene of the ruckus. The men had let go of Belinda. Belinda had a steno pad in her hand and a camera around her neck. She was talking like crazy to Susan in Italian. Did Susan speak Italian? The plainclothesmen from the car behind us were glancing over as they went to join the first pair, who were standing behind the video cameras right by the doors. Dan was watching Belinda. Belinda let loose with another loud, shrill riff of Italian, obviously complaining about the people at the press door. Susan was nodding. Susan had her arm around Belinda, was clearly trying to calm her down.

"Move forward," G.G. said between his teeth. "You keep looking and the cops will be all over her. Move."

I was trying to do what he was telling me, trying to put one foot before the other. Susan was there. Susan would handle it. And then I saw Belinda's eyes again, looking right at me, through the little knot of people around her, and I saw her beautiful little babymouth suddenly smile.

I was paralyzed. Blair shoved right past me and G.G. He was throwing more kisses to the crowd. He let the cloak swirl around him.

"Five minutes till midnight, ladies and gentlemen, time to put on your best Midnight Mink."

More screams, catcalls, whistles. He beckoned for us to follow him now.

"Jeremy, go to the door," G.G. whispered.

Another roar went up as Alex stepped out of the car. Then there was solid applause, respectful applause, moving back from the ropes all through the people on the sidewalk on both sides of the street.

Alex nodded his thanks in all directions, took a long slow bow. Then he put his hand on my arm and gently propelled me forward as he greeted those who pressed in.

"No, darlin', I'm not in the movie, just here to see a really good film." "Yes, sweetheart, good to see you." He stopped to sign an autograph. "Yes, darlin', thank you, thank you, yes, and you want to know a secret? That was my favorite film, too."

The plainclothesmen were watching us. Not her, us. Two of them turned and went on into the lobby. Dan hung back.

Belinda and Susan were at the press door. Belinda gave Susan a peck on the cheek, then went inside.

All right, she was in! I let G.G. practically shove me into the lobby, too. Dan and the last two plainclothesmen brought up the rear.

I was as close to heart failure as ever in my life. The lobby too was jammed, with ropes marking off our path to the doors. We couldn't see over to the right side, where Belinda had gone in.

But within seconds we were inside the theater proper. And I saw the very back row of the center section had been marked off for us. The plainclothes guys sat down across the aisle from us in the back row of the side section. Dan stayed with them. The three rows in front of us, clear across the center, were already full of reporters, some of whom had just been outside my house. There were columnists from all the local papers, several beautifully turned out socialites, and a number of other writers and people connected with the local arts, some of them turning to nod or give a little wave. Andy Blatky and Sheila, who'd gotten their special passes, were already down front. Sheila threw me a kiss. Andy gave a right-on fist.

And there was Belinda standing over on the right side, chewing a wad of gum as she scribbled like mad on her steno pad. She looked up, squinted at us through the glasses, then started across the center section through the empty row right in front of the roped-off seats.

"Mr. Walker, you give me an autograph!" she screamed in the Italian accent. Everybody was looking at her. I was petrified. That's it, I thought. My heart is going to give out now.

Alex and Blair had gone on into the row ahead of me. So had G.G., and I could see him watching her, blank-faced, probably as scared as I was. Susan was standing in the aisle with her thumbs in her belt.

Belinda came right up to me, her mouth working fast with the gum, and shoved the exhibit catalog in front of me along with a ballpoint pen.

For a second I couldn't do anything but look right at her, at her blue eyes peering out from under the brown eyelashes and brown eyebrows and the slick brown hair. I tried to breathe, to move, to take the pen, but I couldn't.

She was smiling. Oh, beautiful Belinda, my Belinda. And I could feel my lips moving, feel my own smile coming back. The fucking hell with the whole world if it was watching.

"Sign the kid's autograph, Walker," Susan said. "Before they let in the thundering herd."

I looked down at the catalog and saw the color print of *Belinda, Come Back* circled in red. Under it was written:

"I love you." Her unmistakable script.

I took the pen out of her hand, my hand shaking so badly I could scarcely control it, and I wrote:

"Marry me?" the pen skittering like skates on ice.

She nodded, winked at me, then let loose in Italian again to Susan. The plainclothesmen weren't even looking at her. What the hell was she saying?

Suddenly Susan broke up. She threw back her head and let go with a loud, deep laugh and, doubling her right hand into a fist, she hit me on the arm:

"Sit down, Walker!" she said.

The doors to the lobby were being opened. I moved into the seat next to G.G. as Susan took the aisle seat next to me. And then Belinda sat down in the aisle seat across from us, right in front of the plainclothesmen, utterly oblivious to them, and flashed another great big smile.

"Susan!" I whispered in panic.

"Shut up," she whispered back.

The crowd was already streaming down all four aisles.

My heart was so loud I wondered if the plainclothes guys could hear it. Belinda, when I could catch a glimpse of her through the people passing us, was scribbling again.

"Now what do we do?" G.G. whispered to me.

"How the fuck should I know?" I asked.

I couldn't tell whether Alex had recognized her or not, he was chatting with the ladies in front of him, and Blair had a similar conversation going with a young reporter I recognized from the Stanford Court.

Susan sat there, with her red hat on, and her long fingers spread out on her knees, just watching the people stream in.

It didn't take long for the theater to fill. Pretty soon only a few people were left combing the place for seats together, then splitting up to take the last empties on the far aisles.

The lights went dim. Somebody tapped Susan on the shoulder. And she started slowly down the main aisle towards the stage.

Belinda was staring right at me, but I didn't dare look directly at her. Then I saw that G.G. was looking at her and she was beaming at him.

"G.G., she doesn't know the cops are behind her!" I whispered.

"The cops are everywhere, Jeremy," he whispered back. "Just try to keep very calm."

Then Belinda turned and asked one of the cops very loudly in that accent if it was OK to smoke in the theater, and he said no, and she threw up her hand in exasperation, and then I heard him lean forward and say something in Italian to her, very apologetic in tone.

Suddenly she was talking to him in Italian. And he was talking to her.

"Christ, G.G.," I whispered. "The fucking cop is Italian."

"Just take a deep breath, Jeremy," G.G. said. "Let her handle it. She's an actress, remember? So she's going for the Academy Award."

All I could catch were a lot of place names, Firenzei, Siena, si, si. North Beach. North Beach! I was going to lose my mind.

But Susan had just gone up the little steps to the stage. The spotlight hit her, setting her red satin clothes beautifully on fire. The theater was alive with enthusiastic applause.

Susan smiled, took off her cowboy hat, got another big volley of whistles and claps, and then she gestured for quiet.

"Thank you all for coming out tonight," she said. "This San Francisco premiere of *Final Score* is kind of a special event for us, and I know we all wish Belinda could be here, too, to see the show."

Loud applause. Everybody was clapping, even the cool people in the press rows in front of us. Everybody that is, except the cops, and Belinda who was again scribbling on her pad.

"Well, I'm just here to remind you of what I think you really do know . . . that there are lots of other people in this movie, lots of people who helped to make it a special experience, including actress Sandy Miller, who is really the star." More applause. "Sandy would be here tonight if she wasn't in Brazil scouting locations for a picture. And I know she thanks y'all for your warm applause. Now y'all will pay close attention to the credits, won't you, because all of these people did a fine job, but I can't leave this microphone without thanking Belinda's mother, Bonnie

Blanchard, for financing this picture. Because without Bonnie it would never have been made."

She didn't wait for the crowd's reaction on that one, but left the stage immediately, and there was only one beat, maybe two, of hesitation before the crowd applauded again.

The lights were out by the time Susan reached her seat. The theater fell dead silent. *Final Score* had begun.

I could scarcely see the first few scenes—or hear them. I was sweating under the boiled shirt and hot dinner jacket. I rested my head in my hands.

And then I was jolted suddenly by Blair pushing his way out of the row, whispering, "Stay where you are," as he went by.

Susan waited a couple of seconds, then followed him.

Belinda took out her cigarettes and her lighter, glanced back at the cop and shrugged, and went out to the lobby, too.

"We're going to sit here like two little birds on a perch," G.G. whispered.

I started watching the movie just so I wouldn't start yelling and screaming. Then Susan came back.

But Blair and Belinda did not.

"So what's happening?" I whispered to her.

She made a little gesture for me to be quiet.

By the end of the first forty-five minutes of the movie, two things were clear. Blair and Belinda were flat out gone. And this movie was a viable commercial hit.

Of course, I knew every syllable of it from watching it during those drunken days in New Orleans right before G.G. and Alex had come down. But no videotape is a substitute for the theater experience. Only here could I feel the pace, the responsiveness of the audience, the way the timing and the humor, which was considerable, worked.

When Belinda finally appeared on horseback, the audience broke into spontaneous applause. Then the crowd went dead quiet during the love scene in the white bedroom of the little house. I felt a frisson all through my body when the moment came, the moment I had painted, Belinda's head back, Sandy's lips on her chin.

As soon as the scene was over, the applause broke out again.

Then I got up and I went out into the lobby. I couldn't stand it a moment longer. I had to at least get up and move my legs. And damn it, Susan had to get her ass out here and tell me something. I was going to drag her out if she didn't come.

I went to the candy counter and asked for some popcorn. The little knot of people talking on the balcony stairs had gone quiet.

Two of the plainclothesmen came out and passed behind me over to the ashtray by the men's room door.

"The popcorn's on us, Jeremy," said the girl behind the counter.

"You remember Belinda?" I asked. "All the times we came in together?"

The girl nodded. "I hope it works out all right."

"Thanks, honey," I said.

Susan had just come out. She went to the one door that was open to the street and stood there looking out. She had her hat pressed down really low, and her thumbs were hooked in the back of her pants.

I came up beside her. I saw the limo out there. I saw one of the plainclothesmen tense, like we were going to run.

"Congratulations, lady, it's a bang-up film," I said. "Should have been released a long time before now."

She smiled at me, nodded. She was almost as tall as I was. We were almost eye to eye. But, of course she had on those high-heeled cowboy boots.

Then, without her lips even moving, she whispered: "Reno or bust, OK?"

The chills went down my arms and back. "When you say the word."

She looked outside again. I pushed the popcorn at her. She took a handful, ate it.

"You're sure?" she whispered. "Belinda wants you to be really sure! She said to say Holy Communion to you and Are you sure?"

I smiled and looked out at the limo gleaming like a big white opal in the lights of the marquee. I thought of my house only two blocks around the corner, the fortress of the past two decades, all choked with dolls and toys and clocks and things that had not meant anything for years and years. I thought of Belinda smiling up at me through that lovely disguise.

"Honey, you can't know how sure I am," I said. "Holy Communion, she said it. Reno or bust."

She was satisfied. She turned to go back in. "Nice sitting in the back row," she said in a normal voice, "I can keep my hat on, for a change."

Dan was suddenly standing next to me.

He had lighted a cigarette already, and I could see it shaking between his thumb and middle finger as he tapped the ash onto the rug. The plainclothesmen were still over by the ashtray, their eyes on us.

"Client–lawyer privilege," I said.

"Always," Dan said. But he sounded as if he had no more stamina left in him. He leaned his shoulder against the door.

"You're one of my closest friends in the whole world, you know that, don't you?" I asked.

"You asking my opinion on something?" he asked. "Or are you saying good-bye?" I could see his teeth biting into his lip.

I didn't answer for a moment. I ate some of the popcorn. In fact, I realized I'd been eating the popcorn ever since I bought it. It was probably the first thing I'd really eaten with any gusto in days. I almost laughed.

"Dan, I want you to do something for me," I said.

He looked up as if to say, What now? Then he glanced at me and gave me a warm, but very worn smile.

"Give all the toys to an orphanage or a school or something," I said. "You don't have to say where they came from. Just see they go to some place where kids will enjoy them, OK?"

His lip was trembling, and he drew up his shoulders like he was going to yell. But he didn't. He took another drag on the cigarette and looked out the open door again.

"And Andy's sculpture, you've got to get that out of my backyard and out someplace where people can see it."

He nodded. "I'll handle it." Then I saw his eyes glass over.

"Dan, I'm sorry about all this as far as you're concerned."

"Jer, save it. At least until you get my bill." But then he gave me another of his rare and very genuine smiles. So quick maybe nobody else would have caught it. "I just hope you make it," he said, as he looked out the door again.

[8]

Two seconds after the last shot faded, after the applause started, Susan was out the doors with me and G.G. right behind her, striding through the lobby and across the pavement to the limousine.

Alex had not followed, and I knew this was deliberate. But I saw the plainclothesmen just coming out, with the crowd flowing right behind them, as I slid after G.G. into the backseat.

I don't think I realized until the motor started that Susan was at the wheel. The driver was gone. The bars on Castro hadn't closed yet, the streets were relatively deserted, and the limousine moved forward very fast around the cop car in front of it and made a smooth right onto Seventeenth, just as if we were going home.

I glanced back. The cops had not even unlocked the door of their car. Dan was talking to the one with the keys in his hand.

Then we were off, roaring past Hartford, G.G. and I thrown forward, the limo gaining speed as it ran through the stop sign on Noe and went on past my house and screeched into a left-hand turn at Sanchez Street.

"Jesus, Susan, you'll kill us," G.G. whispered.

I could hear the sirens suddenly screaming behind us, and then I looked out and saw the flashing light.

"Hell, damn!" Susan said. She slammed on the brakes, and we skidded into the intersection, barely missing an old man crossing the street, who had obviously made Susan stop. He turned, yelled at us, gave us the finger.

The cop car was blazing across Noe.

Susan swerved left on Sanchez and raced ahead.

"Fuckers saw us turn, damn it, hang on," Susan said.

She threw us into a left turn on Market and then a sharp right, roaring into another left.

I saw the lights of the Golden Bear Motel above us, the balconies. She had driven us around back, out of sight of the street, and come to a stop in a parking lot.

"Move it, both of you!" she said.

The sirens were multiplying. But they were racing down Sanchez. They hadn't made the turn on Market Street.

A big silver Lincoln Continental had pulled up right behind us, and Susan opened the passenger door. G.G. and I slid into the back. Blair was driving, wearing a red baseball cap over his bald head.

"Get down, all of you," he said in that ferocious voice of his.

Sirens were screaming past on Market now, right out front.

I could feel the car rolling steadily out of the driveway then turning right as if we had all the time in the world. We were cruising back towards Castro.

A squad car roared by, light revolving. I didn't dare look, but I thought it turned left.

"So far, so good!" Blair said. "Now Walker, how the hell do I get to Fifth and Mission from here? Fast!"

I glanced up over the back of the seat and saw squad cars all over Castro. The crowd was pouring out of the theater still.

"Let's get the fuck out of here," I said. "Go straight up the hill, up Seventeenth."

There were so many sirens now it sounded like a five-alarm fire.

But Blair went up the hill at old-geezer speed until I told him to take a right again, and then led him back down again on Market up near Fifteenth.

Within minutes we were in the early-morning glare and waste of downtown, away from the sirens and away from the Castro, and nobody was the wiser. Nobody had even seen Susan make that lightning turn into the motel.

When we finally turned off Mission into the big multistory parking lot opposite the Chronicle Building, Blair said, "Get ready for another change."

This time it was a big cushy silver van we piled into, the kind with shaggy upholstery and tinted glass. Susan took the wheel again, Blair rode shotgun beside her and, when I opened the side door of the van, I saw Belinda in there, and I climbed up inside and into her arms.

I squeezed her so tight I might have hurt her as we pulled out. For this one second I didn't care about anything in the world—people chasing us, looking for us, it didn't matter. I had her. I was kissing her, her mouth, her eyes, feeling her kisses just as heated and crazy as mine, and I'd defy the whole world to separate us now.

The van was back on Mission. Sirens again, but they were blocks away.

Only reluctantly did I let her go and let her turn towards G.G. and embrace him, too.

I sat down in the backseat, winded, anxious, and deliriously happy and just feasted my eyes on her and G.G. hugging, those two who looked more like twins than father and daughter, enjoying their own version of the moment I was feeling right now.

"All right, gang," Susan said, "we ain't home free yet. The Bay Bridge, where is it? And if you see a squad car or any funny-looking car for that matter, get down!" I saw she'd taken off her cowboy hat—in fact, she had on one of those baseball hats just like Blair. Two nice vacationers, they looked like. And nobody could see us on account of the tinted glass.

"Straight ahead, Susan, you'll see the sign, last on ramp by the East Bay Terminal," Belinda said.

"Hey, talk to me," I said, pulling her back against me. "Just talk to me. Say anything, say anything at all."

"Jeremy, you crazy guy!" she said. "I love you, you crazy guy. You did it. You really did."

I held her with no intentions of ever letting her escape again. I held her face tightly, kissing her mouth a little too hard perhaps, but she didn't seem to mind at all. Then I started taking the pins out of her shiny brown hair. And she shook it all out. She put her hands on the side of my face, and then she looked like she was about to cry.

G.G. stretched his legs out on the middle seat in front of us, lit a cigarette, and shut his eyes.

"OK, gang, four hours till Reno," Susan said. We were going up the ramp to the bridge. "And when we hit the open freeway, this van's gonna fly."

"Yes, well, please crash-land at the first liquor store you see past Oakland," G.G. said. "I need a drink even if I have to stick the place up."

Everybody laughed. I was positively dopey suddenly. I was so happy with Belinda against me and her arm around me. I was floating.

I looked out the deep window at the silver rafters of the Bay Bridge above. The van was rocking with a hypnotic rhythm as it went over the seams in the bridge beneath us, and in the early morning there was not another car to be seen.

It felt odd to me, like the first time I had come to California when I had been very young and I had everything that mattered to me in one suitcase and dreams of pictures in my head.

Dreams of pictures. I could have seen them now if I shut my eyes.

Out of the radio came a country-and-western song real low, a lady singing one of those preposterous lyrics, like the washing machine broke down after you broke up with me, and I started to laugh. My body felt tired and light and full of energy, the way it hadn't since Belinda left.

Belinda snuggled closer. She was looking at me very intently, eyes even bluer on account of the dark lashes. Her hair had fallen down free over the collar of the horrible leopard coat. I realized there was luggage piled in the van behind us, tons of luggage, and there were boxes and tripods and cameras in black cases and other things.

"Mink coats," she said, as she watched me. "You don't mind getting married in a mink coat?"

"You damn well better not mind!" Blair said over his shoulder. Susan gave a deep-throated laugh.

"I love it," I said.

"You madman," she said. "You really did it all right, and what happens when you realize what you did?"

Then I looked down at her and saw she was afraid.

"You think I don't realize?" I said.

"They're burning your books, Jeremy," she said with a little catch in her voice. "All over the country they're taking them out of the libraries and burning them in the town squares."

"Yeah, and they're hanging him in the New York Museum of Modern Art, aren't they?" Blair yelled. "What the hell do you want?"

"Take it easy, Blair," G.G. said. His voice seemed to capture exactly the anxiety I saw in Belinda's face.

"I'm scared for you, Jeremy," she said. "I was scared for you all the way back on the plane from Rome. I was scared for you every moment till I saw you tonight, and even now I'm scared scared scared. I tried to call you from every phone booth between here and Los Angeles, you know that, don't you? I'd never expected you to do it, Jeremy, not really, and I've been scared ever since I found out you did."

"Belinda, this is the happiest day of my life. It's the happiest day I can ever remember," I said. "I might break into laughter and never be able to stop."

"You wouldn't have done this," she said, "if I hadn't run out on you like that."

"Belinda, it is too late for this foolishness!" Blair said.

"Be quiet, Blair," G.G. said.

"Belinda, what do I have to say to get that expression off your face?

Belinda, I did this for both of us. Both of us, don't you see? Now you have to believe me, and don't you forget what I've said. The first time I ever painted you, I knew I was using you. I told you so. Now what do you think has changed? The fact that now you need me, too?"

I think my smile was convincing her. My manner was convincing her, the fact that I was sitting there so calmly, holding her and trying to drain the anxiety away.

But I could see she couldn't quite understand it. She couldn't quite accept that I knew what I was doing and saying and that I was all right. Either that or she was simply too frightened herself.

"There's one thing that bugs me," I said. I stroked her hair away from her face. She didn't look bad with brown hair. She looked beautiful actually. But I couldn't wait to see it washing off.

"What's that?" she asked.

"Marty and Bonnie being hurt so much. The tabloids are crucifying them, the program's nixed. G.G. didn't want them ruined. Neither did I."

"You're out of your head, Rembrandt," Blair bellowed. "I can't listen to this madness. Turn up the radio, Susan."

"Blair, just pipe down!" G.G. said. "Susan, we've got ten minutes to find a liquor store. Everything shuts down at two A.M."

"OK, gang, we aren't even out of the fucking Bay Area and I'm stopping for liquor, can you believe it?"

She rolled off the freeway into downtown Oakland—or something that looked like downtown Oakland. Then we stopped at a real dirty little place on a corner, and G.G. went in.

"Belinda," I said, "I want you to know I told who you were and who I was, I told our story as best I could without bringing them into it, without slinging any mud."

She looked amazed, absolutely amazed. I don't think I'd ever seen her look so taken off guard.

G.G. came back out with a sackful of bottles and some plastic glasses. He climbed back into the middle seat.

"Take off!" Blair said. Back on the freeway, back on to 580 rolling out of Oakland.

I sat back, taking a deep breath, waiting politely for G.G. to open one of those bottles, whatever they were. Belinda was watching me. She still looked absolutely amazed.

"Jeremy," she said finally, "I want to tell you something. When I got off the plane at LAX yesterday, the first paper I picked up had my picture on the front page and the news that Mom was in the hospital. I thought, What is it this time, pills, a gun, razor blades? I ran to the phone, Jeremy, I ran. Even before I tried to call you, I called Mom. I called Sally Tracy, Mom's agent, and I got her to call the hospital, to get me through to the phone right by Mom's bed. And I said, 'Mom, this is Belinda, I'm alive, Mom, and I'm OK.' Do you know what she said, Jeremy? She said, 'This is not my daughter,' and she hung up the phone. She knew it was me, Jeremy. I know she did. She knew. And when she checked out the next morning, she told the reporters she believed her daughter was dead."

Nobody said a word. Then Susan made a long low sound like a disgusted sigh. Blair gave a little ironic laugh, and G.G. just smiled sort of bitter and looked from Belinda to me.

We were out of Oakland now, going north through the beautiful rolling hills of Contra Costa County under a dark yet cloudy sky.

G.G. leaned over and kissed Belinda. "I love you, baby," he whispered.

"You want to open one of those bottles, G.G.?" Blair said.

"Right on. You hold the glass there for me, Jeremy," he said, as he lifted the bottle out of the sack. "I think this flight calls for a little champagne."

IT was six A.M. when we rolled into Reno, and everybody was asleep or drunk by that time, except Susan, who was neither. She just kept pushing on the accelerator and singing to the country-and-western music on the radio.

Then Blair checked us into the MGM Grand, into a two-bedroom suite that had the right colored walls so that he could take our pictures after Belinda had washed the dye out of her hair.

G.G. went to help her with the shampooing, and Blair started setting up his Hasselblad camera and tripod and draping sheets over things to make the light absolutely right.

Belinda had to wash her hair five times to get all the brown out, then G.G. went to work on it madly with the hair dryer, and finally we shot the first roll of film against a perfect dark background, Belinda and I both in full-length white mink coats.

I felt perfectly ridiculous, but Blair assured me that merely standing there, looking blank-faced, exhausted, and slightly annoyed worked out just fine. Twice he called photographer Eric Arlington—the man who took most of the Midnight Mink pictures—at his house in Montauk to get advice from him, then he plunged ahead himself.

Meantime Susan was on the phone to her daddy in Houston, making sure his Learjet was on the way. Her daddy was a high-roller in both Las Vegas and Reno, and his pilot made the run all the time. The plane ought to be at the Reno airport anytime.

G.G. then called Alex in LA. Alex had remained at my house in San Francisco until Dan assured him that the police were no longer in "hot pursuit," that we had apparently gotten out of San Francisco without incident and only then did Alex get on the plane for home.

They had issued a warrant for my arrest, and therefore we ought to get married this minute, Alex said, and then why not all come to his house down south?

When I heard about the warrant, I agreed with Alex. Let's get out of this room and get married right now.

THE wedding was a scream.

The nice little lady and her husband in the twenty-four-hour chapel had never heard of us obviously, though we were on the front pages of the papers just down the street. The nice lady thought G.G. looked awfully young to be Belinda's father, however. But G.G. had the certificate which proved it. And then the lady and her husband were all too pleased to do the wedding with organ music and flowers in less than twenty minutes. Just step right in.

And then we all got a little surprise. Not only would the chapel sell us a nice pack of Polaroid pictures of the ceremony, they would videotape it for ninety dollars more. And we could have as many copies of the videotape as we were willing to buy. We ordered ten.

So while Blair shot more film with the Hasselblad, Belinda and I, up to our earlobes in white mink, said the words to each other while the camera rolled.

But when the moment came, when we exchanged the vows, nobody else was there. The little chapel faded, Blair and Susan faded—even G.G. faded. The ugly artificial lights faded. There was no little man reading from the Bible to us, no little lady smiling from behind her Polaroid camera as it made its strange spitting and grinding sounds.

Just Belinda and I stood there in the moment, and we were together the way we had been in the loft in Carmel with the sun shafting through the skylight and in New Orleans with the summer rain coming through the French doors as we lay on Mother's bed. Even the weariness gave a lovely luster to her eyes, a sharpness to her expression that was faintly tragic. And the sadness of the separation—the sadness of the violence and the misunderstandings—was there too, woven into the moment, giving it a softness and a slowness and mingling the happiness with pain.

We looked at each other in silence when it came time to kiss. Her hair was streaming down over the white fur, and her face was naked of all paint and indescribably lovely, her eyelashes golden as her hair.

"Holy Communion, Jeremy," she whispered. And then I said, "Holy

Communion, Belinda." And when she closed her eyes and I saw her lips open and I felt her rise on tiptoe to kiss me, I took her in my arms, crushing her in all this white mink fur, and the world was gone. Simply gone.

So it was done. And now she was Belinda Walker, and we were Belinda and Jeremy Walker. And nobody was going to take her away from me.

Then I saw G.G. crying. Even Blair was moved. Only Susan was smiling, but it was a very beautiful and understanding smile.

"OK, it's a wrap," she said suddenly. "Now out of this place. Y'all need a director, you know it? And this director's starving to death."

We had a wonderful eggs and bacon breakfast in a big shiny American restaurant while they copied the videotapes, then we hit the office of National Courier and sent the tapes by messenger to the three networks in Los Angeles, and to local stations in New York, San Francisco, and LA. Belinda sent a tape to Bonnie's house in Beverly Hills and another to her uncle Daryl's private secretary in Dallas. The Polaroids we sent to newspapers in the three important cities, too. I sent a copy of the tape along with a Polaroid shot to Lieutenant Connery in San Francisco, with the hasty note that I was sorry for all the inconvenience and I thought he was a nice man.

These things would arrive at their destinations within several hours. So there wasn't much more we could do.

We got a bottle of Dom Pérignon and went back to the MGM Grand.

G.G. fell asleep before anybody could decide where to go, what to do next. He was suddenly sprawled out on the sofa and completely unconscious with the empty champagne glass still in his hand.

The next to go was Susan. One minute she was pacing back and forth with the phone in her hand, talking a print of *Final Score* into the right theater in Chicago. Next time I looked, she was sprawled out on the carpet with a pillow mashed under her face.

Blair got up, packed his things and told us all to stay as long as we wanted on his nickel. Nobody on the hotel staff had even seen us. Just relax. As for him, he had to be in a darkroom in New York with Eric Arlington right now!

I helped him pile his stuff in the hallway for the bellhop so that nobody need come into the room. Then he came to kiss Belinda good-bye.

"Where's my hundred Gs," Belinda said softly.

He stopped. "Where the hell's my checkbook?"

"The hell with your checkbook, good-bye." She threw her arms around him and kissed him.

"Love you, baby," he said.

He took the film and left.

"Does that mean we don't get the money?" I asked.

"We have the coats, don't we?" she said. She scrunched down in the white mink and giggled. "And we've got the Dom Pérignon, too. And I'll betcha Marty's making a fat deal for 'Champagne Flight' with cable television—'The story continues uncensored . . . blah, blah, blah.' "

"You really think so?"

She nodded. "Just wait and see." But then her face went dark. A shadow fell over her soul.

"Come here," I said.

We got up together, taking the champagne and glasses with us, and crept into the bedroom and locked the door.

I closed the heavy draperies till there was only a little sunlight coming through. Everything pure and quiet here. Not a sound from the streets below. Belinda put the champagne on the night table.

Then she let the white mink coat drop to the floor.

"No, spread it out on the bed," I said softly. I laid mine out beside it. The bed was completely covered.

Then we took off our clothes and laid down on the white mink.

I kissed her slowly, opening her lips, and then I felt her hips against me, and the white fur of the coat stroking me and so were her fingers, and I could feel her hair all over my arm. Her mouth opened, became hard and soft at the same time.

I kissed her breasts and pressed my face into them and rubbed my rough unshaven beard against them, and I felt her move closer under me, arching her back and pushing against me, her little nest of nether hair prickling and moist against my leg, and then I went in.

I don't think we had ever made love this fast, the heat rising to combustion this quickly, not even the very first time. I felt her rocking under me and then I was coming, and I thought, This is Belinda, and when it was done, I lay there entwined with her, her cheek against my chest, her hair flowing down her naked back, and high above the noise and bustle of Reno in this warm silent room we slept.

It was late afternoon when Susan knocked on the door. Time to blow this town. They were showing the videotapes of the wedding on TV.

All I had to wear was the dinner jacket and rumpled boiled shirt, so I put all that on again and came out into the living room of the suite. Belinda came after me, hastily dressed in jeans and sweater and looking as beautiful as any tousled bride ought to look.

G.G. was on the phone to Alex, but he hung up when we came in.

Susan told us her daddy's jet was ready to take us to Texas. And Susan said that was absolutely the safest place to go. We could wait out the storm there and nobody, absolutely nobody, was going to hassle us on the Jeremiah ranch.

But I could see by Belinda's face that this was not what she wanted to do. She was biting at one of her fingernails, and I saw the shadow again. I saw the worry.

"Running again? All the way to Texas? Susan, you're trying to cast a movie in Los Angeles. You're trying to get a distributor for *Final Score*. And we're going to hole up in Texas? What for?"

"The marriage is legal," I said. "And everybody knows about it by this time. Plus there was no warrant out for me when I split, you know. There's no question of aiding and abetting."

"It would be kind of interesting," Belinda said, "to see what they'd do."

"We can go to LA," G.G. said. "Alex is ready for us. He says he's got your regular room ready for you and Belinda, Jeremy. You know Alex. He'll let the cops and the reporters in and serve them Brie on crackers and Pinot Chardonnay. He says we can stay in Beverly Hills forever if we want."

"Either way you want to play it," Susan said. "We got a Lear jet waiting for us. And I got plenty of work in LA to do."

Belinda was looking at me. "Where do you want to go, Jeremy?" she asked. Her voice was fragile and scared again. "Where do you want us to be, Jeremy?" she asked.

It hurt me, the expression in her eyes.

"Honey, it doesn't make any difference," I said. "If I can buy some canvas and some Windsor and Newton oils, if I can settle into a place to do some work, I don't care if we're in Rio de Janeiro or on a Greek island or a satellite out in space."

"Way to go, Walker!" Susan said. "Let's high out of here for LA."

I FELL into a half-sleep when we were way up there in the clouds. I was sitting back in a big leather recliner, and the champagne was working on me, and in a half-dream I was thinking of paintings. They were developing in my mind like pictures in a darkroom. Scenes from my entire life.

Belinda was telling G.G. in a soft voice about being in Rome again and how lonely it had been but that working at Cinecittà had been OK. She had a nice room in Florence just a block from the Uffizi, and she'd gone there just about every day. On the Ponte Vecchi when she saw all the glove stores she thought of him and how he'd bought her her first pair of white gloves there when she was four years old.

Then G.G. was assuring her it didn't matter about his New York business closing. He could have stayed, fought it out, probably won. He never would know how the rumors started. Maybe it was not Marty, but Marty's men. But now he and Alex "had something," something that was better than it had been with Ollie, and maybe G.G. would set up shop on Rodeo Drive.

"You know, I'm forty years old, Belinda," he said. "I can't be somebody's little boy forever. My luck should have run out before now. But I'll tell you, it's wonderful having one last go at it with Alex Clementine, with the guy I used to watch up there on the screen when I was twelve years old."

"Good for you, Daddy," she said.

It was a real possibility, a Beverly Hills G.G.'s, why not? He had really cashed out in New York, rumors or no rumors. If he sold the Fire Island house, he would have a small fortune. "Oh, but you know," he laughed, "G.G. on Rodeo Drive would make Bonnie sooo mad."

The clouds were just like a blanket outside the window. The late-afternoon sun hit them in a fan of burnt golden rays. The rays came through the window. They struck Belinda and G.G. together, their hair seeming to mingle as it became light.

I was half-dreaming. I saw my house in San Francisco like a ship cut adrift. Good-bye to all the toys, the dolls, the trains, the dollhouse, good-bye to all the roach and rat paintings, good-bye to the china and silver and the grandfather clock and the letters, all the letters from all the little girls.

Awful to think that the little girls felt hurt. Awful to think they were disappointed in me. Please don't let them feel a dark feeling of betrayal and unwholesomeness. Please let them come to see that the Belinda paintings were supposed to be about love and light.

I tried to think of something I wanted from home, something I would ache for later. And there was nothing at all. The Belinda paintings were going all over the world. Only four were not going to museums—they would go to the august Count Solosky, which was almost the same thing.

And nothing called to me from the house in San Francisco. Not even Andy's wonderful sculpture, because I knew Dan would move it to the right place. Maybe Rhinegold would take it with him when he went back to West Fifty-seventh Street. Now that was a fine idea. I hadn't even shown it to Rhinegold. What an inexcusably selfish thing.

But the paintings, now the paintings, that was where my mind, half in sleep and half-awake, really wanted to go. *The May Procession, The Mardi Gras,* I envisioned them again. I could see every detail. But I could see other works, too. I saw those big shaggy police dogs sniffing at the dolls. *Dogs Visit the Toys.* And I saw Alex in his raincoat and fedora walking through Mother's hallway, looking at the peeling wallpaper. "Jeremy, finish up, son, so we can get out of this house!"

Got to paint a picture of Alex, terribly important to paint Alex, Alex who'd been in hundreds of movies, and never been painted right. The dogs would become werewolves sniffing through the porcelain babies and, yes, I'd have to deal with all that darkness again in that one, but it had an inevitable feel to it, and Alex walking through Mother's house, too, all right. But Alex, important to move him out of the dark house. Alex at the garden gate on that morning twenty-five years ago when he said:

"You stay with me when you come out west."

IV

THE FINAL SCORE

THE long weekend at Alex's quiet sprawling canyon house in Beverly Hills was dreamy and slow. Belinda and I made love often in the undisturbed silence of the bedroom. I slept twelve hours at a stretch, deeper than I had ever slept since I was a kid. The eternal southern California sun poured through the many French windows onto vistas of thick carpet, and down on gardens as well-kept as interiors, the stillness unbroken except by the noise of an occasional car on the distant canyon road.

Susan's plane had gotten us back without incident. For the first twenty-four hours at least nobody had known we were here.

And by Monday morning the tabloids had the story: BONNIE'S DAUGHTER MARRIES ARTIST. JEREMY AND BELINDA IN RENO. BELINDA ALIVE AND WELL AND MARRIED. And the videotape of the wedding had been shown by a thousand news outlets all over the world.

The big local news, however, was Blair Sackwell's full-page insert advertisement in the *San Francisco Chronicle* and the national edition of *The New York Times:* BELINDA AND JEREMY FOR MIDNIGHT MINK.

It was just about the first shot of us that Blair had taken. I was unshaven, shaggy headed, a little puzzled in expression, and Belinda, wide-eyed, babylips jutting slightly, had the unselfconscious seriousness of a child. Two faces, blankets of white fur. The lens of the Hasselblad and the size of the negative gave it a startling graven quality—every pore showed, every hair etched. And that is what Blair had wanted. That was what Eric Arlington had always delivered to him.

The picture transcended photography. We appeared more real than real.

Of course, Blair knew he did not have to spend another cent to publicize his picture. By evening, newspapers all over the country had reprinted it. The news magazines would inevitably do the same. Everybody would see Blair's trademark. Midnight Mink was news, the way it had been years ago, when Bonnie had been its first model with the coat half-open all the way down her right side.

Nevertheless, the advertisement would appear in *Vogue* and *Harper's Bazaar* eventually as well as in a host of other magazines. Such was the destiny of those who posed for Midnight Mink.

Dozens of long-stemmed white roses began to arrive on Monday afternoon. By evening the house was full of them. They were all from Blair.

Meantime the news around us was comforting. The LAPD had dropped its warrant for Belinda. Daryl Blanchard claimed "profound relief" that his niece was alive. He would not contest G.G.'s consent to the marriage. The age-old power of the ritual was recognized by this plainspoken and rather confused Texas man. Bonnie wept heartrending tears on network and cable. Marty broke down again.

The San Francisco police decided not to pursue their warrants for me. Quite impossible to press me for crimes against a delinquent minor who was now my legal bride. And I had not been under arrest at the time I had "flown" from San Francisco. So Susan could not formally be charged for her part in the escape.

The lines continued outside the Folsom Street exhibit. And Rhinegold reported that every painting was now spoken for. Two to Paris, one to Berlin, another to New York, one to Dallas, the four to Count Solosky. I had lost track.

Time and *Newsweek,* hitting the stands at Monday noon with a load of obsolete garbage about the "disappearance" and "possible murder," nevertheless gave enormous coverage to the paintings, which their critics begrudgingly praised.

As early as Monday afternoon Susan had a national distributor for *Final Score.* Limelight was taking it over, and the labs were working overtime on the prints, and Susan was in there with the cinematographer making sure that Chicago and Boston and Washington each got a jewel. The papers already carried their ads for a weekend opening in a thousand theaters nationwide.

Susan also had the go-ahead from Galaxy Pictures for *Of Will and Shame* with her script and Belinda, if Belinda was willing, and Sandy Miller was back from Rio with the lowdown on locations. As of the first of the year, Susan was ready to go to Brazil.

As for Alex, he was hotter than ever, as far as we could tell. His champagne commercials were running on schedule, and there was renewed interest in the television miniseries to be based on his autobiography. Would he consent, the producers were asking, to play himself? He had two other television films in the works, and the talk shows were calling him, too.

Susan wanted Alex for *Of Will and Shame* and was trying desperately to get the studio to meet his price, which was enormous, and he was promising to throw up the television offers for a real picture "if the agents could just work things out."

All Alex wanted to do at the moment, however, was lie on the sun-drenched redbrick terrace and turn browner and browner as he talked to G.G. And G.G. insisted he was having the time of his life. The work of opening the Beverly Hills salon would come all too soon, as far as he was concerned.

When the word got out that G.G. was in Beverly Hills, friends of Alex started calling. G.G. could start free-lance any time he chose.

The shadow in paradise was Belinda.

Belinda had not said absolutely go ahead to the movie, which was making Susan a bit nervous, but Belinda was not entirely all right.

There was something tentative about Belinda's every gesture, something clouded and uncertain in her gaze. There were moments when she reminded me uncannily of Bonnie in that Hyatt Regency room.

Over and over she asked me if I was certain that everything was OK with me. But I came to realize as I repeatedly reassured her that she was the one who was agitated and tense. She was the one who could not take a deep breath.

She read every article in the papers about her mother. In silence she watched her mother and Marty scrambling to salvage their reputations and their positions on the evening news.

The tabloids had not let up on Bonnie and Marty. There was talk of "Champagne Flight" being revived on cable, but nothing firm had been announced.

Meantime Belinda had also spoken to her uncle briefly by phone on Sunday afternoon. Not a very pleasant call. The man had not believed her when she said she had called her mother at the hospital several days ago.

Then I took the phone. I explained to Daryl that Belinda was all right now, we were married, and that maybe the best thing was to let all this simmer down. Daryl was confused, plain and simple. It was obvious Bonnie had been lying to him about everything, and so had Marty. He told me that he had pushed for the warrant for Belinda against their wishes, in a desperate effort to find his niece, if she was still alive. Now he didn't know what to do exactly. He wanted to see Belinda. But she would not see him. The call ended with uncomfortable pleasantries. She would write to him. He would write to her.

She was quiet and withdrawn after. She was not all right at all.

She was happiest in the evening when we all sat around the supper table together and Susan was storyboarding *Of Will and Shame* in the air. Sandy Miller, Susan's lover, was constantly with Susan now, throwing in little stories about her madcap adventures in Rio, and Sandy Miller was indeed a voluptuous young woman, every bit as seductive as she had been on the screen.

The Rio picture sounded terrific, I had to admit. The relationship between the teen prostitute, to be played by Belinda, and the female reporter who saves her, played by Sandy, was quite good. And I liked the idea of going with them on location. I wanted to see the majestic harbor of Rio de Janeiro. I wanted to walk the alien and frightening streets of that old city. I wanted to paint pictures by Brazilian light.

But this was Belinda's decision. And Belinda obviously could not make it. Belinda kept saying she needed to think it over. And so I waited, watched, tried to fathom what was holding Belinda back.

Of course, there was one very obvious answer: Bonnie was holding Belinda back.

Tuesday night we all piled into Alex's Mercedes and went down to Sunset for dinner at Le Dome. Susan was in black satin rodeo finery. Sandy Miller was the ripe starlet in beautifully draped white silk. Belinda, in the classic little black dress and pearls, picked up Blair's floor-length mink coat and threw it over her shoulders and kept it on all night long, letting it hang off the chair like a rain poncho. Alex and G.G. went black tie again, because the black dinner jacket and pants were the only decent clothes I had, other than jeans and sweatshirts that Alex's man had bought for me, and Alex and G.G. said we should all match.

So there we all were together in the soft romantic gloom of Le Dome. And the wine was flowing, and the food was delicious and lovely to look at before we ate it. And nobody busted us or bothered us, and lots of people saw us. And Belinda looked gorgeous and miserable, the mink coat hanging on the floor, her hair a cloud of gold around her soft and tortured little face. Belinda just picked at the delicious food. Belinda wasn't getting better. She was getting worse.

So we bide our time. We wait.

Early Wednesday when I awakened, I went out into the fresh air of the garden and saw Belinda slicing back and forth through the clean blue water of the long rectangular pool. She had on the tiniest black bikini in the Western world which Sandy Miller had brought her from Rio. Her hair was pinned up on top of her head. I could hardly stand to watch her little bottom and silky thighs moving through the water. Thank God, Alex was gay, I thought.

If the old familiar Los Angeles smog was there, I could not smell it or taste it. I smelled only the roses and the lemons and the oranges that grew in Alex's garden all year round.

I wandered into the greenhouse off the cabana, a large cool empty place of whitewashed glass and redwood timbers where Alex had set up my easel for me, the same one I'd left with him twenty-five years ago. He'd had his man, Orlando, go all over Los Angeles to find really big and properly stretched canvases, with just enough give in them, and plenty of brushes, turpentine, linseed oil, paints. Alex had rounded up a lot of old china plates for me to use as palettes and given me the old silver knives —the ones banged up by the garbage disposer—to use as I chose.

An artist never had it so good, it seemed to me. Except for the Muse being silently and uncomplainingly miserable. But that just had to change.

Two days ago I had started *The Mardi Gras* on a huge eight-by-ten canvas. And the great shadowy oaks above the torchlighted parade were already painted in, along with two of the glittering papier-mâché floats crowded with revelers.

Today was the day of the drunken black flambeaux carrier, and the torch tipping forward, its oily fire catching the garlands of papier-mâché flowers that skirted the high floor of the float.

It felt so good to be painting again, to be racing over this utterly new and different territory, to be drawing in the simplest little things that I had never created in any form before. Men's faces for one thing, almost never had I done them. It was as if I could feel parts of the circuitry of my brain flooded with life for the first time.

The light poured gently through the opaque white panes of the glass roof. It fell on the purple flags and on the few potted geraniums and callas in this place that smelled of freshness and earth even in the months of winter. It washed over the white canvas, and fell on my hands, making them warm.

Beyond the open doors I saw the low-pitched roof of the rambling white house, and the comforting sight of others talking, moving about. G.G. was just going out to swim with Belinda. Susan Jeremiah had come over from her place on Benedict Canyon Road. She was in beat-up jeans and blue work shirt, and the scuffed snakeskin boots and the dusty white hat that were her true clothes.

I started right in to work. I started in big fast strokes of burnt sienna to do the head and the back of the flambeaux carrier. I was suddenly on "soul control," trusting that somehow a man who could paint a little girl perfectly could do a grown man's muscular arm and knotted hand.

But even as I painted, another picture was obsessing me, something that had come to me in the night. A dark somber portrait of Blair Sackwell in the outrageous lavender tuxedo sitting on the jumpseat of the limo with his arms folded and his legs crossed. Incandescent Blair. If I could just get that mixture of vulgarity and compassion, that mixture of recklessness and magic—ah, this was Rumpelstiltskin, wasn't it, but this time he saved the child!

There were many pictures to be done. So many. Alex had to be done first, really, before Blair. I was certain of that, and then *Dogs Visit the Toys*—that one would haunt me till I finally gave in to it, and went back to the Victorian mentally, just long enough to get it done. Now for the flambeaux carrier, for the lurid glint of the flames against the trees above.

I don't think I looked up from my work until a good two hours had passed. The pool was empty, had been for some time. But Alex was walking towards me across the redbrick terrace, and smile or no smile, I could tell he had something on his mind.

"Hate to break in on you, Jeremy," he said, "but it's time for a little conference with your little girl."

When I came into the living room with him, I knew by the look on Belinda's face that something bad was happening. She sat there in her white tennis skirt and cotton pullover with her hands on her naked knees, not looking at anyone. Her hair was in braids, the way I especially loved it, but it left her face defenseless. She looked like someone had hit her one fine blow between the eyes. She resembled Bonnie when she had that expression, shocked and unable to react. G.G. was sitting beside her. He was holding her hand.

"Ash Levine and Marty are on their way over here," Alex said. "Marty has a deal for Belinda . . . you know, how to make everything OK for Bonnie and him now. You know."

Did I? I think I was a little too stunned to respond. It wasn't merely what Alex had just told me, it was the way he seemed to take it himself. Has everybody known this was going to happen? I had not.

I turned and looked at Belinda. G.G. looked easily as unhappy as she was, but then he said:

"Belinda, just see him. See what he's got to say—do that for yourself."

I understood what G.G. meant.

Ash Levine and Marty arrived fifteen minutes later. Belinda wanted me to remain in the room. But G.G. and Alex disappeared.

This was the first time Marty and I had laid eyes on each other, and I think I was unprepared for the unbroken assurance with which he grabbed my hand and smiled.

"Nice to see you, Jeremy." Was it? He was like a man running for public office rather than a man fighting for his job. The silver gray suit, the gold jewelry, it was all there, along with the jet black hair and the eyes that locked onto you with the feverish look of an addict. You could feel this guy all right when he was still two feet away.

"Hi ya, sweetheart!" he said to Belinda with the same "spontaneous" affection. "So good to see you, honey!" Then he sat beside her, his arm on the couch behind her. But I noticed he did not touch her.

Ash Levine—dark tan, navy blue suit, prematurely gray hair, reed-thin body—had settled in the leather chair by Alex's desk, and he was the one, white teeth flashing, who began to talk.

"Now, Jeremy, the important thing here is for everybody to come out of this smelling like a rose. That's what we're all here for, right? You know how much we admire Alex. We really like Alex. I mean Alex is Hollywood, they don't make stars like Alex anymore, right? But thanks to 'Champagne Flight' he is in the midst of a pretty damned exciting comeback and I think Alex would be the first to admit that what's good for 'Champagne Flight' has been pretty damn good for us all, right—?"

On and on he went as I looked at Belinda and Belinda slowly lifted her eyes and looked at me. A touch of a smile at the end of her lips for only an instant. Then it was lost. But not on Marty, I didn't think. Marty was watching both of us, eyes darting back and forth.

"—a couple of episodes of 'Champagne Flight' featuring Alex and Belinda," Ash Levine was saying, "I mean, the publicity would be fabulous for Alex after all that's happened, and for Belinda! It would be terrific for Belinda. I mean, they've heard about Belinda, and they've seen pictures of Belinda, and then, they'd see Belinda—and not in some grainy foreign film, some glitzy mink advertisement, hey, prime time, it's Belinda. And the focus is on her. We're talking number-one show in the country and, when we go back on the air, hey, we'll break all the records, I mean, the fan mail has been fabulous, simply fabulous, I mean, the fans are outraged that 'Champagne Flight' was preempted, the fans simply don't understand. I mean, if the network won't play ball, hey, we're getting offers from cable, the independents, we can sit down and create our own network for this thing just with the independents, hey, Alex and Belinda in the same episode, give them back the man they miss and

Belinda? I mean we're talking not just number one, we're talking special event!"

Belinda's face was changing. She wasn't smiling, no, but her eyes had the old steadiness. She looked at Ash. She looked at him for a long time, and then slowly her eyes shifted back to me. That curl of a smile again. Bitter? Frankly amused. Was she ready to let out a high-pitched scream?

"Hey, Ash!" Marty said, gesturing for silence. "Hey, no need to address these remarks to Jeremy, hey, Belinda's a smart girl, aren't you, sweetheart? Belinda knows what we're talking about." His voice had changed suddenly with the last phrase. He turned to Belinda. Silence. Silence with Ash sitting there with his fingers laced together on his knee. And me saying nothing as I watched all of them.

"Honey," Marty said, "do this for Bonnie. That's what I'm asking. We can cut the crap, honey. Do this to straighten things out."

Belinda didn't answer. But she had lost the shocked look utterly now. She was looking through the French doors at the garden, at the distant greenhouse maybe. It almost seemed that she hadn't heard Marty. That she was alone in the room.

Marty was looking at me. No expression really, just looking, the face amazingly calm compared with the body, which had the look of an animal about to pounce.

"Let me talk to Jeremy alone a moment, Marty," Belinda said. She got up and I went with her into the hallway. But she didn't say anything to me. She just looked at me, as if she expected me to talk, and so I did.

I put my hands on her shoulders.

"You remember what Ollie Boon said to you about power," I said, "—all you wrote to me in your letter about that?"

She nodded. The numbed expression had definitely melted, and her eyes were quick though not untroubled. She waited for me to go on.

"Honey, he was right," I said. "You don't like to have power over people. And you don't like to use it."

Again she nodded, but she did not give anything back. She was studying me, and as always, with her hair pulled back and up into the tight braids, her face had a simultaneous innocence and determination.

"But I think this is a time," I said, "when you can go against that inclination again, and use the power that you have."

Again no response.

"I know what you're thinking," I said. "You're thinking about G.G. and the rumors. You're thinking about the call you made to your mom."

"And about you, Jeremy," she said. "What they tried to do to you, too."

"I know. And nobody's going to blame you, honey, whatever you decide. But what I'm saying is, if you do this, if you just do what they want and make it all right for them—two episodes of this 'Champagne Flight' thing—well, then, all your life you'll know you got them off the hook and what happens to them after this is their affair."

Her face registered the most subtle surprise. It brightened visibly. It was like watching morning sun slowly fill a daylighted room.

"You mean you're saying *do it?*" she asked me. Amazement just like when we were riding in the van out of San Francisco only a few nights ago.

"Yes, I guess I am. Bail them out. And then you really can just turn on your heel and walk away."

She looked up at me, wonderingly, confused.

"I thought you wouldn't want me to do it," she said. "I thought you would never forgive me, never understand."

"Look, as it stands, there's still a chance to get everybody out of this in one piece—and then we'll all be free."

"Oh, Jeremy," she whispered. She stood on tiptoe and kissed me. "Thank God."

And for the first time since she'd come back, I thought I saw the radiance of my Belinda. The anxiety and the darkness were almost gone.

BONNIE was waiting in the dark limousine just inside the gates. And when we went outside, we saw that Alex was with her. He was sitting in the backseat with the door open, talking to her, and I heard him say, "Excuse me, darlin'," as he got out.

I stood with Ash as Belinda and Marty went towards the car, and then Marty got in. Alex had come to join us and Alex shook Ash's hand and said how beautiful Bonnie looked, that she was really a vision, and Ash said what a pleasure it was to see Alex, always a pleasure, of course.

Marty was now getting out of the car. He looked at Belinda, who was standing there waiting, her braids twisted a little as they came down to her shoulders, her head slightly bowed. He reached out to touch Belinda's arm.

"Get in and talk to her, honey," he said.

I felt myself tense all over as Belinda got into the car. I walked down the gravel path slowly until I could hear her voice, thin and low, but distinct nevertheless.

"Hi, Mom."

"Hello, darlin'."

"You feeling better now, Mom?"

"Yes, darlin', thank you. I'm so glad you're all right."

"Mom, is it OK if maybe, to smooth things over, you know, that I could be in one of the shows?"

"Sure, darlin', that would be nice, just real nice."

"You know, just a small part. They were talking about maybe me and Alex Clementine—"

"Sure, darlin', whatever you want."

Another car, a shiny little BMW, was nosing up the drive. It came to a halt on the other side of the open gate, and Marty made a gesture to the men inside. Three of them got out. They were photographers, one with the old-fashioned accordion-style camera, the other two with Nikons and Canons on black straps around their necks.

Then Marty asked Bonnie and Belinda to step out of the limo, and Belinda came out first and then helped Bonnie, who blinked and lowered her head as she stepped into the bright sun.

A vision she was, even her pallor was exquisite, set off by the vivid red of her carefully tailored wool suit. Her hair was a sleek mass of black silk curving just at the shoulders. Through the thick lenses of her glasses, she appeared to look past us, unseeing, as she put her arm around Belinda's waist. Belinda slipped her arm around her mother. Belinda inclined her head towards her mother ever so slightly. And the photographers went to work.

It couldn't have taken three minutes. The yard was deadly quiet except for the snapping and grinding of the cameras. Then the men got back into the car, and the BMW made a sharp U-turn and drove away.

Belinda helped her mother back into the car and sat beside her again.

And I looked at Marty and realized that we were standing very close to each other, maybe no more than three feet apart.

He had his arm resting on the top of the limo. And he was staring at me, maybe had been for some time. He was just looking at me in a sober, detached way, his black eyes fixed, but rather relaxed.

"Bye, Mom, it was so good to see you," Belinda said.

"Bye, darlin'."

I couldn't tell whether Marty was even listening to them.

When Belinda got out of the car, he continued to look at me, and I saw him give the smallest little nod of his head. I didn't know what it meant. Maybe I never would. But when he reached out to shake my hand, I tried to respond as best I could. We looked at each other, shaking hands, and that was all. Nothing was said.

"Thank you, sweetheart," he said to Belinda. And he pointed his finger at her. "I promised you once I'd write a bang-up episode for you, didn't I? Well, you wait and see."

"Don't make it too good, Marty," she whispered. "I'm on my way to Rio. I don't want to be a TV star."

He smiled, very wide, very genuine, and then he leaned over and kissed her on the cheek.

Then the limousine was rolling out the gates and down the canyon road through the dappled sun and out of sight. I put my arm around Belinda, felt her lean against me gently, felt her head against my cheek. Belinda was watching the darkened windows, the windows we could not see through. Then she lifted her hand as if she had seen somebody, which clearly she hadn't, and she waved.

The car was gone. Then she turned to me, and the old Belinda was suddenly looking right at me out of her face.

"Hey, Jeremy, let's do the Rio thing," she said suddenly, "I mean, you're coming to Rio with us, aren't you? I'm going to call Susan. I mean, this picture is really truly on, isn't it? We're going to go!"

"You bet, baby darling," I said.

I watched her turn and all but dance up the driveway, snapping her fingers, braids swinging.

"I mean, after, you know—what, two episodes with Mom and Marty? —then we're off!" And she vanished into the shadows of the house.

LATE that afternoon came the inevitable press conference. It had to be announced, didn't it? She had to sit in the den with G.G. beside her and give a statement before the inevitable video cameras and lights. They were asking as many questions about G.G.'s new salon in Beverly Hills as they were asking about the show.

Susan had come over with Sandy Miller "to watch the circus." And Alex sat with them out on the bricks by the pool. In pearls and summer lace Sandy sat there with her long fingers curled around Susan's arm. A tomato, is that what Belinda had called her? Sandy was a tomato, all right. And did she ever play up to Alex. Susan just watched the whole thing with a patient smile.

Alex was having a wonderful time entertaining her with stories, and then Susan kept chiding him about upsetting her "price scale" with his demands for *Of Will and Shame*. He teased her back, telling her she hadn't been in this business long enough to get him to make a deal without his agent at a poolside table in his own backyard.

"You want to be remembered for 'Champagne Flight'? I'm offering you a movie, Clementine, a bona fide movie like they used to make in the old days, remember, plot, character, style, meaning, one hour and forty-five minutes without a commercial break, you get my drift?"

I went into the living room and stood for a long time looking up at the portrait of Faye Clementine that I had painted twenty-five years ago.

It still hung above the fireplace where I had put it myself before I left for San Francisco on that last day. Over the years the little mistakes I'd made in perspective had always tormented me when I saw them. But I liked the painting. I felt good about it. I always had.

And now, as I studied it—Faye's dimpled cheek, the way her carefully modeled hand rested on the pink fabric of her dress—I felt a gentle surge of excitement that no one around me need know of, or try to understand. This wasn't a great painting. It didn't have the hallucinatory vibrancy of the Belinda works. But it had been a true beginning, one that I was only fully understanding now that I had come full circle to stand in front of it again.

I didn't hear Alex come up behind me. Then he put his hand on my shoulder and when I turned, he smiled.

"Go ahead," he said. "Say I told you so. You've got a right."

"You mean our old argument? Some little old talk we had about art and money and death and life?"

"Don't leave out the word, truth, Walker. When you don't throw the word truth into every second sentence, I get afraid."

"OK, it was about art, money, death, life, and truth. And now you're telling me I was right."

"I just didn't know how you were so sure it was all going to turn out the way it did."

"Sure? Me? I wasn't sure at all."

"I don't believe you," he answered. "That was Clair Clarke, your agent, on the phone right now. She's talking to me 'cause you won't take her calls—"

"Right now," I said, "I don't need her calls."

"—and you know what she wants, don't you?"

"Belinda as a client. I told Belinda. Clair can wait till Belinda decides."

"No, dear boy, though she'll want that in the bargain, too, obviously, if she can get it. She's getting offers for your story from all over. She wants to know if you want to sell the rights."

"To my story!"

"Yours and Belinda's—the whole kit and caboodle. She wants you to think it over. She doesn't want somebody to rip it off because you're public figures now. You know, the quickie TV movie. They can do that, using your names and all. She wants to scare them off with a major package, seven-figure deal."

I laughed. In fact, I really came apart.

I had to sit down, I was laughing so hard. I wasn't laughing all that loud. It was a different quality of laughter. It went way deep down inside me and it was bringing the water up into my eyes. I sat there staring at Alex.

He was grinning at me, hands in the pockets of his blue-wash pants, his pink cashmere sweater tied over his shoulders, his eyes full of mischief and pure delight.

"Tell your wife about it, Walker," he said. "Rule of thumb in Tinseltown. Always tell your wife before turning down a major package, seven-figure deal."

"Of course, it's her story, too," I said, when I was finally able to catch my breath. "Oh, you bet I'll consult her. Just wait."

"It worked out just like you predicted, gotta hand it to you. It really did. Must have been the right dirt in the right measure after all, don't you think?"

But then his face darkened a little. The worried look. And it was hardly for the first time.

"Jeremy, are you really doing all right?"

"Alex, don't worry about me, seven-figure deal or no seven-figure deal, I am just fine."

"I know you keep saying that, Jeremy, but I'm just keeping an eye out, OK? You remember Oscar Wilde, when he'd go around with the tough young hustlers in London, he called it 'feasting with panthers.' Remember that, hmmm? Well, you know what this town is, Jeremy? It's 'phone calls from panthers, and lunching with panthers, and cocktails with panthers and "catch you later," from panthers'—you have to watch your step."

"Alex, you're being deceived by appearances," I said. "It's not like I'm here suddenly instead of up in San Francisco with all that Victorian trash. I haven't swapped the kiddie books for Tinseltown, it's not like that at all. I've come back to some fork in the road I never should have passed up the first time around. And it hasn't got much to do with Hollywood really. It's got more to do with time and what's directly in front of you and the way you use it, which is why I'm perfectly all right."

"Now that sounds like the old Jeremy," he said, "I have to admit. Throw a little truth into it for me and I'll be convinced."

He gave my shoulder a squeeze, and then he started back out to the patio, where G.G. was sitting with the ladies by the pool. The reporters were gone now. Belinda had come out, peeled off her jeans and shirt to reveal nothing but that wicked little Brazilian bikini before she carefully aimed her sleek breathtaking little body, arms first, into the pool.

* * *

JUST me and Faye again. OK. I love you, Faye.

I looked up at her, and I was thinking pictures again, my kind of pictures, full of incandescent power and gradations of darkness—burning studies of Alex, Blair, G.G., and Belinda, yes, Belinda in some wholly new context, some new adventure utterly transcending what had gone before.

The contour of glitz, yes, I wanted to get it, and the discovery of the shadows that the spotlight always washed away. The color and texture of California, all that I had to do.

But these gilded images were but a small part of what was yet to come for me. The fact was, my world was now filled with a thousand beings of all ages, shapes, attitudes, a thousand settings, patterns of past and present and future unexamined and unseen before. For the first time I could do anything I wanted.

I had passed—thanks to Belinda—out of the world of dreams into the brilliant light of life itself.

The End
Anne Rice
writing as
Anne Rampling
California, 1986